PENGUIN MODERN CLASSICS

Shooting an Elephant

George Orwell (whose real name was Eric Arthur Blair) was born in 1903 in India and then went to Eton when his family moved back to England. From 1922 to 1927 he served with the Indian Imperial Police in Burma, an experience that inspired his first novel, *Burmese Days* (1934). He lived in Paris before returning to England, and *Down and Out in Paris and London* was published in 1936. After writing *The Road to Wigan Pier* and *Homage to Catalonia* (his account of fighting for the Republicans in the Spanish Civil War), Orwell was admitted to a sanatorium in 1938 and from then on was never fully fit. He spent six months in Morocco where he wrote *Coming Up for Air*. During the Second World War Orwell served in the Home Guard and worked for the BBC. His political allegory *Animal Farm* was published in 1945 and it was this novel, together with *Nineteen Eighty-Four* (1949), which brought him worldwide fame. George Orwell was taken seriously ill in the winter of 1948–9 and died in London in 1950.

Jeremy Paxman is a journalist and writer.

GEORGE ORWELL

Shooting an Elephant and Other Essays

with an Introduction by
Jeremy Paxman

PENGUIN BOOKS

PENGUIN CLASSICS

Published by the Penguin Group
Penguin Books Ltd, 80 Strand, London WC2R 0RL, England
Penguin Group (USA) Inc., 375 Hudson Street, New York, New York 10014, USA
Penguin Group (Canada), 90 Eglinton Avenue East, Suite 700, Toronto, Ontario, Canada M4P 2Y3
(a division of Pearson Penguin Canada Inc.)
Penguin Ireland, 25 St Stephen's Green, Dublin 2, Ireland (a division of Penguin Books Ltd)
Penguin Group (Australia), 250 Camberwell Road, Camberwell, Victoria 3124, Australia
(a division of Pearson Australia Group Pty Ltd)
Penguin Books India Pvt Ltd, 11 Community Centre, Panchsheel Park, New Delhi – 110 017, India
Penguin Group (NZ), 67 Apollo Drive, Rosedale, North Shore 0632, New Zealand
(a division of Pearson New Zealand Ltd)
Penguin Books (South Africa) (Pty) Ltd, 24 Sturdee Avenue, Rosebank, Johannesburg 2196, South Africa

Penguin Books Ltd, Registered Offices: 80 Strand, London WC2R 0RL, England

www.penguin.com

The Collected Essays, Journalism and Letters of George Orwell, Volume 1
first published by Martin Secker & Warburg 1968
Published in Penguin Books 1968
Copyright © the Estate of Sonia Brownell Orwell, 1945, 1952, 1953, 1968

The Collected Essays, Journalism and Letters of George Orwell, Volume 2
first published by Martin Secker & Warburg 1968
Published in Penguin Books 1970
Copyright © the Estate of Sonia Brownell Orwell, 1958

The Collected Essays, Journalism and Letters of George Orwell, Volume 3
first published by Martin Secker & Warburg 1968
Published in Penguin Books 1970
Copyright © the Estate of Sonia Brownell Orwell, 1968

The Collected Essays, Journalism and Letters of George Orwell, Volume 4
first published by Martin Secker & Warburg 1968
Published in Penguin Books 1970
Copyright © the Estate of Sonia Brownell Orwell, 1968

This collection first published 2003
Published in Penguin Classics with an Introduction 2009

015

This collection copyright © the Estate of Sonia Brownell Orwell, 2003
Introduction copyright © Jeremy Paxman, 2009
All rights reserved

The moral right of the author of the Introduction has been asserted

Set in 11.75/14.5 pt Monotype Columbus
Typeset by Rowland Phototypesetting Ltd, Bury St Edmunds, Suffolk
Printed in England by Clays Ltd, St Ives plc

Except in the United States of America, this book is sold subject
to the condition that it shall not, by way of trade or otherwise, be lent,
re-sold, hired out, or otherwise circulated without the publisher's
prior consent in any form of binding or cover other than that in
which it is published and without a similar condition including this
condition being imposed on the subsequent purchaser

978-0-141-18739-6

www.greenpenguin.co.uk

Penguin Books is committed to a sustainable
future for our business, our readers and our planet.
This book is made from Forest Stewardship
Council™ certified paper.

Contents

Introduction   vii

Why I Write   1
The Spike   11
A Hanging   23
Shooting an Elephant   31
Bookshop Memories   41
Charles Dickens   49
Boys' Weeklies   115
My Country Right or Left   149
Looking Back on the Spanish War   157
In Defence of English Cooking   185
Good Bad Books   189
The Sporting Spirit   195
Nonsense Poetry   201
The Prevention of Literature   207
Books v. Cigarettes   227
Decline of the English Murder   233
Some Thoughts on the Common Toad   239
Confessions of a Book Reviewer   245
Politics v. Literature: An Examination of *Gulliver's Travels*   251
How the Poor Die   277

Such, Such Were the Joys   291
Reflections on Gandhi   347
Politics and the English Language   358

Introduction

If you want to learn how to write non-fiction, Orwell is your man. He may be known worldwide for his last two novels, *Animal Farm* and *Nineteen-Eighty Four*. But, for me, his best work is his essays.

Who would have imagined that sixteen hundred words in praise of the Common Toad, knocked out to fill a newspaper column in April 1946, would be worth reprinting sixty years later? But here it is, with many of the characteristic Orwell delights, the unglamorous subject matter, the unnoticed detail ('a toad has about the most beautiful eye of any living creature') the baleful glare, the profound belief in humanity. Because what the piece is really about, of course, is not the toad itself, but the thrill of that most promising time of year, the spring, even as seen from Orwell's dingy Islington flat.

When he produced articles like this, hair-shirted fellow socialists got cross. Why wasn't he spending his time promoting discontent, denouncing the establishment, glorifying the machine-driven future? It is a mark of his greatness that Orwell didn't care. They – whoever they might be – cannot stop you enjoying spring. The essay ends, 'The atom bombs are piling up in the factories, the police are prowling through the cities, the lies are streaming from the loudspeakers, but the earth is still going round the sun, and neither the dictators nor the bureaucrats, deeply as they disapprove of the process, are able to prevent it.'

It all reads so effortlessly. And yet it cannot have been produced without toil. He tells us in 'Why I Write' that he found writing a book 'a horrible, exhausting struggle, like a long bout of some painful illness' and even the shorter pieces, knocked out for magazines or newspapers, must often have been a chore. There is the research, for one thing. His generous, insightful analysis of Charles Dickens shows not merely a close familiarity with thirteen of his novels, but also with those of Trollope, Thackeray and a host of long-forgotten writers, too. For his caustic piece on Boys' Weeklies he evidently immersed himself in mountains of the things.

The result of this steeping is a piece so deft and witty that the result has you laughing out loud. Here, for example, is his list of the national characteristics of the foreigners who make occasional appearances in this bizarre genre:

> FRENCHMAN: Excitable. Wears beard, gesticulates wildly.
> SPANIARD, MEXICAN, etc.: Sinister, treacherous.
> ARAB, AFGHAN, etc.: Sinister, treacherous.
> CHINESE: Sinister, treacherous. Wears pigtail's.
> ITALIAN: Excitable. Grinds barrel-organ or carries stiletto.
> SWEDE, DANE, etc.: Kind-hearted, stupid.
> NEGRO: Comic, very faithful.

How one longs for him to have lived long enough to be let loose on the lads' mags culture of the early twenty-first century.

Because something paradoxical has happened to us. The abundance of the mass media offers a greater choice than ever before. We are adrift in a sea of newspapers, magazines, radio, television and the limitless extremities of cyberspace. It is not merely that the more there is of it, the less any individual part of it matters. It is that so little of it seems *intended* to have any meaning. The mechanical processes of printing and broadcasting seem somehow to have been applied to the generation of content, too. To take one small example; no one ever experiences inconvenience as a result of motorway traffic jams or a broken-down train. Instead they – invariably, meaninglessly – suffer 'misery'. They have not, of course. It is just that that is the word the mental function key brings up when someone is required to write about disruption on the transport system.

Orwell is the enemy of laziness, vagueness and staleness. His 1946 essay, 'Politics and the English Language' remains the best starting point for anyone hoping to achieve the deceptively hard task of clear communication. He boils the business down to five instructions:

i. Never use a metaphor, simile, or other figure of speech which you are used to seeing in print.
ii. Never use a long word where a short one will do.
iii. If it is possible to cut a word out, always cut it out.
iv. Never use the passive where you can use the active.
v. Never use a foreign phrase, a scientific word, or a jargon word if you can think of an everyday English equivalent.
vi. Break any of these rules sooner than say anything outright barbarous.

He might have added – for it was certainly true in his case – that it also helps not to have had your head cluttered, your voice strangulated and your writing hand swathed in bandages by attending one of our finer universities.

You will find nothing much here about fashion, Westminster

politics, gossip, relationships, must-have gadgets and holidays, not a mention of the hints dropped by payroll propagandists, nor a word from anonymous 'sources close to' some soon-to-be forgotten minister, and nothing at all about television, pop music, or most of the other subjects which enable our increasingly feeble newspapers to trail their ink across page after page.

What you will find, instead, is an abundance of everything from the life of a book reviewer to how it is to watch a man hanged. The impeccable style is one thing. But if I had to sum up what makes Orwell's essays so remarkable it is that that they always surprise you. Sometimes it is the choice of subject matter: how many journalists can write with any authority on what it is like to queue to be let into an overnight shelter for the homeless? More often, it's the totally unexpected insight. He can write a sixty-page essay on Charles Dickens which frequently seems to be tending to a conclusion that he was a sentimental old fool, but then come to an unexpectedly affectionate final judgement. You have travelled with him on his journey and are rather startled, and pleased, to discover where you have ended up.

The Dickens essay was an attempt to worry away at why he was such a successful writer and is the longest in this collection. But it is infused with the same spirit of personal engagement as everything else. It is that amazing ability to make you believe that you would have felt as he felt that is his genius. Take 'Shooting an Elephant', which recounts an incident during his time as a policeman in Burma. It is a remarkable piece. There is, firstly, the language. When he first sees the elephant, which is said to have run amok, it is standing, beating a bunch of grass against its knees, 'with that preoccupied grandmotherly air that elephants have'. In the seconds after pulling the trigger the beast remains standing, but 'a mysterious, terrible change had come over the elephant ... every line of his body altered ... He looked suddenly stricken, shrunken, immensely old.' Then the elephant sags to its knees, its mouth slobbering. And, the utterly perfect sentence: 'An enormous senility seemed to have settled upon him.'

Being Orwell, of course, the event is put to political purpose, demonstrating the futility of the imperial project. He has already told us that 'every white man's life in the East was one long struggle not to be laughed at'. Then he reveals in the last sentence that he had killed the elephant 'solely to avoid looking a fool'. Yes, you think, that makes perfect sense. It is hard to imagine many people less suited to the job of an imperial policeman than Orwell.

Yet, while he hated imperialism, he could still remark that the British empire was 'a great deal better than the younger empires that are going to supplant it'. In another essay ('My Country Right or Left') he admits to finding it childish that he feels it faintly sacrilegious not to stand to attention during 'God Save the King', but that he would sooner have that instinct 'than be like the left-wing intellectuals who are so "enlightened" that they cannot understand the most ordinary emotions'.

There is something very striking about this patriotism of his. It was laid out most obviously in his manifesto for a post-war revolution, *The Lion and The Unicorn,* but his love of England informs just about everything he wrote. It is there like a defiant bugle call rallying us to appreciate kippers, crumpets, marmalade and stilton cheese in 'In Defence of English Cooking'. It is there like a comforting cup of tea in 'Decline of the English Murder'. Both belong to a time when – seen from this distance – English life appears to have been more settled, less commercial, more neighbourly and less racked by uncertainty of purpose. You cannot read a piece like 'Bookshop Memories' without immediately conjuring up the bad suits and rank smell of dead cigarettes. They could not have been written about any other country on earth.

Yet this is a million miles away from the nostalgic pastiche that John Major once conjured up for a Conservative conference when he talked about the country being a place of warm beer, cricket grounds and 'old maids cycling to holy communion through the morning mist'. It is not just that in Orwell's day there really were old maids on bicycles and that the Sunday place of pilgrimage had not yet become some ugly out-of-town shopping warehouse. It is that Orwell intuitively understood what it was to be English, and that he *felt* the possibilities within that identity. John Major, decent man though he may have been, was perpetrating the politician's attempt to seem an ordinary bloke. Orwell lives and breathes the identity. And it is a specifically *English* identity. What would he have made of our contemporary politicians' attempts to assure us that all is well with the Union, as it suffers the convulsions of its current St Vitus' Dance? Not much, I suspect. He had a devastatingly accurate instinct for cant.

It is, of course, as a 'political' writer that he is now best-known. Sixty years after publication, *Nineteen Eighty-Four* remains the greatest fictional demolition of totalitarianism, and any decently educated twelve-year-old can explain what *Animal Farm* is about. But, in truth, there is almost none of his successful work, either fiction or non-fiction, that is *not* political. It doesn't matter whether he is writing in his early 'Tory Anarchist' state, or as the committed socialist of later years, his work is always about that basic political question – why do we live like this?

What marks it out from other political writing is not merely the quality of the prose, but its moral authority. Where does this come from? Would he, for example, have produced such luminescent work had had he not had his first unsuitable job? If he had not suffered at the hands of oafs at his ghastly prep school? If he had not had the years of failure? I think the answer to all these questions is 'no'.

But he also had the paradoxical good fortune to live in evil times. There could be no accommodation with fascism – it was either resistance or capitulation, and everything he wrote from the outbreak of the Spanish Civil War until his death was infused with the same urgent imperative to resist totalitarianism. Of course, some of it is absurdly overstated (can he really have believed that 'only revolution can save England, that has been obvious for years . . . I dare say the London gutters will have to run with blood,' in 1940?), but evil times force harsh judgements.

Orwell could toss off sentences like that with greater authority than most because of the quality not merely of his writing but of his experience. When he spoke of life at the bottom of the heap he did so as someone who had lived as a scullion and a tramp. When he talked of war and death he did so as someone who had fought in war and seen people die. The experiences had translated a natural hatred of authority into a political manifesto of sorts. In 'Why I Write' he claimed that he was driven more by egoism, aesthetic enthusiasm and curiosity than by any political purpose. Yet in the same essay he claims that those of his books which lacked a political purpose are those which are most ornate and pointless. This apparent contradiction can, of course be explained in the narrow sense in which he talks of his political purpose ('*against* totalitarianism and *for* democratic Socialism.') But anyone can profess a commitment to some ideology or other, and given those particular options, what sensible personal would not make that choice?

I think there is another explanation, too. What Orwell's experiences – both as figure of authority and as scullion – had given him was a lived understanding of the human condition. It was this grounding in reality which bestowed a more profound political instinct than would be available to some sloganeering zealot. He had acquired a capacity to empathise with the foot-soldiers of history, the put-upon people generally taken for granted, ignored or squashed by the great 'isms' of one sort or another. It conferred upon him the remarkable ability to achieve what every journalist and essayist seeks.

He could tell the truth.

Jeremy Paxman, 2009

Why I Write

From a very early age, perhaps the age of five or six, I knew that when I grew up I should be a writer. Between the ages of about seventeen and twenty-four I tried to abandon this idea, but I did so with the consciousness that I was outraging my true nature and that sooner or later I should have to settle down and write books.

I was the middle child of three, but there was a gap of five years on either side, and I barely saw my father before I was eight. For this and other reasons I was somewhat lonely, and I soon developed disagreeable mannerisms which made me unpopular throughout my schooldays. I had the lonely child's habit of making up stories and holding conversations with imaginary persons, and I think from the very start my literary ambitions were mixed up with the feeling of being isolated and under-valued. I knew that I had a facility with words and a power of facing unpleasant facts, and I felt that this created a sort of private world in which I could get my own back for my failure in everyday life. Nevertheless the volume of serious – i.e. seriously intended – writing which I produced all through my childhood and boyhood would not amount to half a dozen pages. I wrote my first poem at the age of four or five, my mother taking it down to dictation. I cannot remember anything about it except that it was about a tiger and the tiger had 'chair-like teeth' – a good enough phrase, but I fancy the poem was a plagiarism of Blake's 'Tiger, Tiger'. At eleven, when the war of 1914–18 broke out, I wrote a patriotic poem which was printed in the local newspaper, as was another, two years later, on the death of Kitchener. From time to time, when I was a bit older, I wrote bad and usually unfinished 'nature poems' in the Georgian style. I also, about twice, attempted a short story which was a ghastly failure. That was the total of the would-be serious work that I actually set down on paper during all those years.

However, throughout this time I did in a sense engage in literary activities. To begin with there was the made-to-order stuff which I produced quickly, easily and without much pleasure to myself. Apart from school work, I wrote *vers d'occasion*, semi-comic poems which I could turn out at what now seems to me astonishing speed – at fourteen I wrote a whole rhyming play, in imitation of Aristophanes, in about a week – and helped to edit school magazines, both printed and in manuscript. These magazines were the most pitiful burlesque stuff that you could imagine, and I took far less trouble with them than I now would with the cheapest journalism. But side by side with all this, for fifteen years or more, I was carrying out a literary exercise of a quite different kind: this was the making up of a continuous 'story' about myself, a sort of diary existing only in the mind. I believe this is a common habit of children and adolescents. As a very small child I used to imagine that I was, say, Robin Hood, and picture myself as the hero of thrilling adventures, but quite soon my 'story' ceased to be narcissistic in a crude way and became more and more a mere description of what I was doing and the things I saw. For minutes at a time this kind of thing would be running through my head: 'He pushed the door open and entered the room. A yellow beam of sunlight, filtering through the muslin curtains, slanted on to the table, where a matchbox, half open, lay beside the inkpot. With his right hand in his pocket he moved across to the window. Down in the street a tortoiseshell cat was chasing a dead leaf,' etc. etc. This habit continued till I was about twenty-five, right through my non-literary years. Although I had to search, and did search, for the right words, I seemed to be making this descriptive effort almost against my will, under a kind of compulsion from outside. The 'story' must, I suppose, have reflected the styles of the various writers I admired at different ages, but so far as I remember it always had the same meticulous descriptive quality.

When I was about sixteen I suddenly discovered the joy of mere words, i.e. the sounds and associations of words. The lines from *Paradise Lost*,

> So hee with difficulty and labour hard
> Moved on: with difficulty and labour hee,

which do not now seem to me so very wonderful, sent shivers down my backbone; and the spelling 'hee' for 'he' was an added pleasure. As for the need to describe things, I knew all about it already. So it is clear what kind of books I wanted to write, in so far as I could be said to want to write books at that time. I wanted to write enormous naturalistic novels with unhappy endings, full of detailed descriptions and arresting similes, and also full of purple passages in which words were used partly for the sake of their sound. And in fact my first complete novel, *Burmese Days*, which I wrote when I was thirty but projected much earlier, is rather that kind of book.

I give all this background information because I do not think one can assess a writer's motives without knowing something of his early development. His subject-matter will be determined by the age he lives in – at least this is true in tumultuous, revolutionary ages like our own – but before he ever begins to write he will have acquired an emotional attitude from which he will never completely escape. It is his job, no doubt, to discipline his temperament and avoid getting stuck at some immature stage, or in some perverse mood: but if he escapes from his early influences altogether, he will have killed his impulse to write. Putting aside the need to earn a living, I think there are four great motives for writing, at any rate for writing prose. They exist in different degrees in every writer, and in any one writer the proportions will vary from time to time, according to the atmosphere in which he is living. They are:

1. Sheer egoism. Desire to seem clever, to be talked about, to be remembered after death, to get your own back on grown-ups who snubbed you in childhood, etc. etc. It is humbug to pretend that this is not a motive, and a strong one. Writers share this characteristic with scientists, artists, politicians, lawyers, soldiers, successful businessmen – in short, with the whole top crust of humanity. The great mass of human beings are not acutely selfish. After the age of about thirty they abandon individual ambition – in many cases, indeed, they almost abandon the sense of being individuals at all – and live chiefly for others, or are simply smothered under drudgery. But there is also the minority of gifted, wilful people who are determined to live their own lives to the end, and writers belong in this class. Serious writers, I should say, are on the whole more vain and self-centred than journalists, though less interested in money.

2. Aesthetic enthusiasm. Perception of beauty in the external world, or, on the other hand, in words and their right arrangement. Pleasure in the impact or one sound on another, in the firmness of good prose or the rhythm of a good story. Desire to share an experience which one feels is valuable and ought not to be missed. The aesthetic motive is very feeble in a lot of writers, but even a pamphleteer or a writer of textbooks will have pet words and phrases which appeal to him for non-utilitarian reasons; or he may feel strongly about typography, width of margins, etc. Above the level of a railway guide, no book is quite free from aesthetic considerations.

3. Historical impulse. Desire to see things as they are, to find out true facts and store them up for the use of posterity.

4. Political purpose – using the word 'political' in the widest possible sense. Desire to push the world in a certain direction, to alter other people's idea of the kind of society that they should strive after. Once again, no book is genuinely free from political bias. The opinion that art should have nothing to do with politics is itself a political attitude.

It can be seen how these various impulses must war against one another, and how they must fluctuate from person to person and from time to time. By nature – taking your 'nature' to be the state you have attained when you are first adult – I am a person in whom the first three motives would outweigh the fourth. In a peaceful age I might have written ornate or merely descriptive books, and might have remained almost unaware of my political loyalties. As it is I have been forced into becoming a sort of pamphleteer. First I spent five years in a unsuitable profession (the Indian Imperial Police, in Burma), and then I underwent poverty and the sense of failure. This increased my natural hatred of authority and made me for the first time fully aware of the existence of the working classes, and the job in Burma had given me some understanding of the nature of imperialism: but these experiences were not enough to give me an accurate political orientation. Then came Hitler, the Spanish Civil War, etc. By the end of 1935 I had still failed to reach a firm decision. I remember a little poem that I wrote at that date, expressing my dilemma:

> A happy vicar I might have been
> Two hundred years ago,
> To preach upon eternal doom
> And watch my walnuts grow
>
> But born, alas, in an evil time,
> I missed that pleasant haven,
> For the hair has grown on my upper lip
> And the clergy are all clean-shaven.
>
> And later still the times were good,
> We were so easy to please,
> We rocked our troubled thoughts to sleep
> On the bosoms of the trees.
>
> All ignorant we dared to own
> The joys we now dissemble;
> The greenfinch on the apple bough
> Could make my enemies tremble.
>
> But girls' bellies and apricots,
> Roach in a shaded stream,
> Horses, ducks in flight at dawn,
> All these are a dream.

It is forbidden to dream again;
We maim our joys or hide them;
Horses are made of chromium steel
And little fat men shall ride them.

I am the worm who never turned,
The eunuch without a harem;
Between the priest and the commissar
I walk like Eugene Aram;

And the commissar is telling my fortune
While the radio plays,
But the priest has promised an Austin Seven,
For Duggie always pays.

I dreamed I dwelt in marble halls,
And woke to find it true;
I wasn't born for an age like this;
Was Smith? Was Jones? Were you?[1]

The Spanish war and other events in 1936–7 turned the scale and thereafter I knew where I stood. Every line of serious work that I have written since 1936 has been written, directly or indirectly, *against* totalitarianism and *for* democratic Socialism, as I understand it. It seems to me nonsense, in a period like our own, to think that one can avoid writing of such subjects. Everyone writes of them in one guise or another. It is simply a question of which side one takes and what approach one follows. And the more one is conscious of one's political bias, the more chance one has of acting politically without sacrificing one's aesthetic and intellectual integrity.

[1] This poem first appeared in the *Adelphi*, December 1936.

What I have most wanted to do throughout the past ten years is to make political writing into an art. My starting point is always a feeling of partisanship, a sense of injustice. When I sit down to write a book, I do not say to myself, 'I am going to produce a work of art.' I write it because there is some lie that I want to expose, some fact to which I want to draw attention, and my initial concern is to get a hearing. But I could not do the work of writing a book, or even a long magazine article, if it were not also an aesthetic experience. Anyone who cares to examine my work will see that even when it is downright propaganda it contains much that a full-time politician would consider irrelevant. I am not able, and I do not want, completely to abandon the world-view that I acquired in childhood. So long as I remain alive and well I shall continue to feel strongly about prose style, to love the surface of the earth, and to take pleasure in solid objects and scraps of useless information. It is no use trying to suppress that side of myself. The job is to reconcile my ingrained likes and dislikes with the essentially public, non-individual activities that this age forces on all of us.

It is not easy. It raises problems of construction and of language, and it raises in a new way the problem of truthfulness. Let me give just one example of the cruder kind of difficulty that arises. My book about the Spanish Civil War, *Homage to Catalonia*, is, of course, a frankly political book, but in the main it is written with a certain detachment and regard for form. I did try very hard in it to tell the whole truth without violating my literary instincts. But among other things it contains a long chapter, full of newspaper quotations and the like, defending Trotskyists who were accused of plotting with Franco. Clearly such a chapter, which after a year or two would lose its interest for any ordinary reader, must ruin the book. A critic whom I respect read me a lecture about it. 'Why did you put in all that stuff?' he said. 'You've turned what might have been a good book into journalism.' What he said was true, but I could not have done otherwise. I happened to know, what very few people in England had been allowed to know, that innocent men were being falsely accused. If I had not been angry about that I should never have written the book.

In one form or another this problem comes up again. The problem of language is subtler and would take too long to discuss. I will only say that of later years I have tried to write less picturesquely and more exactly. In any case I find that by the time you have perfected any style of writing, you have always outgrown it. *Animal Farm* was the first book in which I tried, with full consciousness of what I was doing, to fuse political purpose and artistic purpose into one whole. I have not written a novel for seven years, but I hope to write another fairly soon. It is bound to be a failure, every book is a failure, but I know with some clarity what kind of book I want to write.

Looking back through the last page or two, I see that I have made it appear as though my motives in writing were wholly public-spirited. I don't want to leave that as the final impression. All writers are vain, selfish and lazy, and at the very bottom of their motives there lies a mystery. Writing a book is a horrible, exhausting struggle, like a long bout of some painful illness. One would never undertake such a thing if one were not driven on by some demon whom one can neither resist nor understand. For all one knows that demon is simply the same instinct that makes a baby squall for attention. And yet it is also true that one can write nothing readable unless one constantly struggles to efface one's own personality. Good prose is like a window pane. I cannot say with certainty which of my motives are the strongest, but I know which of them deserve to be followed. And looking back through my work, I see that it is invariably where I lacked a *political* purpose that I wrote lifeless books and was betrayed into purple passages, sentences without meaning, decorative adjectives and humbug generally.

1946

The Spike

It was late afternoon. Forty-nine of us, forty-eight men and one woman, lay on the green waiting for the spike to open. We were too tired to talk much. We just sprawled about exhaustedly, with home-made cigarettes sticking out of our scrubby faces. Overhead the chestnut branches were covered with blossom, and beyond that great woolly clouds floated almost motionless in a clear sky. Littered on the grass, we seemed dingy, urban riff-raff. We defiled the scene, like sardine-tins and paper bags on the seashore.

What talk there was ran on the Tramp Major of this spike. He was a devil, everyone agreed, a tartar, a tyrant, a bawling, blasphemous, uncharitable dog. You couldn't call your soul your own when he was about, and many a tramp had he kicked out in the middle of the night for giving a back answer. When you came to be searched he fair held you upside down and shook you. If you were caught with tobacco there was hell to pay, and if you went in with money (which is against the law) God help you.

I had eightpence on me. 'For the love of Christ, mate,' the old hands advised me, 'don't you take it in. You'd get seven days for going into the spike with eightpence!'

So I buried my money in a hole under the hedge, marking

the spot with a lump of flint. Then we set about smuggling our matches and tobacco, for it is forbidden to take these into nearly all spikes, and one is supposed to surrender them at the gate. We hid them in our socks, except for the twenty or so per cent who had no socks, and had to carry the tobacco in their boots, even under their very toes. We stuffed our ankles with contraband until anyone seeing us might have imagined an outbreak of elephantiasis. But it is an unwritten law that even the sternest Tramp Majors do not search below the knee, and in the end only one man was caught. This was Scotty, a little hairy tramp with a bastard accent sired by cockney out of Glasgow. His tin of cigarette ends fell out of his sock at the wrong moment, and was impounded.

At six the gates swung open and we shuffled in. An official at the gate entered our names and other particulars in the register and took our bundles away from us. The woman was sent off to the workhouse, and we others into the spike. It was a gloomy, chilly, limewashed place, consisting only of a bathroom and dining-room and about a hundred narrow stone cells. The terrible Tramp Major met us at the door and herded us into the bathroom to be stripped and searched. He was a gruff, soldierly man of forty, who gave the tramps no more ceremony than sheep at the dipping-pond, shoving them this way and that and shouting oaths in their faces. But when he came to myself, he looked hard at me, and said:

'You are a gentleman?'

'I suppose so,' I said.

He gave me another long look. 'Well, that's bloody bad luck, guv'nor,' he said, 'that's bloody bad luck, that is.' And thereafter he took it into his head to treat me with compassion, even with a kind of respect.

It was a disgusting sight, that bathroom. All the indecent secrets of our underwear were exposed; the grime, the rents and patches, the bits of string doing duty for buttons, the layers upon layers of fragmentary garments, some of them mere collections of holes, held together by dirt. The room became a press of steaming nudity, the sweaty odours of the tramps competing with the sickly, sub-faecal stench native to the spike. Some of the men refused the bath, and washed only their 'toe-rags', the horrid, greasy little clouts which tramps bind round their feet. Each of us had three minutes in which to bathe himself. Six greasy, slippery roller towels had to serve for the lot of us.

When we had bathed our own clothes were taken away from us, and we were dressed in the workhouse shirts, grey cotton things like nightshirts, reaching to the middle of the thigh. Then we were sent into the diningroom, where supper was set out on the deal tables. It was the invariable spike meal, always the same, whether breakfast, dinner or supper – half a pound of bread, a bit of margarine, and a pint of so-called tea. It took us five minutes to gulp down the cheap, noxious food. Then the Tramp Major served us with three cotton blankets each, and drove us off to our cells for the night. The doors were locked on the outside a little before seven in the evening, and would stay locked for the next twelve hours.

The cells measured eight feet by five, and had no lighting apparatus except a tiny, barred window high up in the wall, and a spyhole in the door. There were no bugs, and we had bedsteads and straw palliasses, rare luxuries both. In many spikes one sleeps on a wooden shelf, and in some on the bare floor, with a rolled-up coat for a pillow. With a cell to myself, and a bed, I was hoping for a sound night's rest. But I did not get it, for there is always something wrong in the spike, and the peculiar shortcoming here, as I discovered immediately, was the cold. May had begun, and in honour of the season – a little sacrifice to the gods of spring, perhaps – the authorities had cut off the steam from the hot pipes. The cotton blankets were almost useless. One spent the night in turning from side to side, falling asleep for ten minutes and waking half frozen, and watching for dawn.

As always happens in the spike, I had at last managed to fall comfortably asleep when it was time to get up. The Tramp Major came marching down the passage with his heavy tread, unlocking the doors and yelling to us to show a leg. Promptly the passage was full of squalid shirt-clad figures rushing for the bathroom, for there was only one tub full of water between us all in the morning, and it was first come first served. When I arrived twenty tramps had already washed their faces. I gave one glance at the black scum on top of the water, and decided to go dirty for the day.

We hurried into our clothes, and then went to the dining-room to bolt our breakfast. The bread was much worse than usual, because the military-minded idiot of a Tramp Major had cut it into slices overnight, so that it was as hard as ship's biscuit. But we were glad of our tea after the cold, restless night. I do not know what tramps would do without tea, or rather the stuff they miscall tea. It is their food, their medicine, their panacea for all evils. Without the half gallon or so of it that they suck down a day, I truly believe they could not face existence.

After breakfast we had to undress again for the medical inspection, which is a precaution against smallpox. It was three quarters of an hour before the doctor arrived, and one had time now to look about him and see what manner of men we were. It was an instructive sight. We stood shivering naked to the waist in two long ranks in the passage. The filtered light, bluish and cold, lighted us up with unmerciful clarity. No one can imagine, unless he has seen such a thing, what pot-bellied, degenerate curs we looked. Shock heads, hairy, crumpled faces, hollow chests, flat feet, sagging muscles — every kind of malformation and physical rottenness were there. All were flabby and discoloured, as all tramps are under their deceptive sunburn. Two or three figures seen there stay ineradicably in my mind. Old 'Daddy', aged seventy-four, with his truss, and his red, watering eyes: a herring-gutted starveling, with sparse beard and sunken cheeks, looking like the corpse of Lazarus in some primitive picture: an imbecile, wandering hither and thither with vague giggles, coyly pleased because his trousers constantly slipped down and left him nude. But few of us were greatly better than these; there were not ten decently built men among us, and half, I believe, should have been in hospital.

This being Sunday, we were to be kept in the spike over the week-end. As soon as the doctor had gone we were herded back to the dining-room, and its door shut upon us. It was a lime-washed, stone-floored room, unspeakably dreary with its furniture of deal boards and benches, and its prison smell. The windows were so high up that one could not look outside, and the sole ornament was a set of Rules threatening dire penalties to any casual who misconducted himself. We packed the room so tight that one could not move an elbow without jostling somebody. Already, at eight o'clock in the morning, we were bored with our captivity. There was nothing to talk about except the petty gossip of the road, the good and bad spikes, the charitable and uncharitable counties, the iniquities of the police and the Salvation Army. Tramps hardly ever get away from these subjects; they talk, as it were, nothing but shop. They have nothing worthy to be called conversation, because emptiness of belly leaves no speculation in their souls. The world is too much with them. Their next meal is never quite secure, and so they cannot think of anything except the next meal.

Two hours dragged by. Old Daddy, witless with age, sat silent, his back bent like a bow and his inflamed eyes dripping slowly on to the floor. George, a dirty old tramp notorious for the queer habit of sleeping in his hat, grumbled about a parcel of tommy that he had lost on the road. Bill the moocher, the best built man of us all, a Herculean sturdy beggar who smelt of beer even after twelve hours in the spike, told tales of mooching, of pints stood him in the boozers, and of a parson who had preached to the police and got him seven days. William and Fred, two young ex-fishermen from Norfolk, sang a sad song about Unhappy Bella, who was betrayed and died in the snow. The imbecile drivelled about an imaginary toff who had once given him two hundred and fifty-seven golden sovereigns. So the time passed, with dull talk and dull obscenities. Everyone was smoking, except Scotty, whose tobacco had been seized, and he was so miserable in his smokeless state that I stood him the making of a cigarette. We smoked furtively, hiding our cigarettes like schoolboys when we heard the Tramp Major's step, for smoking, though connived at, was officially forbidden.

Most of the tramps spent ten consecutive hours in this dreary room. It is hard to imagine how they put up with it. I have come to think that boredom is the worst of all a tramp's evils, worse than hunger and discomfort, worse even than the constant feeling of being socially disgraced. It is a silly piece of cruelty to confine an ignorant man all day with nothing to do; it is like chaining a dog in a barrel. Only an educated man, who has consolations within himself, can endure confinement. Tramps, unlettered types as nearly all of them are, face their poverty with blank, resourceless minds. Fixed for ten hours on a comfortless bench, they know no way of occupying themselves, and if they think at all it is to whimper about hard luck and pine for work. They have not the stuff in them to endure the horrors of idleness. And so, since so much of their lives is spent in doing nothing, they suffer agonies from boredom.

I was much luckier than the others, because at ten o'clock the Tramp Major picked me out for the most coveted of all jobs in the spike, the job of helping in the workhouse kitchen. There was not really any work to be done there, and I was able to make off and hide in a shed used for storing potatoes, together with some workhouse paupers who were skulking to avoid the Sunday-morning service. There was a stove burning there, and comfortable packing cases to sit on, and back numbers of the *Family Herald*, and even a copy of *Raffles* from the workhouse library. It was paradise after the spike.

Also, I had my dinner from the workhouse table, and it was one of the biggest meals I have ever eaten. A tramp does not see such a meal twice in the year, in the spike or out of it. The paupers told me that they always gorged to the bursting point on Sundays, and went hungry six days of the week. When the meal was over the cook set me to do the washing up, and told me to throw away the food that remained. The wastage was astonishing; great dishes of beef, and bucketfuls of bread and vegetables, were pitched away like rubbish, and then defiled with tea-leaves. I filled five dustbins to overflowing with good food. And while I did so my fellow tramps were sitting two hundred yards away in the spike, their bellies, half filled with the spike dinner of the everlasting bread and tea, and perhaps two cold boiled potatoes each in honour of Sunday. It appeared that the food was thrown away from deliberate policy, rather than that it should be given to the tramps.

At three I left the workhouse kitchen and went back to the spike. The boredom in that crowded, comfortless room was now unbearable. Even smoking had ceased, for a tramp's only tobacco is picked-up cigarette ends, and, like a browsing beast, he starves if he is long away from the pavement-pasture. To occupy the time I talked with a rather superior tramp, a young carpenter who wore a collar and tie, and was on the road, he said, for lack of a set of tools. He kept a little aloof from the other tramps, and held himself more like a free man than a casual. He had literary tastes, too, and carried one of Scott's novels on all his wanderings. He told me he never entered a spike unless driven there by hunger, sleeping under hedges and behind ricks in preference. Along the south coast he had begged by day and slept in bathing-machines for weeks at a time.

We talked of life on the road. He criticized the system which makes a tramp spend fourteen hours a day in the spike, and the other ten in walking and dodging the police. He spoke of his own case – six months at the public charge for want of three pounds' worth of tools. It was idiotic, he said.

Then I told him about the wastage of food in the workhouse kitchen, and what I thought of it. And at that he changed his tune immediately. I saw that I had awakened the pew-renter who sleeps in every English workman. Though he had been famished along with the rest, he at once saw reasons why the food should have been thrown away rather than given to the tramps. He admonished me quite severely.

'They have to do it,' he said. 'If they made these places too pleasant you'd have all the scum of the country flocking into them. It's only the bad food as keeps all that scum away. These tramps are too lazy to work, that's all that's wrong with them. You don't want to go encouraging of them. They're scum.'

I produced arguments to prove him wrong, but he would not listen. He kept repeating:

'You don't want to have any pity on these tramps – scum, they are. You don't want to judge them by the same standards as men like you and me. They're scum, just scum.'

It was interesting to see how subtly he disassociated himself from his fellow tramps. He has been on the road six months, but in the sight of God, he seemed to imply, he was not a tramp. His body might be in the spike, but his spirit soared far away, in the pure aether of the middle classes.

The clock's hands crept round with excruciating slowness. We were too bored even to talk now, the only sound was of oaths and reverberating yawns. One would force his eyes away from the clock for what seemed an age, and then look back again to see that the hands had advanced three minutes. Ennui clogged our souls like cold mutton fat. Our bones ached because of it. The clock's hands stood at four, and supper was not till six, and there was nothing left remarkable beneath the visiting moon.

At last six o'clock did come, and the Tramp Major and his assistant arrived with supper. The yawning tramps brisked up like lions at feeding-time. But the meal was a dismal disappointment. The bread, bad enough in the morning, was now positively uneatable; it was so hard that even the strongest jaws could make little impression on it. The older men went almost supperless, and not a man could finish his portion, hungry though most of us were. When we had finished, the blankets were served out immediately, and we were hustled off once more to the bare, chilly cells.

Thirteen hours went by. At seven we were awakened, and rushed forth to squabble over the water in the bathroom, and bolt our ration of bread and tea. Our time in the spike was up, but we could not go until the doctor had examined us again, for the authorities have a terror of smallpox and its distribution by tramps. The doctor kept us waiting two hours this time, and it was ten o'clock before we finally escaped.

At last it was time to go, and we were let out into the yard. How bright everything looked, and how sweet the winds did blow, after the gloomy, reeking spike! The Tramp Major handed each man his bundle of confiscated possessions, and a hunk of bread and cheese for midday dinner, and then we took the road, hastening to get out of sight of the spike and its discipline. This was our interim of freedom. After a day and two nights of wasted time we had eight hours or so to take our recreation, to scour the roads for cigarette ends, to beg, and to look for work. Also, we had to make our ten, fifteen, or it might be twenty miles to the next spike, where the game would begin anew.

I disinterred my eightpence and took the road with Nobby, a respectable, downhearted tramp who carried a spare pair of boots and visited all the Labour Exchanges. Our late companions were scattering north, south, east and west, like bugs into a mattress. Only the imbecile loitered at the spike gates, until the Tramp Major had to chase him away.

Nobby and I set out for Croydon. It was a quiet road, there were no cars passing, the blossom covered the chestnut trees like great wax candles. Everything was so quiet and smelt so clean, it was hard to realize that only a few minutes ago we had been packed with that band of prisoners in a stench of drains and soft soap. The others had all disappeared; we two seemed to be the only tramps on the road.

Then I heard a hurried step behind me, and felt a tap on my arm. It was little Scotty, who had run panting after us. He pulled a rusty tin box from his pocket. He wore a friendly smile, like a man who is repaying an obligation.

'Here y'are, mate,' he said cordially. 'I owe you some fag ends. You stood me a smoke yesterday. The Tramp Major give me back my box of fag ends when we come out this morning. One good turn deserves another – here y'are.'

And he put four sodden, debauched, loathly cigarette ends into my hand.

1931

A Hanging

It was in Burma, a sodden morning of the rains. A sickly light, like yellow tinfoil, was slanting over the high walls into the jail yard. We were waiting outside the condemned cells, a row of sheds fronted with double bars, like small animal cages. Each cell measured about ten feet by ten and was quite bare within except for a plank bed and a pot of drinking water. In some of them brown silent men were squatting at the inner bars, with their blankets draped round them. These were the condemned men, due to be hanged within the next week or two.

One prisoner had been brought out of his cell. He was a Hindu, a puny wisp of a man, with a shaven head and vague liquid eyes. He had a thick, sprouting moustache, absurdly too big for his body, rather like the moustache of a comic man on the films. Six tall Indian warders were guarding him and getting him ready for the gallows. Two of them stood by with rifles and fixed bayonets, while the others handcuffed him, passed a chain through his handcuffs and fixed it to their belts, and lashed his arms tight to his sides. They crowded very close about him, with their hands always on him in a careful, caressing grip, as though all the while feeling him to make sure he was there. It was like men handling a fish which is still alive and may jump back into the water. But he stood quite unresisting, yielding his arms limply to the ropes, as though he hardly noticed what was happening.

Eight o'clock struck and a bugle call, desolately thin in the wet air, floated from the distant barracks. The superintendent of the jail, who was standing apart from the rest of us, moodily prodding the gravel with his stick, raised his head at the sound. He was an army doctor, with a grey toothbrush moustache and a gruff voice. 'For God's sake hurry up, Francis,' he said irritably. 'The man ought to have been dead by this time. Aren't you ready yet?'

Francis, the head jailer, a fat Dravidian in a white drill suit and gold spectacles, waved his black hand. 'Yes sir, yes sir,' he bubbled. 'All iss satisfactorily prepared. The hangman iss waiting. We shall proceed.'

'Well, quick march, then. The prisoners can't get their breakfast till this job's over.'

We set out for the gallows. Two warders marched on either side of the prisoner, with their rifles at the slope; two others marched close against him, gripping him by arm and shoulder, as though at once pushing and supporting him. The rest of us, magistrates and the like, followed behind. Suddenly, when we had gone ten yards, the procession stopped short without any order or warning. A dreadful thing had happened – a dog, come goodness knows whence, had appeared in the yard. It came bounding among us with a loud volley of barks, and leapt round us wagging its whole body, wild with glee at finding so many human beings together. It was a large woolly dog, half Airedale, half pariah. For a moment it pranced round us, and then, before anyone could stop it, it had made a dash for the prisoner, and jumping up tried to lick his face. Everyone stood aghast, too taken aback even to grab at the dog.

'Who let that bloody brute in here?' said the superintendent angrily. 'Catch it, someone!'

A warder, detached from the escort, charged clumsily after the dog, but it danced and gambolled just out of his reach, taking everything as part of the game. A young Eurasian jailer picked up a handful of gravel and tried to stone the dog away, but it dodged the stones and came after us again. Its yaps echoed from the jail walls. The prisoner, in the grasp of the two warders, looked on incuriously, as though this was another formality of the hanging. It was several minutes before someone managed to catch the dog. Then we put my handkerchief through its collar and moved off once more, with the dog still straining and whimpering.

It was about forty yards to the gallows. I watched the bare brown back of the prisoner marching in front of me. He walked clumsily with his bound arms, but quite steadily, with that bobbing gait of the Indian who never straightens his knees. At each step his muscles slid neatly into place, the lock of hair on his scalp danced up and down, his feet printed themselves on the wet gravel. And once, in spite of the men who gripped him by each shoulder, he stepped slightly aside to avoid a puddle on the path.

It is curious, but till that moment I had never realized what it means to destroy a healthy, conscious man. When I saw the prisoner step aside to avoid the puddle, I saw the mystery, the unspeakable wrongness, of cutting a life short when it is in full tide. This man was not dying, he was alive just as we were alive. All the organs of his body were working – bowels digesting food, skin renewing itself, nails growing, tissues forming – all toiling away in solemn foolery. His nails would still be growing when he stood on the drop, when he was falling through the air with a tenth of a second to live. His eyes saw the yellow gravel and the grey walls, and his brain still remembered, foresaw, reasoned – reasoned even about puddles. He and we were a party of men walking together, seeing, hearing, feeling, understanding the same world; and in two minutes, with a sudden snap, one of us would be gone – one mind less, one world less.

The gallows stood in a small yard, separate from the main grounds of the prison, and overgrown with tall prickly weeds. It was a brick erection like three sides of a shed, with planking on top, and above that two beams and a crossbar with the rope dangling. The hangman, a grey-haired convict in the white uniform of the prison, was waiting beside his machine. He greeted us with a servile crouch as we entered. At a word from Francis the two warders, gripping the prisoner more closely than ever, half led, half pushed him to the gallows and helped him clumsily up the ladder. Then the hangman climbed up and fixed the rope round the prisoner's neck.

We stood waiting, five yards away. The warders had formed in a rough circle round the gallows. And then, when the noose was fixed, the prisoner began crying out on his god. It was a high, reiterated cry of 'Ram! Ram! Ram! Ram!', not urgent and fearful like a prayer or a cry for help, but steady, rhythmical, almost like the tolling of a bell. The dog answered the sound with a whine. The hangman, still standing on the gallows, produced a small cotton bag like a flour bag and drew it down over the prisoner's face. But the sound, muffled by the cloth, still persisted, over and over again: 'Ram! Ram! Ram! Ram! Ram!'

The hangman climbed down and stood ready, holding the lever. Minutes seemed to pass. The steady, muffled crying from the prisoner went on and on, 'Ram! Ram! Ram!' never faltering for an instant. The superintendent, his head on his chest, was slowly poking the ground with his stick; perhaps he was counting the cries, allowing the prisoner a fixed number – fifty, perhaps, or a hundred. Everyone had changed colour. The Indians had gone grey like bad coffee, and one or two of the bayonets were wavering. We looked at the lashed, hooded man on the drop, and listened to his cries – each cry another second of life; the same thought was in all our minds: oh, kill him quickly, get it over, stop that abominable noise!

Suddenly the superintendent made up his mind. Throwing up his head he made a swift motion with his stick. 'Chalo!' he shouted almost fiercely.

There was a clanking noise, and then dead silence. The prisoner had vanished, and the rope was twisting on itself. I let go of the dog, and it galloped immediately to the back of the gallows; but when it got there it stopped short, barked, and then retreated into a corner of the yard, where it stood among the weeds, looking timorously out at us. We went round the gallows to inspect the prisoner's body. He was dangling with his toes pointed straight downwards, very slowly revolving, as dead as a stone.

The superintendent reached out with his stick and poked the bare body; it oscillated, slightly. '*He's* all right,' said the superintendent. He backed out from under the gallows, and blew out a deep breath. The moody look had gone out of his face quite suddenly. He glanced at his wrist-watch. 'Eight minutes past eight. Well, that's all for this morning, thank God.'

The warders unfixed bayonets and marched away. The dog, sobered and conscious of having misbehaved itself, slipped after them. We walked out of the gallows yard, past the condemned cells with their waiting prisoners, into the big central yard of the prison. The convicts, under the command of warders armed with lathis, were already receiving their breakfast. They squatted in long rows, each man holding a tin pannikin, while two warders with buckets marched round ladling out rice; it seemed quite a homely, jolly scene, after the hanging. An enormous relief had come upon us now that the job was done. One felt an impulse to sing, to break into a run, to snigger. All at once everyone began chattering gaily.

The Eurasian boy walking beside me nodded towards the way we had come, with a knowing smile: 'Do you know, sir, our friend (he meant the dead man), when he heard his appeal had been dismissed, he pissed on the floor of his cell. From fright. – Kindly take one of my cigarettes, sir. Do you not admire my new silver case, sir? From the boxwallah, two rupees eight annas. Classy European style.'

Several people laughed – at what, nobody seemed certain.

Francis was walking by the superintendent, talking garrulously: 'Well, sir, all hass passed off with the utmost satisfactoriness. It wass all finished – flick! like that. It iss not always so – oah, no! I have known cases where the doctor wass obliged to go beneath the gallows and pull the prisoner's legs to ensure decease. Most disagreeable!'

'Wriggling about, eh? That's bad,' said the superintendent.

'Ach, sir, it iss worse when they become refractory! One man, I recall, clung to the bars of hiss cage when we went to take him out. You will scarcely credit, sir, that it took six warders to dislodge him, three pulling at each leg. We reasoned with him. "My dear fellow," we said, "think of all the pain and trouble you are causing to us!" But no, he would not listen! Ach, he wass very troublesome!'

I found that I was laughing quite loudly. Everyone was laughing. Even the superintendent grinned in a tolerant way. 'You'd better all come out and have a drink,' he said quite genially. 'I've got a bottle of whisky in the car. We could do with it.'

We went through the big double gates of the prison, into the road. 'Pulling at his legs!' exclaimed a Burmese magistrate suddenly, and burst into a loud chuckling. We all began laughing again. At that moment Francis's anecdote seemed extraordinarily funny. We all had a drink together, native and European alike, quite amicably. The dead man was a hundred yards away.

1931

Shooting an Elephant

In Moulmein, in Lower Burma, I was hated by large numbers of people – the only time in my life that I have been important enough for this to happen to me. I was sub-divisional police officer of the town, and in an aimless, petty kind of way anti-European feeling was very bitter. No one had the guts to raise a riot, but if a European woman went through the bazaars alone somebody would probably spit betel juice over her dress. As a police officer I was an obvious target and was baited whenever it seemed safe to do so. When a nimble Burman tripped me up on the football field and the referee (another Burman) looked the other way, the crowd yelled with hideous laughter. This happened more than once. In the end the sneering yellow faces of young men that met me everywhere, the insults hooted after me when I was at a safe distance, got badly on my nerves. The young Buddhist priests were the worst of all. There were several thousands of them in the town and none of them seemed to have anything to do except stand on street corners and jeer at Europeans.

All this was perplexing and upsetting. For at that time I had already made up my mind that imperialism was an evil thing and the sooner I chucked up my job and got out of it the better. Theoretically – and secretly, of course – I was all for the Burmese and all against their oppressors, the British. As for the job I was doing, I hated it more bitterly than I can perhaps make clear. In a job like that you see the dirty work of Empire at close quarters. The wretched prisoners huddling in the stinking cages of the lock-ups, the grey, cowed faces of the long-term convicts, the scarred buttocks of the men who had been flogged with bamboos – all these oppressed me with an intolerable sense of guilt. But I could get nothing into perspective. I was young and ill-educated and I had had to think out my problems in the utter silence that is imposed on every Englishman in the East. I did not even know that the British Empire is dying, still less did I know that it is a great deal better than the younger empires that are going to supplant it. All I knew was that I was stuck between my hatred of the empire I served and my rage against the evil-spirited little beasts who tried to make my job impossible. With one part of my mind I thought of the British Raj as an unbreakable tyranny, as something clamped down, *in saecula saeculorum*, upon the will of prostrate peoples; with another part I thought that the greatest joy in the world would be to drive a bayonet into a Buddhist priest's guts. Feelings like these are the normal by-products of imperialism; ask any Anglo-Indian official, if you can catch him off duty.

One day something happened which in a roundabout way was enlightening. It was a tiny incident in itself, but it gave me a better glimpse than I had had before of the real nature of imperialism – the real motives for which despotic governments act. Early one morning the sub-inspector at a police station the other end of town rang me up on the phone and said that an elephant was ravaging the bazaar. Would I please come and do something about it? I did not know what I could do, but I wanted to see what was happening and I got on to a pony and started out. I took my rifle, an old .44 Winchester and much too small to kill an elephant, but I thought the noise might be useful *in terrorem*. Various Burmans stopped me on the way and told me about the elephant's doings. It was not, of course, a wild elephant, but a tame one which had gone 'must'. It had been chained up as tame elephants always are when their attack of 'must' is due, but on the previous night it had broken its chain and escaped. Its mahout, the only person who could manage it when it was in that state, had set out in pursuit, but he had taken the wrong direction and was now twelve hours' journey away, and in the morning the elephant had suddenly reappeared in the town. The Burmese population had no weapons and were quite helpless against it. It had already destroyed somebody's bamboo hut, killed a cow and raided some fruit-stalls and devoured the stock; also it had met the municipal rubbish van, and, when the driver jumped out and took to his heels, had turned the van over and inflicted violence upon it.

The Burmese sub-inspector and some Indian constables were waiting for me in the quarter where the elephant had been seen. It was a very poor quarter, a labyrinth of squalid bamboo huts, thatched with palm-leaf, winding all over a steep hillside. I remember that it was a cloudy stuffy morning at the beginning of the rains. We began questioning the people as to where the elephant had gone, and, as usual, failed to get any definite information. That is invariably the case in the East; a story always sounds clear enough at a distance, but the nearer you get to the scene of events the vaguer it becomes. Some of the people said that the elephant had gone in one direction, some said that he had gone in another, some professed not even to have heard of any elephant. I had almost made up my mind that the whole story was a pack of lies, when we heard yells a little distance away. There was a loud, scandalized cry of 'Go away, child! Go away this instant!' and an old woman with a switch in her hand came round the corner of a hut, violently shooing away a crowd of naked children. Some more women followed, clicking their tongues and exclaiming; evidently there was something there that the children ought not to have seen. I rounded the hut and saw a man's dead body sprawling in the mud. He was an Indian, a black Dravidian coolie, almost naked, and he could not have been dead many minutes. The people said that the elephant had come suddenly upon him round the corner of the hut, caught him with its trunk, put its foot on his back and ground him into the earth. This was the rainy season and the ground was soft, and his face had scored a trench a foot deep and a couple of yards long. He was lying on his belly with arms crucified and head sharply twisted to one side. His face was coated with mud, the eyes wide open, the teeth bared and grinning with an expression of unendurable agony. (Never tell me, by the way, that the dead look peaceful. Most of the corpses I have seen looked devilish.) The friction of the great beast's foot had stripped the skin from his back as neatly as one skins a rabbit. As soon as I saw the dead man I sent an orderly to a friend's house near by to borrow an elephant rifle. I had already sent back the pony, not wanting it to go mad with fright and throw me if it smelled the elephant.

The orderly came back in a few minutes with a rifle and five cartridges, and meanwhile some Burmans had arrived and told us that the elephant was in the paddy fields below, only a few hundred yards away. As I started forward practically the whole population of the quarter flocked out of their houses and followed me. They had seen the rifle and were all shouting excitedly that I was going to shoot the elephant. They had not shown much interest in the elephant when he was merely ravaging their homes, but it was different now that he was going to be shot. It was a bit of fun to them, as it would be to an English crowd; besides, they wanted the meat. It made me vaguely uneasy. I had no intention of shooting the elephant – I had merely sent for the rifle to defend myself if necessary – and it is always unnerving to have a crowd following you. I marched down the hill, looking and feeling a fool, with the rifle over my shoulder and an ever-growing army of people jostling at my heels. At the bottom when you got away from the huts there was a metalled road and beyond that a miry waste of paddy fields a thousand yards across, not yet ploughed but soggy from the first rains and dotted with coarse grass. The elephant was standing eighty yards from the road, his left side towards us. He took not the slightest notice of the crowd's approach. He was tearing up bunches of grass, beating them against his knees to clean them and stuffing them into his mouth.

I had halted on the road. As soon as I saw the elephant I knew with perfect certainty that I ought not to shoot him. It is a serious matter to shoot a working elephant – it is comparable to destroying a huge and costly piece of machinery – and obviously one ought not to do it if it can possibly be avoided. And at that distance, peacefully eating, the elephant looked no more dangerous than a cow. I thought then and I think now that his attack of 'must' was already passing off; in which case he would merely wander harmlessly about until the mahout came back and caught him. Moreover, I did not in the least want to shoot him. I decided that I would watch him for a little while to make sure that he did not turn savage again, and then go home.

But at that moment I glanced round at the crowd that had followed me. It was an immense crowd, two thousand at the least and growing every minute. It blocked the road for a long distance on either side. I looked at the sea of yellow faces above the garish clothes – faces all happy and excited over this bit of fun, all certain that the elephant was going to be shot. They were watching me as they would watch a conjurer about to perform a trick. They did not like me, but with the magical rifle in my hands I was momentarily worth watching. And suddenly I realized that I should have to shoot the elephant after all. The people expected it of me and I had got to do it; I could feel their two thousand wills pressing me forward, irresistibly. And it was at this moment, as I stood there with the rifle in my hands, that I first grasped the hollowness, the futility of the white man's dominion in the East. Here was I, the white man with his gun, standing in front of the unarmed native crowd – seemingly the leading actor of the piece; but in reality I was only an absurd puppet pushed to and fro by the will of those yellow faces behind. I perceived in this moment that when the white man turns tyrant it is his own freedom that he destroys. He becomes a sort of hollow, posing dummy, the conventionalized figure of a sahib. For it is the condition of his rule that he shall spend his life in trying to impress the 'natives' and so in every crisis he has got to do what the 'natives' expect of him. He wears a mask, and his face grows to fit it. I had got to shoot the elephant. I had committed myself to doing it when I sent for the rifle. A sahib has got to act like a sahib; he has got to appear resolute, to know his own mind and do definite things. To come all that way, rifle in hand, with two thousand people marching at my heels, and then to trail feebly away, having done nothing – no, that was impossible. The crowd would laugh at me. And my whole life, every white man's life in the East, was one long struggle not be be laughed at.

But I did not want to shoot the elephant. I watched him beating his bunch of grass against his knees, with that preoccupied grandmotherly air that elephants have. It seemed to me that it would be murder to shoot him. At that age I was not squeamish about killing animals, but I had never shot an elephant and never wanted to. (Somehow it always seems worse to kill a *large* animal.) Besides, there was the beast's owner to be considered. Alive, the elephant was worth at least a hundred pounds; dead, he would only be worth the value of his tusks – five pounds, possibly. But I had got to act quickly. I turned to some experienced-looking Burmans who had been there when we arrived, and asked them how the elephant had been behaving. They all said the same thing: he took no notice of you if you left him alone, but he might charge if you went too close to him.

It was perfectly clear to me what I ought to do. I ought to walk up to within, say, twenty-five yards of the elephant and test his behaviour. If he charged I could shoot, if he took no notice of me it would be safe to leave him until the mahout came back. But also I knew that I was going to do no such thing. I was a poor shot with a rifle and the ground was soft mud into which one would sink at every step. If the elephant charged and I missed him, I should have about as much chance as a toad under a steam-roller. But even then I was not thinking particularly of my own skin, only the watchful yellow faces behind. For at that moment, with the crowd watching me, I was not afraid in the ordinary sense, as I would have been if I had been alone. A white man mustn't be frightened in front of 'natives'; and so, in general, he isn't frightened. The sole thought in my mind was that if anything went wrong those two thousand Burmans would see me pursued, caught, trampled on and reduced to a grinning corpse like that Indian up the hill. And if that happened it was quite probable that some of them would laugh. That would never do. There was only one alternative. I shoved the cartridges into the magazine and lay down on the road to get a better aim.

The crowd grew very still, and a deep, low, happy sigh, as of people who see the theatre curtain go up at last, breathed from innumerable throats. They were going to have their bit of fun after all. The rifle was a beautiful German thing with cross-hair sights. I did not then know that in shooting an elephant one should shoot to cut an imaginary bar running from ear-hole to ear-hole. I ought therefore, as the elephant was sideways on, to have aimed straight at his ear-hole; actually I aimed several inches in front of this, thinking the brain would be further forward.

When I pulled the trigger I did not hear the bang or feel the kick – one never does when a shot goes home – but I heard the devilish roar of glee that went up from the crowd. In that instant, in too short a time, one would have thought, even for the bullet to get there, a mysterious, terrible change had come over the elephant. He neither stirred nor fell, but every line of his body had altered. He looked suddenly stricken, shrunken, immensely old, as though the frightful impact of the bullet had paralysed him without knocking him down. At last, after what seemed a long time – it might have been five seconds, I dare say – he sagged flabbily to his knees. His mouth slobbered. An enormous senility seemed to have settled upon him. One could have imagined him thousands of years old. I fired again into the same spot. At the second shot he did not collapse but climbed with desperate slowness to his feet and stood weakly upright, with legs sagging and head drooping. I fired a third time. That was the shot that did for him. You could see the agony of it jolt his whole body and knock the last remnant of strength from his legs. But in falling he seemed for a moment to rise, for as his hind legs collapsed beneath him he seemed to tower upwards like a huge rock toppling, his trunk reaching skyward like a tree. He trumpeted, for the first and only time. And then down he came, his belly towards me, with a crash that seemed to shake the ground even where I lay.

I got up. The Burmans were already racing past me across the mud. It was obvious that the elephant would never rise again, but he was not dead. He was breathing very rhythmically with long rattling gasps, his great mound of a side painfully rising and falling. His mouth was wide open – I could see far down into caverns of pale pink throat. I waited a long time for him to die, but his breathing did not weaken. Finally I fired two remaining shots into the spot where I thought his heart must be. The thick blood welled out of him like red velvet, but still he did not die. His body did not even jerk when the shots hit him, the tortured breathing continued without a pause. He was dying, very slowly and in great agony, but in some world remote from me where not even a bullet could damage him further. I felt that I had got to put an end to that dreadful noise. It seemed dreadful to see the great beast lying there, powerless to move and yet powerless to die, and not even to be able to finish him. I sent back for my small rifle and poured shot after shot into his heart and down his throat. They seemed to make no impression. The tortured gasps continued as steadily as the ticking of a clock.

In the end I could not stand it any longer and went away. I heard later that it took him half an hour to die. Burmans were arriving with dahs and baskets even before I left, and I was told they had stripped his body almost to the bones by the afternoon.

Afterwards, of course, there were endless discussions about the shooting of the elephant. The owner was furious, but he was only an Indian and could do nothing. Besides, legally I had done the right thing, for a mad elephant has to be killed, like a mad dog, if its owner fails to control it. Among the Europeans opinion was divided. The older men said I was right, the younger men said it was a damn shame to shoot an elephant for killing a coolie, because an elephant was worth more than any damn Coringhee coolie. And afterwards I was very glad that the coolie had been killed; it put me legally in the right and it gave me a sufficient pretext for shooting the elephant. I often wondered whether any of the others grasped that I had done it solely to avoid looking a fool.

1936

Bookshop Memories

When I worked in a second-hand bookshop – so easily pictured, if you don't work in one, as a kind of paradise where charming old gentlemen browse eternally among calf-bound folios – the thing that chiefly struck me was the rarity of really bookish people. Our shop had an exceptionally interesting stock, yet I doubt whether ten per cent of our customers knew a good book from a bad one. First edition snobs were much commoner than lovers of literature, but oriental students haggling over cheap textbooks were commoner still, and vague-minded women looking for birthday presents for their nephews were commonest of all.

Many of the people who came to us were of the kind who would be a nuisance anywhere but have special opportunities in a bookshop. For example, the dear old lady who 'wants a book for an invalid' (a very common demand, that), and the other dear old lady who read such a nice book in 1897 and wonders whether you can find her a copy. Unfortunately she doesn't remember the title or the author's name or what the book was about, but she does remember that it had a red cover. But apart from these there are two well-known types of pest by whom every second-hand bookshop is haunted. One is the decayed person smelling of old breadcrusts who comes every day, sometimes several times a day, and tries to sell you worthless books. The other is the person who orders large quantities of books for which he has not the smallest intention of paying. In our shop we sold nothing on credit, but we would put books aside, or order them if necessary, for people who arranged to fetch them away later. Scarcely half the people who ordered books from us ever came back. It used to puzzle me at first. What made them do it? They would come in and demand some rare and expensive book, would make us promise over and over again to keep it for them, and then would vanish never to return. But many of them, of course, were unmistakable paranoiacs. They used to talk in a grandiose manner about themselves and tell the most ingenious stories to explain how they had happened to come out of doors without any money – stories which, in many cases, I am sure they themselves believed. In a town like London there are always plenty of not quite certifiable lunatics walking the streets, and they tend to gravitate towards bookshops, because a bookshop is one of the few places where you can hang about for a long time without spending any money. In the end one gets to know these people almost at a glance. For all their big talk there is something moth-eaten and aimless about them. Very often, when we were dealing with an obvious paranoiac, we would put aside the books he asked for and then put them back on the shelves the moment he had gone. None of them, I noticed, ever attempted to take books away without paying for them; merely to order them was enough – it gave them, I suppose, the illusion that they were spending real money.

Like most second-hand bookshops we had various sidelines. We sold second-hand typewriters, for instance, and also stamps

– used stamps, I mean. Stamp-collectors are a strange, silent, fish-like breed, of all ages, but only of the male sex; women, apparently, fail to see the peculiar charm of gumming bits of coloured paper into albums. We also sold sixpenny horoscopes compiled by somebody who claimed to have foretold the Japanese earthquake. They were in sealed envelopes and I never opened one of them myself, but the people who bought them often came back and told us how 'true' their horoscopes had been. (Doubtless any horoscope seems 'true' if it tells you that you are highly attractive to the opposite sex and your worst fault is generosity.) We did a good deal of business in children's books, chiefly 'remainders'. Modern books for children are rather horrible things, especially when you see them in the mass. Personally I would sooner give a child a copy of Petronius Arbiter than *Peter Pan*, but even Barrie seems manly and wholesome compared with some of his later imitators. At Christmas time we spent a feverish ten days struggling with Christmas cards and calendars, which are tiresome things to sell but good business while the season lasts. It used to interest me to see the brutal cynicism with which Christian sentiment is exploited. The touts from the Christmas card firms used to come round with their catalogues as early as June. A phrase from one of their invoices sticks in my memory. It was: '2 doz. Infant Jesus with rabbits'.

But our principal sideline was a lending library – the usual 'twopenny no-deposit' library of five or six hundred volumes, all fiction. How the book thieves must love those libraries! It is the easiest crime in the world to borrow a book at one shop for twopence, remove the label and sell it at another shop for a shilling. Nevertheless booksellers generally find that it pays them better to have a certain number of books stolen (we used to lose about a dozen a month) than to frighten customers away by demanding a deposit.

Our shop stood exactly on the frontier between Hampstead and Camden Town, and we were frequented by all types from baronets to bus-conductors. Probably our library subscribers were a fair cross-section of London's reading public. It is therefore worth noting that of all the authors in our library the one who 'went out' the best was – Priestley? Hemingway? Walpole? Wodehouse? No, Ethel M. Dell, with Warwick Deeping a good second and Jeffrey Farnol, I should say, third. Dell's novels, of course, are read solely by women, but by women of all kinds and ages and not, as one might expect, merely by wistful spinsters and the fat wives of tobacconists. It is not true that men don't read novels, but it is true that there are whole branches of fiction that they avoid. Roughly speaking, what one might call the average novel – the ordinary, good-bad, Galsworthy-and-water stuff which is the norm of the English novel – seems to exist only for women. Men read either the novels it is possible to respect, or detective stories. But their consumption of detective stories is terrific. One of our subscribers to my knowledge read four or five detective stories every week for over a year, besides others which he got from another library. What chiefly surprised me was that he never read the same book twice. Apparently the whole of that frightful torrent of trash (the pages read every year would, I calculated, cover nearly three quarters of an acre) was stored for ever in his memory. He took no notice of titles or author's names, but he could tell by merely glancing into a book whether he had 'had it already'.

In a lending library you see people's real tastes, not their pretended ones, and one thing that strikes you is how completely the 'classical' English novelists have dropped out of favour. It is simply useless to put Dickens, Thackeray, Jane Austen, Trollope, etc. into the ordinary lending library; nobody takes them out. At the mere sight of a nineteenth-century novel people say, 'Oh, but that's *old*!' and shy away immediately. Yet it is always fairly easy to *sell* Dickens, just as it is always easy to sell Shakespeare. Dickens is one of those authors whom people are 'always meaning to' read, and, like the Bible, he is widely known at second hand. People know by hearsay that Bill Sikes was a burglar and that Mr Micawber had a bald head, just as they know by hearsay that Moses was found in a basket of bulrushes and saw the 'back parts' of the Lord. Another thing that is very noticeable is the growing unpopularity of American books. And another – the publishers get into a stew about this every two or three years – is the unpopularity of short stories. The kind of person who asks the librarian to choose a book for him nearly always starts by saying 'I don't want short stories', or 'I do not desire little stories', as a German customer of ours used to put it. If you ask them why, they sometimes explain that it is too much fag to get used to a new set of characters with every story; they like to 'get into' a novel which demands no further thought after the first chapter. I believe, though, that the writers are more to blame here than the readers. Most modern short stories, English and American, are utterly lifeless and worthless, far more so than most novels. The short stories which *are* stories are popular enough, *vide* D. H. Lawrence, whose short stories are as popular as his novels.

Would I like to be a bookseller *de métier*? On the whole – in spite of my employer's kindness to me, and some happy days I spent in the shop – no.

Given a good pitch and the right amount of capital, any educated person ought to be able to make a small secure living out of a bookshop. Unless one goes in for 'rare' books it is not a difficult trade to learn, and you start at a great advantage if you know anything about the insides of books. (Most booksellers don't. You can get their measure by having a look at the trade papers where they advertise their wants. If you don't see an ad. for Boswell's *Decline and Fall* you are pretty sure to see one for *The Mill on the Floss* by T. S. Eliot.) Also it is a humane trade which is not capable of being vulgarized beyond a certain point. The combines can never squeeze the small independent bookseller out of existence as they have squeezed the grocer and the milkman. But the hours of work are very long – I was only a part-time employee, but my employer put in a seventy-hour week, apart from constant expeditions out of hours to buy books – and it is an unhealthy life. As a rule a bookshop is horribly cold in winter, because if it is too warm the windows get misted over, and a bookseller lives on his windows. And books give off more and nastier dust than any other class of objects yet invented, and the top of a book is the place where every bluebottle prefers to die.

But the real reason why I should not like to be in the book trade for life is that while I was in it I lost my love of books. A bookseller has to tell lies about books, and that gives him a distaste for them; still worse is the fact that he is constantly dusting them and hauling them to and fro.

There was a time when I really did love books – loved the sight and smell and feel of them, I mean, at least if they were fifty or more years old. Nothing pleased me quite so much as to buy a job lot of them for a shilling at a country auction. There is a peculiar flavour about the battered unexpected books you pick up in that kind of collection: minor eighteenth-century poets, out-of-date gazetteers, odd volumes of forgotten novels, bound numbers of ladies' magazines of the sixties. For casual reading – in your bath, for instance, or late at night when you are too tired to go to bed, or in the odd quarter of an hour before lunch – there is nothing to touch a back number of the *Girl's Own Paper*. But as soon as I went to work in the bookshop I stopped buying books. Seen in the mass, five or ten thousand at a time, books were boring and even slightly sickening. Nowadays I do buy one occasionally, but only if it is a book that I want to read and can't borrow, and I never buy junk. The sweet smell of decaying paper appeals to me no longer. It is too closely associated in my mind with paranoiac customers and dead bluebottles.

1936

Charles Dickens

I

Dickens is one of those writers who are well worth stealing. Even the burial of his body in Westminster Abbey was a species of theft, if you come to think of it.

When Chesterton wrote his Introductions to the Everyman Edition of Dickens's works, it seemed quite natural to him to credit Dickens with his own highly individual brand of medievalism, and more recently a Marxist writer, Mr T. A. Jackson,[1] has made spirited efforts to turn Dickens into a bloodthirsty revolutionary. The Marxist claims him as 'almost' a Marxist, the Catholic claims him as 'almost' a Catholic, and both claim him as a champion of the proletariat (or 'the poor', as Chesterton would have put it). On the other hand, Nadezhda Krupskaya, in her little book on Lenin, relates that towards the end of his life Lenin went to see a dramatized version of *The Cricket on the Hearth*, and found Dickens's 'middle-class sentimentality' so intolerable that he walked out in the middle of a scene.

Taking 'middle-class' to mean what Krupskaya might be

[1] *Charles Dickens: The Progress of a Radical* By T. A. Jackson, 1937.

expected to mean by it, this was probably a truer judgement than those of Chesterton and Jackson. But it is worth noticing that the dislike of Dickens implied in this remark is something unusual. Plenty of people have found him unreadable, but very few seem to have felt any hostility towards the general spirit of his work. Some years ago Mr Bechhofer Roberts published a full-length attack on Dickens in the form of a novel (*This Side Idolatry*), but it was a merely personal attack, concerned for the most part with Dickens's treatment of his wife. It dealt with incidents which not one in a thousand of Dickens's readers would ever hear about, and which no more invalidate his work than the second-best bed invalidates *Hamlet*. All that the book really demonstrated was that a writer's literary personality has little or nothing to do with his private character. It is quite possible that in private life Dickens was just the kind of insensitive egoist that Mr Bechhofer Roberts makes him appear. But in his published work there is implied a personality quite different from this, a personality which has won him far more friends than enemies. It might well have been otherwise, for even if Dickens was a bourgeois, he was certainly a subversive writer, a radical, one might truthfully say a rebel. Everyone who has read widely in his work has felt this. Gissing, for instance, the best of the writers on Dickens, was anything but a radical himself, and he disapproved of this strain in Dickens and wished it were not there, but it never occurred to him to deny it. In *Oliver Twist, Hard Times, Bleak House, Little Dorrit*, Dickens attacked English institutions with a ferocity that has never since been approached. Yet he managed to do it without making himself hated, and, more than this, the very people he attacked have swallowed him so completely that he has become a national institution himself. In its attitude towards Dickens the English public has always been a little like the elephant which feels a blow with a walking stick as a delightful tickling. Before I was ten years old I was having Dickens ladled down my throat by schoolmasters in whom even at that age I could see a strong resemblance to Mr Creakle, and one knows without needing to be told that lawyers delight in Serjeant Buzfuz and that *Little Dorrit* is a favourite in the Home Office. Dickens seems to have succeeded in attacking everybody and antagonizing nobody. Naturally this makes one wonder whether after all there was something unreal in his attack upon society. Where exactly does he stand, socially, morally and politically? As usual, one can define his position more easily if one starts by deciding what he was *not*.

In the first place he was *not*, as Messrs Chesterton and Jackson seem to imply, a 'proletarian' writer. To begin with, he does not write about the proletariat, in which he merely resembles the overwhelming majority of novelists, past and present. If you look for the working classes in fiction, and especially English fiction, all you find is a hole. This statement needs qualifying perhaps. For reasons that are easy enough to see, the agricultural labourer (in England a proletarian) gets a fairly good showing in fiction, and a great deal has been written about criminals, derelicts and, more recently, the working-class intelligentsia. But the ordinary town proletariat, the people who make the wheels go round, have always been ignored by novelists. When they do find their way between the covers of a book, it is nearly always as objects of pity or as comic relief. The central action of Dickens's stories almost invariably takes place in middle-class surroundings. If one examines his novels in detail one finds that his real subject-matter is the London commercial bourgeoisie and their hangers-on – lawyers, clerks, tradesmen, innkeepers, small craftsmen and servants. He has no portrait of an agricultural worker, and only one (Stephen Blackpool in *Hard Times*) of an industrial worker. The Plornishes in *Little Dorrit* are probably his best picture of a working-class family – the Peggottys, for instance, hardly belong to the working class – but on the whole he is not successful with this type of character. If you ask any ordinary reader which of Dickens's proletarian characters he can remember, the three he is almost certain to mention are Bill Sikes, Sam Weller and Mrs Gamp. A burglar, a valet and a drunken midwife – not exactly a representative cross-section of the English working class.

Secondly, in the ordinarily accepted sense of the word, Dickens is not a 'revolutionary' writer. But his position here needs some defining.

Whatever else Dickens may have been, he was not a hole-and-corner soul-saver, the kind of well-meaning idiot who thinks that the world will be perfect if you amend a few by-laws and abolish a few anomalies. It is worth comparing him with Charles Reade, for instance. Reade was a much better informed man than Dickens, and in some ways more public-spirited. He really hated the abuses he could understand, he showed them up in a series of novels which for all their absurdity are extremely readable, and he probably helped to alter public opinion on a few minor but important points. But it was quite beyond him to grasp that, given the existing form of society, certain evils *cannot* be remedied. Fasten upon this or that minor abuse, expose it, drag it into the open, bring it before a British jury, and all will be well – that is how he sees it. Dickens at any rate never imagined that you can cure pimples by cutting them off. In every page of his work one can see a consciousness that society is wrong somewhere at the root. It is when one asks 'Which root?' that one begins to grasp his position.

The truth is that Dickens's criticism of society is almost exclusively moral. Hence the utter lack of any constructive suggestion anywhere in his work. He attacks the law, parliamentary government, the educational system and so forth, without ever clearly suggesting what he would put in their places. Of course it is not necessarily the business of a novelist, or a satirist, to make constructive suggestions, but the point is that Dickens's attitude is at bottom not even *destructive*. There is no clear sign that he wants the existing order to be overthrown, or that he believes it would make very much difference if it *were* overthrown. For in reality his target is not so much society as 'human nature'. It would be difficult to point anywhere in his books to a passage suggesting that the economic system is wrong *as a system*. Nowhere, for instance, does he make any attack on private enterprise or private property. Even in a book like *Our Mutual Friend*, which turns on the power of corpses to interfere with living people by means of idiotic wills, it does not occur to him to suggest that individuals ought not to have this irresponsible power. Of course one can draw this inference for oneself, and one can draw it again from the remarks about Bounderby's will at the end of *Hard Times*, and indeed from the whole of Dickens's work one can infer the evil of *laissez-faire* capitalism; but Dickens makes no such inference himself. It is said that Macaulay refused to review *Hard Times* because he disapproved of its 'sullen Socialism'. Obviously Macaulay is here using the word 'Socialism' in the same sense in which, twenty years ago, a vegetarian meal or a Cubist picture used to be referred to as 'Bolshevism'. There is not a line in the book that can properly be called Socialistic; indeed, its tendency if anything is pro-capitalist, because its whole moral is that capitalists ought to be kind, not that workers ought to be rebellious. Bounderby is a bullying windbag and Gradgrind has been morally blinded, but if they were better men, the system would work well enough – that, all through, is the implication. And so far as social criticism goes, one can never extract much more from Dickens than this, unless one deliberately reads meanings into him. His whole 'message' is one that at first glance looks like an enormous platitude: If men would behave decently the world would be decent.

Naturally this calls for a few characters who are in positions of authority and who *do* behave decently. Hence that recurrent Dickens figure, the Good Rich Man. This character belongs especially to Dickens's early optimistic period. He is usually a 'merchant' (we are not necessarily told what merchandise he deals in), and he is always a superhumanly kind-hearted old gentleman who 'trots' to and fro, raising his employees' wages, patting children on the head, getting debtors out of jail and, in general, acting the fairy godmother. Of course he is a pure dream figure, much further from real life than, say, Squeers or Micawber. Even Dickens must have reflected occasionally that anyone who was so anxious to give his money away would never have acquired it in the first place. Mr Pickwick, for instance, had 'been in the city', but it is difficult to imagine him making a fortune there. Nevertheless this character runs like a connecting thread through most of the earlier books. Pickwick, the Cheerybles, old Chuzzlewit, Scrooge – it is the same figure over and over again, the good rich man, handing out guineas. Dickens does however show signs of development here. In the books of the middle period the good rich man fades out to some extent. There is no one who plays this part in *A Tale of*

Two Cities, nor in *Great Expectations* – *Great Expectations* is, in fact definitely an attack on patronage – and in *Hard Times* it is only very doubtfully played by Gradgrind after his reformation. The character reappears in a rather different form as Meagles in *Little Dorrit* and John Jarndyce in *Bleak House* – one might perhaps add Betsy Trotwood in *David Copperfield*. But in these books the good rich man has dwindled from a 'merchant' to a *rentier*. This is significant. A *rentier* is part of the possessing class, he can and, almost without knowing it, does make other people work for him, but he has very little direct power. Unlike Scrooge or the Cheerybles, he cannot put everything right by raising everybody's wages. The seeming inference from the rather despondent books that Dickens wrote in the fifties is that by that time he had grasped the helplessness of well-meaning individuals in a corrupt society. Nevertheless in the last completed novel, *Our Mutual Friend* (published 1864-5), the good rich man comes back in full glory in the person of Boffin. Boffin is a proletarian by origin and only rich by inheritance, but he is the usual *deus ex machina*, solving everybody's problems by showering money in all directions. He even 'trots' like the Cheerybles. In several ways *Our Mutual Friend* is a return to the earlier manner, and not an unsuccessful return either. Dickens's thoughts seem to have come full circle. Once again, individual kindliness is the remedy for everything.

One crying evil of his time that Dickens says very little about is child labour. There are plenty of pictures of suffering children in his books, but usually they are suffering in schools rather than in factories. The one detailed account of child labour that he gives is the description in *David Copperfield* of little David washing bottles in Murdstone & Grinby's warehouse. This, of course, is autobiography. Dickens himself, at the age of ten, had worked in Warren's blacking factory in the Strand, very much as he describes it here. It was a terribly bitter memory to him, partly because he felt the whole incident to be discreditable to his parents, and he even concealed it from his wife till long after they were married. Looking back on this period, he says in *David Copperfield:*

It is a matter of some surprise to me, even now, that I can have been so easily thrown away at such an age. A child of excellent abilities and with strong powers of observation, quick, eager, delicate, and soon hurt bodily or mentally, it seems wonderful to me that nobody should have made any sign in my behalf. But none was made; and I became, at ten years old, a little labouring hind in the service of Murdstone & Grinby.

And again, having described the rough boys among whom he worked:

No words can express the secret agony of my soul as I sunk into this companionship ... and felt my hopes of growing up to be a learned and distinguished man crushed in my bosom.

Obviously it is not David Copperfield who is speaking, it is Dickens himself. He uses almost the same words in the autobiography that he began and abandoned a few months earlier. Of course Dickens is right in saying that a gifted child ought not to work ten hours a day pasting labels on bottles, but what he does not say is that *no* child ought to be condemned to such a fate, and there is no reason for inferring that he thinks it. David escapes from the warehouse, but Mick Walker and Mealy Potatoes and the others are still there, and there is no sign that this troubles Dickens particularly. As usual, he displays no consciousness that the *structure* of society can be changed.

He despises politics, does not believe that any good can come out of Parliament – he had been a parliamentary shorthand writer, which was no doubt a disillusioning experience – and he is slightly hostile to the most hopeful movement of his day, trade unionism. In *Hard Times* trade unionism is represented as something not much better than a racket, something that happens because employers are not sufficiently paternal. Stephen Blackpool's refusal to join the union is rather a virtue in Dickens's eyes. Also, as Mr Jackson has pointed out, the apprentices' association in *Barnaby Rudge*, to which Sim Tappertit belongs, is probably a hit at the illegal or barely legal unions of Dickens's own day, with their secret assemblies, passwords and so forth. Obviously he wants the workers to be decently treated, but there is no sign that he wants them to take their destiny into their own hands, least of all by open violence.

As it happens, Dickens deals with revolution in the narrower sense in two novels, *Barnaby Rudge* and *A Tale of Two Cities*. In *Barnaby Rudge* it is a case of rioting rather than revolution. The Gordon Riots of 1780, though they had religious bigotry as a pretext, seem to have been little more than a pointless outburst of looting. Dickens's attitude to this kind of thing is sufficiently indicated by the fact that his first idea was to make the ringleaders of the riots three lunatics escaped from an asylum. He was dissuaded from this, but the principal figure of the book is in fact a village idiot. In the chapters dealing with the riots Dickens shows a most profound horror of mob violence. He delights in describing scenes in which the 'dregs' of the population behave with atrocious bestiality. These chapters are of great psychological interest, because they show how deeply he had brooded on this subject. The things he describes can only have come out of his imagination, for no riots on anything like the same scale had happened in his lifetime. Here is one of his descriptions, for instance:

> If Bedlam gates had been flung open wide, there would not have issued forth such maniacs as the frenzy of that night had made. There were men there who danced and trampled on the beds of flowers as though they trod down human enemies, and wrenched them from their stalks, like savages who twisted human necks. There were men who cast their lighted torches in the air, and suffered them to fall upon their heads and faces, blistering the skin with deep unseemly burns. There were men who rushed up to the fire, and paddled in it with their hands as if in water; and others who were restrained by force from plunging in, to gratify their deadly longing. On the skull of one drunken lad – not twenty, by his looks – who lay upon the ground with a bottle to his mouth, the lead from the roof came streaming down in a shower of liquid fire, white hot, melting his head like wax . . . But of all the howling throng not one learnt mercy from, or sickened at, these sights; nor was the fierce, besotted, senseless rage of one man glutted.

You might almost think you were reading a description of 'red' Spain by a partisan of General Franco. One ought, of course, to remember that when Dickens was writing, the London 'mob' still existed. (Nowadays there is no mob, only a flock.) Low wages and the growth and shift of population had brought into existence a huge, dangerous slum-proletariat, and until the early middle of the nineteenth century there was hardly such a thing as a police force. When the brickbats began to fly there was nothing between shuttering your windows and ordering the troops to open fire. In *A Tale of Two Cities* he is dealing with a revolution which was really *about* something, and Dickens's attitude is different, but not entirely different. As a matter of fact, *A Tale of Two Cities* is a book which tends to leave a false impression behind, especially after a lapse of time.

The one thing that everyone who has read *A Tale of Two Cities* remembers is the Reign of Terror. The whole book is dominated by the guillotine – tumbrils thundering to and fro, bloody knives, heads bouncing into the basket, and sinister old women knitting as they watch. Actually these scenes only occupy a few chapters, but they are written with terrible intensity, and the rest of the book is rather slow going. But *A Tale of Two Cities* is not a companion volume to *The Scarlet Pimpernel*. Dickens sees clearly enough that the French Revolution was bound to happen and that many of the people who were executed deserved what they got. If, he says, you behave as the French aristocracy had behaved, vengeance will follow. He repeats this over and over again. We are constantly being reminded that while 'my lord' is lolling in bed, with four liveried footmen serving his chocolate and the peasants starving outside, somewhere in the forest a tree is growing which will presently be sawn into planks for the platform of the guillotine, etc. etc. etc. The inevitability of the Terror, given its causes, is insisted upon in the clearest terms:

It was too much the way... to talk of this terrible Revolution as if it were the only harvest ever known under the skies that had not been sown – as if nothing had ever been done, or omitted to be done, that had led to it – as if observers of the wretched millions in France, and of the misused and perverted resources that should have made them prosperous, had not seen it inevitably coming, years before, and had not in plain terms recorded what they saw.

And again:

> All the devouring and insatiate monsters imagined since imagination could record itself, are fused in the one realization, Guillotine. And yet there is not in France, with its rich variety of soil and climate, a blade, a leaf, a root, a sprig, a peppercorn, which will grow to maturity under conditions more certain than those that have produced this horror. Crush humanity out of shape once more, under similar hammers, and it will twist itself into the same tortured forms.

In other words, the French aristocracy had dug their own graves. But there is no perception here of what is now called historic necessity. Dickens sees that the results are inevitable, given the causes, but he thinks that the causes might have been avoided. The Revolution is something that happens because centuries of oppression have made the French peasantry sub-human. If the wicked nobleman could somehow have turned over a new leaf, like Scrooge, there would have been no Revolution, no *jacquerie*, no guillotine – and so much the better. This is the opposite of the 'revolutionary' attitude. From the 'revolutionary' point of view the class-struggle is the main source of progress, and therefore the nobleman who robs the peasant and goads him to revolt is playing a necessary part, just as much as the Jacobin who guillotines the nobleman. Dickens never writes anywhere a line that can be interpreted as meaning this. Revolution as he sees it is merely a monster that is begotten by tyranny and always ends by devouring its own instruments. In Sydney Carton's vision at the foot of the guillotine, he foresees Defarge and the other leading spirits of the Terror all perishing under the same knife – which, in fact, was approximately what happened.

And Dickens is very sure that revolution *is* a monster. That is why everyone remembers the revolutionary scenes in *A Tale of Two Cities*; they have the quality of nightmare, and it is Dickens's own nightmare. Again and again he insists upon the meaningless horrors of revolution – the mass-butcheries, the injustice, the ever-present terror of spies, the frightful blood-lust of the mob. The descriptions of the Paris mob – the description, for instance, of the crowd of murderers struggling round the grindstone to sharpen their weapons before butchering the prisoners in the September massacres – outdo anything in *Barnaby Rudge*. The revolutionaries appear to him simply as degraded savages – in fact, as lunatics. He broods over their frenzies with a curious imaginative intensity. He describes them dancing the 'Carmagnole', for instance:

> There could not be fewer than five hundred people, and they were dancing like five thousand demons ... They danced to the popular Revolution song, keeping a ferocious time that was like a gnashing of teeth in unison ... They advanced, retreated, struck at one another's hands, clutched at one another's heads, spun round alone, caught one another, and spun round in pairs, until many of them dropped ... Suddenly they stopped again, paused, struck out the time afresh, forming into lines the width of the public way, and, with their heads low down and their hands high up, swooped screaming off. No fight could have been half so terrible as this dance. It was so emphatically a fallen sport – a something, once innocent, delivered over to all devilry.

He even credits some of these wretches with a taste for guillotining children. The passage I have abridged above ought to be read in full. It and others like it show how deep was Dickens's horror of revolutionary hysteria. Notice, for instance, that touch, 'with their heads low down and their hands high up' etc., and the evil vision it conveys. Madame Defarge is a truly dreadful figure, certainly Dickens's most successful attempt at a *malignant* character. Defarge and others are simply 'the new oppressors who have risen on the destruction of the old', the revolutionary courts are presided over by 'the lowest, cruellest and worst populace', and so on and so forth. All the way through Dickens insists upon the nightmare insecurity of a revolutionary period, and in this he shows a great deal of prescience. 'A law of the suspected, which struck away all security for liberty or life, and delivered over any good and innocent person to any bad and guilty one; prisons gorged with people who had committed no offence, and could obtain no hearing' – it would apply pretty accurately to several countries today.

The apologists of any revolution generally try to minimize its horrors; Dickens's impulse is to exaggerate them – and from a historical point of view he has certainly exaggerated. Even the Reign of Terror was a much smaller thing than he makes it appear. Though he quotes no figures, he gives the impression of a frenzied massacre lasting for years, whereas in reality the whole of the Terror, so far as the number of deaths goes, was a joke compared with one of Napoleon's battles. But the bloody knives and the tumbrils rolling to and fro create in his mind a special, sinister vision which he has succeeded in passing on to generations of readers. Thanks to Dickens, the very word 'tumbril' has a murderous sound; one forgets that a tumbril is only a sort of farm-cart. To this day, to the average Englishman, the French Revolution means no more than a pyramid of severed heads. It is a strange thing that Dickens, much more in sympathy with the ideas of the Revolution than most Englishmen of his time, should have played a part in creating this impression.

If you hate violence and don't believe in politics, the only major remedy remaining is education. Perhaps society is past praying for, but there is always hope for the individual human being, if you can catch him young enough. This belief partly accounts for Dickens's preoccupation with childhood.

No one, at any rate no English writer, has written better about childhood than Dickens. In spite of all the knowledge that has accumulated since, in spite of the fact that children are now comparatively sanely treated, no novelist has shown the same power of entering into the child's point of view. I must have been about nine years old when I first read *David Copperfield*. The mental atmosphere of the opening chapters was so immediately intelligible to me that I vaguely imagined they had been written *by a child*. And yet when one re-reads the book as an adult and sees the Murdstones, for instance, dwindle from gigantic figures of doom into semi-comic monsters, these passages lose nothing. Dickens has been able to stand both inside and outside the child's mind, in such a way that the same scene can be wild burlesque or sinister reality, according to the age at which one reads it. Look, for instance, at the scene in which David Copperfield is unjustly suspected of eating the mutton chops; or the scene in which Pip, in *Great Expectations*, coming back from Miss Havisham's house and finding himself completely unable to describe what he has seen, takes refuge in a series of outrageous lies – which, of course, are eagerly believed. All the isolation of childhood is there. And how accurately he has recorded the mechanisms of the child's mind, its visualizing tendency, its sensitiveness to certain kinds of impression. Pip relates how in his childhood his ideas about his dead parents were derived from their tombstones:

> The shape of the letters on my father's, gave me an odd idea that he was a square, stout, dark man, with curly black hair. From the character and turn of the inscription, 'ALSO GEORGIANA, WIFE OF THE ABOVE', I drew a childish conclusion that my mother was freckled and sickly. To five little stone lozenges, each about a foot and a half long, which were arranged in a neat row beside their grave, and were sacred to the memory of five little brothers of mine ... I am indebted for a belief I religiously entertained that they had all been born on their backs with their hands in their trouser-pockets, and had never taken them out in this state of existence.

There is a similar passage in *David Copperfield*. After biting Mr Murdstone's hand, David is sent away to a school and obliged to wear on his back a placard saying, 'Take care of him. He bites.' He looks at the door in the playground where the boys have carved their names, and from the appearance of each name he seems to know in just what tone of voice the boy will read out the placard:

> There was one boy – a certain J. Steerforth – who cut his name very deep and very often, who, I conceived, would read it in a rather strong voice, and afterwards pull my hair. There was another boy, one Tommy Traddles, who I dreaded would make game of it, and pretend to be dreadfully frightened of me. There was a third, George Demple, who I fancied would sing it.

When I read this passage as a child, it seemed to me that those were exactly the pictures that those particular names would call up. The reason, of course, is the sound-associations of the words (Demple – 'temple'; Traddles – probably 'skedaddle'). But how many people, before Dickens, had ever noticed such things? A sympathetic attitude towards children was a much rarer thing in Dickens's day than it is now. The early nineteenth century was not a good time to be a child. In Dickens's youth children were still being 'solemnly tried at a criminal bar, where they were held up to be seen', and it was not so long since boys of thirteen had been hanged for petty theft. The doctrine of 'breaking the child's spirit' was in full vigour, and *The Fairchild Family*[1] was a standard book for children till late into the century. This evil book is now issued in pretty-pretty expurgated editions, but it is well worth reading in the original version. It gives one some idea of the lengths to which child-discipline was sometimes carried. Mr Fairchild, for instance, when he catches his children quarrelling, first thrashes them, reciting Doctor Watts's 'Let dogs delight to bark and bite' between blows of the cane, and then takes them to spend the afternoon beneath a gibbet where the rotting corpse of a murderer is hanging. In the earlier part of the century scores of thousands of children, aged sometimes as young as six, were literally worked to death in the mines or cotton mills, and even at the fashionable public schools boys were flogged till they ran with blood for a mistake in their Latin verses. One thing which Dickens seems to have recognized, and which most of his contemporaries did not, is the sadistic sexual element in flogging. I think this can be inferred from *David Copperfield* and *Nicholas Nickleby*. But mental cruelty to a child infuriates him as much as physical, and though there is a fair number of exceptions, his schoolmasters are generally scoundrels.

---

[1] *The History of the Fairchild Family* by Mary M. Sherwood, 3 parts, 1818–47.

Except for the universities and the big public schools, every kind of education then existing in England gets a mauling at Dickens's hands. There is Doctor Blimber's Academy, where little boys are blown up with Greek until they burst, and the revolting charity schools of the period, which produced specimens like Noah Claypole and Uriah Heep, and Salem House, and Dotheboys Hall, and the disgraceful little dame-school kept by Mr Wopsle's great-aunt. Some of what Dickens says remains true even today. Salem House is the ancestor of the modern 'prep school', which still has a good deal of resemblance to it; and as for Mr Wopsle's great-aunt, some old fraud of much the same stamp is carrying on at this moment in nearly every small town in England. But, as usual, Dickens's criticism is neither creative nor destructive. He sees the idiocy of an educational system founded on the Greek lexicon and the wax-ended cane; on the other hand, he has no use for the new kind of school that is coming up in the fifties and sixties, the 'modern' school, with its gritty insistence on 'facts'. What, then, *does* he want? As always, what he appears to want is a moralized version of the existing thing — the old type of school, but with no caning, no bullying or underfeeding, and not quite so much Greek. Doctor Strong's school, to which David Copperfield goes after he escapes from Murdstone & Grinby's, is simply Salem House with the vices left out and a good deal of 'old grey stones' atmosphere thrown in:

Doctor Strong's was an excellent school, as different from Mr Creakle's as good is from evil. It was very gravely and decorously ordered, and on a sound system; with an appeal, in everything, to the honour and good faith of the boys . . . which worked wonders. We all felt that we had a part in the management of the place, and in sustaining its character and dignity. Hence, we soon became warmly attached to it – I am sure I did for one, and I never knew, in all my time, of any boy being otherwise – and learnt with a good will, desiring to do it credit. We had noble games out of hours, and plenty of liberty; but even then, as I remember, we were well spoken of in the town, and rarely did any disgrace, by our appearance or manner, to the reputation of Doctor Strong and Doctor Strong's boys.

In the woolly vagueness of this passage one can see Dickens's utter lack of any educational theory. He can imagine the *moral* atmosphere of a good school, but nothing further. The boys 'learnt with a good will', but what did they learn? No doubt it was Doctor Blimber's curriculum, a little watered down. Considering the attitude to society that is everywhere implied in Dickens's novels, it comes as rather a shock to learn that he sent his eldest son to Eton and sent all his children through the ordinary educational mill. Gissing seems to think that he may have done this because he was painfully conscious of being under-educated himself. Here perhaps Gissing is influenced by his own love of classical learning. Dickens had had little or no formal education, but he lost nothing by missing it, and on the whole he seems to have been aware of this. If he was unable to imagine a better school than Doctor Strong's, or, in real life, than Eton, it was probably due to an intellectual deficiency rather different from the one Gissing suggests.

It seems that in every attack Dickens makes upon society he is always pointing to a change of spirit rather than a change of structure. It is hopeless to try and pin him down to any definite remedy, still more to any political doctrine. His approach is always along the moral plane, and his attitude is sufficiently summed up in that remark about Strong's school being as different from Creakle's 'as good is from evil'. Two things can be very much alike and yet abysmally different. Heaven and Hell are in the same place. Useless to change institutions without a 'change of heart' – that, essentially, is what he is always saying.

If that were all, he might be no more than a cheer-up writer, a reactionary humbug. A 'change of heart' is in fact *the* alibi of people who do not wish to endanger the *status quo*. But Dickens is not a humbug, except in minor matters, and the strongest single impression one carries away from his books is that of a hatred of tyranny. I said earlier that Dickens is not *in the accepted sense* a revolutionary writer. But it is not at all certain that a merely moral criticism of society may not be just as 'revolutionary' – and revolution, after all, means turning things upside down – as the politico-economic criticism which is fashionable at this moment. Blake was not a politician, but there is more understanding of the nature of capitalist society in a poem like 'I wander through each charter'd street' than in three quarters of Socialist literature. Progress is not an illusion, it happens, but it is slow and invariably disappointing. There is always a new tyrant waiting to take over from the old – generally not quite so bad, but still a tyrant. Consequently two view-points are always tenable. The one, how can you improve human nature until you have changed the system? The other, what is the use of changing the system before you have improved human nature? They appeal to different individuals, and they probably show a tendency to alternate in point of time. The moralist and the revolutionary are constantly undermining one another. Marx exploded a hundred tons of dynamite beneath the moralist position, and we are still living in the echo of that tremendous crash. But already, somewhere or other, the sappers are at work and fresh dynamite is being stamped in place to blow Marx at the moon. Then Marx, or somebody like him, will come back with yet more dynamite, and so the process continues, to an end we cannot yet foresee. The central problem – how to prevent power from being abused – remains unsolved. Dickens, who had not the vision to see that private property is an obstructive nuisance, had the vision to see that. 'If men would behave decently the world would be decent' is not such a platitude as it sounds.

II

More completely than most writers, perhaps, Dickens can be explained in terms of his social origin, though actually his family history was not quite what one would infer from his novels. His father was a clerk in government service, and through his mother's family he had connexions with both the army and the navy. But from the age of nine onwards he was brought up in London in commercial surroundings, and generally in an atmosphere of struggling poverty. Mentally he belongs to the small urban bourgeoisie, and he happens to be an exceptionally fine specimen of this class, with all the 'points', as it were, very highly developed. That is partly what makes him so interesting. If one wants a modern equivalent, the nearest would be H. G. Wells, who has had a rather similar history and who obviously owes something to Dickens as a novelist. Arnold Bennett was essentially of the same type, but, unlike the other two, he was a midlander, with an industrial and Nonconformist rather than commercial and Anglican background.

The great disadvantage, and advantage, of the small urban bourgeois is his limited outlook. He sees the world as a middle-class world, and everything outside those limits is either laughable or slightly wicked. On the one hand, he has no contact with industry or the soil; on the other, no contact with the governing classes. Anyone who has studied Wells's novels in detail will have noticed that though he hates the aristocrat like poison, he has no particular objection to the plutocrat, and no enthusiasm for the proletarian. His most hated types, the people he believes to be responsible for all human ills, are kings, landowners, priests, nationalists, soldiers, scholars and peasants. At first sight a list beginning with kings and ending with peasants looks like a mere omnium gatherum, but in reality all these people have a common factor. All of them are archaic types, people who are governed by tradition and whose eyes are turned towards the past – the opposite, therefore, of the rising bourgeois who has put his money on the future and sees the past simply as a dead hand.

Actually, although Dickens lived in a period when the bourgeoisie was really a rising class, he displays this characteristic less strongly than Wells. He is almost unconscious of the future and has a rather sloppy love of the picturesque (the 'quaint old church' etc.). Nevertheless his list of most hated types is like enough to Wells's for the similarity to be striking. He is vaguely on the side of the working class – has a sort of generalized sympathy with them because they are oppressed – but he does not in reality know much about them; they come into his books chiefly as servants, and comic servants at that. At the other end of the scale he loathes the aristocrat and – going one better than Wells in this – loathes the big bourgeois as well. His real sympathies are bounded by Mr Pickwick on the upper side and Mr Barkis on the lower. But the term 'aristocrat', for the type Dickens hates, is vague and needs defining.

Actually Dickens's target is not so much the great aristocracy, who hardly enter into his books, as their petty offshoots, the cadging dowagers who live up mews in Mayfair, and the bureaucrats and professional soldiers. All through his books there are countless hostile sketches of these people, and hardly any that are friendly. There are practically no friendly pictures of the land-owning class, for instance. One might make a doubtful exception of Sir Leicester Dedlock; otherwise there is only Mr Wardle (who is a stock figure – the 'good old squire') and Haredale in *Barnaby Rudge*, who has Dickens's sympathy because he is a persecuted Catholic. There are no friendly pictures of soldiers (i.e. officers), and none at all of naval men. As for his bureaucrats, judges and magistrates, most of them would feel quite at home in the Circumlocution Office. The only officials whom Dickens handles with any kind of friendliness are, significantly enough, policemen.

Dickens's attitude is easily intelligible to an Englishman, because it is part of the English puritan tradition, which is not dead even at this day. The class Dickens belonged to, at least by adoption, was growing suddenly rich after a couple of centuries of obscurity. It had grown up mainly in the big towns, out of contact with agriculture, and politically impotent; government, in its experience, was something which either interfered or persecuted. Consequently it was a class with no tradition of public service and not much tradition of usefulness. What now strikes us as remarkable about the new moneyed class of the nineteenth century is their complete irresponsibility; they see everything in terms of individual success, with hardly any consciousness that the community exists. On the other hand, a Tite Barnacle, even when he was neglecting his duties, would have some vague notion of what duties he was neglecting. Dickens's attitude is never irresponsible, still less does he take the money-grubbing Smilesian line; but at the back of his mind there is usually a half-belief that the whole apparatus of government is unnecessary. Parliament is simply Lord Coodle and Sir Thomas Doodle, the Empire is simply Major Bagstock and his Indian servant, the army is simply Colonel Chowser and Doctor Slammer, the public services are simply Bumble and the Circumlocution Office – and so on and so forth. What he does not see, or only intermittently sees, is that Coodle and Doodle and all the other corpses left over from the eighteenth century *are* performing a function which neither Pickwick nor Boffin would ever bother about.

And of course this narrowness of vision is in one way a great advantage to him, because it is fatal for a caricaturist to see too much. From Dickens's point of view 'good' society is simply a collection of village idiots. What a crew! Lady Tippins! Mrs Gowan! Lord Verisopht! The Honourable Bob Stables! Mrs Sparsit (whose husband was a Powler)! The Tite Barnacles! Nupkins! It is practically a case-book in lunacy. But at the same time his remoteness from the landowning-military-bureaucratic class incapacitates him for full-length satire. He only succeeds with this class when he depicts them as mental defectives. The accusation which used to be made against Dickens in his life-time, that he 'could not paint a gentleman', was an absurdity, but it is true in this sense, that what he says against the 'gentleman' class is seldom very damaging. Sir Mulberry Hawk, for instance, is a wretched attempt at the wicked-baronet type. Harthouse in *Hard Times* is better, but he would be only an ordinary achievement for Trollope or Thackeray. Trollope's thoughts hardly move outside the 'gentleman' class, but Thackeray has the great advantage of having a foot in two moral camps. In some ways his outlook is very similar to Dickens's. Like Dickens, he identifies with the puritanical moneyed class against the card-playing, debt-bilking aristocracy. The eighteenth century, as he sees it, is sticking out into the nineteenth in the person of the wicked Lord Steyne. *Vanity Fair* is a full-length version of what Dickens did for a few chapters in *Little Dorrit*. But by origins and upbringing Thackeray happens to be somewhat nearer to the class he is satirizing. Consequently he can produce such comparatively subtle types as, for instance, Major Pendennis and Rawdon Crawley. Major Pendennis is a shallow old snob, and Rawdon Crawley is a thick-headed ruffian who sees nothing wrong in living for years by swindling tradesmen; but what Thackeray realizes is that according to their tortuous code they are neither of them bad men. Major Pendennis would not sign a dud cheque, for instance. Rawdon certainly would, but on the other hand he would not desert a friend in a tight corner. Both of them would behave well on the field of battle – a thing that would not particularly appeal to Dickens. The result is that at the end one is left with a kind of amused tolerance for Major Pendennis and with something approaching respect for Rawdon; and yet one sees, better than any diatribe could make one, the utter rottenness of that kind of cadging, toadying life on the fringes of smart society. Dickens would be quite incapable of this. In his hands both Rawdon and the Major would dwindle to traditional caricatures. And, on the whole, his attacks on 'good' society are rather perfunctory. The aristocracy and the big bourgeoisie exist in his books chiefly as a kind of 'noises off', a haw-hawing chorus somewhere in the wings, like Podsnap's dinner-parties. When he produces a really subtle and damaging portrait, like John Dorrit or Harold Skimpole, it is generally of some rather middling, unimportant person.

One very striking thing about Dickens, especially considering the time he lived in, is his lack of vulgar nationalism. All peoples who have reached the point of becoming nations tend to despise foreigners, but there is not much doubt that the English-speaking races are the worst offenders. Once can see this from the fact that as soon as they become fully aware of any foreign race, they invent an insulting nickname for it. Wop, Dago, Froggy, Squarehead, Kike, Sheeny, Nigger, Wog, Chink, Greaser, Yellowbelly – these are merely a selection. Any time before 1870 the list would have been shorter because the map of the world was different from what it is now, and there were only three or four foreign races that had fully entered into the English consciousness. But towards these, and especially towards France, the nearest and best-hated nation, the English attitude of patronage was so intolerable that English 'arrogance' and 'xenophobia' are still a legend. And of course they are not a completely untrue legend even now. Till very recently nearly all English children were brought up to despise the southern European races, and history as taught in schools was mainly a list of battles won by England. But one has got to read, say, the *Quarterly Review* of the thirties to know what boasting really is. Those were the days when the English built up their legend of themselves as 'sturdy islanders' and 'stubborn hearts of oak' and when it was accepted as a kind of scientific fact that one Englishman was the equal of three foreigners. All through nineteenth-century novels and comic papers there runs the traditional figure of the 'Froggy' – a small ridiculous man with a tiny beard and a pointed top-hat, always jabbering and gesticulating, vain, frivolous and fond of boasting of his martial exploits, but generally taking to flight when real danger appears. Over against him was John Bull, the 'sturdy English yeoman', or (a more public-school version) the 'strong, silent Englishman' of Charles Kingsley, Tom Hughes and others.

Thackeray, for instance, has this outlook very strongly, though there are moments when he sees through it and laughs at it. The one historical fact that is firmly fixed in his mind is that the English won the battle of Waterloo. One never reads far in his books without coming upon some reference to it. The English, as he sees it, are invincible because of their tremendous physical strength, due mainly to living on beef. Like most Englishmen of his time, he has the curious illusion that the English are larger than other people (Thackeray, as it happened, *was* larger than most people), and therefore he is capable of writing passages like this:

> I say to you that you are better than a Frenchman. I would lay even money that you who are reading this are more than five feet seven in height, and weigh eleven stone; while a Frenchman is five feet four and does not weigh nine. The Frenchman has after his soup a dish of vegetables, where you have one of meat. You are a different and superior animal – a French-beating animal (the history of hundreds of years has shown you to be so), etc. etc.

There are similar passages scattered all through Thackeray's works. Dickens would never be guilty of anything of the kind. It would be an exaggeration to say that he nowhere pokes fun at foreigners, and of course, like nearly all nineteenth-century Englishmen, he is untouched by European culture. But never anywhere does he indulge in the typical English boasting, the 'island race', 'bulldog breed', 'right little, tight little island' style of talk. In the whole of *A Tale of Two Cities* there is not a line that could be taken as meaning, 'Look how those wicked Frenchmen behave!' The one place where he seems to display a normal hatred of foreigners is in the American chapters of *Martin Chuzzlewit*. This, however, is simply the reaction of a generous mind against cant. If Dickens were alive today he would make a trip to Soviet Russia and come back with a book rather like Gide's *Retour de l'U.R.S.S.* But he is remarkably free from the idiocy of regarding nations as individuals. He seldom even makes jokes turning on nationality. He does not exploit the comic Irishman and the comic Welshman, for instance, and not because he objects to stock characters and ready-made jokes, which obviously he does not. It is perhaps more significant that he shows no prejudice against Jews. It is true that he takes it for granted (*Oliver Twist* and *Great Expectations*) that a receiver of stolen goods will be a Jew, which at the time was probably justified. But the 'Jew joke', endemic in English literature until the rise of Hitler, does not appear in his books, and in *Our Mutual Friend* he makes a pious though not very convincing attempt to stand up for the Jews.

Dickens's lack of vulgar nationalism is in part the mark of a real largeness of mind, and in part results from his negative, rather unhelpful political attitude. He is very much an Englishman, but he is hardly aware of it – certainly the thought of being an Englishman does not thrill him. He has no imperialist feeling, no discernible views on foreign politics, and is untouched by the military tradition. Temperamentally he is much nearer to the small Nonconformist tradesman who looks down on the 'red-coats' and thinks that war is wicked – a one-eyed view, but, after all, war *is* wicked. It is noticeable that Dickens hardly writes of war, even to denounce it. With all his marvellous powers of description, and of describing things he had never seen, he never describes a battle, unless one counts the attack on the Bastille in *A Tale of Two Cities*. Probably the subject would not strike him as interesting, and in any case he would not regard a battlefield as a place where anything worth settling could be settled. It is one up to the lower-middle-class, puritan mentality.

III

Dickens had grown up near enough to poverty to be terrified of it, and in spite of his generosity of mind, he is not free from the special prejudices of the shabby-genteel. It is usual to claim him as a 'popular' writer, a champion of the 'oppressed masses'. So he is, so long as he thinks of them as oppressed; but there are two things that condition his attitude. In the first place, he is a south of England man, and a cockney at that, and therefore out of touch with the bulk of the real oppressed masses, the industrial and agricultural labourers. It is interesting to see how Chesterton, another cockney, always presents Dickens as the spokesman of 'the poor', without showing much awareness of who 'the poor' really are. To Chesterton 'the poor' means small shopkeepers and servants. Sam Weller, he says, 'is the great symbol in English literature of the populace peculiar to England'; and Sam Weller is a valet! The other point is that Dickens's early experiences have given him a horror of proletarian roughness. He shows this unmistakably whenever he writes of the poorest of the poor, the slum-dwellers. His descriptions of the London slums are always full of undisguised repulsion:

> The ways were foul and narrow; the shops and houses wretched; and people half naked, drunken, slipshod and ugly. Alleys and archways, like so many cesspools, disgorged their offences of smell, and dirt, and life, upon the straggling streets; and the whole quarter reeked with crime, and filth, and misery, etc. etc.

There are many similar passages in Dickens. From them one gets the impression of whole submerged populations whom he regards as being beyond the pale. In rather the same way the modern doctrinaire Socialist contemptuously writes off a large block of the population as 'lumpenproletariat'. Dickens also shows less understanding of criminals than one would expect of him. Although he is well aware of the social and economic causes of crime, he often seems to feel that when a man has once broken the law he has put himself outside human society. There is a chapter at the end of *David Copperfield* in which David visits the prison where Littimer and Uriah Heep are serving their sentences. Dickens actually seems to regard the horrible 'model' prisons, against which Charles Reade delivered his memorable attack in *It is Never Too Late to Mend*, as too humane. He complains that the food is too good! As soon as he comes up against crime or the worst depths of poverty, he shows traces of the 'I've always kept myself respectable' habit of mind. The attitude of Pip (obviously the attitude of Dickens himself) towards Magwitch in *Great Expectations* is extremely interesting. Pip is conscious all along of his ingratitude towards Joe, but far less so of his ingratitude towards Magwitch. When he discovers that the person who has loaded him with benefits for years is actually a transported convict, he falls into frenzies of disgust. 'The abhorrence in which I held the man, the dread I had of him, the repugnance with which I shrank from him, could not have been exceeded if he had been some terrible beast', etc. etc. So far as one can discover from the text, this is not because when Pip was a child he had been terrorized by Magwitch in the churchyard; it is because Magwitch is a criminal and a convict. There is an even more 'kept-myself-respectable' touch in the fact that Pip feels as a matter of course that he cannot take Magwitch's money. The money is not the product of a crime, it has been honestly acquired; but it is an ex-convict's money and therefore 'tainted'. There is nothing psychologically false in this, either. Psychologically the latter part of *Great Expectations* is about the best thing Dickens ever did; throughout this part of the book one feels 'Yes, that is just how Pip would have behaved.' But the point is that in the matter of Magwitch, Dickens identifies with Pip, and his attitude is at bottom snobbish. The result is that Magwitch belongs to the same queer class of characters as Falstaff and, probably, Don Quixote – characters who are more pathetic than the author intended.

When it is a question of the non-criminal poor, the ordinary, decent, labouring poor, there is of course nothing contemptuous in Dickens's attitude. He has the sincerest admiration for people like the Peggottys and the Plornishes. But it is questionable whether he really regards them as equals. It is of the greatest interest to read Chapter XI of *David Copperfield* and side by side with it the autobiographical fragment (parts of this are given in Forster's *Life*, in which Dickens expresses his feelings about the blacking-factory episode a great deal more strongly than in the novel. For more than twenty years afterwards the memory was so painful to him that he would go out of his way to avoid that part of the Strand. He says that to pass that way 'made me cry, after my eldest child could speak'. The text makes it quite clear that what hurt him most of all, then and in retrospect, was the enforced contact with 'low' associates:

> No words can express the secret agony of my soul as I sunk into this companionship; compared these everyday associates with those of happier childhood ... But I held some station at the blacking warehouse too ... I soon became at least as expeditious and as skilful with my hands as either of the other boys. Though perfectly familiar with them, my conduct and manners were different enough from theirs to place a space between us. They, and the men, always spoke of me as 'the young gentleman'. A certain man ... used to call me 'Charles' sometimes in speaking to me; but I think it was mostly when we were very confidential ... Poll Green uprose once, and rebelled against the 'young gentleman' usage; but Bob Fagin settled him speedily.

It was as well that there should be 'a space between us', you see. However much Dickens may admire the working classes, he does not wish to resemble them. Given his origins, and the time he lived in, it could hardly be otherwise. In the early nineteenth century class-animosities may have been no sharper than they are now, but the surface differences between class and class were enormously greater. The 'gentleman' and the 'common man' must have seemed like different species of animal. Dickens is quite genuinely on the side of the poor against the rich, but it would be next door to impossible for him not to think of a working-class exterior as a stigma. In one of Tolstoy's fables the peasants of a certain village judge every stranger who arrives from the state of his hands. If his palms are hard from work, they let him in; if his palms are soft, out he goes. This would be hardly intelligible to Dickens; all his heroes have soft hands. His younger heroes – Nicholas Nickleby, Martin Chuzzlewit, Edward Chester, David Copperfield, John Harmon – are usually of the type known as 'walking gentlemen'. He likes a bourgeois exterior and a bourgeois (not aristocratic) accent. One curious symptom of this is that he will not allow anyone who is to play a heroic part to speak like a working man. A comic hero like Sam Weller, or a merely pathetic figure like Stephen Blackpool, can speak with a broad accent, but the *jeune premier* always speaks the then equivalent of BBC. This is so, even when it involves absurdities. Little Pip, for instance, is brought up by people speaking broad Essex, but talks upper-class English from his earliest childhood; actually he would have talked the same dialect as Joe, or at least as Mrs Gargery. So also with Biddy Wopsle, Lizzie Hexam, Sissie Jupe, Oliver Twist – one ought perhaps to add Little Dorrit. Even Rachel in *Hard Times* has barely a trace of Lancashire accent, an impossibility in her case.

One thing that often gives the clue to a novelist's real feelings on the class question is the attitude he takes up when class collides with sex. This is a thing too painful to be lied about, and consequently it is one of the points at which the 'I'm-not-a-snob' pose tends to break down.

One sees that at its most obvious where a class-distinction is also a colour-distinction. And something resembling the colonial atitude ('native' women are fair game, white women are sacrosanct) exists in a veiled form in all-white communities, causing bitter resentment on both sides. When this issue arises, novelists often revert to crude class-feelings which they might disclaim at other times. A good example of 'class-conscious' reaction is a rather forgotten novel, *The People of Clopton*, by Andrew Barton. The author's moral code is quite clearly mixed up with class-hatred. He feels the seduction of a poor girl by a rich man to be something atrocious, a kind of defilement, something quite different from her seduction by a man in her own walk of life. Trollope deals with this theme twice (*The Three Clerks* and *The Small House at Allington*) and, as one might expect, entirely from the upper-class angle. As he sees it, an affair with a barmaid or a landlady's daughter is simply an 'entanglement' to be escaped from. Trollope's moral standards are strict, and he does not allow the seduction actually to happen, but the implication is always that a working-class girl's feelings do not greatly matter. In *The Three Clerks* he even gives the typical class-reaction by noting that the girl 'smells'. Meredith (*Rhoda Fleming*) takes more the 'class-conscious' viewpoint. Thackeray, as often, seems to hesitate. In *Pendennis* (Fanny Bolton) his attitude is much the same as Trollope's; in *A Shabby Genteel Story* it is nearer to Meredith's.

One could divine a good deal about Trollope's social origin, or Meredith's, or Barton's, merely from their handling of the class-sex theme. So one can with Dickens, but what emerges, as usual, is that he is more inclined to identify himself with the middle class than with the proletariat. The one incident that seems to contradict this is the tale of the young peasant-girl in Doctor Manette's manuscript in *A Tale of Two Cities*. This, however, is merely a costume-piece put in to explain the implacable hatred of Madame Defarge, which Dickens does not pretend to approve of. In *David Copperfield*, where he is dealing with a typical nineteenth-century seduction, the class-issue does not seem to strike him as paramount. It is a law of Victorian novels that sexual misdeeds must not go unpunished, and so Steerforth is drowned on Yarmouth sands, but neither Dickens, nor old Peggotty, nor even Ham, seems to feel that Steerforth has added to his offence by being the son of rich parents. The Steerforths are moved by class-motives, but the Peggottys are not — not even in the scene between Mrs Steerforth and old Peggotty; if they were, of course, they would probably turn against David as well as against Steerforth.

In *Our Mutual Friend* Dickens treats the episode of Eugene Wrayburn and Lizzie Hexam very realistically and with no appearance of class bias. According to the 'unhand me, monster' tradition, Lizzie ought either to 'spurn' Eugene or to be ruined by him and throw herself off Waterloo Bridge; Eugene ought to be either a heartless betrayer or a hero resolved upon defying society. Neither behaves in the least like this. Lizzie is frightened by Eugene's advances and actually runs away from them, but hardly pretends to dislike them; Eugene is attracted by her, has too much decency to attempt seducing her and dare not marry her because of his family. Finally they are married and no one is any the worse, except perhaps Mr Twemlow, who will lose a few dinner engagements. It is all very much as it might have happened in real life. But a 'class-conscious' novelist would have given her to Bradley Headstone.

But when it is the other way about — when it is a case of a poor man aspiring to some woman who is 'above' him — Dickens instantly retreats into the middle-class attitude. He is rather fond of the Victorian notion of a woman (woman with a capital W) being 'above' a man. Pip feels that Estella is 'above' him, Esther Summerson is 'above' Guppy, Little Dorrit is 'above' John Chivery, Lucy Manette is 'above' Sydney Carton. In some of these the 'above'-ness is merely moral, but in others it is social. There is a scarcely mistakable class-reaction when David Copperfield discovers that Uriah Heep is plotting to marry Agnes Wickfield. The disgusting Uriah suddenly announces that he is in love with her:

'Oh, Master Copperfield, with what a pure affection do I love the ground my Agnes walks on.'

I believe I had the delirious idea of seizing the red-hot poker out of the fire, and running him through with it. It went from me with a shock, like a ball fired from a rifle: but the image of Agnes, outraged by so much as a thought of this red-headed animal's, remained in my mind (when I looked at him, sitting all awry as if his mean soul griped his body) and made me giddy.... 'I believe Agnes Wickfield to be as far above *you* (David says later on), and as far removed from all *your* aspirations, as that moon herself.'

Considering how Heep's general lowness – his servile manners, dropped aitches and so forth – has been rubbed in throughout the book, there is not much doubt about the nature of Dickens's feelings. Heep, of course, is playing a villainous part, but even villains have sexual lives; it is the thought of the 'pure' Agnes in bed with a man who drops his aitches that really revolts Dickens. But his usual tendency is to treat a man in love with a woman who is 'above' him as a joke. It is one of the stock jokes of English literature, from Malvolio onwards. Guppy in *Bleak House* is an example, John Chivery is another, and there is a rather ill-natured treatment of this theme in the 'swarry' in *Pickwick Papers*. Here Dickens describes the Bath footmen as living a kind of fantasy-life, holding dinner-parties in imitation of their 'betters' and deluding themselves that their young mistresses are in love with them. This evidently strikes him as very comic. So it is, in a way, though one might question whether it is not better for a footman even to have delusions of this kind than simply to accept his status in the spirit of the catechism.

In his attitude towards servants, Dickens is not ahead of his age. In the nineteenth century the revolt against domestic service was just beginning, to the great annoyance of everyone with over £500 a year. An enormous number of the jokes in nineteenth-century comic papers deal with the uppishness of servants. For years *Punch* ran a series of jokes called 'Servant Gal-isms', all turning on the then astonishing fact that a servant is a human being. Dickens is sometimes guilty of this kind of thing himself. His books abound with the ordinary comic servants; they are dishonest (*Great Expectations*), incompetent (*David Copperfield*), turn up their noses at good food (*Pickwick Papers*) etc. etc. – all rather in the spirit of the suburban housewife with one down-trodden cook-general. But what is curious, in a nineteenth-century radical, is that when he wants to draw a sympathetic picture of a servant, he creates what is recognizably a feudal type. Sam Weller, Mark Tapley, Clara Peggotty are all of them feudal figures. They belong to the genre of the 'old family retainer'; they identify themselves with their master's family and are at once doggishly faithful and completely familiar. No doubt Mark Tapley and Sam Weller are derived to some extent from Smollett, and hence from Cervantes; but it is interesting that Dickens should have been attracted by such a type. Sam Weller's attitude is definitely medieval. He gets himself arrested in order to follow Mr Pickwick into the Fleet, and afterwards refuses to get married because he feels that Mr Pickwick still needs his services. There is a characteristic scene between them:

'Vages or no vages, board or no board, lodgin' or no lodgin', Sam Veller, as you took from the old inn in the Borough, sticks by you, come what may . . .'

'My good fellow,' said Mr Pickwick, when Mr Weller had sat down again, rather abashed at his own enthusiasm, 'you are bound to consider the young woman also.'

'I do consider the young 'ooman, sir,' said Sam. 'I have considered the young 'ooman. I've spoke to her. I've told her how I'm sitivated; she's ready to vait till I'm ready, and I believe she vill. If she don't, she's not the young 'ooman I take her for, and I give her up with readiness.'

It is easy to imagine what the young woman would have said to this in real life. But notice the feudal atmosphere. Sam Weller is ready as a matter of course to sacrifice years of life to his master, and he can also sit down in his master's presence. A modern manservant would never think of doing either. Dickens's views on the servant question do not get much beyond wishing that master and servant would love one another. Sloppy in *Our Mutual Friend*, though a wretched failure as a character, represents the same kind of loyalty as Sam Weller. Such loyalty, of course, is natural, human and likeable; but so was feudalism.

What Dickens seems to be doing, as usual, is to reach out for an idealized version of the existing thing. He was writing at a time when domestic service must have seemed a completely inevitable evil. There were no labour-saving devices, and there was huge inequality of wealth. It was an age of enormous families, pretentious meals and inconvenient houses, when the slavery drudging fourteen hours a day in the basement kitchen was something too normal to be noticed. And given the *fact* of servitude, the feudal relationship is the only tolerable one. Sam Weller and Mark Tapley are dream figures, no less than the Cheerybles. If there have got to be masters and servants, how much better that the master should be Mr Pickwick and the servant should be Sam Weller. Better still, of course, if servants did not exist at all – but this Dickens is probably unable to imagine. Without a high level of mechanical development, human equality is not practically possible; Dickens goes to show that it is not imaginable either.

IV

It is not merely a coincidence that Dickens never writes about agriculture and writes endlessly about food. He was a cockney, and London is the centre of the earth in rather the same sense that the belly is the centre of the body. It is a city of consumers, of people who are deeply civilized but not primarily useful. A thing that strikes one when one looks below the surface of Dickens's books is that, as nineteenth-century novelists go, he is rather ignorant. He knows very little about the way things really happen. At first sight this statement looks flatly untrue, and it needs some qualification.

Dickens had had vivid glimpses of 'low life' – life in a debtor's prison, for example – and he was also a popular novelist and able to write about ordinary people. So were all the characteristic English novelists of the nineteenth century. They felt at home in the world they lived in, whereas a writer nowadays is so hopelessly isolated that the typical modern novel is a novel about a novelist. Even when Joyce, for instance, spends a decade or so in patient efforts to make contact with the 'common man', his 'common man' finally turns out to be a Jew, and a bit of a highbrow at that. Dickens at least does not suffer from this kind of thing. He has no difficulty in introducing the common motives, love, ambition, avarice, vengeance and so forth. What he does not noticeably write about, however, is *work*.

In Dickens's novels anything in the nature of work happens off-stage. The only one of his heroes who has a plausible profession is David Copperfield, who is first a shorthand writer and then a novelist, like Dickens himself. With most of the others, the way they earn their living is very much in the background. Pip, for instance, 'goes into business' in Egypt; we are not told what business, and Pip's working life occupies about half a page of the book. Clennam has been in some unspecified business in China, and later goes into another barely specified business with Doyce. Martin Chuzzlewit is an architect, but does not seem to get much time for practising. In no case do their adventures spring directly out of their work. Here the contrast between Dickens and, say, Trollope is startling. And one reason for this is undoubtedly that Dickens knows very little about the professions his characters are supposed to follow. What exactly went on in Gradgrind's factories? How did Podsnap make his money? How did Merdle work his swindles? One knows that Dickens could never follow up the details of parliamentary elections and Stock Exchange rackets as Trollope could. As soon as he has to deal with trade, finance, industry or politics he takes refuge in vagueness, or in satire. This is the case even with legal processes, about which actually he must have known a good deal. Compare any lawsuit in Dickens with the lawsuit in *Orley Farm*, for instance.

And this partly accounts for the needless ramifications of

Dickens's novels, the awful Victorian 'plot'. It is true that not all his novels are alike in this. *A Tale of Two Cities* is a very good and fairly simple story, and so in its different way is *Hard Times*; but these are just the two which are always rejected as 'not like Dickens' — and incidentally they were not published in monthly numbers.[1] The two first-person novels are also good stories, apart from their sub-plots. But the typical Dickens novel, *Nicholas Nickleby, Oliver Twist, Martin Chuzzlewit, Our Mutual Friend*, always exists round a framework of melodrama. The last thing anyone remembers about these books is their central story. On the other hand, I suppose no one has ever read them without carrying the memory of individual pages to the day of his death. Dickens sees human beings with the most intense vividness, but he sees them always in private life, as 'characters', not as functional members of society; that is to say, he sees them statically. Consequently his greatest success is *The Pickwick Papers*, which is not a story at all, merely a series of sketches; there is little attempt at development — the characters simply go on and on, behaving like idiots, in a kind of eternity. As soon as he tries to bring his characters into action, the melodrama begins. He cannot make the action revolve round their ordinary occupations; hence the crossword puzzle of coincidences, intrigues, murders, disguises, buried wills, long-lost brothers, etc. etc. In the end even people like Squeers and Micawber get sucked into the machinery.

[1] *Hard Times* was published as a serial in *Household Words* and *Great Expectations* and *A Tale of Two Cities* in *All the Year Round*. Forster says that the shortness of the weekly instalments made it 'much more difficult to get sufficient interest into each'. Dickens himself complained of the lack of 'elbow-room'. In other words, he had to stick more closely to the story. [Author's footnote.]

Of course it would be absurd to say that Dickens is a vague or merely melodramatic writer. Much that he wrote is extremely factual, and in the power of evoking visual images he has probably never been equalled. When Dickens has once described something you see it for the rest of your life. But in a way the concreteness of his vision is a sign of what he is missing. For, after all, that is what the merely casual onlooker always sees — the outward appearance, the non-functional, the surfaces of things. No one who is really involved in the landscape ever sees the landscape. Wonderfully as he can describe an *appearance*, Dickens does not often describe a *process*. The vivid pictures that he succeeds in leaving in one's memory are nearly always the pictures of things seen in leisure moments, in the coffee-rooms of country inns or through the windows of a stagecoach; the kind of things he notices are inn-signs, brass door-knockers, painted jugs, the interiors of shops and private houses, clothes, faces and, above all, food. Everything is seen from the consumer-angle. When he writes about Coketown he manages to evoke, in just a few paragraphs, the atmosphere of a Lancashire town as a slightly disgusted southern visitor would see it. 'It had a black canal in it, and a river that ran purple with evil-smelling dye, and vast piles of buildings full of windows where there was a rattling and a trembling all day long, and where the piston of the steam-engine worked monotonously up and down, like the head of an elephant in a state of melancholy madness.' That is as near as Dickens ever gets to the machinery of the mills. An engineer or a cotton-broker would see it differently; but then neither of them would be capable of that impressionistic touch about the heads of the elephants.

In a rather different sense his attitude to life is extremely unphysical. He is a man who lives through his eyes and ears rather than through his hands and muscles. Actually his habits were not so sedentary as this seems to imply. In spite of rather poor health and physique, he was active to the point of restlessness; throughout his life he was a remarkable walker, and he could at any rate carpenter well enough to put up stage scenery. But he was not one of those people who feel a need to use their hands. It is difficult to imagine him digging at a cabbage-patch, for instance. He gives no evidence of knowing anything about agriculture, and obviously knows nothing about any kind of game or sport. He has no interest in pugilism, for instance. Considering the age in which he was writing, it is astonishing how little physical brutality there is in Dickens's novels. Martin Chuzzlewit and Mark Tapley, for instance, behave with the most remarkable mildness towards the Americans who are constantly menacing them with revolvers and bowie-knives. The average English or American novelist would have had them handing out socks on the jaw and exchanging pistol-shots in all directions. Dickens is too decent for that; he sees the stupidity of violence, and also he belongs to a cautious urban class which does not deal in socks on the jaw, even in theory. And this attitude towards sport is mixed up with social feelings. In England, for mainly geographical reasons, sport, especially field-sports, and snobbery are inextricably mingled. English Socialists are often flatly incredulous when told that Lenin, for instance, was devoted to shooting. In their eyes shooting, hunting, etc. are simply snobbish observances of the landed gentry; they forget that these things might appear differently in a huge virgin country like Russia. From Dickens's point of view almost any kind of sport is at best a subject of satire. Consequently one side of nineteenth-century life – the boxing, racing, cock-fighting, badger-digging, poaching, rat-catching side of life, so wonderfully embalmed in Leech's illustrations to Surtees – is outside his scope.

What is more striking, in a seemingly 'progressive' radical, is that he is not mechanically minded. He shows no interest either in the details of machinery or in the things machinery can do. As Gissing remarks, Dickens nowhere describes a railway journey with anything like the enthusiasm he shows in describing journeys by stage-coach. In nearly all of his books one has a curious feeling that one is living in the first quarter of the nineteenth century, and in fact, he does tend to return to this period. *Little Dorrit*, written in the middle fifties, deals with the late twenties; *Great Expectations* (1861) is not dated, but evidently deals with the twenties and thirties. Several of the inventions and discoveries which have made the modern world possible (the electric telegraph, the breech-loading gun, india-rubber, coal gas, wood-pulp paper) first appeared in Dickens's lifetime, but he scarcely notes them in his books. Nothing is queerer than the vagueness with which he speaks of Doyce's 'invention' in *Little Dorrit*. It is represented as something extremely ingenious and revolutionary, 'of great importance to his country and his fellow creatures', and it is also an important minor link in the book; yet we are never told what the 'invention' is! On the other hand, Doyce's physical appearance is hit off with the typical Dickens touch; he has a peculiar way of moving his thumb, a way characteristic of engineers. After that, Doyce is firmly anchored in one's memory; but, as usual, Dickens has done it by fastening on something external.

There are people (Tennyson is an example) who lack the mechanical faculty but can see the social possibilities of machinery. Dickens has not this stamp of mind. He shows very little consciousness of the future. When he speaks of human progress it is usually in terms of *moral* progress – men growing better; probably he would never admit that men are only as good as their technical development allows them to be. At this point the gap between Dickens and his modern analogue, H. G. Wells, is at its widest. Wells wears the future round his neck like a millstone, but Dickens's unscientific cast of mind is just as damaging in a different way. What it does is to make any *positive* attitude more difficult for him. He is hostile to the feudal, agricultural past and not in real touch with the industrial present. Well, then, all that remains is the future (meaning science, 'progress' and so forth), which hardly enters into his thoughts. Therefore, while attacking everything in sight, he has no definable standard of comparison. As I have pointed out already, he attacks the current educational system with perfect justice. And yet, after all, he has no remedy to offer except kindlier schoolmasters. Why did he not indicate what a school *might* have been? Why did he not have his own sons educated according to some plan of his own, instead of sending them to public schools to be stuffed with Greek? Because he lacked that kind of imagination. He has an infallible moral sense, but very little intellectual curiosity. And here one comes upon something which really is an enormous deficiency in Dickens, something that really does make the nineteenth century seem remote from us – that he has no ideal of *work*.

With the doubtful exception of David Copperfield (merely Dickens himself), one cannot point to a single one of his central characters who is primarily interested in his job. His heroes work in order to make a living and to marry the heroine, not because they feel a passionate interest in one particular subject.

Martin Chuzzlewit, for instance, is not burning with zeal to be an architect; he might just as well be a doctor or a barrister. In any case, in the typical Dickens novel, the *deus ex machina* enters with a bag of gold in the last chapter and the hero is absolved from further struggle. The feeling, 'This is what I came into the world to do. Everything else is uninteresting. I will do this even if it means starvation', which turns men of differing temperaments into scientists, inventors, artists, priests, explorers and revolutionaries – this motif is almost entirely absent from Dickens's books. He himself, as is well known, worked like a slave and believed in his work as few novelists have ever done. But there seems to be no calling except novel-writing (and perhaps acting) towards which he can imagine this kind of devotion. And, after all, it is natural enough, considering his rather negative attitude towards society. In the last resort there is nothing he admires except common decency. Science is uninteresting and machinery is cruel and ugly (the heads of the elephants). Business is only for ruffians like Bounderby. As for politics – leave that to the Tite Barnacles. Really there is no objective except to marry the heroine, settle down, live solvently and be kind. And you can do that much better in private life.

Here, perhaps, one gets a glimpse of Dickens's secret imaginative background. What did he think of as the most desirable way to live? When Martin Chuzzlewit had made it up with his uncle, when Nicholas Nickleby had married money, when John Harmon had been enriched by Boffin – what did they *do*?

The answer evidently is that they did nothing. Nicholas Nickleby invested his wife's money with the Cheerybles and 'became a rich and prosperous merchant', but as he immediately retired into Devonshire, we can assume that he did not work very hard. Mr and Mrs Snodgrass 'purchased and cultivated a small farm, more for occupation than profit'. That is the spirit in which most of Dickens's books end – a sort of radiant idleness. Where he appears to disapprove of young men who do not work (Harthouse, Harry Gowan, Richard Carstone, Wrayburn before his reformation), it is because they are cynical and immoral or because they are a burden on somebody else; if you are 'good', and also self-supporting, there is no reason why you should not spend fifty years in simply drawing your dividends. Home life is always enough. And, after all, it was the general assumption of his age. The 'genteel sufficiency', the 'competence', the 'gentleman of independent means' (or 'in easy circumstances') – the very phrases tell one all about the strange, empty dream of the eighteenth- and nineteenth-century middle bourgeoisie. It was a dream of *complete idleness*. Charles Reade conveys its spirit perfectly in the ending of *Hard Cash*. Alfred Hardie, hero of *Hard Cash*, is the typical nineteenth-century novel hero (public-school style), with gifts which Reade describes as amounting to 'genius'. He is an old Etonian and a scholar of Oxford, he knows most of the Greek and Latin classics by heart, he can box with prize-fighters and win the Diamond Sculls at Henley. He goes through incredible adventures in which, of course, he behaves with faultless heroism, and then, at the age of twenty-five, he inherits a fortune, marries his Julia Dodd and settles down in the suburbs of Liverpool, in the same house as his parents-in-law:

> They lived together at Albion Villa, thanks to Alfred ... Oh, you happy little villa! You were as like Paradise as any mortal dwelling can be. A day came, however, when your walls could no longer hold

all the happy inmates. Julia presented Alfred with a lovely boy; enter two nurses and the villa showed symptoms of bursting. Two months more, and Alfred and his wife overflowed into the next villa. It was but twenty yards off; and there was a double reason for the migration. As often happens after a long separation, Heaven bestowed on Captain and Mrs Dodd another infant to play about their knees, etc. etc. etc.

This is the type of the Victorian happy ending – a vision of a huge, loving family of three or four generations, all crammed together in the same house and constantly multiplying, like a bed of oysters. What is striking about it is the utterly soft, sheltered, effortless life that it implies. It is not even a violent idleness, like Squire Western's. That is the significance of Dickens's urban background and his non-interest in the blackguardly-sporting-military side of life. His heroes, once they had come into money and 'settled down', would not only do no work; they would not even ride, hunt, shoot, fight duels, elope with actresses or lose money at the races. They would simply live at home in feather-bed respectability, and preferably next door to a blood-relation living exactly the same life:

The first act of Nicholas, when he became a rich and prosperous merchant, was to buy his father's old house. As time crept on, and there came gradually about him a group of lovely children, it was altered and enlarged; but none of the old rooms were ever pulled down, no old tree was ever rooted up, nothing with which there was any association of bygone times was ever removed or changed.

Within a stone's-throw was another retreat enlivened by children's pleasant voices too; and here was Kate ... the same true, gentle creature, the same fond sister, the same in the love of all about her, as in her girlish days.

It is the same incestuous atmosphere as in the passage quoted from Reade. And evidently this is Dickens's ideal ending. It is perfectly attained in *Nicholas Nickleby, Martin Chuzzlewit* and *Pickwick*, and it is approximated to in varying degrees in almost all the others. The exceptions are *Hard Times* and *Great Expectations* – the latter actually has a 'happy ending', but it contradicts the general tendency of the book, and it was put in at the request of Bulwer Lytton.

The ideal to be striven after, then, appears to be something like this: a hundred thousand pounds, a quaint old house with plenty of ivy on it, a sweetly womanly wife, a horde of children, and no work. Everything is safe, soft, peaceful and, above all, domestic. In the moss-grown churchyard down the road are the graves of the loved ones who passed away before the happy ending happened. The servants are comic and feudal, the children prattle round your feet, the old friends sit at your fireside, talking of past days, there is the endless succession of enormous meals, the cold punch and sherry negus, the feather beds and warming-pans, the Christmas parties with charades and blind man's bluff; but nothing ever happens, except the yearly child-birth. The curious thing is that it is a genuinely happy picture, or so Dickens is able to make it appear. The thought of that kind of existence is satisfying to him. This alone would be enough to tell one that more than a hundred years have passed since Dicken's first book was written. No modern man could combine such purposelessness with so much vitality.

V

By this time anyone who is a lover of Dickens, and who has read as far as this, will probably be angry with me.

I have been discussing Dickens simply in terms of his 'message', and almost ignoring his literary qualities. But every writer, especially every novelist, *has* a 'message', whether he admits it or not, and the minutest details of his work are influenced by it. All art is propaganda. Neither Dickens himself nor the majority of Victorian novelists would have thought of denying this. On the other hand, not all propaganda is art. As I said earlier, Dickens is one of those writers who are felt to be worth stealing. He has been stolen by Marxists, by Catholics and, above all, by Conservatives. The question is, What is there to steal? Why does anyone care about Dickens? Why do *I* care about Dickens?

That kind of question is never easy to answer. As a rule, an aesthetic preference is either something inexplicable or it is so corrupted by non-aesthetic motives as to make one wonder whether the whole of literary criticism is not a huge network of humbug. In Dickens's case the complicating factor is his familiarity. He happens to be one of those 'great authors' who are ladled down everyone's throat in childhood. At the time this causes rebellion and vomiting, but it may have different after-effects in later life. For instance, nearly everyone feels a sneaking affection for the patriotic poems that he learned by heart as a child, 'Ye Mariners of England', 'The Charge of the Light Brigade' and so forth. What one enjoys is not so much the poems themselves as the memories they call up. And with

Dickens the same forces of association are at work. Probably there are copies of one or two of his books lying about in an actual majority of English homes. Many children begin to know his characters by sight before they can even read, for on the whole Dickens was lucky in his illustrators. A thing that is absorbed as early as that does not come up against any critical judgement. And when one thinks of this, one thinks of all that is bad and silly in Dickens – the cast-iron 'plots', the characters who don't come off, the *longueurs*, the paragraphs in blank verse, the awful pages of 'pathos'. And then the thought arises, when I say I like Dickens, do I simply mean that I like thinking about my childhood? Is Dickens merely an institution?

If so, he is an institution that there is no getting away from. How often one really thinks about any writer, even a writer one cares for, is a difficult thing to decide; but I should doubt whether anyone who has actually read Dickens can go a week without remembering him in one context or another. Whether you approve of him or not, he is *there* like the Nelson Column. At any moment some scene or character, which may come from some book you cannot even remember the name of, is liable to drop into your mind. Micawber's letters! Winkle in the witness box! Mrs Gamp! Mrs Wititterly and Sir Tumley Snuffim! Todger's! (George Gissing said that when he passed the Monument it was never of the Fire of London that he thought, always of Todger's.) Mrs Leo Hunter! Squeers! Silas Wegg and the Decline and Fall-off of the Russian Empire! Miss Mills and the Desert of Sahara! Wopsle acting Hamlet! Mrs Jellyby! Mantalini! Jerry Cruncher! Barkis! Pumblechook! Tracy Tupman! Skimpole! Joe Gargery! Pecksniff! – and so it goes on and on. It is not so much a series of books, it is more like a world. And not a purely comic world either, for part of what one remembers in Dickens is his Victorian morbidness and necrophilia and the blood-and-thunder scenes – the death of Sikes, Krook's spontaneous combustion, Fagin in the condemned cell, the women knitting round the guillotine. To a surprising extent all this has entered even into the minds of people who do not care about it. A music-hall comedian can (or at any rate could quite recently) go on the stage and impersonate Micawber or Mrs Gamp with a fair certainty of being understood, although not one in twenty of the audience had ever read a book of Dickens's right through. Even people who affect to despise him quote him unconsciously.

Dickens is a writer who can be imitated, up to a certain point. In genuinely popular literature – for instance, the Elephant and Castle version of *Sweeny Todd* – he has been plagiarized quite shamelessly. What has been imitated, however, is simply a tradition that Dickens himself took from earlier novelists and developed, the cult of 'character', i.e. eccentricity. The thing that cannot be imitated is his fertility of invention, which is invention not so much of characters, still less of 'situations', as of turns of phrase and concrete details. The outstanding, unmistakable mark of Dickens's writing is the *unnecessary detail*. Here is an example of what I mean. The story given below is not particularly funny, but there is one phrase in it that is as individual as a fingerprint. Mr Jack Hopkins, at Bob Sawyer's party, is telling the story of the child who swallowed its sister's necklace:

Next day, child swallowed two beads; the day after that, he treated himself to three, and so on, till in a week's time he had got through the necklace – five-and-twenty beads in all. The sister, who was an industrious girl and seldom treated herself to a bit of finery, cried her eyes out at the loss of the necklace; looked high and low for it; but I needn't say, didn't find it. A few days afterwards, the family were at dinner – baked shoulder of mutton and potatoes under it – the child, who wasn't hungry, was playing about the room, when suddenly there was heard the devil of a noise, like a small hailstorm. 'Don't do that, my boy,' says the father. 'I ain't a-doin' nothing,' said the child. 'Well, don't do it again,' said the father. There was a short silence, and then the noise began again, worse than ever. 'If you don't mind what I say, my boy,' said the father, 'you'll find yourself in bed, in something less than a pig's whisper.' He gave the child a shake to make him obedient, and such a rattling ensued as nobody ever heard before. 'Why, dam' me, it's *in* the child,' said the father; 'he's got the croup in the wrong place!' 'No, I haven't, father,' said the child, beginning to cry, 'it's the necklace; I swallowed it, father.' The father caught the child up, and ran with him to the hospital, the beads in the boy's stomach rattling all the way with the jolting; and the people looking up in the air, and down in the cellars, to see where the unusual sound came from. 'He's in the hospital now,' said Jack Hopkins, 'and he makes such a devil of a noise when he walks about, that they're obliged to muffle him in a watchman's coat, for fear he should wake the patients.'

As a whole, this story might come out of any nineteenth-century comic paper. But the unmistakable Dickens touch, the thing nobody else would have thought of, is the baked shoulder of mutton and potatoes under it. How does this advance the story? The answer is that it doesn't. It is something totally unnecessary, a florid little squiggle on the edge of the page; only, it is by just these squiggles that the special Dickens atmosphere is created. The other thing one would notice here is that Dickens's way of telling a story takes a long time. An interesting example, too long to quote, is Sam Weller's story of the obstinate patient in Chapter XLIV of *The Pickwick Papers*. As it happens, we have a standard of comparison here, because Dickens is plagiarizing, consciously or unconsciously. The story is also told by some ancient Greek writer. I cannot now find the passage, but I read it years ago as a boy at school, and it runs more or less like this:

A certain Thracian, renowned for his obstinacy, was warned by his physician that if he drank a flagon of wine it would kill him. The Thracian thereupon drank the flagon of wine and immediately jumped off the house-top and perished. 'For,' said he, 'in this way I shall prove that the wine did not kill me.'

As the Greek tells it, that is the whole story – about six lines. As Sam Weller tells it, it takes round about a thousand words. Long before getting to the point we have been told all about the patient's clothes, his meals, his manners, even the newspapers he reads, and about the peculiar construction of the doctor's carriage, which conceals the fact that the coachman's trousers do not match his coat. Then there is the dialogue between the doctor and the patient. ' "Crumpets is wholesome, sir," said the patient. "Crumpets is *not* wholesome sir," says the doctor, wery fierce,' etc. etc. In the end the original story has been buried under the details. And in all of Dickens's most characteristic passages it is the same. His imagination overwhelms everything, like a kind of weed. Squeers stands up to address his boys, and immediately we are hearing about Bolder's father who was two pounds ten short, and Mobb's stepmother who took to her bed on hearing that Mobbs wouldn't eat fat and hoped Mr Squeers would flog him into a happier state of mind. Mrs Leo Hunter writes a poem, 'Expiring Frog';

two full stanzas are given. Boffin takes a fancy to pose as a miser, and instantly we are down among the squalid biographies of eighteenth-century misers, with names like Vulture Hopkins and the Rev. Blewberry Jones, and chapter headings like 'The Story of the Mutton Pies' and 'The Treasures of a Dunghill'. Mrs Harris, who does not even exist, has more detail piled on to her than any three characters in an ordinary novel. Merely in the middle of a sentence we learn, for instance, that her infant nephew has been seen in a bottle at Greenwich Fair, along with the pink-eyed lady, the Prussian dwarf and the living skeleton. Joe Gargery describes how the robbers broke into the house of Pumblechook, the corn and seed merchant – 'and they took his till, and they took his cashbox, and they drinked his wine, and they partook of his wittles, and they slapped his face, and they pulled his nose, and they tied him up to his bedpust, and they give him a dozen, and they stuffed his mouth full of flowering annuals to perwent his crying out'. Once again the unmistakable Dickens touch, the flowering annuals; but any other novelist would only have mentioned about half of these outrages. Everything is piled up and up, detail on detail, embroidery on embroidery. It is futile to object that this kind of thing is rococo – one might as well make the same objection to a wedding-cake. Either you like it or you do not like it. Other nineteenth century writers Surtees, Barham, Thackeray, even Marryat, have something of Dickens's profuse, overflowing quality, but none of them on anything like the same scale. The appeal of all these writers now depends partly on period flavour, and though Marryat is still officially a 'boys' writer' and Surtees has a sort of legendary fame among hunting men, it is probable that they are read mostly by bookish people.

Significantly, Dickens's most successful books (not his *best* books) are *The Pickwick Papers*, which is not a novel, and *Hard Times* and *A Tale of Two Cities*, which are not funny. As a novelist his natural fertility greatly hampers him, because the burlesque which he is never able to resist is constantly breaking into what ought to be serious situations. There is a good example of this in the opening chapter of *Great Expectations*. The escaped convict, Magwitch, has just captured the six-year-old Pip in the churchyard. The scene starts terrifyingly enough, from Pip's point of view. The convict, smothered in mud and with his chain trailing from his leg, suddenly starts up among the tombs, grabs the child, turns him upside down and robs his pockets. Then he begins terrorizing him into bringing food and a file:

He held me by the arms in an upright position on the top of the stone, and went on in these fearful terms:

'You bring me, tomorrow morning early, that file and them wittles. You bring the lot to me, at that old Battery over yonder. You do it, and you never dare to say a word or dare to make a sign concerning your having seen such a person as me, or any person sumever, and you shall be let to live. You fail, or you go from my words in any partickler, no matter how small it is, and your heart and liver shall be tore out, roasted and ate. Now, I ain't alone, as you may think I am. There's a young man hid with me, in comparison with which young man I am a Angel. That young man hears the words I speak. That young man has a secret way pecooliar to himself, of getting at a boy, and at his heart, and at his liver. It is in wain for a boy to attempt to hide himself from that young man. A boy may lock his door, may be warm in bed, may tuck himself up, may draw the clothes over his head, may think himself comfortable and safe, but that young man will softly creep and creep his way to him and tear him open. I am keeping that young man from harming you at the present moment, but with great difficulty. I find it wery hard to hold that young man off of your inside. Now, what do you say?'

Here Dickens has simply yielded to temptation. To begin with, no starving and hunted man would speak in the least like that. Moreover, although the speech shows a remarkable knowledge of the way in which a child's mind works, its actual words are quite out of tune with what is to follow. It turns Magwitch into a sort of pantomime wicked uncle, or, if one sees him through the child's eyes, into an appalling monster. Later in the book he is to be represented as neither, and his exaggerated gratitude, on which the plot turns, is to be incredible because of just this speech. As usual, Dickens's imagination has overwhelmed him. The picturesque details were too good to be left out. Even with characters who are more of a piece than Magwitch he is liable to be tripped up by some seductive phrase. Mr Murdstone, for instance, is in the habit of ending David Copperfield's lessons every morning with a dreadful sum in arithmetic. 'If I go into a cheesemonger's shop, and buy five thousand double-Gloucester cheeses at fourpence halfpenny each, present payment,' it always begins. Once again the typical Dickens detail, the double-Gloucester cheeses. But it is far too human a touch for Murdstone; he would have made it five thousand cashboxes. Every time this note is struck, the unity of the novel suffers. Not that it matters very much, because Dickens is obviously a writer whose parts are greater than his wholes. He is all fragments, all details – rotten architecture, but wonderful gargoyles – and never better than when he is building up some character who will later on be forced to act inconsistently.

Of course it is not usual to urge against Dickens that he

makes his characters behave inconsistently. Generally he is accused of doing just the opposite. His characters are supposed to be mere 'types', each crudely representing some single trait and fitted with a kind of label by which you recognize him. Dickens is 'only a caricaturist' – that is the usual accusation, and it does him both more and less than justice. To begin with, he did not think of himself as a caricaturist, and was constantly setting into action characters who ought to have been purely static. Squeers, Micawber, Miss Mowcher,[1] Wegg, Skimpole, Pecksniff and many others are finally involved in 'plots' where they are out of place and where they behave quite incredibly. They start off as magic-lantern slides and they end by getting mixed up in a third-rate movie. Sometimes one can put one's finger on a single sentence in which the original illusion is destroyed. There is such a sentence in *David Copperfield*. After the famous dinner-party (the one where the leg of mutton was underdone), David is showing his guests out. He stops Traddles at the top of the stairs:

'Traddles,' said I, 'Mr Micawber don't mean any harm, poor fellow: but if I were you I wouldn't lend him anything.'

'My dear Mr Copperfield,' returned Traddles smiling, 'I haven't got anything to lend.'

'You have got a name, you know,' I said.

At the place where one reads it this remark jars a little, though something of the kind was inevitable sooner or later. The story is a fairly realistic one, and David is growing up; ultimately he is bound to see Mr Micawber for what he is, a

---

[1] Dickens turned Miss Mowcher into a sort of heroine because the real woman whom he had caricatured had read the earlier chapters and was bitterly hurt. He had previously meant her to play a villainous part. But *any* action by such a character would seem incongruous. [Author's footnote.]

cadging scoundrel. Afterwards. of course, Dickens's sentimentality overcomes him and Micawber is made to turn over a new leaf. But from then on the original Micawber is never quite recaptured, in spite of desperate efforts. As a rule, the 'plot' in which Dickens's characters get entangled is not particularly credible, but at least it makes some pretence at reality, whereas the world to which they belong is a never-never land, a kind of eternity. But just here one sees that 'only a caricaturist' is not really a condemnation. The fact that Dickens is always thought of as a caricaturist, although he was constantly trying to be something else, is perhaps the surest mark of his genius. The monstrosities that he created are still remembered as monstrosities, in spite of getting mixed up in would-be probable melodramas. Their first impact is so vivid that nothing that comes afterwards effaces it. As with the people one knew in childhood, one seems always to remember them in one particular attitude, doing one particular thing. Mrs Squeers is always ladling out brimstone and treacle, Mrs Gummidge is always weeping, Mrs Gargery is always banging her husband's head against the wall, Mrs Jellyby is always scribbling tracts while her children fall into the area – and there they all are, fixed for ever like little twinkling miniatures painted on snuff-box lids, completely fantastic and incredible, and yet somehow more solid and infinitely more memorable than the efforts of serious novelists. Even by the standards of his time Dickens was an exceptionally artificial writer. As Ruskin said, he 'chose to work in a circle of stage fire'. His characters are even more distorted and simplified than Smollett's. But there are no rules in novel writing, and for any work of art there is only one test worth bothering about – survival. By this test Dickens's characters have succeeded, even if the people who remember them hardly think of them as human beings. They are monsters but at any rate they *exist*.

But all the same there is a disadvantage in writing about monsters. It amounts to this, that it is only certain moods that Dickens can speak to. There are large areas of the human mind that he never touches. There is no poetic feeling anywhere in his books, and no genuine tragedy, and even sexual love is almost outside his scope. Actually his books are not so sexless as they are sometimes declared to be, and considering the time in which he was writing, he is reasonably frank. But there is not a trace in him of the feeling that one finds in *Manon Lescaut, Salammbô, Carmen, Wuthering Heights*. According to Aldous Huxley, D. H. Lawrence once said that Balzac was 'a gigantic dwarf', and in a sense the same is true of Dickens. There are whole worlds which he either knows nothing about or does not wish to mention. Except in a rather roundabout way, one cannot *learn* very much from Dickens. And to say this is to think almost immediately of the great Russian novelists of the nineteenth century. Why is it that Tolstoy's grasp seems to be so much larger then Dickens's – why is it that he seems able to tell you so much more *about yourself*? It is not that he is more gifted, or even, in the last analysis, more intelligent. It is because he is writing about people who are growing. His characters are struggling to make their souls, whereas Dickens's are already finished and perfect. In my own mind Dickens's people are present far more often and far more vividly than Tolstoy's, but always in a single unchangeable attitude, like pictures or pieces of furniture. You cannot hold an imaginary conversation with a Dickens character as you can with, say, Pierre Bezukhov. And this is not merely because of Tolstoy's greater seriousness, for there are also comic characters that you can imagine yourself talking to – Bloom, for instance, or Pécuchet, or even Wells's Mr Polly. It is because Dickens's characters have no mental life. They say perfectly the thing that they have to say, but they cannot be conceived as talking about anything else. They never learn, never speculate. Perhaps the most meditative of his characters is Paul Dombey, and his thoughts are mush. Does this mean that Tolstoy's novels are 'better' than Dickens's? The truth is that it is absurd to make such comparisons in terms of 'better' and 'worse'. If I were forced to compare Tolstoy with Dickens, I should say that Tolstoy's appeal will probably be wider in the long run, because Dickens is scarcely intelligible outside the English-speaking culture; on the other hand, Dickens is able to reach simple people, which Tolstoy is not. Tolstoy's characters can cross a frontier, Dickens's can be portrayed on a cigarette card.[1] But one is no more obliged to choose between them than between a sausage and a rose. Their purposes barely intersect.

VI

If Dickens had been *merely* a comic writer, the chances are that no one would now remember his name. Or at best a few of his books would survive in rather the same way as books like *Frank Fairleigh*, *Mr Verdant Green* and *Mrs Caudle's Curtain Lectures*,[2] as

---

[1] Messrs John Player & Sons issued two series of cigarette cards entitled 'Characters from Dickens' in 1913; they reissued them as a single series in 1923.
[2] *Frank Fairleigh* by F. E. Smedley, 1850; *The Adventures of Mr Verdant Green* by Cuthbert Bede (pseud. of Edward Bradley), 1853; *Mrs Caudle's Curtain Lectures* by Douglas Jerrold (reprinted from *Punch*, 1846).

a sort of hangover of the Victorian atmosphere, a pleasant little whiff of oysters and brown stout. Who has not felt sometimes that it was 'a pity' that Dickens ever deserted the vein of *Pickwick* for things like *Little Dorrit* and *Hard Times*? What people always demand of a popular novelist is that he shall write the same book over and over again, forgetting that a man who would write the same book twice could not even write it once. Any writer who is not utterly lifeless moves upon a kind of parabola, and the downward curve is implied in the upward one. Joyce has to start with the frigid competence of *Dubliners* and end with the dream-language of *Finnegans Wake*, but *Ulysses* and *Portrait of the Artist* are part of the trajectory. The thing that drove Dickens forward into a form of art for which he was not really suited, and at the same time caused us to remember him, was simply the fact that he was a moralist, the consciousness of 'having something to say'. He is always preaching a sermon, and that is the final secret of his inventiveness. For you can only create if you can *care*. Types like Squeers and Micawber could not have been produced by a hack writer looking for something to be funny about. A joke worth laughing at always has an idea behind it, and usually a subversive idea. Dickens is able to go on being funny because he is in revolt against authority, and authority is always there to be laughed at. There is always room for one more custard pie.

His radicalism is of the vaguest kind, and yet one always knows that it is there. That is the difference between being a moralist and a politician. He has no constructive suggestions, not even a clear grasp of the nature of the society he is attacking, only an emotional perception that something is wrong. All he can finally say is, 'Behave decently', which, as I suggested earlier, is not necessarily so shallow as it sounds. Most revolutionaries are potential Tories, because they imagine that everything can be put right by altering the *shape* of society; once that change is effected, as it sometimes is, they see no need for any other. Dickens has not this kind of mental coarseness. The vagueness of his discontent is the mark of its permanence. What he is out against is not this or that institution, but, as Chesterton put it, 'an expression on the human face'. Roughly speaking, his morality is the Christian morality, but in spite of his Anglican upbringing he was essentially a Bible-Christian, as he took care to make plain when writing his will. In any case he cannot properly be described as a religious man. He 'believed', undoubtedly, but religion in the devotional sense does not seem to have entered much into his thoughts.[1] Where he is Christian is in his quasi-instinctive siding with the oppressed against the oppressors. As a matter of course he is on the side of the underdog, always and everywhere. To carry this to its logical conclusion one has got to change sides when the underdog becomes an upperdog, and in fact Dickens does tend to do so. He loathes the Catholic Church, for instance, but as soon as the Catholics are persecuted (*Barnaby Rudge*) he

---

[1] From a letter to his youngest son (in 1868): 'You will remember that you have never at home been harassed about religious observances, or mere formalities. I have always been anxious not to weary my children with such things, before they are old enough to form opinions respecting them. You will therefore understand the better that I now most solemnly impress upon you the truth and beauty of the Christian Religion, as it came from Christ Himself, and the impossibility of your going far wrong if you humbly but heartily respect it ... Never abandon the wholesome practice of saying your own private prayers, night and morning. I have never abandoned it myself, and I know the comfort of it.' [Author's footnote.]

is on their side. He loathes the aristocratic class even more, but as soon as they are really overthrown (the revolutionary chapters in *A Tale of Two Cities*) his sympathies swing round. Whenever he departs from this emotional attitude he goes astray. A well-known example is at the ending of *David Copperfield*, in which everyone who reads it feels that something has gone wrong. What is wrong is that the closing chapters are pervaded, faintly but noticeably, by the cult of success. It is the gospel according to Smiles, instead of the gospel according to Dickens. The attractive, out-at-elbow characters are got rid of, Micawber makes a fortune, Heep gets into prison – both of these events are flagrantly impossible – and even Dora is killed off to make way for Agnes. If you like, you can read Dora as Dickens's wife and Agnes as his sister-in-law, but the essential point is that Dickens has 'turned respectable' and done violence to his own nature. Perhaps that is why Agnes is the most disagreeable of his heroines, the real legless angel of Victorian romance, almost as bad as Thackeray's Laura.

No grown-up person can read Dickens without feeling his limitations, and yet there does remain his native generosity of mind, which acts as a kind of anchor and nearly always keeps him where he belongs. It is probably the central secret of his popularity. A good-tempered antinomianism rather of Dickens's type is one of the marks of western popular culture. One sees it in folk-stories and comic songs, in dream-figures like Mickey Mouse and Popeye the Sailor (both of them variants of Jack the Giant-Killer), in the history of working-class Socialism, in the popular protests (always ineffective but not always a sham) against imperialism, in the impulse that makes a jury award excessive damages when a rich man's car runs over a poor man; it is the feeling that one is always on the side of the underdog, on the side of the weak against the strong. In one sense it is a feeling that is fifty years out of date. The common man is still living in the mental world of Dickens, but nearly every modern intellectual has gone over to some or other form of totalitarianism. From the Marxist or Fascist point of view, nearly all that Dickens stands for can be written off as 'bourgeois morality'. But in moral outlook no one could be more 'bourgeois' than the English working classes. The ordinary people in the western countries have never entered, mentally, into the world of 'realism' and power politics. They may do so before long, in which case Dickens will be as out of date as the cab-horse. But in his own age and ours he has been popular chiefly because he was able to express in a comic, simplified and therefore memorable form the native decency of the common man. And it is important that from this point of view people of very different types can be described as 'common'. In a country like England, in spite of its class-structure there does exist a certain cultural unity. All through the Christian ages, and especially since the French Revolution, the western world has been haunted by the idea of freedom and equality; it is only an *idea*, but it has penetrated to all ranks of society. The most atrocious injustices, cruelties, lies, snobberies exist everywhere, but there are not many people who can regard these things with the same indifference as, say, a Roman slave-owner. Even the millionaire suffers from a vague sense of guilt, like a dog eating a stolen leg of mutton. Nearly everyone, whatever his actual conduct may be, responds emotionally to the idea of human brotherhood. Dickens voiced a code which was and on the whole still is believed in, even by people who violate it. It is difficult otherwise to explain why he could be both read by working people (a thing that has happened to no other novelist of his stature) and buried in Westminster Abbey.

When one reads any strongly individual piece of writing, one has the impression of seeing a face somewhere behind the page. It is not necessarily the actual face of the writer. I feel this very strongly with Swift, with Defoe, with Fielding, Stendhal, Thackeray, Flaubert, though in several cases I do not know what these people looked like and do not want to know. What one sees is the face that the writer *ought* to have. Well, in the case of Dickens I see a face that is not quite the face of Dickens's photographs, though it resembles it. It is the face of a man of about forty, with a small beard and a high colour. He is laughing, with a touch of anger in his laughter, but no triumph, no malignity. It is the face of a man who is always fighting against something, but who fights in the open and is not frightened, the face of a man who is *generously angry* — in other words, of a nineteenth-century liberal, a free intelligence, a type hated with equal hatred by all the smelly little orthodoxies which are now contending for our souls.

1939

Boys' Weeklies

You never walk through any poor quarter in any big town without coming upon a small newsagent's shop. The general appearance of these shops is always very much the same: a few posters for the *Daily Mail* and the *News of the World* outside, a poky little window with sweet-bottles and packets of Players, and a dark interior smelling of liquorice allsorts and festooned from floor to ceiling with vilely printed twopenny papers, most of them with lurid cover illustrations in three colours.

Except for the daily and evening papers, the stock of these shops hardly overlaps at all with that of the big newsagents. Their main selling line is the twopenny weekly, and the number and variety of these are almost unbelievable. Every hobby and pastime – cage-birds, fretwork, carpentering, bees, carrier-pigeons, home conjuring, philately, chess – has at least one paper devoted to it, and generally several. Gardening and livestock-keeping must have at least a score between them. Then there are the sporting papers, the radio papers, the children's comics, the various snippet papers such as *Tit-Bits*, the large range of papers devoted to the movies and all more or less exploiting women's legs, the various trade papers, the women's story-papers (the *Oracle*, *Secrets*, *Peg's Paper*, etc. etc.), the needlework papers – these so numerous that a display of them alone will often fill an entire window – and in addition the long series of 'Yanks Mags' (*Fight Stories, Action Stories, Western Short Stories*, etc.), which are imported shop-soiled from America and sold at twopence-halfpenny or threepence. And the periodical proper shades off into the fourpenny novelette, the *Aldine Boxing Novels*, the *Boys' Friend Library*, the *School-girls' Own Library* and many others.

Probably the contents of these shops is the best available indication of what the mass of the English people really feels and thinks. Certainly nothing half so revealing exists in documentary form. Best-seller novels, for instance, tell one a great deal, but the novel is aimed almost exclusively at people above the £4-a-week level. The movies are probably a very unsafe guide to popular taste, because the film industry is virtually a monopoly, which means that it is not obliged to study its public at all closely. The same applies to some extent to the daily papers, and most of all to the radio. But it does not apply to the weekly paper with a smallish circulation and specialized subject-matter. Papers like the *Exchange and Mart*, for instance, or *Cage-Birds*, or the *Oracle*, or *Prediction*, or the *Matrimonial Times*, only exist because there is a definite demand for them, and they reflect the minds of their readers as a great national daily with a circulation of millions cannot possibly do.

Here I am only dealing with a single series of papers, the boys' twopenny weeklies, often inaccurately described as 'penny dreadfuls'. Falling strictly within this class there are at present ten papers, the *Gem, Magnet, Modern Boy, Triumph* and *Champion*, all owned by the Amalgamated Press, and the *Wizard, Rover, Skipper, Hotspur* and *Adventure*, all owned by D. C. Thomson & Co. What the circulations of these papers are, I do not know. The editors and proprietors refuse to name any figures, and in any case the circulation of a paper carrying serial stories is bound to fluctuate widely. But there is no question that the combined public of the ten papers is a very large one. They are on sale in every town in England, and nearly every boy who reads at all goes through a phase of reading one or more of them. The *Gem* and *Magnet*, which are much the oldest of these papers, are of rather different type from the rest, and they have evidently lost some of their popularity during the past few years. A good many boys now regard them as old-fashioned and 'slow'. Nevertheless I want to discuss them first, because they are more interesting psychologically than the others, and also because the mere survival of such papers into the nineteen-thirties is a rather startling phenomenon.

The *Gem* and *Magnet* are sister-papers (characters out of one paper frequently appear in the other), and were both started more than thirty years ago. At that time, together with *Chums* and the old B[oy's] O[wn] P[aper], they were the leading players for boys, and they remained dominant till quite recently. Each of them carries every week a fifteen- or twenty-thousand word school story, complete in itself, but usually more or less connected with the story of the week before. The *Gem* in addition to its school story carries one or more adventure serials. Otherwise the two papers are so much alike that they can be treated as one, though the *Magnet* has always been the better known of the two, probably because it possesses a really first-rate character in the fat boy, Billy Bunter.

The stories are stories of what purports to be public-school life, and the schools (Greyfriars in the *Magnet* and St Jim's in the *Gem*) are represented as ancient and fashionable foundations of the type of Eton or Winchester. All the leading characters are fourth-form boys aged fourteen or fifteen, older or younger boys only appearing in very minor parts. Like Sexton Blake and Nelson Lee, these boys continue week after week and year after year, never growing any older. Very occasionally a new boy arrives or a minor character drops out, but in at any rate the last twenty-five years the personnel has barely altered. All the principal characters in both papers – Bob Cherry, Tom Merry, Harry Wharton, Johnny Bull, Billy Bunter and the rest of them – were at Greyfriars or St Jim's long before the Great War, exactly the same age as at present, having much the same kind of adventures and talking almost exactly the same dialect. And not only the characters but the whole atmosphere of both the *Gem* and *Magnet* has been preserved unchanged, partly by means of very elaborate stylization. The stories in the *Magnet* are signed 'Frank Richards' and those in the *Gem* 'Martin Clifford', but a series lasting thirty years could hardly be the work of the same person every week.[1] Consequently they have to be written in a style that is easily imitated – an extraordinary, artificial, repetitive style, quite different from anything else now existing in English literature. A couple of extracts will do as illustrations. Here is one from the *Magnet*:

> Groan!
> 'Shut up, Bunter!'
> Groan!
> Shutting up was not really in Billy Bunter's line. He seldom shut up, though often requested to do so. On the present awful occasion

---

[1] This is quite incorrect. These stories have been written throughout the whole period by 'Frank Richards' and 'Martin Clifford', who are one and the same person! See articles in *Horizon*, May 1940, and *Summer Pie*, summer 1944. [Author's footnote 1945.]

the fat Owl of Greyfriars was less inclined than ever to shut up. And he did not shut up! He groaned, and groaned, and went on groaning.

Even groaning did not fully express Bunter's feeling. His feelings, in fact, were inexpressible.

There were six of them in the soup! Only one of the six uttered sounds of woe and lamentation. But that one, William George Bunter, uttered enough for the whole party and a little over.

Harry Wharton & Co. stood in a wrathy and worried group. They were landed and stranded, diddled, dished and done! etc. etc. etc.

Here is one from the *Gem:*

'Oh cwumbs!'
'Oh gum!'
'Oooogh!'
'Urrggh!'

Arthur Augustus sat up dizzily. He grabbed his handkerchief and pressed it to his damaged nose. Tom Merry sat up, gasping for breath. They looked at one another.

'Bai Jove! This is a go, deah boy!' gurgled Arthur Augustus. 'I have been thwown into a quite a fluttah! Oogh! The wottahs! The wuffians! The fearful outsidahs! Wow!' etc. etc. etc.

Both of these extracts are entirely typical; you would find something like them in almost every chapter of every number, today or twenty-five years ago. The first thing that anyone would notice is the extraordinary amount of tautology (the first of these two passages contains a hundred and twenty-five words and could be compressed into about thirty), seemingly designed to spin out the story, but actually playing its part in creating the atmosphere. For the same reason various facetious expressions are repeated over and over again; 'wrathy', for instance, is a great favourite, and so is 'diddled, dished and done'. 'Oooogh!' 'Grooo!' and 'Yaroo!' (stylized cries of pain) recur constantly, and so does 'Ha! ha! ha!', always given a line to itself, so that sometimes a quarter of a column or thereabouts consists of 'Ha! ha! ha!' The slang ('Go and eat coke!', 'What the thump!', 'You frabjous ass!', etc. etc.) has never been altered, so that the boys are now using slang which is at least thirty years out of date. In addition, the various nicknames are rubbed in on every possible occasion. Every few lines we are reminded that Harry Wharton & Co. are 'the Famous Five', Bunter is always 'the fat Owl' or 'the Owl of the Remove', Vernon-Smith is always 'the Bounder of Greyfriars', Gussy (the Honourable Arthur Augustus D'Arcy) is always 'the swell of St Jim's', and so on and so forth. There is a constant, untiring effort to keep the atmosphere intact and to make sure that every new reader learns immediately who is who. The result has been to make Greyfriars and St Jim's into an extraordinary little world of their own, a world which cannot be taken seriously by anyone over fifteen, but which at any rate is not easily forgotten. By a debasement of the Dickens technique a series of stereotyped 'characters' has been built up, in several cases very successfully. Billy Bunter, for instance, must be one of the best-known figures in English fiction; for the mere number of people who know him he ranks with Sexton Blake, Tarzan, Sherlock Holmes and a handful of characters in Dickens.

Needless to say, these stories are fantastically unlike life at a real public school. They run in cycles of rather differing types, but in general they are the clean-fun, knockabout type of story, with interest centring round horseplay, practical jokes, ragging masters, fights, canings, football, cricket and food. A constantly recurring story is one in which a boy is accused of some misdeed committed by another and is too much of a sportsman to reveal the truth. The 'good' boys are 'good' in the clean-living Englishman tradition – they keep in hard training, wash behind their ears, never hit below the belt, etc. etc. – and by way of contrast there is a series of 'bad' boys, Racke, Crooke, Loder and others, whose badness consists in betting, smoking cigarettes and frequenting public houses. All these boys are constantly on the verge of expulsion, but as it would mean a change of personnel if any boy were actually expelled, no one is ever caught out in any really serious offence. Stealing, for instance, barely enters as a motif. Sex is completely taboo, especially in the form in which it actually arises at public schools. Occasionally girls enter into the stories, and very rarely there is something approaching a mild flirtation, but it is always entirely in the spirit of clean fun. A boy and a girl enjoy going for bicycle rides together – that is all it ever amounts to. Kissing, for instance, would be regarded as 'soppy'. Even the bad boys are presumed to be completely sexless. When the *Gem* and *Magnet* were started, it is probably that there was a deliberate intention to get away from the guilty sex-ridden atmosphere that pervaded so much of the earlier literature for boys. In the nineties the *Boy's Own Paper*, for instance, used to have its correspondence columns full of terrifying warnings against masturbation, and books like *St Winifred's* and *Tom Brown's Schooldays* were heavy with homosexual feeling, though no doubt the authors were not fully aware of it. In the *Gem* and *Magnet* sex simply does not exist as a problem. Religion is also taboo; in the whole thirty years' issue of the two papers the word 'God' probably does not occur, except in 'God save the King'. On the other hand, there has always been a very strong 'temperance' strain. Drinking and, by association, smoking are regarded as rather disgraceful even in an adult ('shady' is the usual word), but at the same time as something irresistibly fascinating, a sort of substitute for sex. In their moral atmosphere the *Gem* and *Magnet* have a great deal in common with the Boy Scout movement, which started at about the same time.

All literature of this kind is partly plagiarism. Sexton Blake, for instance, started off quite frankly as an imitation of Sherlock Holmes, and still resembles him fairly strongly; he has hawk-like features, lives in Baker Street, smokes enormously and puts on a dressing-gown when he wants to think. The *Gem* and *Magnet* probably owe something to the school story writers who were flourishing when they began, Gunby Hadath, Desmond Coke and the rest, but they owe more to nineteenth-century models. In so far as Greyfriars and St Jim's are like real schools at all, they are much more like Tom Brown's Rugby than a modern public school. Neither school has an OTC for instance, games are not compulsory, and the boys are even allowed to wear what clothes they like. But without doubt the main origin of these papers is *Stalky & Co*. This book has had an immense influence on boys' literature, and it is one of those books which have a sort of traditional reputation among people who have never even seen a copy of it. More than once in boys' weekly papers I have come across a reference to *Stalky & Co.* in which the word was spelt 'Storky'. Even the name of the chief comic among the Greyfriars masters, Mr Prout, is taken from *Stalky & Co.* and so is much of the slang: 'jape', 'merry', 'giddy', 'bizney' (business), 'frabjous', 'don't' for 'doesn't' – all of them out of date even when *Gem* and *Magnet* started. There are also traces of earlier origins. The name 'Greyfriars' is probably taken from Thackeray, and Gosling, the school porter in the *Magnet*, talks in an imitation of Dickens's dialect.

With all this, the supposed 'glamour' of public-school life is played for all it is worth. There is all the usual paraphernalia – lock-up, roll-call, house matches, fagging, prefects, cosy teas round the study fire, etc. etc. – and constant reference to the 'old school', the 'old grey stones' (both schools were founded in the early sixteenth century), the 'team spirit' of the 'Greyfriars men'. As for the snob-appeal, it is completely shameless. Each school has a titled boy or two whose titles are constantly thrust in the reader's face; other boys have the names of well-known aristocratic families, Talbot, Manners, Lowther. We are for ever being reminded that Gussy is the Honourable Arthur A. D'Arcy, son of Lord Eastwood, that Jack Blake is heir to 'broad acres', that Hurree Jamset Ram Singh (nicknamed Inky) is the Nabob of Bhanipur, that Vernon-Smith's father is a millionaire. Till recently the illustrations in both papers always depicted the boys in clothes imitated from those of Eton; in the last few years Greyfriars has changed over to blazers and flannel trousers, but St Jim's still sticks to the Eton jacket, and Gussy sticks to his top-hat. In the school magazine which appears every week as part of the *Magnet*, Harry Wharton writes an article discussing the pocket-money received by the 'fellows in the Remove', and reveals that some of them get as much as five pounds a week! This kind of thing is a perfectly deliberate incitement to wealth-fantasy. And here it is worth noticing a rather curious fact, and that is that the school story is a thing peculiar to England. So far as I know, there are extremely few school stories in foreign languages. The reason, obviously, is that in England education is mainly a matter of status. The most definite dividing line between the petite bourgeoisie and the working class is that the former pay for their education, and within the bourgeoisie there is another unbridgeable gulf between the 'public' school and the 'private' school. It is quite clear that there are tens and scores of thousands of people to whom every detail of life at a 'posh' public school is wildly thrilling and romantic. They happen to be outside that mystic world of quadrangles and house-colours, but they yearn after it, day-dream about it, live mentally in it for hours at a stretch. The question is, Who are these people? Who reads the *Gem* and *Magnet*?

Obviously one can never be quite certain about this kind of thing. All I can say from my own observation is this. Boys who are likely to go to public schools themselves generally read the *Gem* and *Magnet*, but they nearly always stop reading them when they are about twelve; they may continue for another year from force of habit, but by that time they have ceased to take them seriously. On the other hand, the boys at very cheap private schools, the schools that are designed for people who can't afford a public school but consider the council schools 'common', continue reading the *Gem* and *Magnet* for several years longer. A few years ago I was a teacher at two of these schools myself. I found that not only did virtually all the boys read the *Gem* and *Magnet*, but that they were still taking them fairly seriously when they were fifteen or even sixteen. These boys were the sons of shopkeepers, office employees and small business and professional men, and obviously it is this class that the *Gem* and *Magnet* are aimed at. But they are certainly read by working-class boys as well. They are generally on sale in the poorest quarters of big towns, and I have known them to be read by boys whom one might expect to be completely immune from public-school 'glamour'. I have seen a young coal miner, for instance, a lad who had already worked a year or two underground, eagerly reading the *Gem*. Recently I offered a batch of English papers to some British legionaries of the French Foreign Legion in North Africa; they picked out the *Gem* and *Magnet* first. Both papers are much read by girls,[1] and the Pen Pals' department of the *Gem* shows that it is read in every corner of the British Empire, by Australians, Canadians, Palestine Jews, Malays, Arabs, Straits Chinese, etc. etc. The editors evidently expect their readers to be aged round about fourteen, and the advertisements (milk chocolate, postage stamps, water pistols, blushing cured, home conjuring tricks, itching-powder, the Phine Phun Ring which runs a needle into your friend's hand, etc. etc.) indicate roughly the same age; there are also the Admiralty advertisements, however, which call for youths between seventeen and twenty-two. And there is no question that these papers are also read by adults. It is quite common for people to write to the editor and say that they have read every number of the *Gem* or *Magnet* for the past thirty years. Here, for instance, is a letter from a lady in Salisbury:

> I can say of your splendid yarns of Harry Wharton & Co. of Greyfriars, that they never fail to reach a high standard. Without doubt they are the finest stories of their type on the market to-day, which is saying a good deal. They seem to bring you face to face with Nature. I have taken the *Magnet* from the start, and have followed the adventures of Harry Wharton & Co. with rapt

---

[1] There are several corresponding girls' papers. The *Schoolgirl* is companion-paper to the *Magnet* and has stories by 'Hilda Richards'. The characters are interchangeable to some extent. Bessie Bunter, Billy Bunter's sister, figures in the *Schoolgirl*. [Author's footnote.]

interest. I have no sons, but two daughters, and there's always a rush to be the first to read the grand old paper. My husband, too, was a staunch reader of the *Magnet* until he was suddenly taken away from us.

It is well worth getting hold of some copies of the *Gem* and *Magnet*, especially the *Gem*, simply to have a look at the correspondence columns. What is truly startling is the intense interest with which the pettiest details of life at Greyfriars and St Jim's are followed up. Here, for instance, are a few of the questions sent in by readers:

'What age is Dick Roylance?' 'How old is St Jim's?' 'Can you give me a list of the Shell and their studies?' 'How much did D'Arcy's monocle cost?' 'How is it fellows like Crooke are in the Shell and decent fellows like yourself are only in the Fourth?' 'What are the Form captain's three chief duties?' 'Who is the chemistry master at St Jim's?' (From a girl) 'Where is St Jim's situated? *Could* you tell me how to get there, as I would love to see the building? Are you boys just "phoneys", as I think you are?'

It is clear that many of the boys and girls who write these letters are living a complete fantasy-life. Sometimes a boy will write, for instance, give his age, height, weight, chest and biceps measurements and asking which member of the Shell or Fourth Form he most exactly resembles. The demand for a list of the studies on the Shell passage, with an exact account of who lives in each, is a very common one. The editors, of course, do everything in their power to keep up the illusion. In the *Gem* Jack Blake is supposed to write the answers to correspondents, and in the *Magnet* a couple of pages is always given up to the school magazine (the *Greyfriars Herald*, edited by Harry Wharton), and there is another page in which one or other character is written up each week. The stories run in cycles, two or three characters being kept in the foreground for several weeks at a time. First there will be a series of rollicking adventure stories, featuring the Famous Five and Billy Bunter; then a run of stories turning on mistaken identity, with Wibley (the make-up wizard) in the star part; then a run of more serious stories in which Vernon-Smith is trembling on the verge of expulsion. And here one comes upon the real secret of the *Gem* and *Magnet* and the probable reason why they continue to be read in spite of their obvious out-of-dateness.

It is that the characters are so carefully graded as to give almost every type of reader a character he can identify himself with. Most boys' papers aim at doing this, hence the boy-assistant (Sexton Blake's Tinker, Nelson Lee's Nipper, etc.) who usually accompanies the explorer, detective or what-not on his adventures. But in these cases there is only one boy, and usually it is much the same type of boy. In the *Gem* and *Magnet* there is a model for nearly everybody. There is the normal, athletic, high-spirited boy (Tom Merry, Jack Blake, Frank Nugent), a slightly rowdier version of this type (Bob Cherry), a more aristocratic version (Talbot, Manners), a quieter, more serious version (Harry Wharton), and a stolid, 'bulldog' version (Johnny Bull). Then there is the reckless, dare-devil type of boy (Vernon-Smith), the definitely 'clever', studious boy (Mark Linley, Dick Penfold), and the eccentric boy who is not good at games but possesses some special talent (Skinner, Wibley). And there is the scholarship-boy (Tom Redwing), an important figure in this class of story because he makes it possible for boys from very poor homes to project themselves into the public-school atmosphere. In addition there are Australian, Irish, Welsh, Manx, Yorkshire and Lancashire boys to play upon local patriotism. But the subtlety of characterization goes deeper than this. If one studies the correspondence columns one sees that there is probably *no* character in the *Gem* and *Magnet* whom some or other reader does not identify with, except the out-and-out comics, Coker, Billy Bunter, Fisher T. Fish (the money-grubbing American boy) and, of course, the masters. Bunter, though in his origin he probably owed something to the fat boy in *Pickwick*, is a real creation. His tight trousers against which boots and canes are constantly thudding, his astuteness in search of food, his postal order which never turns up, have made him famous wherever the Union Jack waves. But he is not a subject for day-dreams. On the other hand, another seeming figure of fun, Gussy (the Honourable Arthur A. D'Arcy, 'the swell of St Jim's'), is evidently much admired. Like everything else in the *Gem* and *Magnet*, Gussy is at least thirty years out of date. He is the 'knut' of the early twentieth century or even the 'masher' of the nineties ('Bai Jove, deah boy!' and 'Weally, I shall be obliged to give you a feahful thwashin!'), the monocled idiot who made good on the fields of Mons and Le Cateau. And his evident popularity goes to show how deep the snob-appeal of this type is. English people are extremely fond of the titled ass (cf. Lord Peter Wimsey) who always turns up trumps in the moment of emergency. Here is a letter from one of Gussy's girl admirers:

I think you're too hard on Gussy. I wonder he's still in existence, the way you treat him. He's my hero. Did you know I write lyrics? How's this – to the tune of 'Goody Goody'?

> Gonna get my gas-mask, join the ARP
> 'Cos I'm wise to all those bombs you drop on me.
>> Gonna dig myself a trench
>> Inside the garden fence;
>> Gonna seal my windows up with tin
>> So that the tear gas can't get in;
> Gonna park my cannon right outside the kerb
> With a note to Adolf Hitler: 'Don't disturb!'
>> And if I never fall in Nazi hands
>> That's soon enough for me
>> Gonna get my gas-mask, join the ARP.

PS – Do you get on well with girls?

I quote this in full because (dated April 1939) it is interesting as being probably the earliest mention of Hitler in the *Gem*. In the *Gem* there is also a heroic fat boy, Fatty Wynn, as a set-off against Bunter. Vernon-Smith, 'the Bounder of the Remove', a Byronic character, always on the verge of the sack, is another great favourite. And even some of the cads probably have their following. Loder, for instance, 'the rotter of the Sixth', is a cad, but he is also a highbrow and given to saying sarcastic things about football and the team spirit. The boys of the Remove only think him all the more of a cad for this, but a certain type of boy would probably identify with him. Even Racke, Crooke and Co. are probably admired by small boys who think it diabolically wicked to smoke cigarettes. (A frequent question in the correspondence column: 'What brand of cigarettes does Racke smoke?')

Naturally the politics of the *Gem* and *Magnet* are Conservative, but in a completely pre-1914 style, with no Fascist tinge. In reality their basic political assumptions are two: nothing ever changes, and foreigners are funny. In the *Gem* of 1939 Frenchmen are still Froggies and Italians are still Dagoes. Mossoo, the French master at Greyfriars, is the usual comic-paper Frog, with pointed beard, pegtop trousers, etc. Inky, the Indian boy, though a rajah, and therefore possessing snob-appeal, is also the comic babu of the *Punch* tradition. ('The rowfulness is not the proper caper, my esteemed Bob,' said Inky. 'Let dogs delight in the barkfulness and bitefulness, but the soft answer is the cracked pitcher that goes longest to a bird in the bush, as the English proverb remarks.') Fisher T. Fish is the old-style stage Yankee ('Waal, I guess,' etc.) dating from a period of Anglo-American jealousy. Wun Lung, the Chinese boy (he has rather faded out of late, no doubt because some of the *Magnet*'s readers are Straits Chinese), is the nineteenth-century pantomime Chinaman, with saucer-shaped hat, pigtail and pidgin-English. The assumption all along is not only that foreigners are comics who are put there for us to laugh at, but that they can be classified in much the same way as insects. That is why in all boys' papers, not only the *Gem* and *Magnet*, a Chinese is invariably portrayed with a pigtail. It is the thing you recognize him by, like the Frenchman's beard or the Italian's barrel-organ. In papers of this kind it occasionally happens that when the setting of a story is in a foreign country some attempt is made to describe the natives as individual human beings, but as a rule it is assumed that foreigners of any one race are all alike and will conform more or less exactly to the following patterns:

FRENCHMAN: Excitable. Wears beard, gesticulates wildly.
SPANIARD, MEXICAN etc.: Sinister, treacherous.
ARAB, AFGHAN etc.: Sinister, treacherous.

CHINESE: Sinister, treacherous. Wears pigtails.
ITALIAN: Excitable. Grinds barrel-organ or carries stiletto.
SWEDE, DANE etc.: Kind-hearted, stupid.
NEGRO: Comic, very faithful.

The working classes only enter into the *Gem* and *Magnet* as comics or semi-villains (race-course touts etc.). As for class-friction, trade unionism, strikes, slumps, unemployment, Fascism and civil war – not a mention. Somewhere or other in the thirty years' issue of the two papers you might perhaps find the word 'Socialism', but you would have to look a long time for it. If the Russian Revolution is anywhere referred to, it will be indirectly, in the word 'Bolshy' (meaning a person of violent disagreeable habits). Hitler and the Nazis are just beginning to make their appearance, in the sort of reference I quoted above. The war crisis of September 1938 made just enough impression to produce a story in which Mr Vernon-Smith, the Bounder's millionaire father, cashed in on the general panic by buying up country houses in order to sell them to 'crisis scuttlers'. But that is probably as near to noticing the European situation as the *Gem* and *Magnet* will come, until the war actually starts.[1] That does not mean these papers are unpatriotic – quite the contrary! Throughout the Great War the *Gem* and *Magnet* were perhaps the most consistently and cheerfully patriotic papers in England. Almost every week the boys caught a spy or pushed a conchy into the army, and during the rationing period 'EAT LESS BREAD' was printed in large type on every page. But their patriotism has nothing whatever to do with power politics or

---

[1] This was written some months before the outbreak of war. Up to the end of September 1939 no mention of the war has appeared in either paper. [Author's footnote.]

'ideological' warfare. It is more akin to family loyalty, and actually it gives one a valuable clue to the attitude of ordinary people, especially the huge untouchable block of the middle class and the better-off working class. These people are patriotic to the middle of their bones, but they do not feel that what happens in foreign countries is any of their business. When England is in danger they rally to its defence as a matter of course, but in between times they are not interested. After all, England is always in the right and England always wins, so why worry? It is an attitude that has been shaken during the past twenty years, but not so deeply as is sometimes supposed. Failure to understand it is one of the reasons why left-wing political parties are seldom able to produce an acceptable foreign policy.

The mental world of the *Gem* and *Magnet*, therefore, is something like this:

The year is 1910 – or 1940, but it is all the same. You are at Greyfriars, a rosy-cheeked boy of fourteen in posh, tailor-made clothes, sitting down to tea in your study on the Remove passage after an exciting game of football which was won by an odd goal in the last half-minute. There is a cosy fire in the study, and outside the wind is whistling. The ivy clusters thickly round the old grey stones. The King is on his throne and the pound is worth a pound. Over in Europe the comic foreigners are jabbering and gesticulating, but the grim grey battleships of the British Fleet are steaming up the Channel and at the outposts of Empire the monocled Englishmen are holding the niggers at bay. Lord Mauleverer has just got another fiver and we are all settling down to a tremendous tea of sausages, sardines, crumpets, potted meat, jam and doughnuts. After tea we shall sit round the study fire having a good laugh at Billy Bunter and discussing the team for next week's match against Rookwood. Everything is safe, solid and unquestionable. Everything will be the same for ever and ever. That approximately is the atmosphere.

But now turn from the *Gem* and *Magnet* to the more up-to-date papers which have appeared since the Great War. The truly significant thing is that they have more points of resemblance to the *Gem* and *Magnet* than points of difference. But it is better to consider the differences first.

There are eight of these newer papers, the *Modern Boy, Triumph, Champion, Wizard, Rover, Skipper, Hotspur* and *Adventure*. All of these have appeared since the Great War, but except for the *Modern Boy* none of them is less than five years old. Two papers which ought also to be mentioned briefly here, though they are not strictly in the same class as the rest, are the *Detective Weekly* and the *Thriller*, both owned by the Amalgamated Press. The *Detective Weekly* has taken over Sexton Blake. Both of these papers admit a certain amount of sex-interest into their stories, and though certainly read by boys, they are not aimed at them exclusively. All the others are boys' papers pure and simple, and they are sufficiently alike to be considered together. There does not seem to be any notable difference between Thomson's publications and those of the Amalgamated Press.

As soon as one looks at these papers one sees their technical superiority to the *Gem* and *Magnet*. To begin with, they have the great advantage of not being written entirely by one person. Instead of one long complete story, a number of the *Wizard* or *Hotspur* consists of half a dozen or more serials, none of which goes on for ever. Consequently there is far more variety and far less padding, and none of the tiresome stylization and facetiousness of the *Gem* and *Magnet*. Look at these two extracts, for example:

> Billy Bunter groaned.
>
> A quarter of an hour had elapsed out of the two hours that Bunter was booked for extra French.
>
> In a quarter of an hour there were only fifteen minutes! But every one of those minutes seemed inordinately long to Bunter. They seemed to crawl by like tired snails.
>
> Looking at the clock in Class-room No. 10 the fat Owl could hardly believe that only fifteen minutes had passed. It seemed more like fifteen hours, if not fifteen days!
>
> Other fellows were in extra French as well as Bunter. They did not matter. Bunter did! (*Magnet*.)
>
> After a terrible climb, hacking out handholds in the smooth ice every step of the way up, Sergeant Lionheart Logan of the Mounties was now clinging like a human fly to the face of an icy cliff, as smooth and treacherous as a giant pane of glass.
>
> An Arctic blizzard, in all its fury was buffeting his body, driving the blinding snow into his face, seeking to tear his fingers loose from their handholds and dash him to death on the jagged boulders which lay at the foot of the cliff a hundred feet below.
>
> Crouching among those boulders were eleven villainous trappers who had done their best to shoot down Lionheart and his companion, Constable Jim Rogers – until the blizzard had blotted the two Mounties out of sight from below. (*Wizard*.)

The second extract gets you some distance with the story, the first takes a hundred words to tell you that Bunter is in the detention class. Moreover, by not concentrating on school stories (in point of numbers the school story slightly predominates in all these papers, except the *Thriller* and *Detective Weekly*), the *Wizard, Hotspur*, etc. have far greater opportunities for sensationalism. Merely looking at the cover illustrations of the papers which I have on the table in front of me, here are some of the things I see. On one a cowboy is clinging by his toes to the wing of an aeroplane in mid-air and shooting down another aeroplane with his revolver. On another a Chinese is swimming for his life down a sewer with a swarm of ravenous-looking rats swimming after him. On another an engineer is lighting a stick of dynamite while a steel robot feels for him with its claws. On another a man in airman's costume is fighting bare-handed against a rat somewhat larger than a donkey. On another a nearly naked man of terrific muscular development has just seized a lion by the tail and flung it thirty yards over the wall of an arena, with the words, 'Take back your blooming lion!' Clearly no school story can compete with this kind of thing. From time to time the school buildings may catch fire or the French master may turn out to be the head of an international anarchist gang, but in a general way the interest must centre round cricket, school rivalries, practical jokes, etc. There is not much room for bombs, death-rays, sub-machine-guns, aeroplanes, mustangs, octopuses, grizzly bears or gangsters.

Examination of a large number of these papers shows that, putting aside school stories, the favourite subjects are Wild West, Frozen North, Foreign Legion, crime (always from the detective's angle), the Great War (Air Force or Secret Service, not the infantry), the Tarzan motif in varying forms, professional football, tropical exploration, historical romance (Robin Hood, Cavaliers and Roundheads, etc.) and scientific invention. The Wild West still leads, at any rate as a setting, though the Red Indian seems to be fading out. The one theme that is really new is the scientific one. Death-rays, Martians, invisible men, robots, helicopters and interplanetary rockets figure largely; here and there there are even far-off rumours of psychotherapy and ductless glands. Whereas the *Gem* and *Magnet* derive from Dickens and Kipling, the *Wizard, Champion, Modern Boy*, etc. owe a great deal to H. G. Wells, who, rather than Jules Verne, is the father of 'Scientifiction'. Naturally, it is the magical, Martian aspect of science that is most exploited, but one or two papers include serious articles on scientific subjects, besides quantities of informative snippets. (Examples: 'A Kauri tree in Queensland, Australia, is over 12,000 years old'; 'Nearly 50,000 thunderstorms occur every day'; 'Helium gas costs £1 per 1,000 cubic feet'; 'There are over 500 varieties of spiders in Great Britain'; 'London firemen use 14,000,000 gallons of water annually', etc. etc.) There is a marked advance in intellectual curiosity and, on the whole, in the demand made on the reader's attention. In practice the *Gem* and *Magnet* and the post-war papers are read by much the same public, but the mental age aimed at seems to have risen by a year or two years – an improvement probably corresponding to the improvement in elementary education since 1909.

The other thing that has emerged in the post-war boys' papers, though not to anything like the extent one would expect, is bully-worship and the cult of violence.

If one compares the *Gem* and *Magnet* with a genuinely modern paper, the thing that immediately strikes one is the absence of the leader-principle. There is no central dominating character; instead there are fifteen or twenty characters, all more or less on an equality, with whom readers of different types can identify. In the more modern papers this is not usually the case. Instead of identifying with a schoolboy of more or less his own age, the reader of the *Skipper, Hotspur*, etc. is led to identify with a G-man, with a Foreign Legionary, with some variant of Tarzan, with an air ace, a master spy, an explorer, a pugilist — at any rate with some single all-powerful character who dominates everyone about him and whose usual method of solving any problem is a sock on the jaw. This character is intended as a superman, and as physical strength is the form of power that boys can best understand, he is usually a sort of human gorilla; in the Tarzan type of story he is sometimes actually a giant, eight or ten feet high. At the same time the scenes of violence in nearly all these stories are remarkably harmless and unconvincing. There is a great difference in tone between even the most bloodthirsty English paper and the threepenny Yank Mags, *Fight Stories, Action Stories*, etc. (not strictly boys' papers, but largely read by boys). In the Yank Mags you get real blood-lust, really gory descriptions of the all-in, jump-on-his-testicles style of fighting, written in a jargon that has been perfected by people who brood endlessly on violence. A paper like *Fight Stories*, for instance, would have very little appeal except to sadists and masochists. You can see the comparative gentleness of English civilization by the amateurish way in which prize-fighting is always described in the boys' weeklies. There is no specialized vocabulary. Look at these four extracts, two English, two American:

When the gong sounded, both men were breathing heavily, and each had great red marks on his chest, Bill's chin was bleeding, and Ben had a cut over his right eye.
Into their corners they sank, but when the gong clanged again they were up swiftly, and they went like tigers at each other. (*Rover*.)

He walked in stolidly and smashed a clublike right to my face. Blood spattered and I went back on my heels, but surged in and ripped my right under his heart. Another right smashed full on Sven's already battered mouth, and, spitting out the fragments of a tooth, he crashed a flailing left to my body. (*Fight Stories.*)

It was amazing to watch the black Panther at work. His muscles rippled and slid under his dark skin. There was all the power and grace of a giant cat in his swift and terrible onslaught.

He volleyed blows with a bewildering speed for so huge a fellow. In a moment Ben was simply blocking with his gloves as well as he could. Ben was really a past-master of defence. He had many fine victories behind him. But the Negro's rights and lefts crashed through openings that hardly any other fighter could have found. (*Wizard.*)

Haymakers which packed the bludgeoning weight of forest monarchs crashing down under the ax hurled into the bodies of the two heavies as they swapped punches. (*Fight Stories.*)

Notice how much more knowledgeable the American extracts sound. They are written for devotees of the prize-ring, the others are not. Also, it ought to be emphasized that on its level the moral code of the English boys' papers is a decent one. Crime and dishonesty are never held up to admiration, there is none of the cynicism and corruption of the American gangster story. The huge sale of the Yank Mags in England shows that there is a demand for that kind of thing, but very few English writers seem able to produce it. When hatred of Hitler became a major emotion in America, it was interesting to see how promptly 'anti-Fascism' was adapted to pornographic purposes by the editors of the Yank Mags. One magazine which I have in front of me is given up to a long, complete story, 'When Hell Came to America', in which the agents of a 'blood-maddened European dictator' are trying to conquer the USA with death-rays and invisible aeroplanes. There is the frankest appeal to sadism, scenes in which the Nazis tie bombs to women's backs and fling them off heights to watch them blown to pieces in mid-air, others in which they tie naked girls together by their hair and prod them with knives to make them dance, etc. etc. The editor comments solemnly on all this, and uses it as a plea for tightening up restrictions against immigrants. On another page of the same paper: 'LIVES OF THE HOTCHA CHORUS GIRLS. Reveals all the intimate secrets and fascinating pastimes of the famous Broadway Hotcha girls. NOTHING IS OMITTED. Price 10c.' 'HOW TO LOVE 10c.' 'FRENCH PHOTO RING, 25C.' 'NAUGHTY NUDIES TRANSFERS. From the outside of the glass you see a beautiful girl, innocently dressed. Turn it around and look through the glass and oh! what a difference! Set of 3 transfers 25c.' etc. etc. etc. There is nothing at all like this in any English paper likely to be read by boys. But the process of Americanization is going on all the same. The American ideal, the 'he-man', the 'tough guy', the gorilla who puts everything right by socking everybody else on the jaw, now figures in probably a majority of boys' papers. In one serial now running in the *Skipper* he is always portrayed, ominously enough, swinging a rubber truncheon.

The development of the *Wizard, Hotspur,* etc., as against the earlier boys' papers, boils down to this: better technique, more scientific interest, more bloodshed, more leader-worship. But, after all, it is the *lack* of development that is the really striking thing.

To begin with, there is no political development whatever. The world of the *Skipper* and the *Champion* is still the pre-1914 world of the *Magnet* and the *Gem*. The Wild West story, for instance, with its cattle-rustlers, lynch-law and other paraphernalia belonging to the eighties, is a curiously archaic thing. It is worth noticing that in papers of this type it is always taken for granted that adventures only happen at the ends of the earth, in tropical forests, in Arctic wastes, in African deserts, on Western prairies, in Chinese opium dens – everywhere, in fact, except the place where things really *do* happen. That is a belief dating from thirty or forty years ago, when the new continents were in process of being opened up. Nowadays, of course, if you really want adventure, the place to look for it is in Europe. But apart from the picturesque side of the Great War, contemporary history is carefully excluded. And except that Americans are now admired instead of being laughed at, foreigners are exactly the same figures of fun that they always were. If a Chinese character appears, he is still the sinister pigtailed opium-smuggler of Sax Rohmer; no indication that things have been happening in China since 1912 – no indication that a war is going on there, for instance. If a Spaniard appears, he is still a 'dago' or a 'greaser' who rolls cigarettes and stabs people in the back; no indication that things have been happening in Spain. Hitler and the Nazis have not yet appeared, or are barely making their appearance. There will be plenty about them in a little while, but it will be from a strictly patriotic angle (Britain versus Germany), with the real meaning of the struggle kept out of sight as much as possible. As for the Russian Revolution, it is extremely difficult to find any reference to it in any of these papers. When Russia is mentioned at all it is usually in an information snippet (example: 'There are 29,000 centenarians in the USSR'), and any reference to the Revolution is indirect and twenty years out of date. In one story in the *Rover*, for instance, somebody has a tame bear, and as it is a Russian bear, it is nicknamed Trotsky – obviously an echo of the 1917–23 period and not of recent controversies. The clock has stopped at 1910. Britannia rules the waves, and no one has heard of slumps, booms, unemployment, dictatorships, purges or concentration camps.

And in social outlook there is hardly any advance. The snobbishness is somewhat less open than in the *Gem* and *Magnet* – that is the most one can possibly say. To begin with, the school story, always partly dependent on snob-appeal, is by no means eliminated. Every number of a boys' paper includes at least one school story, these stories slightly outnumbering the Wild Westerns. The very elaborate fantasy-life of the *Gem* and *Magnet* is not imitated and there is more emphasis on extraneous adventure, but the social atmosphere (old grey stones) is much the same. When a new school is introduced at the beginning of a story we are often told in just about those words that 'it was a very posh school'. From time to time a story appears which is ostensibly directed *against* snobbery. The scholarship-boy (cf. Tom Redwing in the *Magnet*) makes fairly frequent appearances, and what is essentially the same theme is sometimes presented in this form; there is great rivalry between two schools, one of which considers itself more 'posh' than the other, and there are fights, practical jokes, football matches, etc. always ending in the discomfiture of the snobs. If one glances very superficially at some of these stories it is possible to imagine that a democratic spirit has crept into the boys' weeklies, but when one looks more closely one sees that they merely reflected the bitter jealousies that exist within the white-collar class. Their real function is to allow the boy who goes to a cheap private school (*not* a Council school) to feel that his school is just as 'posh' in the sight of God as Winchester or Eton. The sentiment of school loyalty ('We're better than the fellows down the road'), a thing almost unknown to the real working class, is still kept up. As these stories are written by many different hands, they do, of course, vary a good deal in tone. Some are reasonably free from snobbishness, in others money and pedigree are exploited even more shamelessly than in the *Gem* and *Magnet*. In one that I came across an actual *majority* of the boys mentioned were titled.

Where working-class characters appear, it is usually either as comics (jokes about tramps, convicts, etc.) or as prize-fighters, acrobats, cowboys, professional footballers and Foreign Legionaries – in other words, as adventurers. There is no facing of the facts about working-class life, or, indeed, about *working* life of any description. Very occasionally one may come across a realistic description of, say, work in a coal mine, but in all probability it will only be there as the background of some lurid adventure. In any case the central character is not likely to be a coalminer. Nearly all the time the boy who reads these papers – in nine cases out of ten a boy who is going to spend his life working in a shop, in a factory or in some subordinate job in an office – is led to identify with people in positions of command, above all with people who are never troubled by shortage of money. The Lord Peter Wimsey figure, the seeming idiot who drawls and wears a monocle but is always to the fore in moments of danger, turns up over and over again. (This character is a great favourite in Secret Service stories.) And, as usual, the heroic characters all have to talk BBC; they may talk Scottish or Irish or American, but no one in a star part is ever permitted to drop an aitch. Here it is worth comparing the social atmosphere of the boys' weeklies with that of the women's weeklies, the *Oracle*, the *Family Star*, *Peg's Paper*, etc.

The women's papers are aimed at an older public and are read for the most part by girls who are working for a living. Consequently they are on the surface much more realistic. It is taken for granted, for example, that nearly everyone has to live in a big town and work at a more or less dull job. Sex, so far from being taboo, is *the* subject. The short, complete stories, the special feature of these papers, are generally of the 'came the dawn' type: the heroine narrowly escapes losing her 'boy' to a designing rival, or the 'boy' loses his job and has to postpone marriage, but presently gets a better job. The changeling-fantasy (a girl brought up in a poor home is 'really' the child of rich parents) is another favourite. Where sensationalism comes in, usually in the serials, it arises out of the more domestic type of crime, such as bigamy, forgery or sometimes murder; no Martians, death-rays or international anarchist gangs. These papers are at any rate aiming at credibility, and they have a link with real life in their correspondence columns, where genuine problems are being discussed. Ruby M. Ayres's column of advice in the *Oracle*, for instance, is extremely sensible and well written. And yet the world of the *Oracle* and *Peg's Paper* is a pure fantasy-world. It is the same fantasy all the time, pretending to be richer than you are. The chief impression that one carries away from almost every story in these papers is of frightful, overwhelming 'refinement'. Ostensibly the characters are working-class people, but their habits, the interiors of their houses, their clothes, their outlook and, above all, their speech are entirely middle class. They are all living at several pounds a week above their income. And needless to say, that is just the impression that is intended. The idea is to give the bored factory-girl or worn-out mother of five a dream-life in which she pictures herself – not actually as a duchess (that convention has gone out) but as, say, the wife of a bank-manager. Not only is a five-to-six-pound-a-week standard of life set up as the ideal, it is tacitly assumed that that is how working-class people really *do* live. The major facts are simply not faced. It is admitted, for instance, that people sometimes lose their jobs; but then the dark clouds roll away and they get better jobs instead. No mention of unemployment as sometimes permanent and inevitable, no mention of the dole, no mention of trade unionism. No suggestion anywhere that there can be anything wrong with the system *as a system*; there are only individual misfortunes, which are generally due to somebody's wickedness and can in any case be put right in the last chapter. Always the dark clouds roll away, the kind employer raises Alfred's wages, and there are jobs for everybody except the drunks. It is still the world of the *Wizard* and the *Gem*, except that there are orange-blossoms instead of machine-guns.

The outlook inculcated by all these papers is that of a rather exceptionally stupid member of the Navy League in the year 1910. Yes, it may be said, but what does it matter? And in any case, what else do you expect?

Of course no one in his senses would want to turn the so-called penny dreadful into a realistic novel or a Socialist tract. An adventure story must of its nature be more or less remote from real life. But, as I have tried to make clear, the unreality of the *Wizard* and the *Gem* is not so artless as it looks. These papers exist because of a specialized demand, because boys at certain ages find it necessary to read about Martians, death-rays, grizzly bears and gangsters. They get what they are looking for, but they get it wrapped up in the illusions which their future employers think suitable for them. To what extent people draw their ideas from fiction is disputable. Personally I believe that most people are influenced far more than they would care to admit by novels, serial stories, films and so forth, and that from this point of view the worst books are often the most important, because they are usually the ones that are read earliest in life. It is probable that many people who could consider themselves extemely sophisticated and 'advanced' are actually carrying through life an imaginative background which they acquired in childhood from (for instance) Sapper and Ian Hay. If that is so, the boys' twopenny weeklies are of the deepest importance. Here is the stuff that is read somewhere between the ages of twelve and eighteen by a very large proportion, perhaps an actual majority, of English boys, including many who will never read anything else except newspapers; and along with it they are absorbing a set of beliefs which would be regarded as hopelessly out of date in the Central Office of the Conservative Party. All the better because it is done indirectly, there is being pumped into them the conviction that the major problems of our time do not exist, that there is nothing wrong with *laissez-faire* capitalism, that foreigners are unimportant comics and that the British Empire is a sort of charity-concern which will last for ever. Considering who owns these papers, it is difficult to believe that this is unintentional. Of the twelve papers I have been discussing (i.e. twelve including the *Thriller* and *Detective Weekly*) seven are the property of the Amalgamated Press, which is one of the biggest press-combines in the world and controls more than a hundred different papers. The *Gem* and *Magnet*, therefore, are closely linked up with the *Daily Telegraph* and the *Financial Times*. This in itself would be enough to rouse certain suspicions, even if it were not obvious that the stories in the boys' weeklies are politically vetted. So it appears that if you feel the need of a fantasy-life in which you travel to Mars and fight lions bare-handed (and what boy doesn't?) you can only have it by delivering yourself over, mentally, to people like Lord Camrose. For there is no competition. Throughout the whole of this run of papers the differences are negligible, and on this level no others exist. This raises the question, why is there no such thing as a left-wing boys' paper?

At first glance such an idea merely makes one slightly sick. It is so horribly easy to imagine what a left-wing boys' paper would be like, if it existed. I remember in 1920 or 1921 some optimistic person handing round Communist tracts among a crowd of public-school boys. The tract I received was of the question-and-answer kind:

Q. 'Can a Boy Communist be a Boy Scout, Comrade?'
A. 'No, Comrade.'
Q. 'Why, Comrade?'
A. 'Because, Comrade, a Boy Scout must salute the
Union Jack, which is the symbol of tyranny and
oppression,' etc. etc.

Now, suppose that at this moment somebody started a left-wing paper deliberately aimed at boys of twelve or fourteen. I do not suggest that the whole of its contents would be exactly like the tract I have quoted above, but does anyone doubt that they would be *something* like it? Inevitably such a paper would either consist of dreary uplift or it would be under Communist influence and given over to adulation of Soviet Russia; in either case no normal boy would ever look at it. Highbrow literature apart, the whole of the existing left-wing press, in so far as it is at all vigorously 'left', is one long tract.

The one Socialist paper in England which could live a week on its merits *as a paper* is the *Daily Herald*, and how much Socialism is there in the *Daily Herald*? At this moment, therefore, a paper with a 'left' slant and at the same time likely to have an appeal to ordinary boys in their teens is something almost beyond hoping for.

But it does not follow that it is impossible. There is no clear reason why every adventure story should necessarily be mixed up with snobbishness and gutter patriotism. For, after all, the stories in the *Hotspur* and the *Modern Boy* are not Conservative tracts; they are merely adventure stories with a Conservative bias. It is fairly easy to imagine the process being reversed. It is possible, for instance, to imagine a paper as thrilling and lively as the *Hotspur*, but with subject-matter and 'ideology' a little more up to date. It is even possible (though this raises other difficulties) to imagine a women's paper at the same literary level as the *Oracle*, dealing in approximately the same kind of story, but taking rather more account of the realities of working-class life. Such things have been done before, though not in England. In the last years of the Spanish monarchy there was a large output in Spain of left-wing novelettes, some of them evidently of Anarchist origin. Unfortunately at the time when they were appearing I did not see their social significance, and I lost the collection of them that I had, but no doubt copies would still be procurable. In get-up and style of story they were very similar to the English fourpenny novelette, except that their inspiration was 'left'. If, for instance, a story described police pursuing Anarchists through the mountains, it would be from the point of view of the Anarchists and not of the police. An example nearer to hand is the Soviet film *Chapayev*, which has been shown a number of times in London.

Technically, by the standards of the time when it was made, *Chapayev* is a first-rate film, but mentally, in spite of the unfamiliar Russian background, it is not so very remote from Hollywood. The one thing that lifts it out of the ordinary is the remarkable performance by the actor who takes the part of the White officer (the fat one) – a performance which looks very like an inspired piece of gagging. Otherwise the atmosphere is familiar. All the usual paraphernalia is there – heroic fight against odds, escape at the last moment, shots of galloping horses, love interest, comic relief. The film is in fact a fairly ordinary one, except that its tendency is 'left'. In a Hollywood film of the Russian Civil War the Whites would probably be angels and the Reds demons. In the Russian version the Reds are angels and the Whites demons. That also is a lie, but, taking the long view, it is a less pernicious lie than the other.

Here several difficult problems present themselves. Their general nature is obvious enough, and I do not want to discuss them. I am merely pointing to the fact that, in England, popular imaginative literature is a field that left-wing thought has never begun to enter. *All* fiction from the novels in the mushroom libraries downwards is censored in the interests of the ruling class. And boys' fiction above all, the blood-and-thunder stuff which nearly every boy devours at some time or other, is sodden in the worst illusions of 1910. The fact is only unimportant if one believes that what is read in childhood leaves no impression behind. Lord Camrose and his colleagues evidently believe nothing of the kind, and, after all, Lord Camrose ought to know.

1939

My Country Right or Left

Contrary to popular belief, the past was not more eventful than the present. If it seems so it is because when you look backward things that happened years apart are telescoped together, and because very few of your memories come to you genuinely virgin. It is largely because of the books, films and reminiscences that have come between that the war of 1914–18 is now supposed to have had some tremendous, epic quality that the present one lacks.

But if you were alive during that war, and if you disentangle your real memories from their later accretions, you find that it was not usually the big events that stirred you at the time. I don't believe that the Battle of the Marne, for instance, had for the general public the melodramatic quality that it was afterwards given. I do not even remember hearing the phrase 'Battle of the Marne' till years later. It was merely that the Germans were twenty-two miles from Paris – and certainly that was terrifying enough, after the Belgian atrocity stories – and then for some reason they had turned back. I was eleven when the war started. If I honestly sort out my memories and disregard what I have learned since, I must admit that nothing in the whole war moved me so deeply as the loss of the *Titanic* had done a few years earlier. This comparatively petty disaster shocked the whole world, and the shock has not quite died away even yet. I remember the terrible, detailed accounts read out at the breakfast table (in those days it was a common habit to read the newspaper aloud), and I remember that in all the long list of horrors the one that most impressed me was that at the last the *Titanic* suddenly up-ended and sank bow foremost, so that the people clinging to the stern were lifted no less than three hundred feet into the air before they plunged into the abyss. It gave me a sinking sensation in the belly which I can still all but feel. Nothing in the war ever gave me quite that sensation.

Of the outbreak of war I have three vivid memories which, being petty and irrelevant, are uninfluenced by anything that has come later. One is of the cartoon of the 'German Emperor' (I believe the hated name 'Kaiser' was not popularized till a little later) that appeared in the last days of July. People were mildly shocked by this guying of royalty ('But he's such a handsome man, really!') although we were on the edge of war. Another is of the time when the army commandeered all the horses in our little country town, and a cabman burst into tears in the market-place when his horse, which had worked for him for years, was taken away from him. And another is of a mob of young men at the railway station, scrambling for the evening papers that had just arrived on the London train. And I remember the pile of peagreen papers (some of them were still green in those days), the high collars, the tightish trousers and the bowler hats, far better than I can remember the names of the terrific battles that were already raging on the French frontier.

Of the middle years of the war, I remember chiefly the

square shoulders, bulging calves and jingling spurs of the artillerymen, whose uniform I much preferred to that of the infantry. As for the final period, if you ask me to say truthfully what is my chief memory, I must answer simply – margarine. It is an instance of the horrible selfishness of children that by 1917 the war had almost ceased to affect us, except through our stomachs. In the school library a huge map of the Western Front was pinned on an easel, with a red silk thread running across on a zig-zag of drawing-pins. Occasionally the thread moved half an inch this way or that, each movement meaning a pyramid of corpses. I paid no attention. I was at school among boys who were above the average level of intelligence, and yet I do not remember that a single major event of the time appeared to us in its true significance. The Russian Revolution, for instance, made no impression, except on the few whose parents happened to have money invested in Russia. Among the very young the pacifist reaction had set in long before the war ended. To be as slack as you dared on OTC parades, and to take no interest in the war, was considered a mark of enlightenment. The young officers who had come back, hardened by their terrible experience and disgusted by the attitude of the younger generation to whom this experience meant just nothing, used to lecture us for our softness. Of course they could produce no argument that we were capable of understanding. They could only bark at you that war was 'a good thing', it 'made you tough', 'kept you fit', etc. etc. We merely sniggered at them. Ours was the one-eyed pacifism that is peculiar to sheltered countries with strong navies. For years after the war, to have any knowledge of or interest in military matters, even to know which end of a gun the bullet comes out of, was suspect in 'enlightened' circles. 1914–18 was written off as a meaningless slaughter, and even the men who had been slaughtered were held to be in some way to blame. I have often laughed to think of the recruiting poster, 'What did you do in the Great War, daddy?' (a child is asking this question of its shame-stricken father), and of all the men who must have been lured into the army by just that poster and afterwards despised by their children for not being Conscientious Objectors.

But the dead men had their revenge after all. As the war fell back into the past, my particular generation, those who had been 'just too young', became conscious of the vastness of the experience they had missed. You felt yourself a little less than a man, because you had missed it. I spent the years 1922–7 mostly among men a little older than myself who had been through the war. They talked about it unceasingly, with horror, of course, but also with a steadily growing nostalgia. You can see this nostalgia perfectly clearly in the English war-books. Besides, the pacifist reaction was only a phase, and even the 'just too young' had all been trained for war. Most of the English middle class are trained for war from the cradle onwards, not technically but morally. The earliest political slogan I can remember is 'We want eight (eight dreadnoughts) and we won't wait'. At seven years old I was a member of the Navy League and wore a sailor suit with 'HMS *Invincible*' on my cap. Even before my public-school OTC I had been in a private-school cadet corps. On and off, I have been toting a rifle ever since I was ten, in preparation not only for war but for a particular kind of war, a war in which the guns rise to a frantic orgasm of sound, and at the appointed moment you clamber out of the trench, breaking your nails on the sandbags, and stumble across mud and wire into the machine-gun barrage. I am convinced that part of the reason for the fascination that the Spanish Civil War had for people of about my age was that it was so like the Great War. At certain moments Franco was able to scrape together enough aeroplanes to raise the war to a modern level, and these were the turning-points. But for the rest it was a bad copy of 1914–18, a positional war of trenches, artillery, raids, snipers, mud, barbed wire, lice and stagnation. In early 1937 the bit of the Aragon front that I was on must have been very like a quiet sector in France in 1915. It was only the artillery that was lacking. Even on the rare occasions when all the guns in Huesca and outside it were firing simultaneously, there were only enough of them to make a fitful unimpressive noise like the ending of a thunderstorm. The shells from Franco's six-inch guns crashed loudly enough, but there were never more than a dozen of them at a time. I know that what I felt when I first heard artillery fired 'in anger', as they say, was at least partly disappointment. It was so different from the tremendous, unbroken roar that my senses had been waiting for for twenty years.

I don't quite know in what year I first knew for certain that the present war was coming. After 1936, of course, the thing was obvious to anyone except an idiot. For several years the coming war was a nightmare to me, and at times I even made speeches and wrote pamphlets against it. But the night before the Russo-German pact was announced I dreamed that the war had started. It was one of those dreams which, whatever Freudian inner meaning they may have, do sometimes reveal to you the real state of your feelings. It taught me two things, first, that I should be simply relieved when the long-dreaded war started, secondly, that I was patriotic at heart, would not sabotage or act against my own side, would support the war, would fight in it if possible. I came downstairs to find the newspaper announcing Ribbentrop's flight to Moscow.[1] So war was coming, and the Government, even the Chamberlain Government, was assured of my loyalty. Needless to say this loyalty was and remains merely a gesture. As with almost everyone I know, the Government has flatly refused to employ me in any capacity whatever, even as a clerk or a private soldier. But that does not alter one's feelings. Besides, they will be forced to make use of us sooner or later.

If I had to defend my reasons for supporting the war, I believe I could do so. There is no real alternative between resisting Hitler and surrendering to him, and from a Socialist point of view I should say that it is better to resist; in any case I can see no argument for surrender that does not make nonsense of the Republican resistance in Spain, the Chinese resistance to Japan, etc. etc. But I don't pretend that that is the emotional basis of my actions. What I knew in my dream that night was that the long drilling in patriotism which the middle classes go through had done its work, and that once England was in a serious jam it would be impossible for me to sabotage. But let no one mistake the meaning of this. Patriotism has nothing to do with conservatism. It is devotion to something that is changing but is felt to be mystically the same, like the devotion of the ex-White Bolshevik to Russia. To be loyal both to Chamberlain's England and to the England of tomorrow might seem an impossibility, if one did not know it to be an everyday phenomenon. Only revolution can save England, that has been obvious for years, but now the revolution has started, and it may proceed quite quickly if only we can

---

[1] On 21 August 1939 Ribbentrop was invited to Moscow and on 23 August he and Molotov signed the Russo-German Pact.

keep Hitler out. Within two years, maybe a year, if only we can hang on, we shall see changes that will surprise the idiots who have no foresight. I dare say the London gutters will have to run with blood. All right, let them, if it is necessary. But when the red militias are billeted in the Ritz I shall still feel that the England I was taught to love so long ago and for such different reasons is somehow persisting.

I grew up in an atmosphere tinged with militarism, and afterwards I spent five boring years within the sound of bugles. To this day it gives me a faint feeling of sacrilege not to stand to attention during 'God save the King'. That is childish, of course, but I would sooner have had that kind of upbringing than be like the left-wing intellectuals who are so 'enlightened' that they cannot understand the most ordinary emotions. It is exactly the people whose hearts have *never* leapt at the sight of a Union Jack who will flinch from revolution when the moment comes. Let anyone compare the poem John Cornford wrote not long before he was killed ('Before the Storming of Huesca') with Sir Henry Newbolt's 'There's a breathless hush in the Close tonight'. Put aside the technical differences, which are merely a matter of period, and it will be seen that the emotional content of the two poems is almost exactly the same. The young Communist who died heroically in the International Brigade was public school to the core. He had changed his allegiance but not his emotions. What does that prove? Merely the possibility of building a Socialist on the bones of a Blimp, the power of one kind of loyalty to transmute itself into another, the spiritual need for patriotism and the military virtues, for which, however little the boiled rabbits of the Left may like them, no substitute has yet been found.

1940

Looking Back on the Spanish War

I

First of all the physical memories, the sound, the smells and the surfaces of things.

It is curious that more vividly than anything that came afterwards in the Spanish war I remember the week of so-called training that we received before being sent to the front – the huge cavalry barracks in Barcelona with its draughty stables and cobbled yards, the icy cold of the pump where one washed, the filthy meals made tolerable by pannikins of wine, the trousered militia-women chopping firewood, and the roll-call in the early mornings where my prosaic English name made a sort of comic interlude among the resounding Spanish ones, Manuel Gonzalez, Pedro Aguilar, Ramon Fenellosa, Roque Ballaster, Jaime Domenech, Sebastian Viltron, Ramon Nuvo Bosch. I name those particular men because I remember the faces of all of them. Except for two who were mere riff-raff and have doubtless become good Falangists by this time, it is probable that all of them are dead. Two of them I know to be dead. The eldest would have been about twenty-five, the youngest sixteen.

One of the essential experiences of war is never being able

to escape from disgusting smells of human origin. Latrines are an overworked subject in war literature, and I would not mention them if it were not that the latrine in our barracks did its necessary bit towards puncturing my own illusions about the Spanish Civil War. The Latin type of latrine, at which you have to squat, is bad enough at its best, but these were made of some kind of polished stone so slippery that it was all you could do to keep on your feet. In addition they were always blocked. Now I have plenty of other disgusting things in my memory, but I believe it was these latrines that first brought home to me the thought, so often to recur; 'Here we are, soldiers of a revolutionary army, defending democracy against Fascism, fighting a war which is *about* something, and the detail of our lives is just as sordid and degrading as it could be in prison, let alone in a bourgeois army.' Many other things reinforced this impression later; for instance, the boredom and animal hunger of trench life, the squalid intrigues over scraps of food, the mean, nagging quarrels which people exhausted by lack of sleep indulge in.

The essential horror of army life (whoever has been a soldier will know what I mean by the essential horror of army life) is barely affected by the nature of the war you happen to be fighting in. Discipline, for instance, is ultimately the same in all armies. Orders have to be obeyed and enforced by punishment if necessary, the relationship of officer and man has to be the relationship of superior and inferior. The picture of war set forth in books like *All Quiet on the Western Front* is substantially true. Bullets hurt, corpses stink, men under fire are often so frightened that they wet their trousers. It is true that the social background from which an army springs will colour its training, tactics and general efficiency, and also that the consciousness of being in the right can bolster up morale, though this affects the civilian population more than the troops. (People forget that a soldier anywhere near the front line is usually too hungry, or frightened, or cold, or, above all, too tired to bother about the political origins of the war.) But the laws of nature are not suspended for a 'red' army any more than for a 'white' one. A louse is a louse and a bomb is a bomb, even though the cause you are fighting for happens to be just.

Why is it worth while to point out anything so obvious? Because the bulk of the British and American intelligentsia were manifestly unaware of it then, and are now. Our memories are short nowadays, but look back a bit, dig out the files of *New Masses* or the *Daily Worker*, and just have a look at the romantic warmongering muck that our left-wingers were spilling at that time. All the stale old phrases! And the unimaginative callousness of it! The sang-froid with which London faced the bombing of Madrid! Here I am not bothering about the counter-propagandists of the Right, the Lunns, Garvins *et hoc genus*; they go without saying. But here were the very people who for twenty years had hooted and jeered at the 'glory' of war, at atrocity stories, at patriotism, even at physical courage, coming out with stuff that with the alteration of a few names would have fitted into the *Daily Mail* of 1918. If there was one thing that the British intelligentsia were committed to, it was the debunking version of war, the theory that war is all corpses and latrines and never leads to any good result. Well, the same people who in 1933 sniggered pityingly if you said that in certain circumstances you would fight for your country, in 1937 were denouncing you as a Trotsky-Fascist if you suggested that the stories in *New Masses* about freshly wounded men clamouring to get back into the fighting might be exaggerated. And the Left intelligentsia made their swing-over from 'War is hell' to 'War is glorious' not only with no sense of incongruity but almost without any intervening stage. Later the bulk of them were to make other transitions equally violent. There must be a quite large number of people, a sort of central core of the intelligentsia, who approved the 'King and Country' declaration in 1935, shouted for a 'firm line' against Germany in 1937, supported the People's Convention in 1940, and are demanding a Second Front now.

As far as the mass of the people go, the extraordinary swings of opinion which occur nowadays, the emotions which can be turned on and off like a tap, are the result of newspaper and radio hypnosis. In the intelligentsia I should say they result rather from money and mere physical safety. At a given moment they may be 'pro-war' or 'anti-war', but in either case they have no realistic picture of war in their minds. When they enthused over the Spanish war they knew, of course, that people were being killed and that to be killed is unpleasant, but they did feel that for a soldier in the Spanish Republican army the experience of war was somehow not degrading. Somehow the latrines stank less, discipline was less irksome. You have only to glance at the *New Statesman* to see that they believed that; exactly similar blah is being written about the Red Army at this moment. We have become too civilized to grasp the obvious. For the truth is very simple. To survive you often have to fight, and to fight you have to dirty yourself. War is evil, and it is often the lesser evil. Those who take the sword perish by the sword, and those who don't take the sword perish by smelly diseases. The fact that such a platitude is worth writing down shows what the years of *rentier* capitalism have done to us.

II

In connexion with what I have just said, a footnote on atrocities.

I have little direct evidence about the atrocities in the Spanish Civil War. I know that some were committed by the Republicans, and far more (they are still continuing) by the Fascists. But what impressed me then, and has impressed me ever since, is that atrocities are believed in or disbelieved in solely on grounds of political predilection. Everyone believes in the atrocities of the enemy and disbelieves in those of his own side, without ever bothering to examine the evidence. Recently I drew up a table of atrocities during the period between 1918 and the present; there was never a year when atrocities were not occurring somewhere or other, and there was hardly a single case when the Left and Right believed in the same stories simultaneously. And stranger yet, at any moment the situation can suddenly reverse itself and yesterday's proved-to-the-hilt atrocity story can become a ridiculous lie, merely because the political landscape has changed.

In the present war we are in the curious situation that our 'atrocity campaign' was done largely before the war started, and done mostly by the Left, the people who normally pride themselves on their incredulity. In the same period the Right, the atrocity-mongers of 1914–18, were gazing at Nazi Germany and flatly refusing to see any evil in it. Then as soon as war broke out it was the pro-Nazis of yesterday who were repeating horror stories, while the anti-Nazis suddenly found themselves doubting whether the Gestapo really existed. Nor was this solely the result of the Russo-German Pact. It was partly because before the war the Left had wrongly believed that

Britain and Germany would never fight and were therefore able to be anti-German and anti-British simultaneously; partly also because official war propaganda, with its disgusting hypocrisy and self-righteousness, always tends to make thinking people sympathize with the enemy. Part of the price we paid for the systematic lying of 1914–18 was the exaggerated pro-German reaction which followed. During the years 1918–33 you were hooted at in left-wing circles if you suggested that Germany bore even a fraction of responsibility for the war. In all the denunciations of Versailles I listened to during those years I don't think I ever once heard the question, 'What would have happened if Germany had won?' even mentioned, let alone discussed. So also with atrocities. The truth, it is felt, becomes untruth when your enemy utters it. Recently I noticed that the very people who swallowed any and every horror story about the Japanese in Nanking in 1937 refused to believe exactly the same stories about Hong Kong in 1942. There was even a tendency to feel that the Nanking atrocities had become, as it were retrospectively untrue because the British Government now drew attention to them.

But unfortunately the truth about atrocities is far worse than that they are lied about and made into propaganda. The truth is that they happen. The fact often adduced as a reason for scepticism – that the same horror stories come up in war after war – merely makes it rather more likely that these stories are true. Evidently they are widespread fantasies, and war provides an opportunity of putting them into practice. Also, although it has ceased to be fashionable to say so, there is little question that what one may roughly call the 'whites' commit far more and worse atrocities than the 'reds'. There is not the slightest doubt, for instance, about the behaviour of the Japanese in

China. Nor is there much doubt about the long tale of Fascist outrages during the last ten years in Europe. The volume of testimony is enormous, and a respectable proportion of it comes from the German press and radio. These things really happened, that is the thing to keep one's eye on. They happened even though Lord Halifax said they happened. The raping and butchering in Chinese cities, the tortures in the cellars of the Gestapo, the elderly Jewish professors flung into cesspools, the machine-gunning of refugees along the Spanish roads – they all happened, and they did not happen any the less because the *Daily Telegraph* has suddenly found out about them when it is five years too late.

III

Two memories, the first not proving anything in particular, the second, I think, giving one a certain insight into the atmosphere of a revolutionary period.

Early one morning another man and I had gone out to snipe at the Fascists in the trenches outside Huesca. Their line and ours here lay three hundred yards apart, at which range our aged rifles would not shoot accurately, but by sneaking out to a spot about a hundred yards from the Fascist trench you might, if you were lucky, get a shot at someone through a gap in the parapet. Unfortunately the ground between was a flat beet-field with no cover except a few ditches, and it was necessary to go out while it was still dark and return soon after dawn, before the light became too good. This time no Fascists appeared, and we stayed too long and were caught by the dawn. We were in a ditch, but behind us were two hundred yards of flat ground with hardly enough cover for a rabbit. We were still trying to nerve ourselves to make a dash for it when there was an uproar and a blowing of whistles in the Fascist trench. Some of our aeroplanes were coming over. At this moment a man, presumably carrying a message to an officer, jumped out of the trench and ran along the top of the parapet in full view. He was half-dressed and was holding up his trousers with both hands as he ran. I refrained from shooting at him. It is true that I am a poor shot and unlikely to hit a running man at a hundred yards, and also that I was thinking chiefly about getting back to our trench while the Fascists had their attention fixed on the aeroplanes. Still, I did not shoot partly because of that detail about the trousers. I had come here to shoot at 'Fascists'; but a man who is holding up his trousers isn't a 'Fascist', he is visibly a fellow creature, similar to yourself, and you don't feel like shooting at him.

What does this incident demonstrate? Nothing very much, because it is the kind of thing that happens all the time in all wars. The other is different. I don't suppose that in telling it I can make it moving to you who read it, but I ask you to believe that it is moving to me, as an incident characteristic of the moral atmosphere of a particular moment in time.

One of the recruits who joined us while I was at the barracks was a wild-looking boy from the back streets of Barcelona. He was ragged and barefooted. He was also extremely dark (Arab blood, I dare say), and made gestures you do not usually see a European make; one in particular – the arm outstretched, the palm vertical – was a gesture characteristic of Indians. One day a bundle of cigars, which you could still buy dirt cheap at that time, was stolen out of my bunk. Rather foolishly I reported this to the officer, and one of the scallywags I have already mentioned promptly came forward and said quite untruly that twenty-five pesetas had been stolen from his bunk. For some reason the officer instantly decided that the brown-faced boy must be the thief. They were very hard on stealing in the militia, and in theory people could be shot for it. The wretched boy allowed himself to be led off to the guardroom to be searched. What most struck me was that he barely attempted to protest his innocence. In the fatalism of his attitude you could see the desperate poverty in which he had been bred. The officer ordered him to take his clothes off. With a humility which was horrible to me he stripped himself naked, and his clothes were searched. Of course neither the cigars nor the money were there; in fact he had not stolen them. What was most painful of all was that he seemed no less ashamed after his innocence had been established. That night I took him to the pictures and gave him brandy and chocolate. But that too was horrible – I mean the attempt to wipe out an injury with money. For a few minutes I had half believed him to be a thief, and that could not be wiped out.

Well, a few weeks later at the front I had trouble with one of the men in my section. By this time I was a 'cabo', or corporal, in command of twelve men. It was static warfare, horribly cold, and the chief job was getting sentries to stay awake and at their posts. One day a man suddenly refused to go to a certain post, which he said quite truly was exposed to enemy fire. He was a feeble creature, and I seized hold of him and began to drag him towards his post. This roused the feelings of the others against me, for Spaniards, I think, resent being touched more than we do. Instantly I was surrounded by a ring of shouting men: 'Fascist! Fascist! Let that man go! This isn't a bourgeois army. Fascist!' etc. etc. As best I could in my bad Spanish I shouted back that orders had got to be obeyed, and the row developed into one of those enormous arguments by means of which discipline is gradually hammered out in revolutionary armies. Some said I was right, others said I was wrong. But the point is that the one who took my side the most warmly of all was the brown-faced boy. As soon as he saw what was happening he sprang into the ring and began passionately defending me. With his strange, wild, Indian gesture he kept exclaiming, 'He's the best corporal we've got!' (¡*No hay cabo como el!*) Later on he applied for leave to exchange into my section.

Why is this incident touching to me? Because in any normal circumstances it would have been impossible for good feelings ever to be re-established between this boy and myself. The implied accusation of theft would not have been made any better, probably somewhat worse, by my efforts to make amends. One of the effects of safe and civilized life is an immense oversensitiveness which makes all the primary emotions seem somewhat disgusting. Generosity is as painful as meanness, gratitude as hateful as ingratitude. But in Spain in 1936 we were not living in a normal time. It was a time when generous feelings and gestures were easier than they ordinarily are. I could relate a dozen similar incidents, not really communicable but bound up in my own mind with the special atmosphere of the time, the shabby clothes and the gay-coloured revolutionary posters, the universal use of the word 'comrade', the anti-Fascist ballads printed on flimsy paper and sold for a penny, the phrases like 'international proletarian solidarity', pathetically repeated by ignorant men who believed them to mean something. Could you feel friendly towards somebody, and stick up for him in a quarrel, after you had been ignominiously searched in his presence for property you were supposed to have stolen from him? No, you couldn't; but you might if you had both been through some emotionally widening experience. That is one of the by-products of revolution, though in this case it was only the beginnings of a revolution, and obviously foredoomed to failure.

IV

The struggle for power between the Spanish Republican parties is an unhappy, far-off thing which I have no wish to revive at this date. I only mention it in order to say: believe nothing, or next to nothing, of what you read about internal affairs on the Government side. It is all, from whatever source, party propaganda – that is to say, lies. The broad truth about the war is simple enough. The Spanish bourgeoisie saw their chance of crushing the labour movement, and took it, aided by the Nazis and by the forces of reaction all over the world. It is doubtful whether more than that will ever be established.

I remember saying once to Arthur Koestler, 'History stopped in 1936,' at which he nodded in immediate understanding. We were both thinking of totalitarianism in general, but more particularly of the Spanish Civil War. Early in life I had noticed that no event is ever correctly reported in a newspaper, but in Spain, for the first time, I saw newspaper reports which did not bear any relation to the facts, not even the relationship which is implied in an ordinary lie. I saw great battles reported where there had been no fighting, and complete silence where hundreds of men had been killed. I saw troops who had fought bravely denounced as cowards and traitors, and others who had never seen a shot fired hailed as the heroes of imaginary victories, and I saw newspapers in London retailing these lies and eager intellectuals building emotional superstructures over events that had never happened. I saw, in fact, history being written not in terms of what happened but of what ought to have happened according to various 'party lines'. Yet in a way, horrible as all this was, it was unimportant. It concerned secondary issues — namely, the struggle for power between the Comintern and the Spanish left-wing parties, and the efforts of the Russian Government to prevent revolution in Spain. But the broad picture of the war which the Spanish Government presented to the world was not untruthful. The main issues were what it said they were. But as for the Fascists and their backers, how could they come even as near to the truth as that? How could they possibly mention their real aims? Their version of the war was pure fantasy, and in the circumstances it could not have been otherwise.

The only propaganda line open to the Nazis and Fascists was to represent themselves as Christian patriots saving Spain from a Russian dictatorship. This involved pretending that life in Government Spain was just one long massacre (*vide* the *Catholic Herald* or the *Daily Mail* — but these were child's play compared with the continental Fascist press), and it involved immensely exaggerating the scale of Russian intervention. Out of the huge pyramid of lies which the Catholic and reactionary press all over the world built up, let me take just one point — the presence in Spain of a Russian army. Devout Franco partisans all believed in this; estimates of its strength went as high as half a million. Now, there was no Russian army in Spain. There may have been a handful of airmen and other technicians, a few hundred at the most, but an army there was not. Some thousands of foreigners who fought in Spain, not to mention millions of Spaniards, were witnesses of this. Well, their testimony made no impression at all upon the Franco propagandists, not one of whom had set foot in Government Spain. Simultaneously these people refused utterly to admit the fact of German or Italian intervention, at the same time as the German and Italian press were openly boasting about the exploits of their 'legionaries'. I have chosen to mention only one point, but in fact the whole of Fascist propaganda about the war was on this level.

This kind of thing is frightening to me, because it often gives me the feeling that the very concept of objective truth is fading out of the world. After all, the chances are that those lies, or at any rate similar lies, will pass into history. How will the history of the Spanish war be written? If Franco remains in power his nominees will write the history books, and (to stick to my chosen point) that Russian army which never existed will become historical fact, and schoolchildren will learn about it generations hence. But suppose Fascism is finally defeated and some kind of democratic government restored in Spain in the fairly near future; even then, how is the history of the war to be written? What kind of records will Franco have left behind him? Suppose even that the records kept on the Government side are recoverable – even so, how is a true history of the war to be written? For, as I have pointed out already, the Government also dealt extensively in lies. From the anti-Fascist angle one could write a broadly truthful history of the war, but it would be a partisan history, unreliable on every minor point. Yet, after all, *some* kind of history will be written, and after those who actually remember the war are dead, it will be universally accepted. So for all practical purposes the lie will have become truth.

I know it is the fashion to say that most of recorded history is lies anyway. I am willing to believe that history is for the most part inaccurate and biased, but what is peculiar to our own age is the abandonment of the idea that history *could* be truthfully written. In the past people deliberately lied, or they unconsciously coloured what they wrote, or they struggled after the truth, well knowing that they must make many mistakes; but in each case they believed that 'the facts' existed and were more or less discoverable. And in practice there was always a considerable body of fact which would have been agreed to by almost everyone. If you look up the history of the last war in, for instance, the *Encyclopaedia Britannica*, you will find that a respectable amount of the material is drawn from German sources. A British and a German historian would disagree deeply on many things, even on fundamentals, but there would still be that body of, as it were, neutral fact on which neither would seriously challenge the other. It is just this common basis of agreement, with its implication that human beings are all one species of animal, that totalitarianism destroys. Nazi theory indeed specifically denies that such a thing as 'the truth' exists. There is, for instance, no such thing as 'science'. There is only 'German science', 'Jewish science' etc. The implied objective of this line of thought is a nightmare world in which the Leader, or some ruling clique, controls not only the future but *the past*. If the Leader says of such and such an event, 'It never happened' – well, it never happened. If he says that two and two are five – well, two and two are five. This prospect frightens me much more than bombs – and after our experiences of the last few years that is not a frivolous statement.

But is it perhaps childish or morbid to terrify oneself with visions of a totalitarian future? Before writing off the totalitarian world as a nightmare that can't come true, just remember that in 1925 the world of today would have seemed a nightmare that couldn't come true. Against that shifting phantasmagoric world in which black may be white tomorrow and yesterday's weather can be changed by decree, there are in reality only two safeguards. One is that however much you deny the truth, the truth goes on existing, as it were, behind your back, and you consequently can't violate it in ways that impair military efficiency. The other is that so long as some parts of the earth remain unconquered, the liberal tradition can be kept alive. Let Fascism, or possibly even a combination of several Fascisms, conquer the whole world, and those two conditions no longer exist. We in England underrate the danger of this kind of thing, because our traditions and our past security have given us a sentimental belief that it all comes right in the end and the thing you most fear never really happens. Nourished for hundreds of years on a literature in which Right invariably triumphs in the last chapter, we believe half-instinctively that evil always defeats itself in the long run. Pacifism, for instance, is founded largely on this belief. Don't resist evil, and it will somehow destroy itself. But why should it? What evidence is there that it does? And what instance is there of a modern industrialized state collapsing unless conquered from the outside by military force?

Consider for instance the re-institution of slavery. Who could have imagined twenty years ago that slavery would return to Europe? Well, slavery has been restored under our noses. The forced-labour camps all over Europe and North Africa where Poles, Russians, Jews and political prisoners of every race toil at road-making or swamp-draining for their bare rations, are simple chattel slavery. The most one can say is that the buying and selling of slaves by individuals is not yet permitted. In other ways – the breaking-up of families, for instance – the conditions are probably worse than they were on the American cotton plantations. There is no reason for thinking that this state of affairs will change while any totalitarian domination endures. We don't grasp its full implications, because in our mystical way we feel that a régime founded on slavery *must* collapse. But it is worth comparing the duration of the slave empires of antiquity with that of any modern state. Civilizations founded on slavery have lasted for such periods as four thousand years.

When I think of antiquity, the detail that frightens me is that those hundreds of millions of slaves on whose backs civilization rested generation after generation have left behind them no record whatever. We do not even know their names. In the whole of Greek and Roman history, how many slaves' names are known to you? I can think of two, or possibly three. One is Spartacus and the other is Epictetus. Also, in the Roman room at the British Museum there is a glass jar with the maker's name inscribed on the bottom, '*Felix fecit*'. I have a vivid mental picture of poor Felix (a Gaul with red hair and a metal collar round his neck), but in fact he may not have been a slave; so there are only two slaves whose names I definitely know, and probably few people can remember more. The rest have gone down into utter silence.

V

The backbone of the resistance against Franco was the Spanish working class, especially the urban trade-union members. In the long run – it is important to remember that it is only in the long run – the working class remains the most reliable enemy of Fascism, simply because the working class stands to gain most by a decent reconstruction of society. Unlike other classes or categories, it can't be permanently bribed.

To say this is not to idealize the working class. In the long struggle that has followed the Russian Revolution it is the manual workers who have been defeated, and it is impossible not to feel that it was their own fault. Time after time, in country after country, the organized working-class movements have been crushed by open, illegal violence, and their comrades abroad, linked to them in theoretical solidarity, have simply looked on and done nothing; and underneath this, secret cause of many betrayals, has lain the fact that between white and coloured workers there is not even lip-service to solidarity. Who can believe in the class-conscious international proletariat after the events of the past ten years? To the British working class the massacre of their comrades in Vienna, Berlin, Madrid, or wherever it might be, seemed less interesting and less important than yesterday's football match. Yet this does not alter the fact that the working class will go on struggling against Fascism after the others have caved in. One feature of the Nazi conquest of France was the astonishing defections among the intelligentsia, including some of the left-wing political intelligentsia. The intelligentsia are the people who squeal loudest against Fascism, and yet a respectable proportion of them collapse into defeatism when the pinch comes. They are far-sighted enough to see the odds against them, and moreover they can be bribed – for it is evident that the Nazis think it worth while to bribe intellectuals. With the working class it is the other way about. Too ignorant to see through the trick that is being played on them, they easily swallow the promises of Fascism, yet sooner or later they always take up the struggle again. They must do so, because in their own bodies they always discover that the promises of Fascism cannot be fulfilled. To win over the working class permanently, the Fascists would have to raise the general standard of living, which they are unable and probably unwilling to do. The struggle of the working class is like the growth of a plant. The plant is blind and stupid, but it knows enough to keep pushing upwards towards the light, and it will do this in the face of endless discouragements. What are the workers struggling for? Simply for the decent life which they are more and more aware is now technically possible. Their consciousness of this aim ebbs and flows. In Spain, for a while, people were acting consciously, moving towards a goal which they wanted to reach and believed they could reach. It accounted for the curiously buoyant feeling that life in Government Spain had during the early months of the war. The common people knew in their bones that the Republic was their friend and Franco was their enemy. They knew that they were in the right, because they were fighting for something which the world owed them and was able to give them.

One has to remember this to see the Spanish war in its true perspective. When one thinks of the cruelty, squalor, and futility of war – and in this particular case of the intrigues, the persecutions, the lies and the misunderstandings – there is always the temptation to say: 'One side is as bad as the other. I am neutral.' In practice, however, one cannot be neutral, and there is hardly such a thing as a war in which it makes no difference who wins. Nearly always one side stands more or less for progress, the other side more or less for reaction. The hatred which the Spanish Republic excited in millionaires, dukes, cardinals, play-boys, Blimps and what-not would in itself be enough to show one how the land lay. In essence it was a class war. If it had been won, the cause of the common people everywhere would have been strengthened. It was lost, and the dividend-drawers all over the world rubbed their hands. That was the real issue; all else was froth on its surface.

VI

The outcome of the Spanish war was settled in London, Paris, Rome, Berlin – at any rate not in Spain. After the summer of 1937 those with eyes in their heads realized that the Government could not win the war unless there was some profound change in the international set-up, and in deciding to fight on Negrin and the others may have been partly influenced by the expectation that the world war which actually broke out in 1939 was coming in 1938. The much-publicized disunity on the Government side was not a main cause of defeat. The Government militias were hurriedly raised, ill-armed and unimaginative in their military outlook, but they would have been the same if complete political agreement had existed from the start. At the outbreak of war the average Spanish factory-worker did not even know how to fire a rifle (there had never been universal conscription in Spain), and the traditional pacifism of the Left was a great handicap. The thousands of foreigners who served in Spain made good infantry, but there were very few experts of any kind among them. The Trotskyist thesis that the war could have been won if the revolution had not been sabotaged was probably false. To nationalize factories, demolish churches, and issue revolutionary manifestos would not have made the armies more efficient. The Fascists won because they were the stronger; they had modern arms and the others hadn't. No political strategy could offset that.

The most baffling thing in the Spanish war was the behaviour of the great powers. The war was actually won for Franco by the Germans and Italians, whose motives were obvious enough. The motives of France and Britain are less easy to understand. In 1936 it was clear to everyone that if Britain would only help the Spanish Government, even to the extent of a few million pounds' worth of arms, Franco would collapse and German strategy would be severely dislocated. By that time one did not need to be a clairvoyant to foresee that war between Britain and Germany was coming; one could even foretell within a year or two when it would come. Yet in the most mean, cowardly, hypocritical way the British ruling class did all they could to hand Spain over to Franco and the Nazis. Why? Because they were pro-Fascist, was the obvious answer. Undoubtedly they were, and yet when it came to the final showdown they chose to stand up to Germany. It is still very uncertain what plan they acted on in backing Franco, and they may have had no clear plan at all. Whether the British ruling class are wicked or merely stupid is one of the most difficult questions of our time, and at certain moments a very important question. As to the Russians, their motives in the Spanish war are completely inscrutable. Did they, as the pinks believed, intervene in Spain in order to defend democracy and thwart the Nazis? Then why did they intervene on such a niggardly scale and finally leave Spain in the lurch? Or did they, as the Catholics maintained, intervene in order to foster revolution in Spain? They why did they do all in their power to crush the Spanish revolutionary movements, defend private property and hand power to the middle class as against the working class? Or did they, as the Trotskyists suggested, intervene simply in order to *prevent* a Spanish revolution? Then why not have backed Franco? Indeed, their actions are most easily explained if one assumes that they were acting on several contradictory motives. I believe that in the future we shall come to feel that Stalin's foreign policy, instead of being so diabolically clever as it is claimed to be, has been merely opportunistic and stupid. But at any rate, the Spanish Civil War demonstrated that the Nazis knew what they were doing and their opponents did not. The war was fought at a low technical level and its major strategy was very simple. That side which had arms would win. The Nazis and the Italians gave arms to their Spanish Fascist friends, and the western democracies and the Russians didn't give arms to those who should have been their friends. So the Spanish Republic perished, having 'gained what no republic missed'.

Whether it was right, as all left-wingers in other countries undoubtedly did, to encourage the Spaniards to go on fighting when they could not win is a question hard to answer. I myself think it was right, because I believe that it is better even from the point of view of survival to fight and be conquered than to surrender without fighting. The effects on the grand strategy of the struggle against Fascism cannot be assessed yet. The ragged, weaponless armies of the Republic held out for two and a half years, which was undoubtedly longer than their enemies expected. But whether that dislocated the Fascist timetable, or whether, on the other hand, it merely postponed the major war and gave the Nazis extra time to get their war machine into trim, is still uncertain.

VII

I never think of the Spanish war without two memories coming into my mind. One is of the hospital ward at Lerida and the rather sad voices of the wounded militiamen singing some song with a refrain that ended:

Una resolucion,
Luchar hast' al fin!

Well, they fought to the end all right. For the last eighteen months of the war the Republican armies must have been fighting almost without cigarettes, and with precious little food. Even when I left Spain in the middle of 1937, meat and bread were scarce, tobacco a rarity, coffee and sugar almost unobtainable.

The other memory is of the Italian militiaman who shook my hand in the guardroom, the day I joined the militia. I wrote about this man at the beginning of my book on the Spanish war,[1] and do not want to repeat what I said there. When I remember – oh, how vividly! – his shabby uniform and fierce, pathetic, innocent face, the complex side-issues of the war seem to fade away and I see clearly that there was at any rate no

[1] *Homage to Catalonia.*

doubt as to who was in the right. In spite of power politics and journalistic lying, the central issue of the war was the attempt of people like this to win the decent life which they knew to be their birthright. It is difficult to think of this particular man's probable end without several kinds of bitterness. Since I met him in the Lenin Barracks he was probably a Trotskyist or an Anarchist, and in the peculiar conditions of our time, when people of that sort are not killed by the Gestapo they are usually killed by the GPU. But that does not affect the long-term issues. This man's face, which I saw only for a minute or two, remains with me as a sort of visual reminder of what the war was really about. He symbolizes for me the flower of the European working class, harried by the police of all countries, the people who fill the mass graves of the Spanish battlefields and are now, to the tune of several millions, rotting in forced-labour camps.

When one thinks of all the people who support or have supported Fascism, one stands amazed at their diversity. What a crew! Think of a programme which at any rate for a while could bring Hitler, Pétain, Montagu Norman, Pavelitch, William Randolph Hearst, Streicher, Buchman, Ezra Pound, Juan March, Cocteau, Thyssen, Father Coughlin, the Mufti of Jerusalem, Arnold Lunn, Antonescu, Spengler, Beverly Nichols, Lady Houston, and Marinetti all into the same boat! But the clue is really very simple. They are all people with something to lose, or people who long for a hierarchical society and dread the prospect of a world of free and equal human beings. Behind all the ballyhoo that is talked about 'godless' Russia and the 'materialism' of the working class lies the simple intention of those with money or privileges to cling to them. Ditto, though it contains a partial truth, with all the talk about the worthlessness of social reconstruction not accompanied by a 'change of heart'. The pious ones, from the Pope to the yogis of California, are great on the 'changes of heart', much more reassuring from their point of view than a change in the economic system. Pétain attributes the fall of France to the common people's 'love of pleasure'. One sees this in its right perspective if one stops to wonder how much pleasure the ordinary French peasant's or working-man's life would contain compared with Pétain's own. The damned impertinence of these politicians, priests, literary men, and what not who lecture the working-class Socialist for his 'materialism'! All that the working man demands is what these others would consider the indispensable minimum without which human life cannot be lived at all. Enough to eat, freedom from the haunting terror of unemployment, the knowledge that your children will get a fair chance, a bath once a day, clean linen reasonably often, a roof that doesn't leak, and short enough working hours to leave you with a little energy when the day is done. Not one of those who preach against 'materialism' would consider life liveable without these things. And how easily that minimum could be attained if we chose to set our minds to it for only twenty years! To raise the standard of living of the whole world to that of Britain would not be a greater undertaking than the war we are now fighting. I don't claim, and I don't know who does, that that would solve anything in itself. It is merely that privation and brute labour have to be abolished before the real problems of humanity can be tackled. The major problem of our time is the decay of the belief in personal immortality, and it cannot be dealt with while the average human being is either drudging like an ox or shivering in fear of the secret police. How right the working classes are in their 'materialism'! How right they are to realize that the belly comes before the soul, not in the scale of values but in point of time! Understand that, and the long horror that we are enduring becomes at least intelligible. All the considerations that are likely to make one falter – the siren voices of a Pétain or of a Gandhi, the inescapable fact that in order to fight one has to degrade oneself, the equivocal moral position of Britain, with its democratic phrases and its coolie empire, the sinister development of Soviet Russia, the squalid farce of left-wing politics – all this fades away and one sees only the struggle of the gradually awakening common people against the lords of property and their hired liars and bumsuckers. The question is very simple. Shall people like that Italian soldier be allowed to live the decent, fully human life which is now technically achievable, or shan't they? Shall the common man be pushed back into the mud, or shall he not? I myself believe, perhaps on insufficient grounds, that the common man will win his fight sooner or later, but I want it to be sooner and not later – some time within the next hundred years, say, and not some time within the next ten thousand years. That was the real issue of the Spanish war, and of the present war, and perhaps of other wars yet to come.

I never saw the Italian militiaman again, nor did I ever learn his name. It can be taken as quite certain that he is dead. Nearly two years later, when the war was visibly lost, I wrote these verses in his memory:

> The Italian soldier shook my hand
> Beside the guard-room table;
> The strong hand and the subtle hand
> Whose palms are only able

To meet within the sounds of guns,
But oh! what peace I knew then
In gazing on his battered face
Purer than any woman's!

For the flyblown words that make me spew
Still in his ears were holy,
And he was born knowing that I had learned
Out of books and slowly.

The treacherous guns had told their tale
And we both had bought it,
But my gold brick was made of gold —
Oh! who ever would have thought it?

Good luck go with you, Italian soldier!
But luck is not for the brave;
What would the world give back to you?
Always less than you gave.

Between the shadow and the ghost,
Between the white and the red,
Between the bullet and the lie,
Where would you hide your head?

For where is Manuel Gonzalez,
And where is Pedro Aguilar,
And where is Ramon Fenellosa?
The earthworms know where they are.

Your name and your deeds were forgotten
Before your bones were dry,
And the lie that slew you is buried
Under a deeper lie;

But the thing that I saw in your face
No power can disinherit:
No bomb that ever burst
Shatters the crystal spirit.

1942

In Defence of English Cooking

We have heard a good deal of talk in recent years about the desirability of attracting foreign tourists to this country. It is well known that England's two worst faults, from a foreign visitor's point of view, are the gloom of our Sundays and the difficulty of buying a drink.

Both of these are due to fanatical minorities who will need a lot of quelling, including extensive legislation. But there is one point on which public opinion could bring about a rapid change for the better: I mean cooking.

It is commonly said, even by the English themselves, that English cooking is the worst in the world. It is supposed to be not merely incompetent, but also imitative, and I even read quite recently, in a book by a French writer, the remark: 'The best English cooking is, of course, simply French cooking.'

Now that is simply not true. As anyone who has lived long abroad will know, there is a whole host of delicacies which it is quite impossible to obtain outside the English-speaking countries. No doubt the list could be added to, but here are some of the things that I myself have sought for in foreign countries and failed to find.

First of all, kippers, Yorkshire pudding, Devonshire cream, muffins and crumpets. Then a list of puddings, that would be interminable if I gave it in full: I will pick out for special mention Christmas pudding, treacle tart and apple dumplings. Then an almost equally long list of cakes: for instance, dark plum cake (such as you used to get at Buzzard's before the war), short-bread and saffron buns. Also innumerable kinds of biscuit, which exist, of course, elsewhere, but are generally admitted to be better and crisper in England.

Then there are the various ways of cooking potatoes that are peculiar to our own country. Where else do you see potatoes roasted under the joint, which is far and away the best way of cooking them? Or the delicious potato cakes that you get in the north of England? And it is far better to cook new potatoes in the English way — that is, boiled with mint and then served with a little melted butter or margarine — than to fry them as is done in most countries.

Then there are the various sauces peculiar to England. For instance, bread sauce, horse-radish sauce, mint sauce and apple sauce; not to mention redcurrant jelly, which is excellent with mutton as well as with hare, and various kinds of sweet pickle, which we seem to have in greater profusion than most countries.

What else? Outside these islands I have never seen a haggis, except one that came out of a tin, nor Dublin prawns, nor Oxford marmalade, nor several other kinds of jam (marrow jam and bramble jelly, for instance), nor sausages of quite the same kind as ours.

Then there are the English cheeses. There are not many of them but I fancy that Stilton is the best cheese of its type in the world, with Wensleydale not far behind. English apples are also outstandingly good, particularly the Cox's Orange Pippin.

And finally, I would like to put in a word for English bread. All the bread is good, from the enormous Jewish loaves flavoured with caraway seeds to the Russian rye bread which is the colour of black treacle. Still, if there is anything quite as good as the soft part of the crust from an English cottage loaf (how soon shall we be seeing cottage loaves again?) I do not know of it.

No doubt some of the things I have named above could be obtained in continental Europe, just as it is possible in London to obtain vodka or bird's nest soup. But they are all native to our shores, and over huge areas they are literally unheard of.

South of, say, Brussels, I do not imagine that you would succeed in getting hold of a suet pudding. In French there is not even a word that exactly translates 'suet'. The French, also, never use mint in cookery and do not use black currants except as a basis of a drink.

It will be seen that we have no cause to be ashamed of our cookery, so far as originality goes or so far as the ingredients go. And yet it must be admitted that there is a serious snag from the foreign visitor's point of view. This is, that you practically don't find good English cooking outside a private house. If you want, say, a good, rich slice of Yorkshire pudding you are more likely to get it in the poorest English home than in a restaurant, which is where the visitor necessarily eats most of his meals.

It is a fact that restaurants which are distinctively English and which also sell good food are very hard to find. Pubs, as a rule, sell no food at all, other than potato crips and tasteless sandwiches. The expensive restaurants and hotels almost all imitate French cookery and write their menus in French, while if you want a good cheap meal you gravitate naturally towards a Greek, Italian or Chinese restaurant. We are not likely to succeed in attracting tourists while England is thought of as a country of bad food and unintelligible by-laws. At present one cannot do much about it, but sooner or later rationing will come to an end, and then will be the moment for our national cookery to revive. It is not a law of nature that every restaurant in England should be either foreign or bad, and the first step towards an improvement will be a less long-suffering attitude in the British public itself.

1945

Good Bad Books

Not long ago a publisher commissioned me to write an introduction for a reprint of a novel by Leonard Merrick. This publishing house, it appears, is going to reissue a long series of minor and partly-forgotten novels of the twentieth century. It is a valuable service in these bookless days, and I rather envy the person whose job it will be to scout round the threepenny boxes, hunting down copies of his boyhood favourites.

A type of book which we hardly seem to produce in these days, but which flowered with great richness in the late nineteenth and early twentieth centuries, is what Chesterton called the 'good bad book': that is, the kind of book that has no literary pretensions but which remains readable when more serious productions have perished. Obviously outstanding books in this line are *Raffles* and the Sherlock Holmes stories, which have kept their place when innumerable 'problem novels', 'human documents' and 'terrible indictments' of this or that have fallen into deserved oblivion. (Who has worn better, Conan Doyle or Meredith?) Almost in the same class as these I put R. Austin Freeman's earlier stories – 'The Singing Bone', 'The Eye of Osiris' and others – Ernest Bramah's *Max Carrados*, and, dropping the standard a bit, Guy Boothby's Tibetan thriller, *Dr Nikola*, a sort of schoolboy version of Huc's

Travels in Tartary which would probably make a real visit to Central Asia seem a dismal anticlimax.

But apart from thrillers, there were the minor humorous writers of the period. For example, Pett Ridge — but I admit his full-length books no longer seem readable — E. Nesbit (*The Treasure Seekers*), George Birmingham, who was good so long as he kept off politics, the pornographic Binstead ('Pitcher' of the *Pink 'Un*), and, if American books can be included, Booth Tarkington's Penrod stories. A cut above most of these was Barry Pain. Some of Pain's humorous writings are, I suppose, still in print, but to anyone who comes across it I recommend what must now be a very rare book — *The Octave of Claudius*, a brilliant exercise in the macabre. Somewhat later in time there was Peter Blundell, who wrote in the W.W. Jacobs vein about Far Eastern seaport towns, and who seems to be rather unaccountably forgotten, in spite of having been praised in print by H. G. Wells.

However, all the books I have been speaking of are frankly 'escape' literature. They form pleasant patches in one's memory, quiet corners where the mind can browse at odd moments, but they hardly pretend to have anything to do with real life. There is another kind of good bad book which is more seriously intended, and which tells us, I think, something about the nature of the novel and the reasons for its present decadence. During the last fifty years there has been a whole series of writers — some of them are still writing — whom it is quite impossible to call 'good' by any strictly literary standard, but who are natural novelists and who seem to attain sincerity partly because they are not inhibited by good taste. In this class I put Leonard Merrick himself, W. L. George, J. D. Beresford, Ernest Raymond, May Sinclair, and — at a lower level than the others but still essentially similar – A. S. M. Hutchinson.

Most of these have been prolific writers, and their output has naturally varied in quality. I am thinking in each case of one or two outstanding books: for example, Merrick's *Cynthia*, J. D. Beresford's *A Candidate for Truth*, W. L. George's *Caliban*, May Sinclair's *The Combined Maze* and Ernest Raymond's *We, the Accused*. In each of these books the author has been able to identify himself with his imagined characters, to feel with them and invite sympathy on their behalf, with a kind of abandonment that cleverer people would find it difficult to achieve. They bring out the fact that intellectual refinement can be a disadvantage to a story-teller, as it would be to a music-hall comedian.

Take, for example, Ernest Raymond's *We, the Accused* – a peculiarly sordid and convincing murder story, probably based on the Crippen case. I think it gains a great deal from the fact that the author only partly grasps the pathetic vulgarity of the people he is writing about, and therefore does not despise them. Perhaps it even – like Theodore Dreiser's *An American Tragedy* – gains something from the clumsy long-winded manner in which it is written; detail is piled on detail, with almost no attempt at selection, and in the process an effect of terrible, grinding cruelty is slowly built up. So also with *A Candidate for Truth*. Here there is not the same clumsiness, but there is the same ability to take seriously the problems of commonplace people. So also with *Cynthia* and at any rate the earlier part of *Caliban*. The greater part of what W. L. George wrote was shoddy rubbish, but in this particular book, based on the career of Northcliffe, he achieved some memorable and truthful pictures of lower-middle-class London life. Parts of this book are probably autobiographical, and one of the advantages of good bad writers is their lack of shame in writing autobiography. Exhibitionism and self-pity are the bane of the novelist, and yet if he is too frightened of them his creative gift may suffer.

The existence of good bad literature – the fact that one can be amused or excited or even moved by a book that one's intellect simply refuses to take seriously – is a reminder that art is not the same thing as cerebration. I imagine that by any test that could be devised, Carlyle would be found to be a more intelligent man than Trollope. Yet Trollope has remained readable and Carlyle has not: with all his cleverness he had not even the wit to write in plain straightforward English. In novelists, almost as much as in poets, the connexion between intelligence and creative power is hard to establish. A good novelist may be a prodigy of self-discipline like Flaubert, or he may be an intellectual sprawl like Dickens. Enough talent to set up dozens of ordinary writers has been poured into Wyndham Lewis's so-called novels, such as *Tarr* or *Snooty Baronet*. Yet it would be a very heavy labour to read one of these books right through. Some indefinable quality, a sort of literary vitamin, which exists even in a book like *If Winter Comes*, is absent from them.

Perhaps the supreme example of the 'good bad' book is *Uncle Tom's Cabin*. It is an unintentionally ludicrous book, full of preposterous melodramatic incidents; it is also deeply moving and essentially true; it is hard to say which quality outweighs the other. But *Uncle Tom's Cabin*, after all, is trying to be serious and to deal with the real world. How about the frankly escapist writers, the purveyors of thrills and 'light' humour? How about *Sherlock Holmes, Vice Versa, Dracula, Helen's*

Babies or *King Solomon's Mines*? All of these are definitely absurd books, books which one is more inclined to laugh *at* than *with*, and which were hardly taken seriously even by their authors; yet they have survived, and will probably continue to do so. All one can say is that, while civilization remains such that one needs distraction from time to time, 'light' literature has its appointed place; also that there is such a thing as sheer skill, or native grace, which may have more survival value than erudition or intellectual power. There are music-hall songs which are better poems than three quarters of the stuff that gets into the anthologies:

> Come where the booze is cheaper,
> Come where the pots hold more,
> Come where the boss is a bit of a sport,
> Come to the pub next door!

Or again:

> Two lovely black eyes –
> Oh, what a surprise!
> Only for calling another man wrong,
> Two lovely black eyes!

I would far rather have written either of these than, say, 'The Blessed Damozel' or 'Love in the Valley'. And by the same token I would back *Uncle Tom's Cabin* to outlive the complete works of Virginia Woolf or George Moore, though I know of no strictly literary test which would show where the superiority lies.

1945

The Sporting Spirit

Now that the brief visit of the Dynamo football team[1] has come to an end, it is possible to say publicly what many thinking people were saying privately before the Dynamos ever arrived. That is, that sport is an unfailing cause of ill-will, and that if such a visit as this had any effect at all on Anglo-Soviet relations, it could only be to make them slightly worse than before.

Even the newspapers have been unable to conceal the fact that at least two of the four matches played led to much bad feeling. At the Arsenal match, I am told by someone who was there, a British and a Russian player came to blows and the crowd booed the referee. The Glasgow match, someone else informs me, was simply a free-for-all from the start. And then there was the controversy, typical of our nationalistic age, about the composition of the Arsenal team. Was it really an all-England team, as claimed by the Russians, or merely a league team, as claimed by the British? And did the Dynamos end their tour abruptly in order to avoid playing an all-England team? As usual, everyone answers these questions according to his political predilections. Not quite everyone, however. I noted

---

[1] The Moscow Dynamos, a Russian football team, toured Britain in the autumn of 1945 playing against leading British clubs.

with interest, as an instance of the vicious passions that football provokes, that the sporting correspondent of the russophile *News Chronicle* took the anti-Russian line and maintained that Arsenal was *not* an all-England team. No doubt the controversy will continue to echo for years in the footnotes of history books. Meanwhile the result of the Dynamos' tour, in so far as it has had any result, will have been to create fresh animosity on both sides.

And how could it be otherwise? I am always amazed when I hear people saying that sport creates goodwill between the nations, and that if only the common peoples of the world could meet one another at football or cricket, they would have no inclination to meet on the battlefield. Even if one didn't know from concrete examples (the 1936 Olympic Games, for instance) that international sporting contests lead to orgies of hatred, one could deduce it from general principles.

Nearly all the sports practised nowadays are competitive. You play to win, and the game has little meaning unless you do your utmost to win. On the village green, where you pick up sides and no feeling of local patriotism is involved, it is possible to play simply for the fun and exercise: but as soon as the question of prestige arises, as soon as you feel that you and some larger unit will be disgraced if you lose, the most savage combative instincts are aroused. Anyone who has played even in a school football match knows this. At the international level sport is frankly mimic warfare. But the significant thing is not the behaviour of the players but the attitude of the spectators: and, behind the spectators, of the nations who work themselves into furies over these absurd contests, and seriously believe – at any rate for short periods – that running, jumping and kicking a ball are tests of national virtue.

Even a leisurely game like cricket, demanding grace rather than strength, can cause much ill-will, as we saw in the controversy over body-line bowling and over the rough tactics of the Australian team that visited England in 1921. Football, a game in which everyone gets hurt and every nation has its own style of play which seems unfair to foreigners, is far worse. Worst of all is boxing. One of the most horrible sights in the world is a fight between white and coloured boxers before a mixed audience. But a boxing audience is always disgusting, and the behaviour of the women, in particular, is such that the army, I believe, does not allow them to attend its contests. At any rate, two or three years ago, when Home Guards and regular troops were holding a boxing tournament, I was placed on guard at the door of the hall, with orders to keep the women out.

In England, the obsession with sport is bad enough, but even fiercer passions are aroused in young countries where games playing and nationalism are both recent developments. In countries like India or Burma, it is necessary at football matches to have strong cordons of police to keep the crowd from invading the field. In Burma, I have seen the supporters of one side break through the police and disable the goalkeeper of the opposing side at a critical moment. The first big football match that was played in Spain about fifteen years ago led to an uncontrollable riot. As soon as strong feelings of rivalry are aroused, the notion of playing the game according to the rules always vanishes. People want to see one side on top and the other side humiliated, and they forget that victory gained through cheating or through the intervention of the crowd is meaningless. Even when the spectators don't intervene physically they try to influence the game by cheering their own side and 'rattling' opposing players with boos and insults. Serious sport has nothing to do with fair play. It is bound up with hatred, jealousy, boastfulness, disregard of all rules and sadistic pleasure in witnessing violence: in other words it is war minus the shooting.

Instead of blah-blahing about the clean, healthy rivalry of the football field and the great part played by the Olympic Games in bringing the nations together, it is more useful to inquire how and why this modern cult of sport arose. Most of the games we now play are of ancient origin, but sport does not seem to have been taken very seriously between Roman times and the nineteenth century. Even in the English public schools the games cult did not start till the later part of the last century. Dr Arnold, generally regarded as the founder of the modern public school, looked on games as simply a waste of time. Then, chiefly in England and the United States, games were built up into a heavily-financed activity, capable of attracting vast crowds and rousing savage passions, and the infection spread from country to country. It is the most violently combative sports, football and boxing, that have spread the widest. There cannot be much doubt that the whole thing is bound up with the rise of nationalism – that is, with the lunatic modern habit of identifying oneself with large power units and seeing everything in terms of competitive prestige. Also, organized games are more likely to flourish in urban communities where the average human being lives a sedentary or at least a confined life, and does not get much opportunity for creative labour. In a rustic community a boy or young man works off a good deal of his surplus energy by walking, swimming, snowballing, climbing trees, riding horses, and by various sports involving cruelty to animals, such as fishing, cock-fighting and ferreting for rats. In a big town one must indulge in group activities if one wants an outlet for one's physical strength or for one's sadistic impulses. Games are taken seriously in London and New York, and they were taken seriously in Rome and Byzantium: in the Middle Ages they were played, and probably played with much physical brutality, but they were not mixed up with politics nor a cause of group hatreds.

If you wanted to add to the vast fund of ill-will existing in the world at this moment, you could hardly do it better than by a series of football matches between Jews and Arabs, Germans and Czechs, Indians and British, Russians and Poles, and Italians and Jugoslavs, each match to be watched by a mixed audience of 100,000 spectators. I do not, of course, suggest that sport is one of the main causes of international rivalry; big-scale sport is itself, I think, merely another effect of the causes that have produced nationalism. Still, you do make things worse by sending forth a team of eleven men, labelled as national champions, to do battle against some rival team, and allowing it to be felt on all sides that whichever nation is defeated will 'lose face'.

I hope, therefore, that we shan't follow up the visit of the Dynamos by sending a British team to the USSR. If we must do so, then let us send a second-rate team which is sure to be beaten and cannot be claimed to represent Britain as a whole. There are quite enough real causes of trouble already, and we need not add to them by encouraging young men to kick each other on the shins amid the roars of infuriated spectators.

1945

Nonsense Poetry

In many languages, it is said, there is no nonsense poetry, and there is not a great deal of it even in English. The bulk of it is in nursery rhymes and scraps of folk poetry, some of which may not have been strictly nonsensical at the start, but have become so because their original application has been forgotten. For example, the rhyme about Margery Daw:

> See-saw, Margery Daw,
> Dobbin shall have a new master.
> He shall have but a penny a day
> Because he can't go any faster.

Or the other version that I learned in Oxfordshire as a little boy:

> See-saw, Margery Daw,
> Sold her bed and lay upon straw.
> Wasn't she a silly slut
> To sell her bed and lie upon dirt?

It may be that there was once a real person called Margery Daw, and perhaps there was even a Dobbin who somehow came into the story. When Shakespeare makes Edgar in *King Lear* quote 'Pillicock sat on Pillicock hill', and similar fragments, he is uttering nonsense, but no doubt these fragments come from forgotten ballads in which they once had a meaning. The typical scrap of folk poetry which one quotes almost unconsciously is not exactly nonsense but a sort of musical comment on some recurring event, such as 'One a penny, two a penny, Hot-Cross buns', or 'Polly, put the kettle on, we'll all have tea'. Some of these seemingly frivolous rhymes actually express a deeply pessimistic view of life, the churchyard wisdom of the peasant. For instance:

> Solomon Grundy,
> Born on Monday,
> Christened on Tuesday,
> Married on Wednesday,
> Took ill on Thursday,
> Worse on Friday,
> Died on Saturday,
> Buried on Sunday,
> And that was the end of Solomon Grundy.

which is a gloomy story, but remarkably similar to yours or mine.

Until Surrealism made a deliberate raid on the unconscious, poetry that aimed at being nonsense, apart from the meaningless refrains of songs, does not seem to have been common. This gives a special position to Edward Lear, whose nonsense rhymes have just been edited by Mr R. L. Megroz,[1] who was also responsible for the Penguin edition a year or two before the war. Lear was one of the first writers to deal in pure fantasy, with imaginary countries and made-up words, without any satirical purposes. His poems are not all of them equally nonsensical; some of them get their effect by a perversion of logic, but

---

[1] *The Lear Omnibus* edited by R. L. Megroz.

they are all alike in that their underlying feeling is sad and not bitter. They express a kind of amiable lunacy, a natural sympathy with whatever is weak and absurd. Lear could fairly be called the originator of the limerick, though verses in almost the same metrical form are to be found in earlier writers, and what is sometimes considered a weakness in his limericks — that is, the fact that the rhyme is the same in the first and last lines — is part of their charm. The very slight change increases the impression of ineffectuality, which might be spoiled if there were some striking surprise. For example:

> There was a young lady of Portugal
> Whose ideas were excessively nautical;
> She climbed up a tree
> To examine the sea,
> But declared she would never leave Portugal.

It is significant that almost no limericks since Lear's have been both printable and funny enough to seem worth quoting. But he is really seen at his best in certain longer poems, such as 'The Owl and the Pussy-Cat' or the 'The Courtship of the Yonghy-Bonghy-Bò:

> On the Coast of Coromandel,
> Where the early pumpkins blow,
> In the middle of the woods
> Lived the Yonghy-Bonghy-Bò.
> Two old chairs, and half a candle —
> One old jug without a handle —
> These were all his worldly goods:
> In the middle of the woods,
> These were all the worldly goods

> Of the Yonghy-Bonghy-Bò
> Of the Yonghy-Bonghy-Bò.

Later there appears a lady with some white Dorking hens, and an inconclusive love affair follows. Mr Megroz thinks, plausibly enough, that this may refer to some incident in Lear's own life. He never married, and it is easy to guess that there was something seriously wrong in his sex life. A psychiatrist could no doubt find all kinds of significance in his drawings and in the recurrence of certain made-up words such as 'runcible'. His health was bad, and as he was the youngest of twenty-one children in a poor family, he must have known anxiety and hardship in very early life. It is clear that he was unhappy and by nature solitary, in spite of having good friends.

Aldous Huxley, in praising Lear's fantasies as a sort of assertion of freedom, has pointed out that the 'They' of the limericks represent common sense, legality and the duller virtues generally. 'They' are the realists, the practical men, the sober citizens in bowler hats who are always anxious to stop you doing anything worth doing. For instance:

> There was an Old Man of Whitehaven,
> Who danced a quadrille with a raven;
> But they said, 'It's absurd
> To encourage this bird!'
> So they smashed that Old Man of Whitehaven.

To smash somebody just for dancing a quadrille with a raven is exactly the kind of thing that 'They' would do. Herbert Read has also praised Lear, and is inclined to prefer his verse to that of Lewis Carroll, as being purer fantasy. For myself, I must say that I find Lear funniest when he is least arbitrary and when a touch of burlesque or perverted logic makes its appearance. When he gives his fancy free play, as in his imaginary names, or in things like 'Three Receipts for Domestic Cookery', he can be silly and tiresome. 'The Pobble Who Has No Toes' is haunted by the ghost of logic, and I think it is the element of sense in it that makes it funny. The Pobble, it may be remembered, went fishing in the Bristol Channel:

> And all the Sailors and Admirals cried,
> When they saw him nearing the further side –
> 'He has gone to fish, for his Aunt Jobiska's
> Runcible Cat with crimson whiskers!'

The thing that is funny here is the burlesque touch, the Admirals. What is arbitrary – the word 'runcible', and the cat's crimson whiskers – is merely rather embarrassing. While the Pobble was in the water some unidentified creatures came and ate his toes off, and when he got home his aunt remarked:

> It's a fact the whole world knows,
> That Pobbles are happier without their toes,

which once again is funny because it has a meaning, and one might even say a political significance. For the whole theory of authoritarian governments is summed up in the statement that Pobbles were happier without their toes. So also with the well-known limerick:

> There was an Old Person of Basing,
> Whose presence of mind was amazing;
> He purchased a steed,
> Which he rode at full speed,
> And escaped from the people of Basing.

It is not quite arbitrary. The funniness is in the gentle implied criticism of the people of Basing, who once again are 'They', the respectable ones, the right-thinking, art-hating majority.

The writer closest to Lear among his contemporaries was Lewis Carroll, who, however, was less essentially fantastic — and, in my opinion, funnier. Since then, as Mr Megroz points out in his Introduction, Lear's influence has been considerable, but it is hard to believe that it has been altogether good. The silly whimsiness of present-day children's books could perhaps be partly traced back to him. At any rate, the idea of deliberately setting out to write nonsense, though it came off in Lear's case, is a doubtful one. Probably the best nonsense poetry is produced gradually and accidentally, by communities rather than by individuals. As a comic draughtsman, on the other hand, Lear's influence must have been beneficial. James Thurber, for instance, must surely owe something to Lear, directly or indirectly.

1945

The Prevention of Literature

About a year ago I attended a meeting of the PEN Club, the occasion being the tercentenary of Milton's *Areopagitica* – a pamphlet, it may be remembered, in defence of freedom of the press. Milton's famous phrase about the sin of 'killing' a book was printed on the leaflets, advertising the meeting, which had been circulated beforehand.

There were four speakers on the platform. One of them delivered a speech which did deal with the freedom of the press, but only in relation to India; another said, hesitantly, and in very general terms, that liberty was a good thing; a third delivered an attack on the laws relating to obscenity in literature. The fourth devoted most of his speech to a defence of the Russian purges. Of the speeches from the body of the hall, some reverted to the question of obscenity and the laws that deal with it, others were simply eulogies of Soviet Russia. Moral liberty – the liberty to discuss sex questions frankly in print – seemed to be generally approved, but political liberty was not mentioned. Out of this concourse of several hundred people, perhaps half of whom were directly connected with the writing trade, there was not a single one who could point out that freedom of the press, if it means anything at all, means the freedom to criticize and oppose. Significantly, no speaker quoted from the pamphlet which was ostensibly being commemorated. Nor was there any mention of the various books that have been 'killed' in this country and the United States during the war. In its net effect the meeting was a demonstration in favour of censorship.[1]

There was nothing particularly surprising in this. In our age, the idea of intellectual liberty is under attack from two directions. On the one side are its theoretical enemies, the apologists of totalitarianism, and on the other its immediate, practical enemies, monopoly and bureaucracy. Any writer or journalist who wants to retain his integrity finds himself thwarted by the general drift of society rather than by active persecution. The sort of things that are working against him are the concentration of the press in the hands of a few rich men, the grip of monopoly on radio and the films, the unwillingness of the public to spend money on books, making it necessary for nearly every writer to earn part of his living by hack work, the encroachment of official bodies like the MOI[2] and the British Council, which help the writer to keep alive but also waste his time and dictate his opinions, and the continuous war atmosphere of the past ten years, whose distorting effects no one has been able to escape. Everything in our age conspires to turn the writer, and every other kind of

---

[1] It is fair to say that the PEN Club celebrations, which lasted a week or more, did not always stick at quite the same level. I happened to strike a bad day. But an examination of the speeches (printed under the title *Freedom of Expression*) shows that almost nobody in our own day is able to speak out as roundly in favour of intellectual liberty as Milton could do three hundred years ago – and this in spite of the fact that Milton was writing in a period of civil war. [Author's footnote.]

[2] Ministry of Information

artist as well, into a minor official, working on themes handed to him from above and never telling what seems to him the whole of the truth. But in struggling against his fate he gets no help from his own side: that is, there is no large body of opinion which will assure him that he is in the right. In the past, at any rate throughout the Protestant centuries, the idea of rebellion and the idea of intellectual integrity were mixed up. A heretic – political, moral, religious, or aesthetic – was one who refused to outrage his own conscience. His outlook was summed up in the words of the Revivalist hymn:

> Dare to be a Daniel,
> Dare to stand alone;
> Dare to have a purpose firm,
> Dare to make it known.

To bring this hymn up to date one would have to add a 'Don't' at the beginning of each line. For it is the peculiarity of our age that the rebels against the existing order, at any rate the most numerous and characteristic of them, are also rebelling against the idea of individual integrity. 'Daring to stand alone' is ideologically criminal as well as practically dangerous. The independence of the writer and the artist is eaten away by vague economic forces, and at the same time it is undermined by those who should be its defenders. It is with the second process that I am concerned here.

Freedom of thought and of the press are usually attacked by arguments which are not worth bothering about. Anyone who has experience of lecturing and debating knows them off backwards. Here I am not trying to deal with the familiar claim that freedom is an illusion, or with the claim that there is more freedom in totalitarian countries than in democratic ones, but with the much more tenable and dangerous proposition that freedom is undesirable and that intellectual honesty is a form of antisocial selfishness. Although other aspects of the question are usually in the foreground the controversy over freedom of speech and of the press is at the bottom a controversy over the desirability, or otherwise, of telling lies. What is really at issue is the right to report contemporary events truthfully, or as truthfully as is consistent with the ignorance, bias and self-deception from which every observer necessarily suffers. In saying this I may seem to be saying that straightforward 'reportage' is the only branch of literature that matters: but I will try to show later that at every literary level, and probably in every one of the arts, the same issue arises in more or less subtilized forms. Meanwhile, it is necessary to strip away the irrelevancies in which this controversy is usually wrapped up.

The enemies of intellectual liberty always try to present their case as a plea for discipline versus individualism. The issue truth-versus-untruth is as far as possible kept in the background. Although the point of emphasis may vary, the writer who refuses to sell his opinions is always branded as a mere egoist. He is accused, that is, either of wanting to shut himself up in an ivory tower, or of making an exhibitionist display of his own personality, or of resisting the inevitable current of history in an attempt to cling to unjustified privileges. The Catholic and the Communist are alike in assuming that an opponent cannot be both honest and intelligent. Each of them tacitly claims that 'the truth' has already been revealed, and that the heretic, if he is not simply a fool, is secretly aware of 'the truth' and merely resists it out of selfish motives. In Communist literature the attack on intellectual liberty is usually masked by oratory about 'petty-bourgeois individualism', 'the illusions of nineteenth-century liberalism', etc., and backed up by words of abuse such as 'romantic' and 'sentimental', which, since they do not have any agreed meaning, are difficult to answer. In this way the controversy is manoeuvred away from its real issue. One can accept, and most enlightened people would accept, the Communist thesis that pure freedom will only exist in a classless society, and that one is more nearly free when one is working to bring such a society about. But slipped in with this is the quite unfounded claim that the Communist Party is itself aiming at the establishment of the classless society, and that in the USSR this aim is actually on the way to being realized. If the first claim is allowed to entail the second, there is almost no assault on common sense and common decency that cannot be justified. But meanwhile, the real point has been dodged. Freedom of the intellect means the freedom to report what one has seen, heard, and felt, and not to be obliged to fabricate imaginary facts and feelings. The familiar tirades against 'escapism', 'individualism', 'romanticism' and so forth, are merely a forensic device, the aim of which is to make the perversion of history seem respectable.

Fifteen years ago, when one defended the freedom of the intellect, one had to defend it against Conservatives, against Catholics, and to some extent – for they were not of great importance in England – against Fascists. Today one has to defend it against Communists and 'fellow-travellers'. One ought not to exaggerate the direct influence of the small English Communist Party, but there can be no question about the poisonous effect of the Russian *mythos* on English intellectual life. Because of it, known facts are suppressed and distorted to such an extent as to make it doubtful whether a true history of our times can ever be written. Let me give just one instance out of the hundreds that could be cited. When Germany collapsed, it was found that very large numbers of Soviet Russians – mostly, no doubt, from non-political motives – had changed sides and were fighting for the Germans. Also, a small but not negligible proportion of the Russian prisoners and Displaced Persons refused to go back to the USSR, and some of them, at least, were repatriated against their will. These facts, known to many journalists on the spot, went almost unmentioned in the British press, while at the same time russophile publicists in England continued to justify the purges and deportations of 1936–8 by claiming that the USSR, 'had no quislings'. The fog of lies and misinformation that surrounds such subjects as the Ukraine famine, the Spanish Civil War, Russian policy in Poland, and so forth, is not due entirely to conscious dishonesty, but any writer or journalist who is fully sympathetic to the USSR – sympathetic, that is, in the way the Russians themselves would want him to be – does have to acquiesce in deliberate falsification on important issues. I have before me what must be a very rare pamphlet, written by Maxim Litvinov in 1918 and outlining the recent events in the Russian Revolution. It makes no mention of Stalin, but gives high praise to Trotsky, and also to Zinoviev, Kamenev and others. What could be the attitude of even the most intellectually scrupulous Communist towards such a pamphlet? At best, the obscurantist attitude of saying that it is an undesirable document and better suppressed. And if for some reason it were decided to issue a garbled version of the pamphlet, denigrating Trotsky and inserting references to Stalin, no Communist who remained faithful to his Party could protest. Forgeries almost as gross as this have been committed in recent years. But the significant thing is not that they happen, but that even when they are known about they provoke no reaction from the left-wing intelligentsia as a whole. The argument that to tell the truth would be 'inopportune' or would 'play into the hands of' somebody or other is felt to be unanswerable, and few people are bothered by the prospect of the lies which they condone getting out of the newspapers and into the history books.

The organized lying practised by totalitarian states is not, as is sometimes claimed, a temporary expedient of the same nature as military deception. It is something integral to totalitarianism, something that would still continue even if concentration camps and secret police forces had ceased to be necessary. Among intelligent Communists there is an underground legend to the effect that although the Russian Government is obliged now to deal in lying propaganda, frame-up trials, and so forth, it is secretly recording the true facts and will publish them at some future time. We can, I believe, be quite certain that this is not the case, because the mentality implied by such an action is that of a liberal historian who believes that the past cannot be altered and that a correct knowledge of history is valuable as a matter of course. From the totalitarian point of view history is something to be created rather than learned. A totalitarian state is in effect a theocracy, and its ruling caste, in order to keep its position, has to be thought of as infallible. But since, in practice, no one is infallible, it is frequently necessary to rearrange past events in order to show that this or that mistake was not made, or that this or that imaginary triumph actually happened. Then, again, every major change in policy demands a corresponding change of doctrine and a revaluation of prominent historical figures. This kind of thing happens everywhere, but is clearly likelier to lead to outright falsification in societies where only one opinion is permissible at any given moment. Totalitarianism demands, in fact, the continuous alteration of the past, and in the long run probably demands a disbelief in the very existence of objective truth. The friends of totalitarianism in this country tend to argue that since absolute truth is not attainable, a big lie is no worse than a little lie. It is pointed out that all historical records are biassed and inaccurate, or, on the other hand, that modern physics has proved that what seems to us the real world is an illusion, so that to believe in the evidence of one's senses is simply vulgar philistinism. A totalitarian society which succeeded in perpetuating itself would probably set us a schizophrenic system of thought, in which the laws of common sense held good in everyday life and in certain exact sciences, but could be disregarded by the politician, the historian, and the sociologist. Already there are countless people who would think it scandalous to falsify a scientific text-book, but would see nothing wrong in falsifying an historical fact. It is at the point where literature and politics cross that totalitarianism exerts its greatest pressure on the intellectual. The exact sciences are not, at this date, menaced to anything like the same extent. This partly accounts for the fact that in all countries it is easier for the scientists than for the writers to line up behind their respective governments.

To keep the matter in perspective, let me repeat what I said at the beginning of this essay; that in England the immediate enemies of truthfulness, and hence of freedom of thought, are the press lords, the film magnates, and the bureaucrats, but that on a long view the weakening of the desire for liberty among the intellectuals themselves is the most serious symptom of all. It may seem that all this time I have been talking about the effects of censorship, not on literature as a whole, but merely on one department of political journalism. Granted that Soviet Russia constitutes a sort of forbidden area in the British press, granted that issues like Poland, the Spanish Civil War, the Russo-German Pact, and so forth, are debarred from serious discussion, and that if you possess information that conflicts with the prevailing orthodoxy you are expected to distort it or to keep quiet about it – granted all this, why should literature in the wider sense be affected? Is every writer a politician, and is every book necessarily a work of straightforward 'reportage'? Even under the tightest dictatorship, cannot the individual writer remain free inside his own mind and distil or disguise his unorthodox ideas in such a way that the authorities will be too stupid to recognize them? And in any case, if the writer himself is in agreement with the prevailing orthodoxy, why should it have a cramping effect on him? Is not literature, or any of the arts, likeliest to flourish in societies in which there are no major conflicts of opinion and no sharp distinction between the artist and his audience? Does one have to assume that every writer is a rebel, or even that a writer as such is an exceptional person?

Whenever one attempts to defend intellectual liberty against the claims of totalitarianism, one meets with these arguments in one form or another. They are based on a complete misunderstanding of what literature is, and how – one should perhaps rather say why – it comes into being. They assume that a writer is either a mere entertainer or else a venal hack who can switch from one line of propaganda to another as easily as an organ-grinder changing tunes. But after all, how is it that books ever come to be written? Above a quite low level, literature is an attempt to influence the viewpoint of one's contemporaries by recording experience. And so far as freedom of expression is concerned, there is not much difference between a mere journalist and the most 'unpolitical' imaginative writer. The journalist is unfree, and is conscious of unfreedom, when he is forced to write lies or suppress what seems to him important news: the imaginative writer is unfree when he has to falsify his subjective feelings, which from his point of view are facts. He may distort and caricature reality in order to make his meaning clearer, but he cannot misrepresent the scenery of his own mind: he cannot say with any conviction that he likes what he dislikes, or believes what he disbelieves. If he is forced to do so, the only result is that his creative faculties dry up. Nor can he solve the problem by keeping away from controversial topics. There is no such thing as genuinely non-political literature, and least of all in an age like our own, when fears, hatreds, and loyalties of a directly political kind are near to the surface of everyone's consciousness. Even a single taboo can have an all-round crippling effect upon the mind, because there is always the danger that any thought which is freely followed up may lead to the forbidden thought. It follows that the atmosphere of totalitarianism is deadly to any kind of prose writer, though a poet, at any rate a lyric poet, might possible find it breathable. And in any totalitarian society that survives for more than a couple of generations, it is probable that prose literature, of the kind that has existed during the past four hundred years, must actually come to an end.

Literature has sometimes flourished under despotic régimes, but, as has often been pointed out, the despotisms of the past were not totalitarian. Their repressive apparatus was always inefficient, their ruling classes were usually either corrupt or apathetic or half-liberal in outlook, and the prevailing religious doctrines usually worked against perfectionism and the notion of human infallibility. Even so it is broadly true that prose literature has reached its highest levels in periods of democracy and free speculation. What is new in totalitarianism is that its doctrines are not only unchallengeable but also unstable. They have to be accepted on pain of damnation, but on the other hand they are always liable to be altered at a moment's notice. Consider, for example, the various attitudes, completely incompatible with one another, which an English Communist or 'fellow-traveller' has had to adopt towards the war between Britain and Germany. For years before September 1939 he was expected to be in a continuous stew about 'the horrors of Nazism' and to twist everything he wrote into a denunciation of Hitler: after September 1939, for twenty months, he had to believe that Germany was more sinned against than sinning, and the word 'Nazi', at least so far as print went, had to drop right out of his vocabulary. Immediately after hearing the 8 o'clock news bulletin on the morning of 22 June 1941, he had to start believing once again that Nazism was the most hideous evil the world had ever seen. Now, it is easy for a politician to make such changes: for a writer the case is somewhat different. If he is to switch his allegiance at exactly the right moment, he must either tell lies about his subjective feelings, or else suppress them altogether. In either case he has destroyed his dynamo. Not only will ideas refuse to come to him but the very words he uses will seem to stiffen under his touch. Political writing in our time consists almost entirely of prefabricated phrases bolted together like the pieces of a child's Meccano set. It is the unavoidable result of self-censorship. To write in plain, vigorous language one has to think fearlessly, and if one thinks fearlessly one cannot be politically orthodox. It might be otherwise in an 'age of faith', when the prevailing orthodoxy has been long established and is not taken too seriously. In that case it would be possible, or might be possible, for large areas of one's mind to remain unaffected by what one officially believed. Even so, it is worth noticing that prose literature almost disappeared during the only age of faith that Europe has ever enjoyed. Throughout the whole of the Middle Ages there was almost no imaginative prose literature and very little in the way of historical writing: and the intellectual leaders of society expressed their most serious thoughts in a dead language which barely altered during a thousand years.

Totalitarianism, however, does not so much promise an age of faith as an age of schizophrenia. A society becomes totalitarian when its structure becomes flagrantly artificial: that is, when its ruling class has lost its function but succeeds in clinging to power by force or fraud. Such a society, no matter how long it persists, can never afford to become either tolerant or intellectually stable. It can never permit either the truthful recording of facts, or the emotional sincerity, that literary creation demands. But to be corrupted by totalitarianism one does not have to live in a totalitarian country. The mere prevalence of certain ideas can spread a kind of poison that makes one subject after another impossible for literary purposes. Wherever there is an enforced orthodoxy – or even two orthodoxies, as often happens – good writing stops. This was well illustrated by the Spanish Civil War. To many English intellectuals the war was a deeply moving experience, but not an experience about which they could write sincerely. There were only two things that you were allowed to say, and both of them were palpable lies: as a result, the war produced acres of print but almost nothing worth reading.

It is not certain whether the effects of totalitarianism upon verse need be so deadly as its effects on prose. There is a whole series of converging reasons why it is somewhat easier for a poet than for a prose writer to feel at home in an authoritarian society. To begin with, bureaucrats and other 'practical' men usually despise the poet too deeply to be much interested in what he is saying. Secondly, what the poet is saying – that is, what his poem 'means' if translated into prose – is relatively unimportant even to himself. The thought contained in a poem is always simple, and is no more the primary purpose of the poem than the anecdote is the primary purpose of a picture. A poem is an arrangement of sounds and associations, as a painting is an arrangement of brush-marks. For short snatches, indeed, as in the refrain of a song, poetry can even dispense with meaning altogether. It is therefore fairly easy for a poet to keep away from dangerous subjects and avoid uttering heresies: and even when he does utter them, they may escape notice. But above all, good verse, unlike good prose, is not necessarily an individual product. Certain kinds of poems, such as ballads, or, on the other hand, very artificial verse forms, can be composed co-operatively by groups of people. Whether the ancient English and Scottish ballads were originally produced by individuals, or by the people at large, is disputed, but at any rate they are non-individual in the sense that they constantly change in passing from mouth to mouth. Even in print no two versions of a ballad are ever quite the same. Many primitive peoples compose verse communally. Someone begins to improvise, probably accompanying himself on a musical instrument, somebody else chips in with a line or a rhyme when the first singer breaks down, and so the process continues until there exists a whole song or ballad which has no identifiable author.

In prose, this kind of intimate collaboration is quite impossible. Serious prose, in any case, has to be composed in solitude, whereas the excitement of being part of a group is actually an aid to certain kinds of versification. Verse – and perhaps good verse of its kind, though it would not be the highest kind – might survive under even the most inquisitorial régime. Even in a society where liberty and individuality had been extinguished, there would still be need either for patriotic songs and heroic ballads celebrating victories, or for elaborate exercises in flattery: and these are the kinds of poem that can be written to order, or composed communally, without necessarily lacking artistic value. Prose is a different matter, since the prose writer cannot narrow the range of his thoughts without killing his inventiveness. But the history of totalitarian societies, or of groups of people who have adopted the totalitarian outlook, suggests that loss of liberty is inimical to all forms of literature. German literature almost disappeared during the Hitler régime, and the case was not much better in Italy. Russian literature, so far as one can judge by translations, has deteriorated markedly since the early days of the Revolution, though some of the verse appears to be better than the prose. Few if any Russian novels that it is possible to take seriously have been translated for about fifteen years. In western Europe and America large sections of the literary intelligentsia have either passed through the Communist Party or been warmly sympathetic to it, but this whole leftward movement has produced extraordinarily few books worth reading. Orthodox Catholicism, again, seems to have a crushing effect upon certain literary forms, especially the novel. During a period of three hundred years, how many people have been at once good novelists and good Catholics? The fact is that certain themes cannot be celebrated in words, and tyranny is one of them. No one ever wrote a good book in praise of the Inquisition. Poetry might survive, in a totalitarian age, and certain arts or half-arts, such as architecture, might even find tyranny beneficial, but the prose writer would have no choice between silence and death. Prose literature as we know it is the product of rationalism, of the Protestant centuries, of the autonomous individual. And the destruction of intellectual liberty cripples the journalist, the sociological writer, the historian, the novelist, the critic and the poet, in that order. In the future it is possible that a new kind of literature, not involving individual feeling or truthful observation, may arise, but no such thing is at present imaginable. It seems much likelier that if the liberal culture that we have lived in since the Renaissance actually comes to an end, the literary art will perish with it.

Of course, print will continue to be used, and it is interesting to speculate what kinds of reading matter would survive in a rigidly totalitarian society. Newspapers will presumably continue until television technique reaches a higher level, but apart from newspapers it is doubtful even now whether the great mass of people in the industrialized countries feel the need for any kind of literature. They are unwilling, at any rate, to spend anywhere near as much on reading matter as they spend on several other recreations. Probably novels and stories will be completely superseded by film and radio productions. Or perhaps some kind of low-grade sensational fiction will survive, produced by a sort of conveyor-belt process that reduces human initiative to the minimum.

It would probably not be beyond human ingenuity to write books by machinery. But a sort of mechanizing process can already be seen at work in the film and radio, in publicity and propaganda, and in the lower reaches of journalism. The Disney films, for instance, are produced by what is essentially a factory process, the work being done partly mechanically and partly by teams of artists who have to subordinate their individual style. Radio features are commonly written by tired hacks to whom the subject and the manner of treatment are dictated beforehand: even so, what they write is merely a kind of raw material to be chopped into shape by producers and censors. So also with the innumerable books and pamphlets commissioned by government departments. Even more machine-like is the production of short stories, serials and poems for the very cheap magazines. Papers such as the *Writer* abound with advertisements of Literary Schools, all of them offering you ready-made plots at a few shillings a time. Some, together with the plot, supply the opening and closing sentences of each chapter. Others furnish you with a sort of algebraical formula by the use of which you can construct your plots for yourself. Others offer packs of cards marked with characters and situations, which have only to be shuffled and dealt in order to produce ingenious stories automatically. It is probably in some such way that the literature of a totalitarian society would be produced, if literature were still felt to be necessary. Imagination – even consciousness, so far as possible – would be eliminated from the process of writing. Books would be planned in their broad lines by bureaucrats, and would pass through so many hands that when finished they would be no more an individual product than a Ford car at the end of the assembly line. It goes without saying that anything so produced would be rubbish; but anything that was not rubbish would endanger the structure of the State. As for the surviving literature of the past, it would have to be suppressed or at least elaborately rewritten.

Meanwhile totalitarianism has not fully triumphed everywhere. Our own society is still, broadly speaking, liberal. To exercise your right of free speech you have to fight against economic pressure and against strong sections of public opinion, but not, as yet, against a secret police force. You can say or print almost anything so long as you are willing to do it in a hole-and-corner way. But what is sinister, as I said at the beginning of this essay, is that the conscious enemies of liberty are those to whom liberty ought to mean most. The big public do not care about the matter one way or the other. They are not in favour of persecuting the heretic, and they will not exert themselves to defend him. They are at once too sane and too stupid to acquire the totalitarian outlook. The direct, conscious attack on intellectual decency comes from the intellectuals themselves.

It is possible that the russophile intelligentsia, if they had not succumbed to that particular myth, would have succumbed to another of much the same kind. But at any rate the Russian myth is there, and the corruption it causes stinks. When one sees highly educated men looking on indifferently at oppression and persecution, one wonders which to despise more, their cynicism or their shortsightedness. Many scientists, for example, are the uncritical admirers of the USSR. They appear to think that the destruction of liberty is of no importance so long as their own line of work is for the moment unaffected. The USSR is a large, rapidly developing country which has acute need of scientific workers and, consequently, treats them generously. Provided that they steer clear of dangerous subjects such as psychology, scientists are privileged persons. Writers, on the other hand, are viciously persecuted. It is true that literary prostitutes like Ilya Ehrenburg or Alexei Tolstoy are paid huge sums of money, but the only thing which is of any value to the writer as such – his freedom of expression – is taken away from him. Some, at least, of the English scientists who speak so enthusiastically of the opportunities enjoyed by scientists in Russia are capable of understanding this. But their reflection appears to be: 'Writers are persecuted in Russia. So what? I am not a writer.' They do not see that any attack on intellectual liberty, and on the concept of objective truth, threatens in the long run every department of thought.

For the moment the totalitarian state tolerates the scientist because it needs him. Even in Nazi Germany, scientists, other than Jews, were relatively well treated, and the German scientific community, as a whole, offered no resistance to Hitler. At this stage of history, even the most autocratic ruler is forced to take account of physical reality, partly because of the lingering-on of liberal habits of thought, partly because of the need to prepare for war. So long as physical reality cannot be altogether ignored, so long as two and two have to make four when you are, for example, drawing the blue-print of an aeroplane, the scientist has his function, and can even be allowed a measure of liberty. His awakening will come later, when the totalitarian state is firmly established. Meanwhile, if he wants to safeguard the integrity of science, it is his job to develop some kind of solidarity with his literary colleagues and not regard it as a matter of indifference when writers are silenced or driven to suicide, and newspapers systematically falsified.

But however it may be with the physical sciences, or with

music, painting, and architecture, it is – as I have tried to show – certain that literature is doomed if liberty of thought perishes. Not only is it doomed in any country which retains a totalitarian structure; but any writer who adopts the totalitarian outlook, who finds excuses for persecution and the falsification of reality, thereby destroys himself as a writer. There is no way out of this. No tirades against 'individualism' and 'the ivory tower', no pious platitudes to the effect that 'true individuality is only attained through identification with the community', can get over the fact that a bought mind is a spoiled mind. Unless spontaneity enters at some point or another, literary creation is impossible, and language itself becomes ossified. At some time in the future, if the human mind becomes something totally different from what it now is, we may learn to separate literary creation from intellectual honesty. At present we know only that the imagination, like certain wild animals, will not breed in captivity. Any writer or journalist who denies that fact – and nearly all the current praise of the Soviet Union contains or implies such a denial – is, in effect, demanding his own destruction.

1946

Books v. Cigarettes

A couple of years ago a friend of mine, a newspaper editor, was fire-watching with some factory workers. They fell to talking about his newspaper, which most of them read and approved of, but when he asked them what they thought of the literary section, the answer he got was: 'You don't suppose we read that stuff, do you? Why, half the time you're talking about books that cost twelve and sixpence! Chaps like us couldn't spend twelve and sixpence on a book.' These, he said, were men who thought nothing of spending several pounds on a day trip to Blackpool.

This idea that the buying, or even the reading, of books is an expensive hobby and beyond the reach of the average person is so widespread that it deserves some detailed examination. Exactly what reading costs, reckoned in terms of pence per hour, is difficult to estimate, but I have made a start by inventorying my own books and adding up their total price. After allowing for various other expenses, I can make a fairly good guess at my expenditure over the last fifteen years.

The books that I have counted and priced are the ones I have here, in my flat. I have about an equal number stored in another place, so that I shall double the final figure in order to arrive at the complete amount. I have not counted oddments such as proof copies, defaced volumes, cheap paper-covered editions, pamphlets, or magazines, unless bound up into book form. Nor have I counted the kind of junky books – old school textbooks and so forth – that accumulate in the bottoms of cupboards. I have counted only those books which I have acquired voluntarily, or else would have acquired voluntarily, and which I intend to keep. In this category I find that I have 442 books, acquired in the following ways:

Bought (mostly second-hand)	251
Given to me or bought with book tokens	33
Review copies and complimentary copies	143
Borrowed and not returned	10
Temporarily on loan	5
TOTAL	442

Now as to the method of pricing. Those books that I have bought I have listed at their full price, as closely as I can determine it. I have also listed at their full price the books that have been given to me, and those that I have temporarily borrowed, or borrowed and kept. This is because book-giving, book-borrowing and book-stealing more or less even out. I possess books that do not strictly speaking belong to me, but many other people also have books of mine: so that the books I have not paid for can be taken as balancing others which I have paid for but no longer possess. On the other hand I have listed the review and complimentary copies at half-price. That is about what I would have paid for them second-hand, and they are mostly books that I would only have bought second-hand, if at all. For the prices I have sometimes had to rely on guesswork, but my figures will not be far out. The costs were as follows:

	£	s.	d.
Bought	36	9	0
Gifts	10	10	0
Review copies, etc.	25	11	9

	£	s.	d.
Borrowed and not returned	4	16	9
On Loan	3	10	0
Shelves	2	0	0
TOTAL	82	17	6

Adding the other batch of books that I have elsewhere, it seems that I possess altogether nearly 900 books, at a cost of £165 15s. This is the accumulation of about fifteen years – actually more, since some of these books date from my childhood: but call it fifteen years. This works out at £11 1s. a year, but there are other charges that must be added in order to estimate my full reading expenses. The biggest will be for newspapers and periodicals, and for this I think £8 a year would be a reasonable figure. Eight pounds a year covers the cost of two daily papers, one evening paper, two Sunday papers, one weekly review and one or two monthly magazines. This brings the figure up to £19 1s., but to arrive at the grand total one has to make a guess. Obviously one often spends money on books without afterwards having anything to show for it. There are library subscriptions, and there are also the books, chiefly Penguins and other cheap editions, which one buys and then loses or throws away. However, on the basis of my other figures, it looks as though £6 a year would be quite enough to add for expenditure of this kind. So my total reading expenses over the past fifteen years have been in the neighbourhood of £25 a year.

Twenty-five pounds a year sounds quite a lot until you begin to measure it against other kinds of expenditure. It is nearly 9s. 9d. a week, and at present 9s. 9d. is the equivalent of about 83 cigarettes (Players): even before the war it would have bought you less than 200 cigarettes. With prices as they now are, I am spending far more on tobacco than I do on books. I smoke six ounces a week, at half a crown an ounce, making nearly £40 a year. Even before the war when the same tobacco cost 8d. an ounce, I was spending over £10 a year on it: and if I also averaged a pint of beer a day, at 6d., these two items together will have cost me close on £20 a year. This was probably not much above the national average. In 1938 the people of this country spent nearly £10 per head per annum on alcohol and tobacco: however, 20 per cent of the population were children under fifteen and another 40 per cent were women, so that the average smoker and drinker must have been spending much more than £10. In 1944, the annual expenditure per head on these items was no less than £23. Allow for the women and children as before, and £40 is a reasonable individual figure. Forty pounds a year would just about pay for a packet of Woodbines every day and half a pint of mild six days a week — not a magnificent allowance. Of course, all prices are now inflated, including the price of books: still, it looks as though the cost of reading, even if you buy books instead of borrowing them and take in a fairly large number of periodicals, does not amount to more than the combined cost of smoking and drinking.

It is difficult to establish any relationship between the price of books and the value one gets out of them. 'Books' includes novels, poetry, textbooks, works of reference, sociological treatises and much else, and length and price do not correspond to one another, especially if one habitually buys books second-hand. You may spend ten shillings on a poem of 500 lines, and you may spend sixpence on a dictionary which you consult at odd moments over a period of twenty years. There are books that one reads over and over again, books that become part of the furniture of one's mind and alter one's whole attitude to life, books that one dips into but never reads through, books that one reads at a single sitting and forgets a week later: and the cost in terms of money, may be the same in each case. But if one regards reading simply as a recreation, like going to the pictures, then it is possible to make a rough estimate of what it costs. If you read nothing but novels and 'light' literature, and bought every book that you read, you would be spending – allowing eight shillings as the price of a book, and four hours as the time spent in reading it – two shillings an hour. This is about what it costs to sit in one of the more expensive seats in the cinema. If you concentrated on more serious books, and still bought everything that you read, your expenses would be about the same. The books would cost more but they would take longer to read. In either case you would still possess the books after you had read them, and they would be saleable at about a third of their purchase price. If you bought only second-hand books, your reading expenses would, of course, be much less: perhaps sixpence an hour would be a fair estimate. And on the other hand if you don't buy books, but merely borrow them from the lending library, reading costs you round about a halfpenny an hour: if you borrow them from the public library, it costs you next door to nothing.

I have said enough to show that reading is one of the cheaper recreations: after listening to the radio probably *the* cheapest. Meanwhile, what is the actual amount that the British public spends on books? I cannot discover any figures, though no doubt they exist. But I do know that before the war this country was publishing annually about 15,000 books, which included reprints and school books. If as many as 10,000 copies of each book were sold – and even allowing for the school books, this is probably a high estimate – the average person was only buying, directly or indirectly, about three books a year. These three books taken together might cost £1, or probably less.

These figures are guesswork, and I should be interested if someone would correct them for me. But if my estimate is anywhere near right, it is not a proud record for a country which is nearly 100 per cent literate and where the ordinary man spends more on cigarettes than an Indian peasant has for his whole livelihood. And if our book consumption remains as low as it has been, at least let us admit that it is because reading is a less exciting pastime than going to the dogs, the pictures or the pub, and not because books, whether bought or borrowed, are too expensive.

1946

Decline of the English Murder

It is Sunday afternoon, preferably before the war. The wife is already asleep in the armchair, and the children have been sent out for a nice long walk. You put your feet up on the sofa, settle your spectacles on your nose, and open the *News of the World*. Roast beef and Yorkshire, or roast pork and apple sauce, followed up by suet pudding and driven home, as it were, by a cup of mahogany-brown tea, have put you in just the right mood. Your pipe is drawing sweetly, the sofa cushions are soft underneath you, the fire is well alight, the air is warm and stagnant. In these blissful circumstances, what is it that you want to read about?

Naturally, about a murder. But what kind of murder? If one examines the murders which have given the greatest amount of pleasure to the British public, the murders whose story is known in its general outline to almost everyone and which have been made into novels and rehashed over and over again by the Sunday papers, one finds a fairly strong family resemblance running through the greater number of them. Our great period in murder, our Elizabethan period, so to speak, seems to have been between roughly 1850 and 1925, and the murderers whose reputation has stood the test of time are the following: Dr Palmer of Rugeley, Jack the Ripper, Neill Cream,

Mrs Maybrick, Dr Crippen, Seddon, Joseph Smith, Armstrong, and Bywaters and Thompson. In addition, in 1919 or thereabouts, there was another very celebrated case which fits into the general pattern but which I had better not mention by name, because the accused man was acquitted.

Of the above-mentioned nine cases, at least four have had successful novels based on them, one has been made into a popular melodrama, and the amount of literature surrounding them, in the form of newspaper write-ups, criminological treatises and reminiscences by lawyers and police officers, would make a considerable library. It is difficult to believe that any recent English crime will be remembered so long and so intimately, and not only because the violence of external events has made murder seem unimportant, but because the prevalent type of crime seems to be changing. The principal *cause célèbre* of the war years was the so-called Cleft Chin Murder, which has now been written up in a popular booklet;[1] the verbatim account of the trial was published some time last year by Messrs Jarrolds with an introduction by Mr. Bechhofer-Roberts. Before returning to this pitiful and sordid case, which is only interesting from a sociological and perhaps a legal point of view, let me try to define what it is that the readers of Sunday papers mean when they say fretfully that 'you never seem to get a good murder nowadays'.

In considering the nine murders I named above, one can start by excluding the Jack the Ripper case, which is in a class by itself. Of the other eight, six were poisoning cases, and eight of the ten criminals belonged to the middle class. In one way or another, sex was a powerful motive in all but two cases,

---

[1] *The Cleft Chin Murder* by R. Alwyn Raymond.

and in at least four cases respectability – the desire to gain a secure position in life, or not to forfeit one's social position by some scandal such as a divorce – was one of the main reasons for committing murder. In more than half the cases, the object was to get hold of a certain known sum of money such as a legacy or an insurance policy, but the amount involved was nearly always small. In most of the cases the crime only came to light slowly, as the result of careful investigation which started off with the suspicions of neighbours or relatives; and in nearly every case there was some dramatic coincidence, in which the finger of Providence could be clearly seen, or one of those episodes that no novelist would dare to make up, such as Crippen's flight across the Atlantic with his mistress dressed as a boy, or Joseph Smith playing 'Nearer, my God, to Thee' on the harmonium while one of his wives was drowning in the next room. The background of all these crimes, except Neill Cream's, was essentially domestic; of twelve victims, seven were either wife or husband of the murderer.

With all this in mind one can construct what would be, from a *News of the World* reader's point of view, the 'perfect' murder. The murderer should be a little man of the professional class – a dentist or a solicitor, say – living an intensely respectable life somewhere in the suburbs, and preferably in a semi-detached house, which will allow the neighbours to hear suspicious sounds through the wall. He should be either chairman of the local Conservative Party branch, or a leading Nonconformist and strong Temperance advocate. He should go astray through cherishing a guilty passion for his secretary or the wife of a rival professional man, and should only bring himself to the point of murder after long and terrible wrestles with his conscience. Having decided on murder, he should plan it all with the utmost cunning, and only slip up over some tiny, unforeseeable detail. The means chosen should, of course, be poison. In the last analysis he should commit murder because this seems to him less disgraceful, and less damaging to his career, than being detected in adultery. With this kind of background, a crime can have dramatic and even tragic qualities which make it memorable and excite pity for both victim and murderer. Most of the crimes mentioned above have a touch of this atmosphere, and in three cases, including the one I referred to but did not name, the story approximates to the one I have outlined.

Now compare the Cleft Chin Murder. There is no depth of feeling in it. It was almost chance that the two people concerned committed that particular murder, and it was only by good luck that they did not commit several others. The background was not domesticity, but the anonymous life of the dance halls and the false values of the American film. The two culprits were an eighteen-year-old ex-waitress named Elizabeth Jones, and an American army deserter, posing as an officer, named Karl Hulten. They were only together for six days, and it seems doubtful whether, until they were arrested, they even learned one another's true names. They met casually in a teashop, and that night went out for a ride in a stolen army truck. Jones described herself as a strip-tease artist, which was not strictly true (she had given one unsuccessful performance in this line), and declared that she wanted to do something dangerous, 'like being a gun-moll'. Hulten described himself as a big-time Chicago gangster, which was also untrue. They met a girl bicycling along the road, and to show how tough he was Hulten ran over her with his truck, after which the pair robbed her of the few shillings that were on her. On another occasion they knocked out a girl to whom they had offered a lift, took her coat and handbag and threw her into a river. Finally, in the most wanton way, they murdered a taxi-driver who happened to have £8 in his pocket. Soon afterwards they parted. Hulten was caught because he had foolishly kept the dead man's car, and Jones made spontaneous confessions to the police. In court each prisoner incriminated the other. In between crimes, both of them seem to have behaved with the utmost callousness: they spent the dead taxi-driver's £8 at the dog races.

Judging from her letters, the girl's case has a certain amount of psychological interest, but this murder probably captured the headlines because it provided distraction amid the doodlebugs and the anxieties of the Battle of France. Jones and Hulten committed their murder to the tune of V1,[1] and were convicted to the tune of V2.[2] There was also considerable excitement because – as has become usual in England – the man was sentenced to death and the girl to imprisonment.

According to Mr Raymond, the reprieving of Jones caused widespread indignation and streams of telegrams to the Home Secretary: in her native town, 'She should hang' was chalked on the walls beside pictures of a figure dangling from a gallows. Considering that only ten women have been hanged in Britain in this century, and that the practice has gone out largely because of popular feeling against it, it is difficult not to feel that this clamour to hang an eighteen-year-old girl was due

---

[1] The V1, an unmanned aircraft developed by the Germans and used by them to bomb London from June 1944: they were nicknamed 'doodlebugs' by the Londoners.
[2] The V2, a rocket bomb used by the Germans on London from September 1944.

partly to the brutalizing effects of war. Indeed, the whole meaningless story, with its atmosphere of dance-halls, movie palaces, cheap perfume, false names and stolen cars, belongs essentially to a war period.

Perhaps it is significant that the most talked-of English murder of recent years should have been committed by an American and an English girl who had become partly americanized. But it is difficult to believe that this case will be so long remembered as the old domestic poisoning dramas, product of a stable society where the all-prevailing hypocrisy did at least ensure that crimes as serious as murder should have strong emotions behind them.

1946

Some Thoughts on the Common Toad

Before the swallow, before the daffodil, and not much later than the snowdrop, the common toad salutes the coming of spring after his own fashion, which is to emerge from a hole in the ground, where he has lain buried since the previous autumn, and crawl as rapidly as possible towards the nearest suitable patch of water. Something — some kind of shudder in the earth, or perhaps merely a rise of a few degrees in the temperature — has told him that it is time to wake up: though a few toads appear to sleep the clock round and miss out a year from time to time — at any rate, I have more than once dug them up, alive and apparently well, in the middle of summer.

At this period, after his long fast, the toad has a very spiritual look, like a strict Anglo-Catholic towards the end of Lent. His movements are languid but purposeful, his body is shrunken, and by contrast his eyes look abnormally large. This allows one to notice, what one might not at another time, that a toad has about the most beautiful eye of any living creature. It is like gold, or more exactly it is like the golden-coloured semi-precious stone which one sometimes sees in signet-rings, and which I think is called a chrysoberyl.

For a few days after getting into the water the toad concentrates on building up his strength by eating small insects. Presently he has swollen to his normal size again, and then he goes through a phase of intense sexiness. All he knows, at least if he is a male toad, is that he wants to get his arms round something, and if you offer him a stick, or even your finger, he will cling to it with surprising strength and take a long time to discover that it is not a female toad. Frequently one comes upon shapeless masses of ten or twenty toads rolling over and over in the water, one clinging to another without distinction of sex. By degrees, however, they sort themselves out into couples, with the male duly sitting on the female's back. You can now distinguish males from females, because the male is smaller, darker and sits on top, with his arms tightly clasped round the female's neck. After a day or two the spawn is laid in long strings which wind themselves in and out of the reeds and soon become invisible. A few more weeks, and the water is alive with masses of tiny tadpoles which rapidly grow larger, sprout hind-legs, then forelegs, then shed their tails: and finally, about the middle of the summer, the new generation of toads, smaller than one's thumb-nail but perfect in every particular, crawl out of the water to begin the game anew.

I mention the spawning of the toads because it is one of the phenomena of spring which most deeply appeal to me, and because the toad, unlike the skylark and the primrose, has never had much of a boost from poets. But I am aware that many people do not like reptiles or amphibians, and I am not suggesting that in order to enjoy the spring you have to take an interest in toads. There are also the crocus, the missel-thrush, the cuckoo, the blackthorn, etc. The point is that the pleasures of spring are available to everybody, and cost nothing. Even in the most sordid street the coming of spring will register itself by some sign or other, if it is only a brighter blue between the chimney pots or the vivid green of an elder sprouting on a blitzed site. Indeed it is remarkable how Nature goes on existing unofficially, as it were, in the very heart of London. I have seen a kestrel flying over the Deptford gasworks, and I have heard a first-rate performance by a blackbird in the Euston Road. There must be some hundreds of thousands, if not millions, of birds living inside the four-mile radius, and it is rather a pleasing thought that none of them pays a halfpenny of rent.

As for spring, not even the narrow and gloomy streets round the Bank of England are quite able to exclude it. It comes seeping in everywhere, like one of those new poison gases which pass through all filters. The spring is commonly referred to as 'a miracle', and during the past five or six years this worn-out figure of speech has taken on a new lease of life. After the sort of winters we have had to endure recently, the spring does seem miraculous, because it has become gradually harder and harder to believe that it is actually going to happen. Every February since 1940 I have found myself thinking that this time winter is going to be permanent. But Persephone, like the toads, always rises from the dead at about the same moment. Suddenly, towards the end of March, the miracle happens and the decaying slum in which I live is transfigured. Down in the square the sooty privets have turned bright green, the leaves are thickening on the chestnut trees, the daffodils are out, the wallflowers are budding, the policeman's tunic looks positively a pleasant shade of blue, the fishmonger greets his customers with a smile, and even the sparrows are quite a different colour, having felt the balminess of the air and nerved themselves to take a bath, their first since last September.

Is it wicked to take a pleasure in spring and other seasonal changes? To put it more precisely, is it politically reprehensible, while we are all groaning, or at any rate ought to be groaning, under the shackles of the capitalist system, to point out that life is frequently more worth living because of a blackbird's song, a yellow elm tree in October, or some other natural phenomenon which does not cost money and does not have what the editors of left-wing newspapers call a class angle? There is no doubt that many people think so. I know by experience that a favourable reference to 'Nature' in one of my articles is liable to bring me abusive letters, and though the key-word in these letters is usually 'sentimental', two ideas seem to be mixed up in them. One is that any pleasure in the actual process of life encourages a sort of political quietism. People, so the thought runs, ought to be discontented, and it is our job to multiply our wants and not simply to increase our enjoyment of the things we have already. The other idea is that this is the age of machines and that to dislike the machine, or even to want to limit its domination, is backward-looking, reactionary and slightly ridiculous. This is often backed up by the statement that a love of Nature is a foible of urbanized people who have no notion what Nature is really like. Those who really have to deal with the soil, so it is argued, do not love the soil, and do not take the faintest interest in birds or flowers, except from a strictly utilitarian point of view. To love the country one must live in the town, merely taking an occasional week-end ramble at the warmer times of year.

This last idea is demonstrably false. Medieval literature, for instance, including the popular ballads, is full of an almost Georgian enthusiasm for Nature, and the art of agricultural peoples such as the Chinese and Japanese centres always round trees, birds, flowers, rivers, mountains. The other idea seems to me to be wrong in a subtler way. Certainly we ought to be discontented, we ought not simply to find out ways of making the best of a bad job, and yet if we kill all pleasure in the actual process of life, what sort of future are we preparing for ourselves? If a man cannot enjoy the return of spring, why should he be happy in a labour-saving Utopia? What will he do with the leisure that the machine will give him? I have always suspected that if our economic and political problems are ever really solved, life will become simpler instead of more complex, and that the sort of pleasure one gets from finding the first primrose will loom larger than the sort of pleasure one gets from eating an ice to the tune of a Wurlitzer. I think that by retaining one's childhood love of such things as trees, fishes, butterflies and – to return to my first instance – toads, one makes a peaceful and decent future a little more probable, and that by preaching the doctrine that nothing is to be admired except steel and concrete, one merely makes it a little surer that human beings will have no outlet for their surplus energy except in hatred and leader worship.

At any rate, spring is here, even in London N.1, and they can't stop you enjoying it. This is a satisfying reflection. How many a time have I stood watching the toads mating, or a pair of hares having a boxing match in the young corn, and thought of all the important persons who would stop me enjoying this if they could. But luckily they can't. So long as you are not actually ill, hungry, frightened or immured in a prison or a holiday camp, spring is still spring. The atom bombs are piling up in the factories, the police are prowling through the cities, the lies are streaming from the loudspeakers, but the earth is still going round the sun, and neither the dictators nor the bureaucrats, deeply as they disapprove of the process, are able to prevent it.

1946

Confessions of a Book Reviewer

In a cold but stuffy bed-sitting room littered with cigarette ends and half-empty cups of tea, a man in a moth-eaten dressing-gown sits at a rickety table, trying to find room for his typewriter among the piles of dusty papers that surround it. He cannot throw the papers away because the wastepaper basket is already overflowing, and besides, somewhere among the unanswered letters and unpaid bills it is possible that there is a cheque for two guineas which he is nearly certain he forgot to pay into the bank. There are also letters with addresses which ought to be entered in his address book. He has lost his address book, and the thought of looking for it, or indeed of looking for anything, afflicts him with acute suicidal impulses.

He is a man of thirty-five, but looks fifty. He is bald, has varicose veins and wears spectacles, or would wear them if his only pair were not chronically lost. If things are normal with him he will be suffering from malnutrition, but if he has recently had a lucky streak he will be suffering from a hangover. At present it is half past eleven in the morning, and according to his schedule he should have started work two hours ago; but even if he had made any serious effort to start he would have been frustrated by almost continuous ringing of the telephone bell, the yells of the baby, the rattle of an electric drill out in the street, and the heavy boots of his creditors clumping up and down the stairs. The most recent interruption was the arrival of the second post, which brought him two circulars and an income-tax demand printed in red.

Needless to say this person is a writer. He might be a poet, a novelist, or a writer of film scripts or radio features, for all literary people are very much alike, but let us say that he is a book reviewer. Half hidden among the pile of papers is a bulky parcel containing five volumes which his editor has sent with a note suggesting that they 'ought to go well together'. They arrived four days ago, but for forty-eight hours the reviewer was prevented by moral paralysis from opening the parcel. Yesterday in a resolute moment he ripped the string off it and found the five volumes to be *Palestine at the Cross Roads, Scientific Dairy Farming, A Short History of European Democracy* (this one is 680 pages and weighs four pounds), *Tribal Customs in Portuguese East Africa*, and a novel, *It's Nicer Lying Down*, probably included by mistake. His review – 800 words, say – has got to be 'in' by midday tomorrow.

Three of these books deal with subjects of which he is so ignorant that he will have to read at least fifty pages if he is to avoid making some howler which will betray him not merely to the author (who of course knows all about the habits of book reviewers), but even to the general reader. By four in the afternoon he will have taken the books out of their wrapping papers but will still be suffering from a nervous inability to open them. The prospects of having to read them, and even the smell of the paper, affects him like the prospect of eating cold ground-rice pudding flavoured with castor oil. And yet curiously enough his copy will get to the office in time. Somehow it always does get there in time. At about nine p.m.

Confessions of a Book Reviewer

his mind will grow relatively clear, and until the small hours he will sit in a room which grows colder and colder, while the cigarette smoke grows thicker and thicker, skipping expertly through one book after another and laying each down with a final comment, 'God, what tripe!' In the morning, blear-eyed, surly and unshaven, he will gaze for an hour or two at a blank sheet of paper until the menacing finger of the clock frightens him into action. Then suddenly he will snap into it. All the stale old phrases – 'a book that no one should miss', 'something memorable on every page', 'of special value are the chapters dealing with, etc. etc.' – will jump into their places like iron filings obeying the magnet, and the review will end up at exactly the right length and with just about three minutes to go. Meanwhile another wad of ill-assorted, unappetizing books will have arrived by post. So it goes on. And yet with what high hopes this downtrodden, nerve-racked creature started his career, only a few years ago.

Do I seem to exaggerate? I ask any regular reviewer – anyone who reviews, say, a minimum of a hundred books a year – whether he can deny in honesty that his habits and character are such as I have described. Every writer, in any case, is rather that kind of person, but the prolonged, indiscriminate reviewing of books is a quite exceptionally thankless, irritating and exhausting job. It not only involves praising trash – though it does involve that, as I will show in a moment – but constantly *inventing* reactions towards books about which one has no spontaneous feelings whatever. The reviewer, jaded though he may be, is professionally interested in books, and out of the thousands that appear annually, there are probably fifty or a hundred that he would enjoy writing about. If he is a top-notcher in his profession he may get hold of ten or twenty of them: more probably he gets hold of two or three. The rest of his work however conscientious he may be in praising or damning, is in essence humbug. He is pouring his immortal spirit down the drain, half a pint at a time.

The great majority of reviews give an inadequate or misleading account of the book that is dealt with. Since the war publishers have been less able than before to twist the tails of literary editors and evoke a paean of praise for every book that they produce, but on the other hand the standard of reviewing has gone down owing to lack of space and other inconveniences. Seeing the results, people sometimes suggest that the solution lies in getting book reviewing out of the hands of hacks. Books on specialized subjects ought to be dealt with by experts, and on the other hand a good deal of reviewing, especially of novels, might well be done by amateurs. Nearly every book is capable of arousing passionate feeling, if it is only a passionate dislike, in some or other reader, whose ideas about it would surely be worth more than those of a bored professional. But, unfortunately, as every editor knows, that kind of thing is very difficult to organize. In practice the editor always finds himself reverting to his team of hacks – his 'regulars', as he calls them.

None of this is remediable so long as it is taken for granted that every book deserves to be reviewed. It is almost impossible to mention books in bulk without grossly overpraising the great majority of them. Until one has some kind of professional relationship with books one does not discover how bad the majority of them are. In much more than nine cases out of ten the only objectively truthful criticism would be 'This book is worthless', while the truth about the reviewer's own reaction would probably be 'This book does not interest me in any way, and I would not write about it unless I were paid to'. But the public will not pay to read that kind of thing. Why should they? They want some kind of guide to the books they are asked to read, and they want some kind of evaluation. But as soon as values are mentioned, standards collapse. For if one says – and nearly every reviewer says this kind of thing at least once a week – that *King Lear* is a good play and *The Four Just Men* is a good thriller, what meaning is there in the word 'good'?

The best practice, it has always seemed to me, would be simply to ignore the great majority of books and to give very long reviews – 1,000 words is a bare minimum – to the few that seem to matter. Short notes of a line or two on forthcoming books can be useful, but the usual middle-length review of about 600 words is bound to be worthless even if the reviewer genuinely wants to write it. Normally he doesn't want to write it, and the week-in, week-out production of snippets soon reduces him to the crushed figure in a dressing gown whom I described at the beginning of this article. However, everyone in this world has someone else whom he can look down on, and I must say, from experience of both trades, that the book reviewer is better off than the film critic, who cannot even do his work at home, but has to attend trade shows at eleven in the morning and, with one or two notable exceptions, is expected to sell his honour for a glass of inferior sherry.

1946

Politics v. Literature:
An Examination of Gulliver's Travels

In *Gulliver's Travels* humanity is attacked, or criticized, from at least three different angles, and the implied character of Gulliver himself necessarily changes somewhat in the process. In Part I he is the typical eighteenth-century voyager, bold, practical and unromantic, his homely outlook skilfully impressed on the reader by the biographical details at the beginning, by his age (he is a man of forty, with two children, when his adventures start), and by the inventory of the things in his pockets, especially his spectacles, which make several appearances. In Part II he has in general the same character, but at moments when the story demands it he has a tendency to develop into an imbecile who is capable of boasting of 'our noble Country, the Mistress of Arts and Arms, the Scourge of France' etc., etc., and at the same time of betraying every available scandalous fact about the country which he professes to love. In Part III he is much as he was in Part I, though, as he is consorting chiefly with the courtiers and men of learning, one has the impression that he has risen in the social scale. In Part IV he conceives a horror of the human race which is not apparent, or only intermittently apparent, in the earlier books, and changes into a sort of unreligious anchorite whose one desire is to live in some desolate spot where he can devote himself to meditating on the goodness of the Houyhnhnms. However, these inconsistencies are forced upon Swift by the fact that Gulliver is there chiefly to provide a contrast. It is necessary, for instance, that he should appear sensible in Part I and at least intermittently silly in Part II, because in both books the essential manoeuvre is the same, i.e. to make the human being look ridiculous by imagining him as a creature six inches high. Whenever Gulliver is not acting as a stooge there is a sort of continuity in his character, which comes out especially in his resourcefulness and his observation of physical detail. He is much the same kind of person, with the same prose style, when he bears off the warships of Blefuscu, when he rips open the belly of the monstrous rat, and when he sails away upon the ocean in his frail coracle made from the skins of Yahoos. Moreover, it is difficult not to feel that in his shrewder moments Gulliver is simply Swift himself, and there is at least one incident in which Swift seems to be venting his private grievance against contemporary society. It will be remembered that when the Emperor of Lilliput's palace catches fire, Gulliver puts it out by urinating on it. Instead of being congratulated on his presence of mind, he finds that he has committed a capital offence by making water in the precincts of the palace, and

> I was privately assured, that the Empress, conceiving the greatest Abhorrence of what I had done, removed to the most distant Side of the Court, firmly resolved that those buildings should never be repaired for her Use; and, in the Presence of her chief Confidents, could not forbear vowing Revenge.

According to Professor G.M. Trevelyan (*England under Queen Anne*), part of the reason for Swift's failure to get preferment was that the Queen was scandalized by *A Tale of a Tub* – a pamphlet in which Swift probably felt he had done a great service to the English Crown, since it scarifies the Dissenters and still more the Catholics while leaving the Established Church alone. In any case no one would deny that *Gulliver's Travels* is a rancorous as well as a pessimistic book, and that especially in Parts I and III it often descends into political partisanship of a narrow kind. Pettiness and magnanimity, republicanism and authoritarianism, love of reason and lack of curiosity, are all mixed up in it. The hatred of the human body with which Swift is especially associated is only dominant in Part IV, but somehow this new preoccupation does not come as a surprise. One feels that all these adventures, and all these changes of mood, could have happened to the same person, and the inter-connexion between Swift's political loyalties and his ultimate despair is one of the most interesting features of the book.

Politically, Swift was one of those people who are driven into a sort of perverse Toryism by the follies of the progressive party of the moment. Part I of *Gulliver's Travels*, ostensibly a satire on human greatness, can be seen, if one looks a little deeper, to be simply an attack on England, on the dominant Whig Party, and on the war with France, which – however bad the motives of the Allies may have been – did save Europe from being tyrannized over by a single reactionary power. Swift was not a Jacobite nor strictly speaking a Tory, and his declared aim in the war was merely a moderate peace treaty and not the outright defeat of England. Nevertheless there is a tinge of quislingism in his attitude, which comes out in the ending of Part I and slightly interferes with the allegory. When Gulliver flees from Lilliput (England) to Blefuscu (France) the assumption that a human being six inches high is inherently contemptible seems to be dropped. Whereas the people of Lilliput have behaved towards Gulliver with the utmost treachery and meanness, those of Blefuscu behave generously and straightforwardly, and indeed this section of the book ends on a different note from the all-round disillusionment of the earliest chapters. Evidently Swift's animus is, in the first place, against *England*. It is 'your Natives' (i.e. Gulliver's fellow countrymen) whom the King of Brobdingnag considers to be 'the most pernicious Race of little odious Vermin that Nature ever suffered to crawl upon the surface of the Earth', and the long passage at the end, denouncing colonization and foreign conquest, is plainly aimed at England, although the contrary is elaborately stated. The Dutch, England's allies and target of one of Swift's most famous pamphlets, are also more or less wantonly attacked in Part III. There is even what sounds like a personal note in the passage in which Gulliver records his satisfaction that the various countries he has discovered cannot be made colonies of the British Crown:

> The *Houyhnhnms*, indeed, appear not to be so well prepared for War, a Science to which they are perfect Strangers, and especially against missive Weapons. However, supposing myself to be a Minister of State, I could never give my advice for invading them ... Imagine twenty thousand of them breaking into the midst of an *European* army, confounding the Ranks, overturning the Carriages, battering the Warriors' Faces into Mummy, by terrible Yerks from their hinder Hoofs ...

Considering that Swift does not waste words, that phrase, 'battering the warriors' faces into mummy', probably indicates a secret wish to see the invincible armies of the Duke of Marlborough treated in a like manner. There are similar touches elsewhere. Even the country mentioned in Part III, where 'the Bulk of the People consist, in a Manner, wholly of Discoverers, Witnesses, Informers, Accusers, Prosecutors, Evidences, Swearers, together with their several subservient and subaltern Instruments, all under the Colours, the Conduct, and Pay of Ministers of State', is called Langdon, which is within one letter of being an anagram of England. (As the early editions of the book contain misprints, it may perhaps have been intended as a complete anagram.) Swift's *physical* repulsion from humanity is certainly real enough, but one has the feeling that his debunking of human grandeur, his diatribes against lords, politicians, court favourites, etc. have mainly a local application and spring from the fact that he belonged to the unsuccessful party. He denounces injustice and oppression, but he gives no evidence of liking democracy. In spite of his enormously greater powers, his implied position is very similar to that of the innumerable silly-clever Conservatives of our own day – people like Sir Alan Herbert, Professor G. M. Young, Lord Elton, the Tory Reform Committee or the long line of Catholic apologists from W. H. Mallock onwards: people who specialize in cracking neat jokes at the expense of whatever is 'modern' and 'progressive', and whose opinions are often all the more extreme because they know that they cannot influence the actual drift of events. After all, such a pamphlet as *An Argument to prove that the Abolishing of Christianity* etc. is very like 'Timothy Shy' having a bit of clean fun with the Brains Trust, or Father Ronald Knox exposing the errors of Bertrand Russell. And the ease with which Swift has been forgiven – and forgiven sometimes, by devout believers – for the blasphemies of *A Tale of a Tub* demonstrates clearly enough the feebleness of religious sentiments as compared with political ones.

However, the reactionary cast of Swift's mind does not show itself chiefly in his political affiliations. The important thing is his attitude towards science, and, more broadly, towards intellectual curiosity. The famous Academy of Lagado, described in Part III of *Gulliver's Travels*, is no doubt a justified satire on most of the so-called scientists of Swift's own day. Significantly, the people at work in it are described as 'Projectors', that is, people not engaged in disinterested research but merely on the look-out for gadgets which will save labour and bring in money. But there is no sign – indeed, all through the book there are many signs to the contrary – that 'pure' science would have struck Swift as a worth-while activity. The more serious kind of scientist has already had a kick in the pants in Part II, when the 'Scholars' patronized by the King of Brobdingnag try to account for Gulliver's small stature:

After much Debate, they concluded unanimously that I was only *Relplum Scalcath*, which is interpreted literally, *Lusus Naturae*; a Determination exactly agreeable to the modern philosophy of *Europe*, whose Professors, disdaining the old Evasion of *occult Causes*, whereby the followers of *Aristotle* endeavoured in vain to disguise their Ignorance, have invented this wonderful Solution of all Difficulties, to the unspeakable Advancement of human Knowledge.

If this stood by itself one might assume that Swift is merely the enemy of *sham* science. In a number of places, however, he goes out of his way to proclaim the uselessness of all learning or speculation not directed towards some practical end:

The Learning of (the Brobdingnagians) is very defective, consisting only in Morality, History, Poetry, and Mathematics, wherein they must be allowed to excel. But, the last of these is wholly applied to what may be useful in Life, to the Improvement of Agriculture, and all mechanical Arts; so that among us it would be little esteemed. And as to Ideas, Entities, Abstractions, and Transcendentals, I could never drive the least Conception into their Heads.

The Houyhnhnms, Swift's ideal beings, are backward even in a mechanical sense. They are unacquainted with metals, have never heard of boats, do not, properly speaking, practise agriculture (we are told that the oats which they live upon 'grow naturally') and appear not to have invented wheels.[1] They have no alphabet, and evidently have not much curiosity about the physical world. They do not believe that any inhabited country exists beside their own, and though they understand the motions of the sun and moon, and the nature of eclipses, 'this is the utmost Progress of their *Astronomy*'. By contrast, the philosophers of the flying island of Laputa are so continuously absorbed in mathematical speculations that before speaking to them one has to attract their attention by flapping them on the ear with a bladder. They have catalogued ten thousand fixed stars, have settled the periods of ninety-three comets, and have discovered, in advance of the astronomers of Europe, that Mars has two moons — all of which information Swift evidently regards as ridiculous, useless and uninteresting. As one might expect, he believes that the scientist's place, if he has a place,

---

[1] Houyhnhnms too old to walk are described as being carried in 'sledges' or in 'a kind of vehicle, drawn like a sledge'. Presumably these had no wheels. [Author's footnote.]

is in the laboratory, and that scientific knowledge has no bearing on political matters:

> What I . . . thought altogether unaccountable, was the strong Disposition I observed in them towards News and Politics, perpetually enquiring into Public Affairs, giving their judgements in Matters of State, and passionately disputing every Inch of a Party Opinion. I have, indeed, observed the same Disposition among most of the Mathematicians I have known in *Europe*, though I could never discover the least Analogy between the two Sciences; unless those People suppose, that, because the smallest Circle hath as many Degrees as the largest, therefore the Regulation and Management of the World require no more Abilities, than the Handling and turning of a Globe.

Is there not something familiar in that phrase 'I could never discover the least analogy between the two sciences'? It has precisely the note of the popular Catholic apologists who profess to be astonished when a scientist utters an opinion on such questions as the existence of God or the immortality of the soul. The scientist, we are told, is an expert only in one restricted field: why should his opinions be of value in any other? The implication is that theology is just as much an exact science as, for instance, chemistry, and that the priest is also an expert whose conclusions on certain subjects must be accepted. Swift in effect makes the same claim for the politician, but he goes one better in that he will not allow the scientist – either the 'pure' scientist or the *ad hoc* investigator – to be a useful person in his own line. Even if he had not written Part III of *Gulliver's Travels*, one could infer from the rest of the book that, like Tolstoy and like Blake, he hates the very idea of studying the processes of Nature. The 'Reason' which he so admires in the Houyhnhnms does not primarily mean the power of drawing logical inferences from observed facts. Although he never defines it, it appears in most contexts to mean either common sense – i.e. acceptance of the obvious and contempt for quibbles and abstractions – or absence of passion and superstition. In general he assumes that we know all that we need to know already, and merely use our knowledge incorrectly. Medicine, for instance, is a useless science, because if we lived in a more natural way, there would be no diseases. Swift, however, is not a simple-lifer or an admirer of the Noble Savage. He is in favour of civilization and the arts of civilization. Not only does he see the value of good manners, good conversation, and even learning of a literary and historical kind, he also sees that agriculture, navigation and architecture need to be studied and could with advantage be improved. But his implied aim is a static, incurious civilization – the world of his own day, a little cleaner, a little saner, with no radical change and no poking into the unknowable. More than one would expect in anyone so free from accepted fallacies, he reveres the past, especially classical antiquity, and believes that modern man has degenerated sharply during the past hundred years.[1] In the island of sorcerers, where the spirits of the dead can be called up at will:

> I desired that the Senate of *Rome* might appear before me in one large Chamber, and a modern Representative in Counterview, in another. The first seemed to be an Assembly of Heroes and

---

[1] The physical decadence which Swift claims to have observed may have been a reality at that date. He attributes it to syphilis, which was a new disease in Europe and may have been more virulent than it is now. Distilled liquors, also, were a novelty in the seventeenth century and must have led at first to a great increase in drunkenness. [Author's footnote.]

Demy-Gods, the other a Knot of Pedlars, Pick-Pockets, Highwaymen, and Bullies.

Although Swift uses this section of Part III to attack the truthfulness of recorded history, his critical spirit deserts him as soon as he is dealing with Greeks and Romans. He remarks, of course, upon the corruption of imperial Rome, but he has an almost unreasoning admiration for some of the leading figures of the ancient world:

> I was struck with profound Veneration at the Sight of *Brutus*, and could easily discover the most consummate Virtue, the greatest Intrepidity and Firmness of Mind, the truest Love of his Country, and general Benevolence for mankind, in every Lineament of his Countenance . . . I had the Honour to have much Conversation with *Brutus*, and was told, that his Ancester *Junius, Socrates, Epaminondas, Cato* the younger, *Sir Thomas More*, and himself, were perpetually together: a *Sextumvirate*, to which all the Ages of the World cannot add a seventh.

It will be noticed that of these six people only one is a Christian. This is an important point. If one adds together Swift's pessimism, his reverence for the past, his incuriosity and his horror of the human body, one arrives at an attitude common among religious reactionaries – that is, people who defend an unjust order of society by claiming that this world cannot be substantially improved and only the 'next world' matters. However, Swift shows no sign of having any religious beliefs, at least in an ordinary sense of the words. He does not appear to believe seriously in life after death, and his idea of goodness is bound up with republicanism, love of liberty, courage, 'benevolence' (meaning in effect public spirit), 'reason' and other pagan qualities. This reminds one that there is another strain in Swift, not quite congruous with his disbelief in progress and his general hatred of humanity.

To begin with, he has moments when he is 'constructive' and even 'advanced'. To be occasionally inconsistent is almost a mark of vitality in Utopia books, and Swift sometimes inserts a word of praise into a passage that ought to be purely satirical. Thus, his ideas about the education of the young are fathered on to the Lilliputians, who have much the same views on this subject as the Houyhnhnms. The Lilliputians also have various social and legal institutions (for instance, there are old age pensions, and people are rewarded for keeping the law as well as punished for breaking it) which Swift would have liked to see prevailing in his own country. In the middle of this passage Swift remembers his satirical intention and adds, 'In relating these and the following Laws, I would only be understood to mean the original Institutions, and not the most scandalous Corruptions into which these people are fallen by the degenerate Nature of Man': but as Lilliput is supposed to represent England, and the laws he is speaking of have never had their parallel in England, it is clear that the impulse to make constructive suggestions has been too much for him. But Swift's greatest contribution to political thought, in the narrower sense of the words, is his attack, especially in Part III, on what would now be called totalitarianism. He has an extraordinarily clear prevision of the spy-haunted 'police-State', with its endless heresy-hunts and treason trials, all really designed to neutralize popular discontent by changing it into war hysteria. And one must remember that Swift is here inferring the whole from a quite small part, for the feeble governments of his own day did not give him illustrations ready-made. For example, there is the professor at the School of Political Projectors who 'shewed me a large Paper of Instructions for discovering Plots and Conspiracies', and who claimed that one can find people's secret thoughts by examining their excrement:

Because Men are never so serious, thoughtful, and intent, as when they are at Stool, which he found by frequent Experiment: for in such Conjectures, when he used merely as a Trial to consider what was the best Way of murdering the King, his Ordure would have a Tincture of Green; but quite different when he thought only of raising an Insurrection, or burning the Metropolis.

The professor and his theory are said to have been suggested to Swift by the – from our point of view – not particularly astonishing or disgusting fact that in a recent State Trial some letters found in somebody's privy had been put in evidence. Later in the same chapter we seem to be positively in the middle of the Russian purges:

In the Kingdom of Tribnia, by the Natives called Langdon . . . the Bulk of the People consist, in a Manner, wholly of Discoverers, Witnesses, Informers, Accusers, Prosecutors, Evidences, Swearers. . . . It is first agreed, and settled among them, what suspected Persons shall be accused of a Plot: Then, 'effectual Care is taken to secure all their Letters and Papers, and put the Owners in Chains. These papers are delivered to a Sett of Artists, very dexterous in finding out the mysterious Meanings of Words, Syllables, and Letters.. . . Where this Method fails, they have two others more effectual, which the Learned among them call *Acrostics* and *Anagrams*. *First*, they can decypher all initial Letters into political Meanings: Thus, N shall signify a Plot, B a Regiment of Horse, L a Fleet at Sea: Or, *Secondly*, by transposing the Letters of the Alphabet in any suspected Paper, they can lay open the deepest Designs of a discontented Party. So, for Example, if I should say in a Letter to a Friend, *Our Brother Tom has just got the Piles*, a skilful Decypherer would discover that the same Letters, which compose that Sentence, may be analysed in the following Words: *Resist – a Plot is brought Home – The Tour*.[1] And this is the anagrammatic Method.

Other professors at the same school invent simplified languages, write books by machinery, educate their pupils by inscribing the lessons on a wafer and causing them to swallow it, or propose to abolish individuality altogether by cutting off part of the brain of one man and grafting it on to the head of another. There is something queerly familiar in the atmosphere of these chapters, because, mixed up with much fooling, there is a perception that one of the aims of totalitarianism is not merely to make sure that people will think the right thoughts, but actually to make them *less conscious*. Then, again, Swift's account of the Leader who is usually to be found ruling over a tribe of Yahoos, and of the 'favourite' who acts first as a dirty-worker and later as a scapegoat, fits remarkably well into the pattern of our own times. But are we to infer from all this that Swift was first and foremost an enemy of tyranny and a champion of the free intelligence? No: his views, so far as one can discern them, are not markedly liberal. No doubt he hates lords, kings, bishops, generals, ladies of fashion, orders, titles and flummery generally, but he does not seem to think better of the common people than of their rulers, or to be in favour of increased social equality, or to be enthusiastic about representative institutions. The Houyhnhnms are organized upon a sort of caste system which is racial in character, the horses

[1] Tower. [Author's footnote.]

which do the menial work being of different colours from their masters and not interbreeding with them. The educational system which Swift admires in the Lilliputians takes hereditary class distinctions for granted, and the children of the poorest class do not go to school, because 'their Business being only to till and cultivate the Earth . . . therefore their Education is of little Consequence to the Public'. Nor does he seem to have been strongly in favour of freedom of speech and the press, in spite of the toleration which his own writings enjoyed. The King of Brobdingnag is astonished at the multiplicity of religious and political sects in England, and considers that those who hold 'opinions prejudicial to the public' (in the context this seems to mean simply heretical opinions), though they need not be obliged to change them, ought to be obliged to conceal them: for 'as it was Tyranny in any Government to require the first, so it was Weakness not to enforce the second'. There is a subtler indication of Swift's own attitude in the manner in which Gulliver leaves the land of the Houyhnhnms. Intermittently, at least, Swift was a kind of anarchist, and Part IV of *Gulliver's Travels* is a picture of an anarchistic society, not governed by law in the ordinary sense, but by the dictates of 'Reason', which are voluntarily accepted by everyone. The General Assembly of the Houyhnhnms 'exhorts' Gulliver's master to get rid of him, and his neighbours put pressure on him to make him comply. Two reasons are given. One is that the presence of this unusual Yahoo may unsettle the rest of the tribe, and the other is that a friendly relationship between a Houyhnhnm and a Yahoo is 'not agreeable to Reason or Nature, or a Thing ever heard of before among them'. Gulliver's master is somewhat unwilling to obey, but the 'exhortation' (a

Houyhnhnm, we are told, is never *compelled* to do anything, he is merely 'exhorted' or 'advised') cannot be disregarded. This illustrates very well the totalitarian tendency which is implicit in the anarchist or pacifist vision of society. In a society in which there is no law, and in theory no compulsion, the only arbiter of behaviour is public opinion. But public opinion, because of the tremendous urge to conformity in gregarious animals, is less tolerant than any system of law. When human beings are governed by 'thou shalt not', the individual can practise a certain amount of eccentricity: when they are supposedly governed by 'love' or 'reason', he is under continuous pressure to make him behave and think in exactly the same way as everyone else. The Houyhnhnms, we are told, were unanimous on almost all subjects. The only question they ever *discussed* was how to deal with the Yahoos. Otherwise there was no room for disagreement among them, because the truth is always either self-evident, or else it is undiscoverable and unimportant. They had apparently no word for 'opinion' in their language, and in their conversations there was no 'difference of sentiments'. They had reached, in fact, the highest stage of totalitarian organization, the stage when conformity has become so general that there is no need for a police force. Swift approves of this kind of thing because among his many gifts neither curiosity nor good nature was included. Disagreement would always seem to him sheer perversity. 'Reason', among the Houyhnhnms, he says, 'is not a Point Problematical, as with us, where men can argue with Plausibility on both Sides of a Question; but strikes you with immediate Conviction; as it must needs do, where it is not mingled, obscured, or discoloured by Passion and Interest'. In other words, we know everything already, so why should dissident opinions be tolerated? The totalitarian society of the Houyhnhnms, where there can be no freedom and no development, follows naturally from this.

We are right to think of Swift as a rebel and iconoclast, but except in certain secondary matters, such as his insistence that women should receive the same education as men, he cannot be labelled 'left'. He is a Tory anarchist, despising authority while disbelieving in liberty, and preserving the aristocratic outlook while seeing clearly that the existing aristocracy is degenerate and contemptible. When Swift utters one of his characteristic diatribes against the rich and powerful, one must probably, as I said earlier, write off something for the fact that he himself belonged to the less successful party, and was personally disappointed. The 'outs', for obvious reasons, are always more radical than the 'ins'.[1] But the most essential thing in Swift is his inability to believe that life – ordinary life on the solid earth, and not some rationalized, deodorized version of it – could be made worth living. Of course, no honest person claims that happiness is *now* a normal condition among adult

---

[1] At the end of the book, as typical specimens of human folly and viciousness, Swift names 'a Lawyer, a Pickpocket, a Colonel, a Fool, a Lord, a Gamester, a Politician, a Whore-master, a Physician, an Evidence, a Suborner, an Attorney, a Traitor, or the like'. One sees here the irresponsible violence of the powerless. The list lumps together those who break the conventional code, and those who keep it. For instance, if you automatically condemn a colonel, as such, on what grounds do you condemn a traitor? Or again, if you want to suppress pickpockets, you must have laws, which means that you must have lawyers. But the whole closing passage, in which the hatred is so authentic, and the reason given for it so inadequate, is somehow unconvincing. One has the feeling that personal animosity is at work. [Author's footnote.]

human beings; but perhaps it *could* be made normal, and it is upon this question that all serious political controversy really turns. Swift has much in common – more, I believe, than has been noticed – with Tolstoy, another disbeliever in the possiblity of happiness. In both men you have the same anarchistic outlook covering an authoritarian cast of mind; in both a similar hostility to science, the same impatience with opponents, the same inability to see the importance of any question not interesting to themselves; and in both cases a sort of horror of the actual process of life, though in Tolstoy's case it was arrived at later and in a different way. The sexual unhappiness of the two men was not of the same kind, but there was this in common, that in both of them a sincere loathing was mixed up with a morbid fascination. Tolstoy was a reformed rake who ended by preaching complete celibacy, while continuing to practise the opposite into extreme old age. Swift was presumably impotent, and had an exaggerated horror of human dung: he also thought about it incessantly, as is evident throughout his works. Such people are not likely to enjoy even the small amount of happiness that falls to most human beings, and, from obvious motives, are not likely to admit that earthly life is capable of much improvement. Their incuriosity, and hence their intolerance, spring from the same root.

Swift's disgust, rancour and pessimism would make sense against the background of a 'next world' to which this one is the prelude. As he does not appear to believe seriously in any such thing, it becomes necessary to construct a paradise supposedly existing on the surface of the earth, but something quite different from anything we know, with all that he disapproves of – lies, folly, change, enthusiasm, pleasure, love and dirt – eliminated from it. As his ideal being he chooses the horse, an animal whose excrement is not offensive. The Houyhnhnms are dreary beasts – this is so generally admitted that the point is not worth labouring. Swift's genius can make them credible, but there can have been very few readers in whom they have excited any feeling beyond dislike. And this is not from wounded vanity at seeing animals preferred to men; for, of the two, the Houyhnhnms are much liker to human beings than are the Yahoos, and Gulliver's horror of the Yahoos, together with his recognition that they are the same kind of creature as himself, contains a logical absurdity. This horror comes upon him at his very first sight of them. 'I never beheld' he says, 'in all my Travels, so disagreeable an Animal, nor one against which I naturally conceived so strong an Antipathy.' But in comparison with what are the Yahoos disgusting? Not with the Houyhnhnms, because at this time Gulliver has not seen a Houyhnhnm. It can only be in comparison with himself, i.e. with a human being. Later, however, we are told that the Yahoos *are* human beings, and human society becomes insupportable to Gulliver because all men are Yahoos. In that case why did he not conceive his disgust of humanity earlier? In effect we are told that the Yahoos are fantastically different from men, and yet are the same. Swift has overreached himself in his fury, and is shouting at his fellow creatures: 'You are filthier than you are!' However, it is impossible to feel much sympathy with the Yahoos, and it is not because they oppress the Yahoos that the Houyhnhnms are unattractive. They are unattractive because the 'Reason' by which they are governed is really a desire for death. They are exempt from love, friendship, curiosity, fear, sorrow and – except in their feelings towards the Yahoos, who occupy rather the same place in their community as the Jews in Nazi Germany – anger and hatred. 'They have no Fondness for their Colts or Foles, but the Care they take, in educating them, proceeds entirely from the Dictates of *Reason*.' They lay store by 'Friendship' and 'Benevolence', but 'these are not confined to particular Objects, but universal to the whole Race'. They also value conversation, but in their conversations there are no differences of opinion, and 'nothing passed but what was useful, expressed in the fewest and most significant Words'. They practise strict birth control, each couple producing two offspring and thereafter abstaining from sexual intercourse. Their marriages are arranged for them by their elders, on eugenic principles, and their language contains no word for 'love', in the sexual sense. When somebody dies they carry on exactly as before, without feeling any grief. It will be seen that their aim is to be as like a corpse as is possible while retaining physical life. One or two of their characteristics, it is true, do not seem to be strictly 'reasonable' in their own usage of the word. Thus, they place a great value not only on physical hardihood but on athleticism, and they are devoted to poetry. But these exceptions may be less arbitrary than they seem. Swift probably emphasizes the physical strength of the Houyhnhnms in order to make clear that they could never be conquered by the hated human race, while a taste for poetry may figure among their qualities because poetry appeared to Swift as the antithesis of science, from his point of view the most useless of all pursuits. In Part III he names 'Imagination, Fancy, and Invention' as desirable faculties in which the Laputan mathematicians (in spite of their love of music) were wholly lacking. One must remember that although Swift was an admirable writer of comic verse, the kind of poetry he thought valuable would probably be didactic poetry. The poetry of the Houyhnhnms, he says, must be allowed to excel (that of) all other Mortals; wherein the Justness of their Similes, and the Minuteness, as well as exactness, of their Descriptions, are, indeed, inimitable. Their Verses abound very much in both of these; and usually contain either some exalted Notions of Friendship and Benevolence, or the Praises of those who were Victors in Races, and other bodily Exercises.

Alas, not even the genius of Swift was equal to producing a specimen by which we could judge the poetry of the Houyhnhnms. But it sounds as though it were chilly stuff (in heroic couplets, presumably), and not seriously in conflict with the principles of 'Reason'.

Happiness is notoriously difficult to describe, and pictures of a just and well-ordered society are seldom either attractive or convincing. Most creators of 'favourable' Utopias, however, are concerned to show what life could be like if it were lived more fully. Swift advocates a simple refusal of life, justifying this by the claim that 'Reason' consists in thwarting your instincts. The Houyhnhnms, creatures without a history, continue for generation after generation to live prudently, maintaining their population at exactly the same level, avoiding all passion, suffering from no diseases, meeting death indifferently, training up their young in the same principles – and all for what? In order that the same process may continue indefinitely. The notions that life here and now is worth living, or that it could be made worth living, or that it must be sacrificed for some future good, are all absent. The dreary world of the Houyhnhnms was about as good a Utopia as Swift could construct, granting that he neither believed in a 'next world' nor could get any pleasure out of certain normal activities. But it is not really set up as something desirable in itself, but as the justification for another attack on humanity. The aim, as usual, is to humiliate Man by reminding him that he is weak and ridiculous, and above all that he stinks; and the ultimate motive, probably, is a kind of envy, the envy of the ghost for the living, of the man who knows he cannot be happy for the others who – so he fears – may be a little happier than himself. The political expression of such an outlook must be either reactionary or nihilistic, because the person who holds it will want to prevent society from developing in some direction in which his pessimism may be cheated. One can do this either by blowing everything to pieces, or by averting social change. Swift ultimately blew everything to pieces in the only way that was feasible before the atomic bomb – that is, he went mad – but, as I have tried to show, his political aims were on the whole reactionary ones.

From what I have written it may have seemed that I am *against* Swift, and that my object is to refute him and even to belittle him. In a political and moral sense I am against him so far as I understand him. Yet curiously enough he is one of the writers I admire with least reserve, and *Gulliver's Travels*, in particular, is a book which it seems impossible for me to grow tired of. I read it first when I was eight – one day short of eight, to be exact, for I stole and furtively read the copy which was to be given me next day on my eighth birthday – and I have certainly not read it less than half a dozen times since. Its fascination seems inexhaustible. If I had to make a list of six books which were to be preserved when all others were destroyed, I would certainly put *Gulliver's Travels* among them. This raises the question: what is the relationship between agreement with a writer's opinions, and enjoyment of his work?

If one is capable of intellectual detachment, one can *perceive* merit in a writer whom one deeply disagrees with, but *enjoyment* is a different matter. Supposing that there is such a thing as good or bad art, then the goodness or badness must reside in the work of art itself – not independently of the observer, indeed, but independently of the mood of the observer. In one sense, therefore, it cannot be true that a poem is good on Monday and bad on Tuesday. But if one judges the poem by the appreciation it arouses, then it can certainly be true, because appreciation, or enjoyment, is a subjective condition which cannot be commanded. For a great deal of his waking life, even the most cultivated person has no aesthetic feelings whatever, and the power to have aesthetic feelings is very easily destroyed. When you are frightened, or hungry, or are suffering from toothache or seasickness, *King Lear* is no better from your point of view than *Peter Pan*. You may know in an intellectual sense that it is better, but that is simply a fact which you remember; you will not *feel* the merit of *King Lear* until you are normal again. And aesthetic judgement can be upset just as disastrously – more disastrously, because the cause is less readily recognized – by political or moral disagreement. If a book angers, wounds or alarms you, then you will not enjoy it, whatever its merits may be. If it seems to you a really pernicious book, likely to influence other people in some undesirable way, then you will probably construct an aesthetic theory to show that it *has* no merits. Current literary criticism consists quite largely of this kind of dodging to and fro between two sets of standards. And yet the opposite process can also happen: enjoyment can overwhelm disapproval, even though one clearly recognizes that one is enjoying something inimical. Swift, whose world-view is so peculiarly unacceptable, but who is nevertheless an extremely popular writer, is a good instance of this. Why is it that we don't mind being called Yahoos, although firmly convinced that we are *not* Yahoos?

It is not enough to make the usual answer that of course Swift was wrong, in fact he was insane, but he was 'a good writer'. It is true that the literary quality of a book is to some small extent separable from its subject-matter. Some people have a native gift for using words, as some people have a naturally 'good eye' at games. It is largely a question of timing and of instinctively knowing how much emphasis to use. As an example near at hand, look back at the passage I quoted earlier, starting 'In the Kingdom of Tribnia, by the Natives called Langdon'. It derives much of its force from the final sentence: 'And this is the anagrammatic Method.' Strictly speaking this sentence is unnecessary, for we have already seen the anagram deciphered, but the mock-solemn repetition, in which one seems to hear Swift's own voice uttering the words, drives home the idiocy of the activities described, like the final tap to a nail. But not all the power and simplicity of Swift's prose, nor the imaginative effort that has been able to make not one but a whole series of impossible words more credible than the majority of history books – none of this would enable us to enjoy Swift if his world-view were truly wounding or shocking. Millions of people, in many countries, must have enjoyed *Gulliver's Travels* while more or less seeing its anti-human implications: and even the child who accepts Parts I and II as a simple story gets a sense of absurdity from thinking of human beings six inches high. The explanation must be that Swift's world-view is felt to be *not* altogether false – or it would probably be more accurate to say, not false all the time. Swift is a diseased writer. He remains permanently in a depressed mood which in most people is only intermittent, rather as though someone suffering from jaundice or the after-effects of influenza should have the energy to write books. But we all know that mood, and something in us responds to the expression of it. Take, for instance, one of his most characteristic works, 'The Lady's Dressing Room': one might add the kindred poem, 'Upon a Beautiful Young Nymph Going to Bed'. Which is truer, the viewpoint expressed in these poems, or the viewpoint implied in Blake's phrase, 'The naked female human form divine'? No doubt Blake is nearer the truth, and yet who can fail to feel a sort of pleasure in seeing that fraud, feminine delicacy, exploded for once? Swift falsifies his picture of the whole world by refusing to see anything in human life except dirt, folly and wickedness, but the part which he abstracts from the whole does exist, and it is something which we all know about while shrinking from mentioning it. Part of our minds — in any normal person it is the dominant part — believes that man is a noble animal and life is worth living: but there is also a sort of inner self which at least intermittently stands aghast at the horror of existence. In the queerest way, pleasure and disgust are linked together. The human body is beautiful: it is also repulsive and ridiculous, a fact which can be verified at any swimming pool. The sexual organs are objects of desire and also of loathing, so much so that in many languages, if not in all languages, their names are used as words of abuse. Meat is delicious, but a butcher's shop makes one feel sick: and indeed all our food springs ultimately from dung and dead bodies, the two things which of all others seem to us the most horrible. A child, when it is past the infantile stage but still looking at the world with fresh eyes, is moved by horror almost as often as by wonder — horror of snot and spittle, of the dogs' excrement on the pavement, the dying toad full of maggots, the sweaty smell of grown-ups, the hideousness of old men, with their bald heads and bulbous noses. In his endless harping on disease, dirt and deformity, Swift is not actually inventing anything, he is merely leaving something out. Human behaviour, too, especially in politics, is as he describes it, although it contains other more important factors which he refuses to admit. So far as we can see, both horror and pain are necessary to the continuance of life on this planet, and it is therefore open to pessimists like Swift to say: 'If horror and pain must always be with us, how can life be significantly improved?' His attitude is in effect the Christian attitude, minus the bribe of a 'next world' – which, however, probably has less hold upon the minds of believers than the conviction that this world is a vale of tears and the grave is a place of rest. It is, I am certain, a wrong attitude, and one which could have harmful effects upon behaviour; but something in us responds to it, as it responds to the gloomy words of the burial service and the sweetish smell of corpses in a country church.

It is often argued, at least by people who admit the importance of subject-matter, that a book cannot be 'good' if it expresses a palpably false view of life. We are told that in our own age, for instance, any book that has genuine literary merit will also be more or less 'progressive' in tendency. This ignores the fact that throughout history a similar struggle between the progress and reaction has been raging, and that the best books of any one age have always been written from several different viewpoints, some of them palpably more false than others. In so far as the writer is a propagandist, the most one can ask of him is that he shall genuinely believe in what he is saying, and that it shall not be something blazingly silly. Today, for example, one can imagine a good book being written by a

Catholic, a Communist, a Fascist, a Pacifist, an Anarchist, perhaps by an old-style Liberal or an ordinary Conservative: one cannot imagine a good book being written by a spiritualist, a Buchmanite or a member of the Ku Klux Klan. The views that a writer holds must be compatible with sanity, in the medical sense, and with the power of continuous thought: beyond that what we ask of him is talent, which is probably another name for conviction. Swift did not possess ordinary wisdom, but he did possess a terrible intensity of vision, capable of picking out a single hidden truth and then magnifying it and distorting it. The durability of *Gulliver's Travels* goes to show that if the force of belief is behind it, a world-view which only just passes the test of sanity is sufficient to produce a great work of art.

1946

How the Poor Die

In the year 1929 I spent several weeks in the Hôpital X, in the fifteenth *arrondissement* of Paris. The clerks put me through the usual third-degree at the reception desk, and indeed I was kept answering questions for some twenty minutes before they would let me in. If you have ever had to fill up forms in a Latin country you will know the kind of questions I mean. For some days past I have been unequal to translating Réaumur into Fahrenheit, but I know that my temperature was round about 103, and by the end of the interview I had some difficulty in standing on my feet. At my back a resigned little knot of patients, carrying bundles done up in coloured handkerchiefs, waiting their turn to be questioned.

After the questioning came the bath – a compulsory routine for all newcomers, apparently, just as in prison or the workhouse. My clothes were taken away from me, and after I had sat shivering for some minutes in five inches of warm water I was given a linen nightshirt and a short blue flannel dressing-gown – no slippers, they had none big enough for me, they said – and led out into the open air. This was a night in February and I was suffering from pneumonia. The ward we were going to was 200 yards away and it seemed that to get to it you had to cross the hospital grounds. Someone stumbled in front of me with a lantern. The gravel path was frosty underfoot, and the wind whipped the nightshirt round my bare calves. When we got into the ward I was aware of a strange feeling of familiarity whose origin I did not succeed in pinning down till later in the night. It was a long, rather low, ill-lit room, full of murmuring voices and with three rows of beds surprisingly close together. There was a foul smell, faecal and yet sweetish. As I lay down I saw on a bed nearly opposite me a small, round-shouldered, sandy-haired man sitting half naked while a doctor and a student performed some strange operation on him. First the doctor produced from his black bag a dozen small glasses like wine glasses, then the student burned a match inside each glass to exhaust the air, then the glass was popped on to the man's back or chest and the vacuum drew up a huge yellow blister. Only after some moments did I realize what they were doing to him. It was something called cupping, a treatment which you can read about in old medical text-books but which till then I had vaguely thought of as one of those things they do to horses.

The cold air outside had probably lowered my temperature, and I watched this barbarous remedy with detachment and even a certain amount of amusement. The next moment, however, the doctor and the student came across to my bed, hoisted me upright and without a word began applying the same set of glasses, which had not been sterilized in any way. A few feeble protests that I uttered got no more response than if I had been an animal. I was very much impressed by the impersonal way in which the two men started on me. I had never been in the public ward of a hospital before, and it was my first experience of doctors who handle you without speaking to you, or, in a human sense, taking any notice of you. They only put on six glasses in my case, but after doing so they scarified the blisters and applied the glasses again. Each glass now drew out about a dessert-spoonful of dark-coloured blood. As I lay down again, humiliated, disgusted and frightened by the thing that had been done to me, I reflected that now at least they would leave me alone. But no, not a bit of it. There was another treatment coming, the mustard poultice, seemingly a matter of routine like the hot bath. Two slatternly nurses had already got the poultice ready, and they lashed it round my chest as tight as a strait jacket while some men who were wandering about the ward in shirt and trousers began to collect round my bed with half-sympathetic grins. I learned later that watching a patient have a mustard poultice was a favourite pastime in the ward. These things are normally applied for a quarter of an hour and certainly they are funny enough if you don't happen to be the person inside. For the first five minutes the pain is severe, but you believe you can bear it. During the second five minutes this belief evaporates, but the poultice is buckled at the back and you can't get it off. This is the period the onlookers most enjoy. During the last five minutes, I noted a sort of numbness supervenes. After the poultice had been removed a waterproof pillow packed with ice was thrust beneath my head and I was left alone. I did not sleep and to the best of my knowledge this was the only night of my life – I mean the only night spent in bed – in which I have not slept at all, not even a minute.

During my first hour in the Hôpital X, I had had a whole series of different and contradictory treatments, but this was misleading, for in general you got very little treatment at all, either good or bad, unless you were ill in some interesting and instructive way. At five in the morning the nurses came round, woke the patients and took their temperatures, but did not wash them. If you were well enough you washed yourself, otherwise you depended on the kindness of some walking patient. It was generally patients, too, who carried the bedbottles and the grim bed-pan, nicknamed *la casserole*. At eight breakfast arrived, called army fashion *la soupe*. It was soup, too, a thin vegetable soup with slimy hunks of bread floating about in it. Later in the day the tall, solemn, black-bearded doctor made his rounds, with an *interne* and a troop of students following at his heels, but there were about sixty of us in the ward and it was evident that he had other wards to attend to as well. There were many beds past which he walked day after day, sometimes followed by imploring cries. On the other hand if you had some disease with which the students wanted to familiarize themselves you got plenty of attention of a kind. I myself, with an exceptionally fine specimen of a bronchial rattle, sometimes had as many as a dozen students queueing up to listen to my chest. It was a queer feeling – queer, I mean, because of their intense interest in learning their job, together with a seeming lack of any perception that the patients were human beings. It is strange to relate, but sometimes as some young student stepped forward to take his turn at manipulating you he would be actually tremulous with excitement, like a boy who has at last got his hands on some expensive piece of machinery. And then ear after ear – ears of young men, of girls, of Negroes – pressed against your back, relays of fingers solemnly but clumsily tapping, and not from any one of them did you get a word of conversation or a look direct in your face. As a non-paying patient, in the uniform nightshirt, you were primarily *a specimen*, a thing I did not resent but could never quite get used to.

After some days I grew well enough to sit up and study the surrounding patients. The stuffy room, with its narrow beds so close together that you could easily touch your neighbour's hand, had every sort of disease in it except, I suppose, acutely infectious cases. My right-hand neighbour was a little red-haired cobbler with one leg shorter than the other, who used to announce the death of any other patient (this happened a number of times, and my neighbour was always the first to hear of it) by whistling to me, exclaiming '*Numéro 43!*' (or whatever it was) and flinging his arms above his head. This man had not much wrong with him, but in most of the other beds within my angle of vision some squalid tragedy or some plain horror was being enacted. In the bed that was foot to foot with mine there lay, until he died (I didn't see him die – they moved him to another bed), a little weazened man who was suffering from I do not know what disease, but something that made his whole body so intensely sensitive that any movement from side to side, sometimes even the weight of the bed-clothes, would make him shout out with pain. His worst suffering was when he urinated, which he did with the greatest difficulty. A nurse would bring him the bed-bottle and then for a long time stand beside his bed, whistling, as grooms are said to do with horses, until at last with an agonized shriek of '*Je pisse!*' he would get started. In the bed next to him the sandy-haired man whom I had seen being cupped used to cough up blood-streaked mucus at all hours. My left-hand neighbour was a tall, flaccid-looking young man who used periodically to have a tube inserted into his back and astonishing quantities of frothy liquid drawn off from some part of his body. In the bed beyond that a veteran of the war of 1870 was dying, a handsome old man with a white imperial, round whose bed, at all hours when visiting was allowed, four elderly female relatives dressed all in black sat exactly like crows, obviously scheming for some pitiful legacy. In the bed opposite me in the further row was an old bald-headed man with drooping moustaches and greatly swollen face and body, who was suffering from some disease that made him urinate almost incessantly. A huge glass receptable stood always beside his bed. One day his wife and daughter came to visit him. At the sight of them the old man's bloated face lit up with a smile of surprising sweetness, and as his daughter, a pretty girl of about twenty, approached the bed I saw that his hand was slowly working its way from under the bed-clothes. I seemed to see in advance the gesture that was coming – the girl kneeling beside the bed, the old man's hand laid on her head in his dying blessing. But no, he merely handed her the bed-bottle, which she promptly took from him and emptied into the receptacle.

About a dozen beds away from me was *numéro 57* – I think that was his number – a cirrhosis of the liver case. Everyone in the ward knew him by sight because he was sometimes the subject of a medical lecture. On two afternoons a week the tall, grave doctor would lecture in the ward to a party of students, and on more than one occasion old *numéro 57* was wheeled on a sort of trolley into the middle of the ward, where the doctor would roll back his nightshirt, dilate with his fingers a huge flabby protuberance on the man's belly – the diseased liver, I suppose – and explain solemnly that this was a disease attributable to alcoholism, commoner in the wine-drinking countries. As usual he neither spoke to his patient nor gave him a smile, a nod or any kind of recognition. While he talked, very grave and upright, he would hold the wasted body beneath his two hands, sometimes giving it a gentle roll to and fro, in just the attitude of a woman handling a rolling-pin. Not that *numéro 57* minded this kind of thing. Obviously he was an old hospital inmate, a regular exhibit at lectures, his liver long since marked down for a bottle in some pathological museum. Utterly uninterested in what was said about him, he would lie with his colourless eyes gazing at nothing, while the doctor showed him off like a piece of antique china. He was a man of about sixty, astonishingly shrunken. His face, pale as vellum, had shrunken away till it seemed no bigger than a doll's.

One morning my cobbler neighbour woke me by plucking at my pillow before the nurses arrived. '*Numéro 57!*' – he flung his arms above his head. There was a light in the ward, enough to see by. I could see old *numéro 57* lying crumpled up on his side, his face sticking out over the side of the bed, and towards me. He had died some time during the night, nobody knew when. When the nurses came they received the news of his death indifferently and went about their work. After a long time, an hour or more, two other nurses marched in abreast like soldiers, with a great clumping of sabots, and knotted the corpse up in the sheets, but it was not removed till some time later. Meanwhile, in the better light, I had time for a good look at *numéro 57*. Indeed I lay on my side to look at him. Curiously enough he was the first dead European I had seen. I had seen dead men before, but always Asiatics and usually people who had died violent deaths. *Numéro 57*'s eyes were still open, his mouth also open, his small face contorted into an expression of agony. What most impressed me however was the whiteness of his face. It had been pale before, but now it was little darker than the sheets. As I gazed at the tiny, screwed-up face it struck me that this disgusting piece of refuse, waiting to be carted away and dumped on a slab in the dissecting room, was an example of 'natural' death, one of the things you pray for in the Litany. There you are, then, I thought, that's what is waiting for you, twenty, thirty, forty years hence: that is how the lucky ones die, the ones who live to be old. One wants to live, of course, indeed one only stays alive by virtue of the fear of death, but I think now, as I thought then, that it's better to die violently and not too old. People talk about the horrors of war, but what weapon has a man invented that even approaches in cruelty some of the commoner diseases? 'Natural' death, almost by definition, means something slow, smelly and painful. Even at that, it makes a difference if you can achieve it in your own home and not in a public institution. This poor old wretch who had just flickered out like a candle-end was not even important enough to have anyone watching by his deathbed. He was merely a number, then a 'subject' for the students' scalpels. And the sordid publicity of dying in such a place! In the Hôpital X the beds were very close together and there were no screens. Fancy, for instance, dying like the little man whose bed was for a while foot to foot with mine, the one who cried out when the bed-clothes touched him! I dare say *Je pisse!* were his last recorded words. Perhaps the dying don't bother about such things – that at least would be the standard answer: nevertheless dying people are often more or less normal in their minds till within a day or so of the end.

In the public wards of a hospital you see horrors that you don't seem to meet with among people who manage to die in their own homes, as though certain diseases only attacked people at the lower income levels. But it is a fact that you would not in any English hospitals see some of the things I saw in the Hôpital X. This business of people just dying like animals, for instance, with nobody standing by, nobody interested, the death not even noticed till the morning – this happened more than once. You certainly would not see that in England, and still less would you see a corpse left exposed to the view of the other patients. I remember that once in a cottage hospital in England a man died while we were at tea, and though there were only six of us in the ward the nurses managed things so adroitly that the man was dead and his body removed without our even hearing about it till tea was over. A thing we perhaps underrate in England is the advantage we enjoy in having large numbers of well-trained and rigidly-disciplined nurses. No doubt English nurses are dumb enough, they may tell fortunes with tea-leaves, wear Union Jack badges and keep photographs of the Queen on their mantelpieces, but at least they don't let you lie unwashed and constipated on an unmade bed, out of sheer laziness. The nurses at the Hôpital X still had a tinge of Mrs Gamp about them, and later, in the military hospitals of Republican Spain, I was to see nurses almost too ignorant to take a temperature. You wouldn't, either, see in England such dirt as existed in the Hôpital X. Later on, when I was well enough to wash myself in the bathroom, I found that there was kept there a huge packing-case into which the scraps of food and dirty dressings from the ward were flung, and the wainscottings were infested by crickets.

When I had got back my clothes and grown strong on my legs I fled from the Hôpital X, before my time was up and without waiting for a medical discharge. It was not the only hospital I have fled from, but its gloom and bareness, its sickly smell and, above all, something in its mental atmosphere stand out in my memory as exceptional. I had been taken there because it was the hospital belonging to my *arrondissement*, and I did not learn till after I was in it that it bore a bad reputation.

A year or two later the celebrated swindler, Madame Hanaud, who was ill while on remand, was taken to the Hôpital X, and after a few days of it she managed to elude her guards, took a taxi and drove back to the prison, explaining that she was more comfortable there. I have no doubt that the Hôpital X was quite untypical of French hospitals even at that date. But the patients, nearly all of them working men, were surprisingly resigned. Some of them seemed to find the conditions almost comfortable, for at least two were destitute malingerers who found this a good way of getting through the winter. The nurses connived because the malingerers made themselves useful by doing odd jobs. But the attitude of the majority was: of course this is a lousy place, but what else do you expect? It did not seem strange to them that you should be woken at five and then wait three hours before starting the day on watery soup, or that people should die with no one at their bedside, or even that your chance of getting medical attention should depend on catching the doctor's eye as he went past. According to their traditions that was what hospitals were like. If you are seriously ill, and if you are too poor to be treated in your own home, then you must go into hospital, and once there you must put up with harshness and discomfort, just as you would in the army. But on top of this I was interested to find a lingering belief in the old stories that have now almost faded from memory in England – stories, for instance, about doctors cutting you open out of sheer curiosity or thinking it funny to start operating before you were properly 'under'. There were dark tales about a little operating room said to be situated just beyond the bathroom. Dreadful screams were said to issue from this room. I saw nothing to confirm these stories and no doubt they were all nonense, though I did see two students kill a sixteen-year-old boy, or nearly kill him (he appeared to be dying when I left the hospital, but he may have recovered later) by mischievous experiment which they probably could not have tried on a paying patient. Well within living memory it used to be believed in London that in some of the big hospitals patients were killed off to get dissection subjects. I didn't hear this tale repeated at the Hôpital X, but I should think some of the men there would have found it credible. For it was a hospital in which not the methods, perhaps, but something of the atmosphere of the nineteenth century had managed to survive, and therein lay its peculiar interest.

During the past fifty years or so there has been a great change in the relationship between doctor and patient. If you look at almost any literature before the later part of the nineteenth century, you find that a hospital is popularly regarded as much the same thing as a prison, and an old-fashioned, dungeon-like prison at that. A hospital is a place of filth, torture and death, a sort of antechamber to the tomb. No one who was not more or less destitute would have thought of going into such a place for treatment. And especially in the early part of the last century, when medical science had grown bolder than before without being any more successful, the whole business of doctoring was looked on with horror and dread by ordinary people. Surgery, in particular, was believed to be no more than a peculiarly gruesome form of sadism, and dissection, possible only with the aid of body-snatchers, was even confused with necromancy. From the nineteenth century you could collect a large horror-literature connected with doctors and hospitals. Think of poor old George III, in his dotage, shrieking for mercy as he sees his surgeons approaching to 'bleed him till he faints'! Think of the conversations of

Bob Sawyer and Benjamin Allen, which no doubt are hardly parodies, or the field hospitals in *La Débâcle* and *War and Peace*, or that shocking description of an amputation in Melville's *Whitejacket*! Even the names given to doctors in nineteenth-century English fiction, Slasher, Carver, Sawyer, Fillgrave and so on, and the generic nickname 'sawbones', are about as grim as they are comic. The anti-surgery tradition is perhaps best expressed in Tennyson's poem, 'The Children's Hospital', which is essentially a pre-chloroform document though it seems to have been written as late as 1880. Moreover, the outlook which Tennyson records in this poem had a lot to be said for it. When you consider what an operation without anaesthetics must have been like, what it notoriously *was* like, it is difficult not to suspect the motives of people who would undertake such things. For these bloody horrors which the students so eagerly looked forward to ('A magnificent sight if Slasher does it!') were admittedly more or less useless: the patient who did not die of shock usually died of gangrene, a result which was taken for granted. Even now doctors can be found whose motives are questionable. Anyone who has had much illness, or who has listened to medical students talking, will know what I mean. But anaesthetics were a turning-point, and disinfectants were another. Nowhere in the world, probably, would you now see the kind of scene described by Axel Munthe in *The Story of San Michele*, when the sinister surgeon in top-hat and frock-coat, his starched shirtfront spattered with blood and pus, carves up patient after patient with the same knife and flings the severed limbs into a pile beside the table. Moreover, national health insurance has partly done away with the idea that a working-class patient is a pauper who deserves little consideration. Well into this century it was usual for 'free' patients at the big hospitals to have their teeth extracted with no anaesthetic. They don't pay, so why should they have anaesthetic – that was the attitude. That too has changed.

And yet every institution will always bear upon it some lingering memory of its past. A barrack-room is still haunted by the ghost of Kipling, and it is difficult to enter a workhouse without being reminded of *Oliver Twist*. Hospitals began as a kind of casual ward for lepers and the like to die in, and they continued as places where medical students learned their art on the bodies of the poor. You can still catch a faint suggestion of their history in their characteristically gloomy architecture. I would be far from complaining about the treatment I have received in any English hospital, but I do know that it is a sound instinct that warns people to keep out of hospitals if possible, and especially out of the public wards. Whatever the legal position may be, it is unquestionable that you have far less control over your own treatment, far less certainty that frivolous experiments will not be tried on you, when it is a case of 'accept the discipline or get out'. And it is a great thing to die in your own bed, though it is better still to die in your boots. However great the kindness and the efficiency, in every hospital death there will be some cruel, squalid detail, something perhaps too small to be told but leaving terribly painful memories behind, arising out of the haste, the crowding, the impersonality of a place where every day people are dying among strangers.

The dread of hospitals probably still survives among the very poor and in all of us it has only recently disappeared. It is a dark patch not far beneath the surface of our minds. I have said earlier that, when I entered the ward at the Hôpital X, I was conscious of a strange feeling of familiarity. What the scene reminded me of, of course, was the reeking, pain-filled hospitals of the nineteenth century, which I had never seen but of which I had a traditional knowledge. And something, perhaps the black-clad doctor with his frowsy black bag, or perhaps only the sickly smell, played the queer trick of unearthing from my memory that poem of Tennyson's, 'The Children's Hospital', which I had not thought of for twenty years. It happened that as a child I had had it read aloud to me by a sick-nurse whose own working life might have stretched back to the time when Tennyson wrote the poem. The horrors and sufferings of the old-style hospitals were a vivid memory to her. We had shuddered over the poem together, and then seemingly I had forgotten it. Even its name would probably have recalled nothing to me. But the first glimpse of the ill-lit, murmurous room, with the beds so close together, suddenly roused the train of thought to which it belonged, and in the night that followed I found myself remembering the whole story and atmosphere of the poem, with many of its lines complete.

1946

Such, Such Were the Joys

I

Soon after I arrived at St Cyprian's (not immediately, but after a week or two, just when I seemed to be settling into the routine of school life) I began wetting my bed. I was now aged eight, so that this was a reversion to a habit which I must have grown out of at least four years earlier.

Nowadays, I believe, bed-wetting in such circumstances is taken for granted. It is a normal reaction in children who have been removed from their homes to a strange place. In those days, however, it was looked on as a disgusting crime which the child committed on purpose and for which the proper cure was a beating. For my part I did not need to be told it was a crime. Night after night I prayed, with a fervour never previously attained in my prayers. 'Please God, do not let me wet my bed! Oh, please God, do not let me wet my bed!', but it made remarkably little difference. Some nights the thing happened, others not. There was no volition about it, no consciousness. You did not properly speaking *do* the deed: you merely woke up in the morning and found that the sheets were wringing wet.

After the second or third offence I was warned that I should be beaten next time, but I received the warning in a curiously roundabout way. One afternoon, as we were filing out from tea, Mrs W –, the Headmaster's wife, was sitting at the head of one of the tables, chatting with a lady of whom I knew nothing, except that she was on an afternoon's visit to the school. She was an intimidating, masculine-looking person wearing a riding-habit, or something that I took to be a riding-habit. I was just leaving the room when Mrs W – called me back, as though to introduce me to the visitor.

Mrs W – was nicknamed Flip, and I shall call her by that name, for I seldom think of her by any other. (Officially, however, she was addressed as Mum, probably a corruption of the 'Ma'am' used by public schoolboys to their housemasters' wives.) She was a stocky square-built woman with hard red cheeks, a flat top to her head, prominent brows and deep-set, suspicious eyes. Although a great deal of the time she was full of false heartiness, jollying one along with mannish slang ('*Buck* up, old chap!' and so forth), and even using one's Christian name, her eyes never lost their anxious, accusing look. It was very difficult to look her in the face without feeling guilty, even at moments when one was not guilty of anything in particular.

'Here is a little boy,' said Flip, indicating me to the strange lady, 'who wets his bed every night. Do you know what I am going to do if you wet your bed again?' she added, turning to me. 'I am going to get the Sixth Form to beat you.'

The strange lady put on an air of being inexpressibly shocked, and exclaimed 'I-should-*think*-so!' And here there occurred one of those wild, almost lunatic misunderstandings which are part of the daily experience of childhood. The Sixth Form were a group of older boys who were selected as having 'character' and were empowered to beat smaller boys. I had not yet learned of their existence, and I mis-heard the phrase 'the Sixth Form' as 'Mrs Form'. I took it as referring to the strange lady – I thought, that is, that her name was Mrs Form. It was an improbable name, but a child has no judgement in such matters. I imagined, therefore, that it was *she* who was to be deputed to beat me. It did not strike me as strange that this job should be turned over to a casual visitor in no way connected with the school. I merely assumed that 'Mrs Form' was a stern disciplinarian who enjoyed beating people (somehow her appearance seemed to bear this out) and I had an immediate terrifying vision of her arriving for the occasion in full riding kit and armed with a hunting-whip. To this day I can feel myself almost swooning with shame as I stood, a very small, round-faced boy in short corduroy knickers, before the two women. I could not speak. I felt that I should die if 'Mrs Form' were to beat me. But my dominant feeling was not fear or even resentment: it was simply shame because one more person, and that a woman, had been told of my disgusting offence.

A little later, I forget how, I learned that it was not after all 'Mrs Form' who would do the beating. I cannot remember whether it was that very night that I wetted my bed again, but at any rate I did wet it again quite soon. Oh, the despair, the feeling of cruel injustice, after all my prayers and resolutions, at once again waking between the clammy sheets! There was no chance of hiding what I had done. The grim statuesque matron, Margaret by name, arrived in the dormitory specially to inspect my bed. She pulled back the clothes, then drew herself up, and the dreaded words seemed to come rolling out of her like a peal of thunder:

'REPORT YOURSELF to the Headmaster after breakfast!'

I put REPORT YOURSELF in capitals because that was how it appeared in my mind. I do not know how many times I heard that phrase during my early years at St Cyprian's. It was only very rarely that it did not mean a beating. The words always had a portentous sound in my ears, like muffled drums or the words of the death sentence.

When I arrived to report myself, Flip was doing something or other at the long shiny table in the ante-room to the study. Her uneasy eyes searched me as I went past. In the study the Headmaster, nicknamed Sambo, was waiting. Sambo was a round-shouldered, curiously oafish-looking man, not large but shambling in gait, with a chubby face which was like that of an overgrown baby, and which was capable of good humour. He knew, of course, why I had been sent to him, and had already taken a bone-handled riding-crop out of the cupboard, but it was part of the punishment of reporting yourself that you had to proclaim your offence with your own lips. When I had said my say, he read me a short but pompous lecture, then seized me by the scruff of the neck, twisted me over and began beating me with the riding-crop. He had a habit of continuing his lecture while he flogged you, and I remember the words 'you dir-ty lit-tle boy' keeping time with the blows. The beating did not hurt (perhaps, as it was the first time, he was not hitting me very hard), and I walked out feeling very much better. The fact that the beating had not hurt was a sort of victory and partially wiped out the shame of the bed-wetting. I was even incautious enough to wear a grin on my face. Some small boys were hanging about in the passage outside the door of the ante-room.

'D'you get the cane?'

'It didn't hurt,' I said proudly.

Flip had heard everything. Instantly her voice came screaming after me:

'Come here! Come here this instant! What was that you said?'

'I said it didn't hurt,' I faltered out.

'How dare you say a thing like that? Do you think that is the proper thing to say? Go in and REPORT YOURSELF AGAIN!'

This time Sambo laid on in real earnest. He continued for a length of time that frightened and astonished me – about five minutes, it seemed – ending up by breaking the riding-crop. The bone handle went flying across the room.

'Look what you've made me do!' he said furiously, holding up the broken crop.

I had fallen into a chair, weakly snivelling. I remember that this was the only time throughout my boyhood when a beating actually reduced me to tears, and curiously enough I was not even now crying because of the pain. The second beating had not hurt very much either. Fright and shame seemed to have anaesthetized me. I was crying partly because I felt that this was expected of me, partly from genuine repentance, but partly also because of a deeper grief which is peculiar to childhood and not easy to convey: a sense of desolate loneliness and helplessness, of being locked up not only in a hostile world but in a world of good and evil where the rules were such that it was actually not possible for me to keep them.

I knew that the bed-wetting was (a) wicked and (b) outside my control. The second fact I was personally aware of, and the first I did not question. It was possible, therefore, to commit a sin without knowing that you committed it, without wanting to commit it, and without being able to avoid it. Sin was not necessarily something that you did: it might be something that happened to you. I do not want to claim that this idea flashed into my mind as a complete novelty at this very moment, under the blows of Sambo's cane: I must have had glimpses of it even before I left home, for my early childhood had not been altogether happy. But at any rate this was the great, abiding lesson of my boyhood: that I was in a world where it was *not possible* for me to be good. And the double beating was a turning-point, for it brought home to me for the first time the harshness of the environment into which I had been flung. Life was more terrible, and I was more wicked, than I had imagined. At any rate, as I sat snivelling on the edge of a chair in Sambo's study, with not even the self-possession to stand up while he stormed at me, I had a conviction of sin and folly and weakness, such as I do not remember to have felt before.

In general, one's memories of any period must necessarily weaken as one moves away from it. One is constantly learning new facts, and old ones have to drop out to make way for them. At twenty I could have written the history of my schooldays with an accuracy which would be quite impossible now. But it can also happen that one's memories grow sharper after a long lapse of time, because one is looking at the past with fresh eyes and can isolate and, as it were, notice facts which previously existed undifferentiated among a mass of others. Here are two things which in a sense I remembered, but which did not strike me as strange or interesting until quite recently. One is that the second beating seemed to me a just and reasonable punishment. To get one beating, and then to get another and far fiercer one on top of it, for being so unwise as to show that the first had not hurt – that was quite natural. The gods are jealous, and when you have good fortune you should conceal it. The other is that I accepted the broken riding-crop as my own crime. I can still recall my feeling as I saw the handle lying on the carpet – the feeling of having done an ill-bred clumsy thing, and ruined an expensive object. *I* had broken it: so Sambo told me, and so I believed. This acceptance of guilt lay unnoticed in my memory for twenty or thirty years.

So much for the episode of bed-wetting. But there is one more thing to be remarked. This is that I did not wet my bed again – at least, I did wet it once again, and received another beating, after which the trouble stopped. So perhaps this barbarous remedy does work, though at a heavy price, I have no doubt.

II

St Cyprian's was an expensive and snobbish school which was in process of becoming more snobbish, and, I imagine, more expensive. The public school with which it had special connexions was Harrow, but during my time an increasing proportion of the boys went on to Eton. Most of them were the children of rich parents, but on the whole they were the un-aristocratic rich, the sort of people who live in huge shrubberied houses in Bournemouth or Richmond, and who have cars and butlers but not country estates. There were a few exotics among them – some South American boys, sons of Argentine beef barons, one or two Russians, and even a Siamese prince, or someone who was described as a prince.

Sambo had two great ambitions. One was to attract titled boys to the school, and the other was to train up pupils to win scholarships at public schools, above all at Eton. He did, towards the end of my time, succeed in getting hold of two boys with real English titles. One of them, I remember, was a wretched drivelling little creature, almost an albino, peering upwards out of weak eyes, with a long nose at the end of which a dewdrop always seemed to be trembling. Sambo always gave these boys their titles when mentioning them to a third person, and for the first few days he actually addressed them to their faces as 'Lord So-and-so'. Needless to say he found ways of drawing attention to them when any visitor was being shown round the school. Once, I remember, the little fair-haired boy had a choking fit at dinner, and a stream of snot ran out of his nose on to his plate in a way horrible to see. Any lesser person would have been called a dirty little beast and ordered out of the room instantly: but Sambo and Flip laughed it off in a 'boys will be boys' spirit.

All the very rich boys were more or less undisguisedly favoured. The school still had a faint suggestion of the Victorian 'private academy' with its 'parlour boarders', and when I later read about that kind of school in Thackeray I immediately saw the resemblance. The rich boys had milk and biscuits in the middle of the morning, they were given riding lessons once or twice a week, Flip mothered them and called them by their Christian names, and above all they were never caned. Apart from the South Americans, whose parents were safely distant, I doubt whether Sambo ever caned any boy whose father's income was much above £2,000 a year. But he was sometimes willing to sacrifice financial profit to scholastic prestige. Occasionally, by special arrangement, he would take at greatly reduced fees some boy who seemed likely to win scholarships and thus bring credit on the school. It was on these terms that I was at St Cyprian's myself: otherwise my parents could not have afforded to send me to so expensive a school.

I did not at first understand that I was being taken at reduced fees; it was only when I was about eleven that Flip and Sambo began throwing the fact in my teeth. For my first two or three years I went through the ordinary educational mill: then, soon after I had started Greek (one started Latin at eight, Greek at ten), I moved into the scholarship class, which was taught, so far as classics went, largely by Sambo himself. Over a period of two or three years the scholarship boys were crammed with learning as cynically as a goose is crammed for Christmas. And with what learning! This business of making a gifted boy's career depend on a competitive examination, taken when he is only twelve or thirteen, is an evil thing at best, but there do appear to be preparatory schools which send scholars to Eton, Winchester, etc. without teaching them to see everything in terms of marks. At St Cyprian's the whole process was frankly a preparation for a sort of confidence trick. Your job was to learn exactly those things that would give an examiner the impression that you knew more than you did know, and as far as possible to avoid burdening your brain with anything else. Subjects which lacked examination-value, such as geography, were almost completely neglected, mathematics was also neglected if you were a 'classical', science was not taught in any form – indeed it was so despised that even an interest in natural history was discouraged – and even the books you were encouraged to read in your spare time were chosen with one eye on the 'English paper'. Latin and Greek, the main scholarship subjects, were what counted, but even these were deliberately taught in a flashy, unsound way. We never, for example, read right through even a single book of a Greek or

Latin author: we merely read short passages which were picked out because they were the kind of thing likely to be set as an 'unseen translation'. During the last year or so before we went up for our scholarships, most of our time was spent in simply working our way through the scholarship papers of previous years. Sambo had sheaves of these in his possession, from every one of the major public schools. But the greatest outrage of all was the teaching of history.

There was in those days a piece of nonsense called the Harrow History Prize, an annual competition for which many preparatory schools entered. It was a tradition for St Cyprian's to win it every year, as well we might, for we had mugged up every paper that had been set since the competition started, and the supply of possible questions was not inexhaustible. They were the kind of stupid question that is answered by rapping out a name or a quotation. Who plundered the Begams? Who was beheaded in an open boat? Who caught the Whigs bathing and ran away with their clothes? Almost all our historical teaching was on this level. History was a series of unrelated, unintelligible but – in some way that was never explained to us – important facts with resounding phrases tied to them. Disraeli brought peace with honour. Clive was astonished at his moderation. Pitt called in the New World to redress the balance of the Old. And the dates, and the mnemonic devices! (Did you know, for example, that the initial letters of 'A black Negress was my aunt: there's her house behind the barn' are also the initial letters of the battles in the Wars of the Roses?) Flip, who 'took' the higher forms in history, revelled in this kind of thing. I recall positive orgies of dates, with the keener boys leaping up and down in their places in their eagerness to shout out the right answers, and at the same time not feeling the faintest interest in the meaning of the mysterious events they were naming.

'1587?'
'Massacre of St Bartholomew!'
'1707?'
'Death of Aurangzeeb!'
'1713?'
'Treaty of Utrecht!'
'1773?'
'Boston Tea Party!'
'1520?'
'Oo, Mum, please, Mum –'
'Please, Mum, please, Mum! Let me tell him, Mum!'
'Well! 1520?'
'Field of the Cloth of Gold!'
And so on.

But history and such secondary subjects were not bad fun. It was in 'classics' that the real strain came. Looking back, I realize that I then worked harder than I have ever done since, and yet at the time it never seemed possible to make quite the effort that was demanded of one. We would sit round the long shiny table, made of some very pale-coloured hard wood, with Sambo goading, threatening, exhorting, sometimes joking, very occasionally praising, but always prodding, prodding away at one's mind to keep it up to the right pitch of concentration, as one might keep a sleepy person awake by sticking pins in him.

'Go on, you little slacker! Go on, you idle, worthless little boy! The whole trouble with you is that you're bone and horn idle. You eat too much, that's why. You wolf down enormous meals, and then when you come here you're half asleep. Go on, now, put your back into it. You're not *thinking*. Your brain doesn't sweat.'

He would tap away at one's skull with his silver pencil, which, in my memory, seems to have been about the size of a banana, and which certainly was heavy enough to raise a bump: or he would pull the short hairs round one's ears, or, occasionally, reach out under the table and kick one's shin. On some days nothing seemed to go right, and then it would be: 'All right, then, I know what you want. You've been asking for it the whole morning. Come along, you useless little slacker. Come into the study.' And then whack, whack, whack, whack, and back one would come, red-wealed and smarting – in later years Sambo had abandoned his riding-crop in favour of a thin rattan cane which hurt very much more – to settle down to work again. This did not happen very often, but I do remember, more than once, being led out of the room in the middle of a Latin sentence, receiving a beating and then going straight ahead with the same sentence, just like that. It is a mistake to think such methods do not work. They work very well for their special purpose. Indeed, I doubt whether classical education ever has been or can be successfully carried on without corporal punishment. The boys themselves believed in its efficacy. There was a boy named Beacham, with no brains to speak of, but evidently in acute need of a scholarship. Sambo was flogging him towards the goal as one might do with a foundered horse. He went up for a scholarship at Uppingham, came back with a consciousness of having done badly, and a day or two later received a severe beating for idleness. 'I wish I'd had that caning before I went up for the exam,' he said sadly – a remark which I felt to be contemptible, but which I perfectly well understood.

The boys of the scholarship class were not all treated alike. If a boy were the son of rich parents to whom the saving of fees was not all-important, Sambo would goad him along in a comparatively fatherly way, with jokes and digs in the ribs and perhaps an occasional tap with the pencil, but no hair-pulling and no caning. It was the poor but 'clever' boys who suffered. Our brains were a gold-mine in which he had sunk money, and the dividends must be squeezed out of us. Long before I had grasped the nature of my financial relationship with Sambo, I had been made to understand that I was not on the same footing as most of the other boys. In effect there were three castes in the school. There was the minority with an aristocratic or millionaire background, there were the children of the ordinary suburban rich, who made up the bulk of the school, and there were a few underlings like myself, the sons of clergymen, Indian civil servants, struggling widows and the like. These poorer ones were discouraged from going in for 'extras' such as shooting and carpentry, and were humiliated over clothes and petty possessions. I never, for instance, succeeded in getting a cricket bat of my own, because 'Your parents wouldn't be able to afford it'. This phrase pursued me throughout my schooldays. At St Cyprian's we were not allowed to keep the money we brought back with us, but had to 'give it in' on the first day of term, and then from time to time were allowed to spend it under supervision. I and similarly-placed boys were always choked off from buying expensive toys like model aeroplanes, even if the necessary money stood to our credit. Flip, in particular, seemed to aim consciously at inculcating a humble outlook in the poorer boys. 'Do you think that's the sort of thing a boy like you should buy?' I remember her saying to somebody — and she said this in front of the whole school: 'You know you're not going to grow up with money, don't you? Your people aren't rich. You must learn to be sensible. Don't get above yourself!' There was also the weekly pocket-money, which we took out in sweets, dispensed by Flip from a large table. The millionaires had sixpence a week, but the normal sum was threepence. I and one or two others were only allowed twopence. My parents had not given instructions to this effect, and the saving of a penny a week could not conceivably have made any difference to them: it was a mark of status. Worse yet was the detail of the birthday cakes. It was usual for each boy, on his birthday, to have a large iced cake with candles, which was shared out at tea between the whole school. It was provided as a matter of routine and went on his parents' bill. I never had such a cake, though my parents would have paid for it readily enough. Year after year, never daring to ask, I would miserably hope that this year a cake would appear. Once or twice I even rashly pretended to my companions that this time I *was* going to have a cake. Then came tea-time, and no cake, which did not make me more popular.

Very early it was impressed upon me that I had no chance of a decent future unless I won a scholarship at a public school. Either I won my scholarship, or I must leave school at fourteen and become, in Sambo's favourite phrase 'a little office boy at forty pounds a year'. In my circumstances it was natural that I should believe this. Indeed, it was universally taken for granted at St Cyprian's that unless you went to a 'good' public school (and only about fifteen schools came under this heading) you were ruined for life. It is not easy to convey to a grown-up person the sense of strain, of nerving oneself for some terrible, all-deciding combat, as the date of the examination crept nearer – eleven years old, twelve years old, then thirteen, the fatal year itself! Over a period of about two years, I do not think there was ever a day when 'the exam', as I called it, was quite out of my waking thoughts. In my prayers it figured invariably: and whenever I got the bigger portion of a wishbone, or picked up a horseshoe, or bowed seven times to the new moon, or succeeded in passing through a wishing-gate without touching the sides, then the wish I earned by doing so went on 'the exam' as a matter of course. And yet curiously enough I was also tormented by an almost irresistible impulse *not* to work. There were days when my heart sickened at the labours ahead of me, and I stood stupid as an animal before the most elementary difficulties. In the holidays, also, I could not work. Some of the scholarship boys received extra tuition from a certain Mr Batchelor, a likeable, very hairy man who wore shaggy suits and lived in a typical bachelor's 'den' – book-lined walls, overwhelming stench of tobacco – somewhere in the town. During the holidays Mr Batchelor used to send us extracts from Latin authors to translate, and we were supposed to send back a wad of work once a week. Somehow I could not do it. The empty paper and the black Latin dictionary lying on the table, the consciousness of a plain duty shirked, poisoned my leisure, but somehow I could not start, and by the end of the holidays I would only have sent Mr Batchelor fifty or a hundred lines. Undoubtedly part of the reason was that Sambo and his cane were far away. But in term-time, also, I would go through periods of idleness and stupidity when I would sink deeper and deeper into disgrace and even achieve a sort of feeble, snivelling defiance, fully conscious of my guilt and yet unable or unwilling – I could not be sure which – to do any better. Then Sambo or Flip would send for me, and this time it would not even be a caning.

Flip would search me with her baleful eyes. (What colour were those eyes, I wonder? I remember them as green, but actually no human being has green eyes. Perhaps they were hazel.) She would start off in her peculiar, wheedling, bullying style, which never failed to get right through one's guard and score a hit on one's better nature.

'I don't think it's awfully decent of you to behave like this, is it? Do you think it's quite playing the game by your mother and father to go on idling your time away, week after week, month after month? Do you *want* to throw all your chances away? You know your people aren't rich, don't you? You know they can't afford the same things as other boys' parents. How are they to send you to a public school if you don't win a scholarship? I know how proud your mother is of you. Do you *want* to let her down?'

'I don't think he wants to go to a public school any longer,' Sambo would say, addressing himself to Flip with a pretence that I was not there. 'I think he's given up that idea. He wants to be a little office boy at forty pounds a year.'

The horrible sensation of tears – a swelling in the breast, a tickling behind the nose – would already have assailed me. Flip would bring out her ace of trumps:

'And do you think it's quite fair to *us*, the way you're behaving? After all we've done for you? You *do* know what we've done for you, don't you?' Her eyes would pierce deep into me, and though she never said it straight out, I did know. 'We've had you here all these years – we even had you here for a week in the holidays so that Mr Batchelor could coach you. We don't *want* to have to send you away, you know, but we can't keep a boy here just to eat up our food, term after term. *I* don't think it's very straight, the way you're behaving. Do you?'

I never had any answer except a miserable 'No, Mum', or 'Yes, Mum', as the case might be. Evidently it was *not* straight, the way I was behaving. And at some point or other the unwanted tear would always force its way out of the corner of my eye, roll down my nose and splash.

Flip never said in plain words that I was a non-paying pupil, no doubt because vague phrases like 'all we've done for you' had a deeper emotional appeal. Sambo, who did not aspire to be loved by his pupils, put it more brutally, though, as was usual with him in pompous language. 'You are living on my bounty' was his favourite phrase in this context. At least once I listened to these words between blows of the cane. I must say that these scenes were not frequent, and except on one occasion they did not take place in the presence of other boys. In public I was reminded that I was poor and that my parents 'wouldn't be able to afford' this or that, but I was not actually reminded of my dependent position. It was a final unanswerable argument, to be brought forth like an instrument of torture when my work became exceptionally bad.

To grasp the effect of this kind of thing on a child of ten or twelve, one has to remember that the child has little sense of proportion or probability. A child may be a mass of egoism and rebelliousness, but it has no accumulated experience to give it confidence in its own judgements. On the whole it will accept what it is told, and it will believe in the most fantastic way in the knowledge and powers of the adults surrounding it. Here is an example.

I have said that at St Cyprian's we were not allowed to keep our own money. However, it was possible to hold back a shilling or two, and sometimes I used furtively to buy sweets which I kept hidden in the loose ivy on the playing-field wall. One day when I had been sent on an errand I went into a sweet-shop a mile or more from the school and bought some chocolates. As I came out of the shop I saw on the opposite pavement a small sharp-faced man who seemed to be staring very hard at my school cap. Instantly a horrible fear went through me. There could be no doubt as to who the man was. He was a spy placed there by Sambo! I turned away unconcernedly, and then, as though my legs were doing it of their own accord, broke into a clumsy run. But when I got round the next corner I forced myself to walk again, for to run was a sign of guilt, and obviously there would be other spies posted here and there about the town. All that day and the next I waited for the summons to the study, and was surprised when it did not come. It did not seem to me strange that the headmaster of a private school should dispose of an army of informers, and I did not even imagine that he would have to pay them. I assumed that any adult, inside the school or outside, would collaborate voluntarily in preventing us from breaking the rules. Sambo was all-powerful; it was natural that his agents should be everywhere. When this episode happened I do not think I can have been less than twelve years old.

I hated Sambo and Flip, with a sort of shamefaced, remorseful hatred, but it did not occur to me to doubt their judgement. When they told me that I must either win a public-school scholarship or become an office boy at fourteen, I believed that those were the unavoidable alternatives before me. And above all, I believed Sambo and Flip when they told me they were my benefactors. I see now, of course, that from Sambo's point of view I was a good speculation. He sank money in me, and he looked to get it back in the form of prestige. If I had 'gone off', as promising boys sometimes do, I imagine that he would have got rid of me swiftly. As it was I won him two scholarships when the time came, and no doubt he made full use of them in his prospectuses. But it is difficult for a child to realize that a school is primarily a commercial venture. A child believes that the school exists to educate and that the school-master disciplines him either for his own good, or from a love of bullying. Flip and Sambo had chosen to befriend me, and their friendship included canings, reproaches and humiliations, which were good for me and saved me from an office stool. That was their version, and I believed in it. It was therefore clear that I owed them a vast debt of gratitude. But I was *not* grateful, as I very well knew. On the contrary, I hated both of them. I could not control my subjective feelings, and I could not conceal them from myself. But it is wicked, is it not, to hate your benefactors? So I was taught, and so I believed. A child accepts the codes of behaviour that are presented to it, even when it breaks them. From the age of eight, or even earlier, the consciousness of sin was never far away from me. If I contrived to seem callous and defiant, it was only a thin cover over a mass of shame and dismay. All through my boyhood I had a profound conviction that I was no good, that I was wasting my time, wrecking my talents, behaving with monstrous folly and wickedness and ingratitude – and all this, it seemed, was inescapable, because I lived among laws which were absolute, like the law of gravity, but which it was not possible for me to keep.

III

No one can look back on his schooldays and say with truth that they were altogether unhappy.

I have good memories of St Cyprian's, among a horde of bad ones. Sometimes on summer afternoons there were wonderful expeditions across the Downs to a village called Birling Gap, or to Beachy Head, where one bathed dangerously among the chalk boulders and came home covered with cuts. And there were still more wonderful mid-summer evenings when, as a special treat, we were not driven off to bed as usual but allowed to wander about the grounds in the long twilight, ending up with a plunge into the swimming bath at about nine o'clock. There was the joy of waking early on summer mornings and getting in an hour's undisturbed reading (Ian Hay, Thackeray, Kipling and H. G. Wells were the favourite authors of my boyhood) in the sunlit, sleeping dormitory. There was also cricket, which I was no good at but with which I conducted a sort of hopeless love affair up to the age of about eighteen. And there was the pleasure of keeping caterpillars – the silky green and purple puss-moth, the ghostly green poplar-hawk, the privet-hawk, large as one's third finger, specimens of which could be illicitly purchased for sixpence at a shop in the town – and, when one could escape long enough from the master who was 'taking the walk', there was the excitement of dredging the dew-ponds on the Downs for enormous newts with orange-coloured bellies. This business of being out for a walk, coming across something of fascinating interest and then being dragged away from it by a yell from the master, like a dog jerked onwards by the leash, is an important feature of school life, and helps to build up the conviction, so strong in many children, that the things you most want to do are always unattainable.

Very occasionally, perhaps once during each summer, it was possible to escape altogether from the barrack-like atmosphere of school, when Brown, the second master, was permitted to take one or two boys for an afternoon of butterfly hunting on a common a few miles away. Brown was a man with white hair and a red face like a strawberry, who was good at natural history, making models and plaster casts, operating magic lanterns, and things of that kind. He and Mr Batchelor were the only adults in any way connected with the school whom I did not either dislike or fear. Once he took me into his room and showed me in confidence a plated, pearl-handled revolver – his 'six-shooter', he called it – which he kept in a box under his bed, and oh, the joy of those occasional expeditions! The ride of two or three miles on a lonely little branch line, the afternoon of charging to and fro with large green nets, the beauty of the enormous dragonflies which hovered over the tops of the grasses, the sinister killing-bottle with its sickly smell, and then tea in the parlour of a pub with large slices of pale-coloured cake! The essence of it was in the railway journey, which seemed to put magic distances between yourself and school.

Flip, characteristically, disapproved of these expeditions, though not actually forbidding them. 'And have you been catching *little butterflies*?' she would say with a vicious sneer when one got back, making her voice as babyish as possible. From her point of view, natural history ('bug-hunting' she would probably have called it) was a babyish pursuit which a boy should be laughed out of as early as possible. Moreover it was somehow faintly plebeian, it was traditionally associated with boys who wore spectacles and were no good at games, it did not help you to pass exams, and above all it smelt of science and therefore seemed to menace classical education. It needed a considerable moral effort to accept Brown's invitation. How I dreaded that sneer of *little butterflies*! Brown, however, who had been at the school since its early days, had built up a certain independence for himself: he seemed to handle Sambo, and ignored Flip a good deal. If it ever happened that both of them were away, Brown acted as deputy headmaster, and on those occasions instead of reading the appointed lesson for the day at morning chapel, he would read us stories from the Apocrypha.

Most of the good memories of my childhood, and up to the age of about twenty, are in some way connected with animals. So far as St Cyprian's goes, it also seems, when I look back, that all my good memories are of summer. In winter your nose ran continually, your fingers were too numb to button your shirt (this was an especial misery on Sundays, when we wore Eton collars), there was the daily nightmare of football – the cold, the mud, the hideous greasy ball that came whizzing at one's face, the gouging knees and trampling boots of the bigger boys. Part of the trouble was that in winter, after about the age of ten, I was seldom in good health, at any rate during term-time. I had defective bronchial tubes and a lesion in one lung which was not discovered till many years later. Hence I not only had a chronic cough, but running was a torment to me. In those days however, 'wheeziness', or 'chestiness', as it was called, was either diagnosed as imagination or was looked on as essentially a moral disorder, caused by overeating. 'You wheeze like a concertina,' Sambo would say disapprovingly as he stood behind my chair; 'You're perpetually stuffing yourself with food, that's why.' My cough was referred to as a 'stomach cough', which made it sound both disgusting and reprehensible. The cure for it was hard running, which, if you kept it up long enough, ultimately 'cleared your chest'.

It is curious, the degree — I will not say of actual hardship, but of squalor and neglect — that was taken for granted in upper-class schools of that period. Almost as in the days of Thackeray, it seemed natural that a little boy of eight or ten should be a miserable, snotty-nosed creature, his face almost permanently dirty, his hands chapped, his nails bitten, his handkerchief a sodden horror, his bottom frequently blue with bruises. It was partly the prospect of actual physical discomfort that made the thought of going back to school lie in one's breast like a lump of lead during the last few days of the holidays. A characteristic memory of St Cyprian's is the astonishing hardness of one's bed on the first night of term. Since this was an expensive school, I took a social step upwards by attending it, and yet the standard of comfort was in every way far lower than in my own home, or indeed, than it would have been in a prosperous working-class home. One only had a hot bath once a week, for instance. The food was not only bad, it was also insufficient. Never before or since have I seen butter or jam scraped on bread so thinly. I do not think I can be imagining the fact that we were underfed, when I remember the lengths we would go in order to steal food. On a number of occasions I remember creeping down at two or three o'clock in the morning through what seemed like miles of pitch-dark stairways and passages — barefooted, stopping to listen after each step, paralysed with about equal fear of Sambo, ghosts and burglars — to steal stale bread from the pantry. The assistant masters had their meals with us, but they had somewhat better food, and if one got half a chance it was usual to steal left-over scraps of bacon rind or fried potato when their plates were removed.

As usual, I did not see the sound commercial reason for this underfeeding. On the whole I accepted Sambo's view that a boy's appetite is a sort of morbid growth which should be kept in check as much as possible. A maxim often repeated to us at St Cyprian's was that it is healthy to get up from a meal feeling as hungry as when you sat down. Only a generation earlier than this it had been common for school dinners to start off with a slab of unsweetened suet pudding, which, it was frankly said, 'broke the boys' appetites'. But the underfeeding was probably less flagrant at preparatory schools, where a boy was wholly dependent on the official diet, than at public schools, where he was allowed – indeed, expected – to buy extra food for himself. At some schools, he would literally not have had enough to eat unless he had bought regular supplies of eggs, sausages, sardines, etc.; and his parents had to allow him money for this purpose. At Eton, for instance, at any rate in College, a boy was given no solid meal after midday dinner. For his afternoon tea he was given only tea and bread and butter, and at eight o'clock he was given a miserable supper of soup or fried fish, or more often bread and cheese, with water to drink. Sambo went down to see his eldest son at Eton and came back in snobbish ecstacies over the luxury in which the boys lived. 'They give them fried fish for supper!' he exclaimed, beaming all over his chubby face. 'There's no school like it in the world.' Fried fish! The habitual supper of the poorest of the working class! At very cheap boarding schools it was no doubt worse. A very early memory of mine is of seeing the boarders at a grammar school – the sons, probably, of farmers and shopkeepers – being fed on boiled lights.

Whoever writes about his childhood must beware of exaggeration and self-pity. I do not claim that I was a martyr or that St Cyprian's was a sort of Dotheboys Hall. But I should be falsifying my own memories if I did not record that they are largely memories of disgust. The overcrowded, underfed, underwashed life that we led *was* disgusting, as I recall it. If I shut my eyes and say 'school', it is of course the physical surroundings that first come back to me: the flat playing-field with its cricket pavilion and the little shed by the rifle range, the draughty dormitories, the dusty splintery passages, the square of asphalt in front of the gymnasium, the raw-looking pinewood chapel at the back. And at almost every point some filthy detail obtrudes itself. For example, there were the pewter bowls out of which we had our porridge. They had overhanging rims, and under the rims there were accumulations of sour porridge, which could be flaked off in long strips. The porridge itself, too, contained more lumps, hairs and unexplained black things than one would have thought possible, unless someone were putting them there on purpose. It was never safe to start on that porridge without investigating it first. And there was the slimy water of the plunge bath – it was twelve or fifteen feet long, the whole school was supposed to go into it every morning, and I doubt whether the water was changed at all frequently – and the always-damp towels with their cheesy smell: and, on occasional visits in the winter, the murky seawater of the local Baths, which came straight in from the beach and on which I once saw floating a human turd. And the sweaty smell of the changing-room with its greasy basins, and, giving on this, the row of filthy, dilapidated lavatories, which had no fastenings of any kind on the doors, so that whenever you were sitting there someone was sure to come crashing in. It is not easy for me to think of my schooldays without seeming to breathe in a whiff of something cold and evil-smelling – a sort of compound of sweaty stockings, dirty towels, faecal smells blowing along corridors, forks with old food between the prongs, neck-of-mutton stew, and the banging doors of the lavatories and the echoing chamber-pots in the dormitories.

It is true that I am by nature not gregarious, and the WC and dirty handkerchief side of life is necessarily more obtrusive when great numbers of human beings are crushed together in a small space. It is just as bad in an army, and worse, no doubt, in a prison. Besides, boyhood is the age of disgust. After one has learned to differentiate, and before one has become hardened – between seven and eighteen, say – one seems always to be walking the tight-rope over a cesspool. Yet I do not think I exaggerate the squalor of school life, when I remember how health and cleanliness were neglected, in spite of the hoo-ha about fresh air and cold water and keeping in hard training. It was common to remain constipated for days together. Indeed, one was hardly encouraged to keep one's bowels open, since the only aperients tolerated were castor oil or another almost equally horrible drink called liquorice powder. One was supposed to go into the plunge bath every morning, but some boys shirked it for days on end, simply making themselves scarce when the bell sounded, or else slipping along the edge of the bath among the crowd, and then wetting their hair with a little dirty water off the floor. A little boy of eight or nine will not necessarily keep himself clean unless there is someone to see that he does it. There was a new boy named Hazel, a pretty, mother's darling of a boy, who came a little while before I left. The first thing I noticed about him was the beautiful pearly whiteness of his teeth. By the end of that term his teeth were an extraordinary shade of green. During all that time, apparently, no one had taken sufficient interest in him to see that he brushed them.

But of course the differences between home and school were more than physical. That bump on the hard mattress, on the first night of term, used to give me a feeling of abrupt awakening, a feeling of: 'This is reality, this is what you are up against.' Your home might be far from perfect, but at least it was a place ruled by love rather than by fear, where you did not have to be perpetually on your guard against the people surrounding you. At eight years old you were suddenly taken out of this warm nest and flung into a world of force and fraud and secrecy, like a gold-fish into a tank full of pike. Against no matter what degree of bullying you had no redress. You could only have defended yourself by sneaking, which, except in a few rigidly defined circumstances, was the unforgivable sin. To write home and ask your parents to take you away would have been even less thinkable, since to do so would have been to admit yourself unhappy and unpopular, which a boy will never do. Boys are Erewhonians: they think that misfortune is disgraceful and must be concealed at all costs. It might perhaps have been considered permissible to complain to your parents about bad food, or an unjustified caning, or some other ill-treatment inflicted by masters and not by boys. The fact that Sambo never beat the richer boys suggests that such complaints were made occasionally. But in my own peculiar circumstances I could never have asked my parents to intervene on my behalf. Even before I understood about the reduced fees, I grasped that they were in some way under an obligation to Sambo, and therefore could not protect me against him. I have mentioned already that throughout my time at St. Cyprian's I never had a cricket bat of my own. I had been told this was because 'your parents couldn't afford it'. One day in the holidays, by some casual remark, it came out that they had provided ten shillings to buy me one: yet no cricket bat appeared. I did not protest to my parents, let alone raise the subject with Sambo. How could I? I was dependent on him, and the ten shillings was merely a fragment of what I owed him. I realize now, of course, that it is immensely unlikely that Sambo had simply stuck to the money. No doubt the matter had slipped his memory. But the point is that I assumed that he had stuck to it, and that he had a right to do so if he chose.

How difficult it is for a child to have any real independence of attitude could be seen in our behaviour towards Flip. I think it would be true to say that every boy in the school hated and feared her. Yet we all fawned on her in the most abject way, and the top layer of our feelings towards her was a sort of guilt-stricken loyalty. Flip, although the discipline of the school depended more on her than on Sambo, hardly pretended to dispense strict justice. She was frankly capricious. An act which might get you a caning one day might next day be laughed off as a boyish prank, or even commended because it 'showed you had guts'. There were days when everyone cowered before those deep-set, accusing eyes, and there were days when she was like a flirtatious queen surrounded by courtier-lovers, laughing and joking, scattering largesse, or the promise of largesse ('And if you win the Harrow History Prize I'll give you a new case for your camera!'), and occasionally even packing three or four favoured boys into her Ford car and carrying them off to a teashop in town, where they were allowed to buy coffee and cakes. Flip was inextricably mixed up in my mind with Queen Elizabeth, whose relations with Leicester and Essex and Raleigh were intelligible to me from a very early age. A word we all constantly used in speaking of Flip was 'favour'. 'I'm in good favour,' we would say, or 'I'm in bad favour.' Except for the handful of wealthy or titled boys, no one was permanently in good favour, but on the other hand even the outcasts had patches of it from time to time. Thus, although my memories of Flip are mostly hostile, I also remember considerable periods when I basked under her smiles, when she called me 'old chap' and used my Christian name, and allowed me to frequent her private library, where I first made acquaintance with *Vanity Fair*. The high-water mark of good favour was to be invited to serve at table on Sunday nights when Flip and Sambo had guests to dinner. In clearing away, of course, one had a chance to finish off the scraps, but one also got a servile pleasure from standing behind the seated guests and darting deferentially forward when something was wanted. Whenever one had the chance to suck up, one did suck up, and at the first smile one's hatred turned into a sort of cringing love. I was always tremendously proud when I succeeded in making Flip laugh. I have even, at her command, written *vers d'occasion*, comic verses to celebrate memorable events in the life of the school.

I am anxious to make it clear that I was not a rebel, except by force of circumstances. I accepted the codes that I found in being. Once, towards the end of my time, I even sneaked to Brown about a suspected case of homosexuality. I did not know very well what homosexuality was, but I knew that it happened and was bad, and that this was one of the contexts in which it was proper to sneak. Brown told me I was 'a good fellow', which made me feel horribly ashamed. Before Flip one seemed as helpless as a snake before the snake-charmer. She had a hardly-varying vocabulary of praise and abuse, a whole series of set phrases, each of which promptly called forth the appropriate response. There was 'Buck up, old chap!', which inspired one to paroxysms of energy; there was 'Don't be such a fool!' (or, 'It's pathetic, isn't it?') which made one feel a born idiot; and there was 'It isn't very straight of you, is it?', which always brought one to the brink of tears. And yet all the while, at the middle of one's heart, there seemed to stand an incorruptible inner self who knew that whatever one did – whether one laughed or snivelled or went into frenzies of gratitude for small favours – one's only true feeling was hatred.

IV

I had learned early in my career that one can do wrong against one's will, and before long I also learned that one can do wrong without ever discovering what one has done or why it was wrong. There were sins that were too subtle to be explained, and there were others that were too terrible to be clearly mentioned. For example, there was sex, which was always smouldering just under the surface and which suddenly blew up into a tremendous row when I was about twelve.

At some preparatory schools homosexuality is not a problem but I think that St Cyprian's may have acquired a 'bad tone' thanks to the presence of the South American boys, who would perhaps mature a year or two earlier than an English boy. At that age I was not interested, so I do not actually know what went on, but I imagine it was group masturbation. At any rate, one day the storm suddenly burst over our heads. There were summonses, interrogations, confessions, floggings, repentances, solemn lectures of which one understood nothing except that some irredeemable sin known as 'swinishness' or 'beastliness' had been committed. One of the ringleaders, a boy named Horne, was flogged, according to eye-witnesses, for a quarter of an hour continuously before being expelled. His yells rang through the house. But we were all implicated, more or less, or felt ourselves to be implicated. Guilt seemed to hang in the air like a pall of smoke. A solemn, black-haired imbecile of an assistant master, who was later to be a Member of Parliament, took the older boys to a secluded room and delivered a talk on the Temple of the Body.

'Don't you realize what a wonderful thing your body is?' he said gravely. 'You talk of your motor-car engines, your Rolls-Royces and Daimlers and so on. Don't you understand that no engine ever made is fit to be compared with your body? And then you go and wreck it, ruin it – for life!'

He turned his cavernous black eyes on me and added quite sadly:

'And you, whom I'd always believed to be quite a decent person after your fashion – you, I hear, are one of the very worst.'

A feeling of doom descended upon me. So I was guilty too. I too had done the dreadful thing, whatever it was, that wrecked you for life, body and soul, and ended in suicide or the lunatic asylum. Till then I had hoped that I was innocent, and the conviction of sin which now took possession of me was perhaps all the stronger because I did not know what I had done. I was not among those who were interrogated and flogged, and it was not until the row was well over that I even learned about the trivial accident that had connected my name with it. Even then I understood nothing. It was not till about two years later that I fully grasped what that lecture on the Temple of the Body had referred to.

At this time I was in an almost sexless state, which is normal, or at any rate common, in boys of that age; I was therefore in the position of simultaneously knowing and not knowing what used to be called the Facts of Life. At five or six, like many children, I had passed through a phase of sexuality. My friends were the plumber's children up the road, and we used sometimes to play games of a vaguely erotic kind. One was called 'playing at doctors', and I remember getting a faint but definitely pleasant thrill from holding a toy trumpet, which was supposed to be a stethoscope, against a little girl's belly. About the same time I fell deeply in love, a far more worshipping kind of love than I have ever felt for anyone since, with a girl named Elsie at the convent school which I attended. She seemed to me grown up, so I suppose she must have been fifteen. After that, as often happens, all sexual feelings seemed to go out of me for many years. At twelve I knew more than I had known as a young child, but I understood less, because I no longer knew the essential fact that there is something pleasant in sexual activity. Between roughly seven and fourteen, the whole subject seemed to me uninteresting and, when for some reason I was forced to think of it, disgusting. My knowledge of the so-called Facts of Life was derived from animals, and was therefore distorted, and in any case was only intermittent. I knew that animals copulated and that human beings had bodies resembling those of animals: but that human beings also copulated I only knew as it were, reluctantly, when something, a phrase in the Bible, perhaps, compelled me to remember it. Not having desire, I had no curiosity, and was willing to leave many questions unanswered. Thus, I knew in principle how the baby gets into the woman, but I did not know how it gets out again, because I had never followed the subject up. I knew all the dirty words, and in my bad moments I would repeat them to myself, but I did not know what the worst of them meant, nor wanted to know. They were abstractly wicked, a sort of verbal charm. While I remained in this state, it was easy for me to remain ignorant of any sexual misdeeds that went on about me, and to be hardly wiser even when the row broke. At most, through the veiled and terrible warnings of Flip, Sambo and all the rest of them, I grasped that the crime of which we were all guilty was somehow connected with the sexual organs. I had noticed, without feeling much interest, that one's penis sometimes stands up of its own accord (this starts happening to a boy long before he has any conscious sexual desires), and I was inclined to believe, or half-believe, that *that* must be the crime. At any rate, it was something to do with the penis – so much I understood. Many other boys, I have no doubt, were equally in the dark.

After the talk on the Temple of the Body (days later, it seems in retrospect: the row seemed to continue for days), a dozen of us were seated at a long shiny table which Sambo used for the scholarship class, under Flip's lowering eye. A long desolate wail rang out from a room somewhere above. A very small boy named Ronalds, aged no more than about ten, who was implicated in some way, was being flogged, or was recovering from a flogging. At the sound, Flip's eyes searched our faces, and settled upon me.

'*You see,*' she said.

I will not swear that she said 'You see what you have done,' but that was the sense of it. We were all bowed down with shame. It was *our* fault. Somehow or other we had led poor Ronalds astray: *we* were responsible for his agony and his ruin. Then Flip turned upon another boy named Heath. It is thirty years ago, and I cannot remember for certain whether she merely quoted a verse from the Bible, or whether she actually brought out the Bible and made Heath read it; but at any rate the text indicated was: 'Whoso shall offend one of these little ones that believe in me, it were better for him that a millstone were hanged about his neck, and that he were drowned in the depth of the sea.'

That, too, was terrible. Ronalds was one of these little ones, we had offended him; it were better that a millstone were hanged about our necks and that we were drowned in the depth of the sea.

'Have you thought about that, Heath – have you thought what it means?' Flip said. And Heath broke down into snivelling tears.

Another boy, Beacham, whom I have mentioned already, was similarly overwhelmed with shame by the accusation that he 'had black rings round his eyes'.

'Have you looked in the glass lately, Beacham?' said Flip. 'Aren't you ashamed to go about with a face like that? Do you think everyone doesn't know what it means when a boy has black rings round his eyes?'

Once again the load of guilt and fear seemed to settle down upon me. Had *I* got black rings round my eyes? A couple of years later I realized that these were supposed to be a symptom by which masturbators could be detected. But already, without knowing this, I accepted black rings as a sure sign of depravity, *some* kind of depravity. And many times, even before I grasped the supposed meaning, I have gazed anxiously into the glass, looking for the first hint of that dreaded stigma, the confession which the secret sinner writes upon his own face.

These terrors wore off, or became merely intermittent, without affecting what one might call my official beliefs. It was still true about the madhouse and the suicide's grave, but it was no longer acutely frightening. Some months later it happened that I once again saw Horne, the ringleader who had been flogged and expelled. Horne was one of the outcasts, the son of poor middle-class parents, which was no doubt part of the reason why Sambo had handled him so roughly. The term after his expulsion he went on to Eastbourne College, the small local public school, which was hideously despised at St Cyprian's and looked on as 'not really' a public school at all. Only a very few boys from St Cyprian's went there, and Sambo always spoke of them with a sort of contemptuous pity. You had no chance if you went to a school like that: at the best your destiny would be a clerkship. I thought of Horne as a person who at thirteen had already forfeited all hope of any decent future. Physically, morally and socially he was finished. Moreover I assumed that his parents had only sent him to Eastbourne College because after his disgrace no 'good' school would have him.

During the following term, when we were out for a walk, we passed Horne in the street. He looked completely normal. He was a strongly-built, rather good-looking boy with black hair. I immediately noticed that he looked better than when I had last seen him – his complexion, previously rather pale, was pinker – and that he did not seem embarrassed at meeting us. Apparently he was not ashamed either of having been expelled, or of being at Eastbourne College. If one could gather anything from the way he looked at us as we filed past, it was that he was glad to have escaped from St Cyprian's. But the encounter made very little impression on me. I drew no inference from the fact that Horne, ruined in body and soul, appeared to be happy and in good health. I still believed in the sexual mythology that had been taught me by Sambo and Flip. The mysterious, terrible dangers were still there. Any morning the black rings might appear round your eyes and you would know that you too were among the lost ones. Only it no longer seemed to matter very much. These contradictions can exist easily in the mind of a child, because of its own vitality. It accepts – how can it do otherwise? – the nonsense that its elders tell it, but its youthful body, and the sweetness of the physical world, tell it another story. It was the same with Hell, which up to the age of about fourteen I officially believed in. Almost certainly Hell existed, and there were occasions when a vivid sermon could scare you into fits. But somehow it never lasted. The fire that waited for you was real fire, it would hurt in the same way as when you burnt your finger, and *for ever*, but most of the time you could contemplate it without bothering.

V

The various codes which were presented to you at St Cyprian's – religious, moral, social and intellectual – contradicted one another if you worked out their implications. The essential conflict was between the tradition of the nineteenth-century asceticism and the actually existing luxury and snobbery of the pre-1914 age. On the one side were low-church Bible Christianity, sex puritanism, insistence on hard work, respect for academic distinction, disapproval of self-indulgence: on the other, contempt for 'braininess', and worship of games, contempt for foreigners and the working class, an almost neurotic dread of poverty, and, above all, the assumption not only that money and privilege are the things that matter, but that it is better to inherit them than to have to work for them. Broadly, you were bidden to be at once a Christian and a social success, which is impossible. At the time I did not perceive that the various ideals which were set before us cancelled out. I merely saw that they were all, or nearly all, unattainable, so far as I was concerned, since they all depended not only on what you did but on what you *were*.

Very early, at the age of ten or eleven, I reached the conclusion – no one told me this, but on the other hand I did not simply make it up out of my own head: somehow it was in the air I breathed – that you were no good unless you had £100,000. I had perhaps fixed on this particular sum as a result of reading Thackeray. The interest on £100,000 would be £4,000 a year (I was in favour of a safe 4 per cent), and this seemed to me the minimum income that you must possess if you were to belong to the real top crust, the people in the country houses. But it was clear that I could never find my way into that paradise, to which you did not really belong unless you were born into it. You could only *make* money, if at all, by a mysterious operation called 'going into the City', and when you came out of the City, having won your £100,000, you were fat and old. But the truly enviable thing about the top-notchers was that they were rich while young. For people like me, the ambitious middle class, the examination-passers, only a bleak, laborious kind of success was possible. You clambered upwards on a ladder of scholarships into the Civil Service or the Indian Civil Service, or possibly you became a barrister. And if at any point you 'slacked' or 'went off' and missed one of the rungs of the ladder, you became 'a little office boy at forty pounds a year'. But even if you climbed to the highest niche that was open to you, you could still only be an underling, a hanger-on of the people who really counted.

Even if I had not learned this from Sambo and Flip, I would have learned it from other boys. Looking back, it is astonishing how intimately, intelligently snobbish we all were, how knowledgeable about names and addresses, how swift to detect small differences in accents and manners and the cut of clothes. There were some boys who seemed to drip money from their pores even in the bleak misery of the middle of a winter term. At the beginning and end of the term, especially, there was naïvely snobbish chatter about Switzerland, and Scotland with its ghillies and grouse moors, and 'my uncle's yacht', and 'our place in the country', and 'my pony' and 'my pater's touring car'. There never was, I suppose, in the history of the world a time when the sheer vulgar fatness of wealth, without any kind of aristocratic elegance to redeem it, was so obtrusive as in those years before 1914. It was the age when crazy millionaires in curly top-hats and lavender waistcoats gave champagne parties in rococo house-boats on the Thames, the age of diabolo and hobble skirts, the age of the 'knut' in his grey bowler and cut-away coat, the age of *The Merry Widow*, Saki's novels, *Peter Pan* and *Where the Rainbow Ends*, the age when people talked about chocs and cigs and ripping and topping and heavenly, when they went for divvy week-ends at Brighton and had scrumptious teas at the Troc. From the whole decade before

1914 there seems to breathe forth a smell of the more vulgar, un-grown-up kind of luxury, a smell of brilliantine and *crème-de-menthe* and soft centred chocolates – an atmosphere, as it were, of eating everlasting strawberry ices on green lawns to the tune of the Eton Boating Song. The extraordinary thing was the way in which everyone took it for granted that this oozing, bulging wealth of the English upper and upper-middle classes would last for ever, and was part of the order of things. After 1918 it was never quite the same again. Snobbishness and expensive habits came back, certainly, but they were self-conscious and on the defensive. Before the war the worship of money was entirely unreflecting and untroubled by any pang of conscience. The goodness of money was as unmistakable as the goodness of health or beauty, and a glittering car, a title or a horde of servants was mixed up in people's minds with the idea of actual moral virtue.

At St Cyprian's, in term-time, the general bareness of life enforced a certain democracy, but any mention of the holidays, and the consequent competitive swanking about cars and butlers and country houses, promptly called class distinctions into being. The school was pervaded by a curious cult of Scotland, which brought out the fundamental contradiction in our standard of values. Flip claimed Scottish ancestry, and she favoured the Scottish boys, encouraging them to wear kilts in their ancestral tartan instead of the school uniform, and even christened her youngest child by a Gaelic name. Ostensibly we were supposed to admire the Scots because they were 'grim' and 'dour' ('stern' was perhaps the key word), and irresistible on the field of battle. In the big schoolroom there was a steel engraving of the charge of the Scots Greys at Waterloo, all looking as though they enjoyed every moment of it. Our picture of Scotland was made up of burns, braes, kilts, sporrans, claymores, bagpipes and the like, all somehow mixed up with the invigorating effects of porridge, Protestantism and a cold climate. But underlying this was something quite different. The real reason for the cult of Scotland was that only very rich people could spend their summers there. And the pretended belief in Scottish superiority was a cover for the bad conscience of the occupying English, who had pushed the Highland peasantry off their farms to make way for the deer forests, and then compensated them by turning them into servants. Flip's face always beamed with innocent snobbishness when she spoke of Scotland. Occasionally she even attempted a trace of Scottish accent. Scotland was a private paradise which a few initiates could talk about and make outsiders feel small.

'You going to Scotland this hols?'

'Rather! We go every year.'

'My pater's got three miles of river.'

'My pater's giving me a new gun for the twelfth. There's jolly good black game where we go. Get out, Smith! What are you listening for? You've never been to Scotland. I bet you don't know what a blackcock looks like.'

Following on this, imitations of the cry of a blackcock, of the roaring of a stag, of the accent of 'our ghillies', etc. etc.

And the questionings that new boys of doubtful social origin were sometimes put through – questions quite surprising in their mean-minded particularity, when one reflects that the inquisitors were only twelve or thirteen!

'How much a year has your pater got? What part of London do you live in? Is that Knightsbridge or Kensington? How many bathrooms has your house got? How many servants do your people keep? Have you got a butler? Well, then, have you got a cook? Where do you get your clothes made? How many shows did you go to in the hols? How much money did you bring back with you?' etc. etc.

I have seen a little new boy, hardly older than eight, desperately lying his way through such a catechism:

'Have your people got a car?'

'Yes.'

'What sort of car?'

'Daimler.'

'How many horse-power?'

(Pause, and leap in the dark.) 'Fifteen.'

'What kind of lights?'

The little boy is bewildered.

'What kind of lights? Electric or acetylene?'

(A longer pause, and another leap in the dark.) 'Acetylene.'

'Coo! He says his pater's car's got acetylene lamps. They went out years ago. It must be as old as the hills.'

'Rot! He's making it up. He hasn't got a car. He's just a navvy. Your pater's a navvy.'

And so on.

By the social standards that prevailed about me, I was no good, and could not be any good. But all the different kinds of virtue seemed to be mysteriously interconnected and to belong to much the same people. It was not only money that mattered: there were also strength, beauty, charm, athleticism and something called 'guts' or 'character', which in reality meant the power to impose your will on others. I did not possess any of these qualities. At games for instance, I was hopeless. I was a fairly good swimmer and not altogether contemptible at cricket, but these had no prestige value, because boys only attach importance to a game if it requires strength and courage. What counted was football, at which I was a funk. I loathed the game, and since I could see no pleasure or usefulness in it, it was very difficult for me to show courage at it. Football, it seemed to me, is not really played for the pleasure of kicking a ball about, but is a species of fighting. The lovers of football are large, boisterous, nobbly boys who are good at knocking down and trampling on slightly smaller boys. That was the pattern of school life – a continuous triumph of the strong over the weak. Virtue consisted in winning: it consisted in being bigger, stronger, handsomer, richer, more popular, more elegant, more unscrupulous than other people – in dominating them, bullying them, making them suffer pain, making them look foolish, getting the better of them in every way. Life was hierarchical and whatever happened was right. There were the strong, who deserved to win and always did win, and there were the weak, who deserved to lose and always did lose, everlastingly.

I did not question the prevailing standards, because so far as I could see there were no others. How could the rich, the strong, the elegant, the fashionable, the powerful, be in the wrong? It was their world, and the rules they made for it must be the right ones. And yet from a very early age I was aware of the impossibility of any *subjective* conformity. Always at the centre of my heart the inner self seemed to be awake, pointing out the difference between the moral obligation and the psychological *fact*. It was the same in all matters, worldly or otherworldly. Take religion, for instance. You were supposed to love God, and I did not question this. Till the age of about fourteen I believed in God, and believed that the accounts given of him were true. But I was well aware that I did not love him. On the contrary, I hated him, just as I hated Jesus and the Hebrew patriarchs. If I had sympathetic feelings towards any character in the Old Testament, it was towards such people as Cain, Jezebel, Haman, Agag, Sisera: in the New Testament my friends, if any, were Ananias, Caiaphas, Judas and Pontius Pilate. But the whole business of religion seemed to be strewn with psychological impossibilities. The Prayer Book told you, for example, to love God and fear him: but how could you love someone whom you feared? With your private affections it was the same. What you *ought* to feel was usually clear enough but the appropriate emotion could not be commanded. Obviously it was my duty to feel grateful towards Flip and Sambo; but I was not grateful. It was equally clear that one ought to love one's father, but I knew very well that I merely disliked my own father, whom I had barely seen before I was eight and who appeared to me simply as a gruff-voiced elderly man forever saying 'Don't'. It was not that one did not want to possess the right qualities or feel the correct emotions, but that one could not. The good and the possible never seemed to coincide.

There was a line of verse that I came across not actually while I was at St Cyprian's, but a year or two later, and which seemed to strike a sort of leaden echo in my heart. It was: 'The armies of unalterable law'. I understood to perfection what it meant to be Lucifer, defeated and justly defeated, with no possibility of revenge. The schoolmasters with their canes, the millionaires with their Scottish castles, the athletes with their curly hair – these were the armies of unalterable law. It was not easy, at that date, to realize that in fact it *was* alterable. And according to that law I was damned. I had no money, I was weak, I was ugly, I was unpopular, I had a chronic cough, I was cowardly, I smelt. This picture, I should add, was not altogether fanciful. I was an unattractive boy, St Cyprian's soon made me so, even if I had not been so before. But a child's belief in its own shortcomings is not much influenced by facts. I believed, for example, that I 'smelt', but this was based simply on general probability. It was notorious that disagreeable people smelt, and therefore presumably I did so too. Again, until after I had left school for good I continued to believe that I was preternaturally ugly. It was what my schoolfellows had told me, and I had no other authority to refer to. The conviction that it was *not possible* for me to be a success went deep enough to influence my actions till far into adult life. Until I was about thirty I always planned my life on the assumption not only that any major undertaking was bound to fail, but that I could only expect to live a few years longer.

But this sense of guilt and inevitable failure was balanced by something else: that is, the instinct to survive. Even a creature that is weak, ugly, cowardly, smelly and in no way justifiable still wants to stay alive and be happy after its own fashion. I could not invert the existing scale of values, or turn myself into a success, but I could accept my failure and make the best of it. I could resign myself to being what I was, and then endeavour to survive on those terms.

To survive, or at least to preserve any kind of independence, was essentially criminal, since it meant breaking rules which you yourself recognized. There was a boy named Johnny Hale who for some months oppressed me horribly. He was a big, powerful, coarsely handsome boy with a very red face and curly black hair, who was forever twisting somebody's arm, wringing somebody's ear, flogging somebody with a riding-crop (he was a member of the Sixth Form), or performing prodigies of activity on the football field. Flip loved him (hence the fact he was habitually called by his Christian name) and Sambo commended him as a boy who 'had character' and 'could keep order'. He was followed about by a group of toadies who nicknamed him Strong Man.

One day, when we were taking off our overcoats in the changing-room, Hale picked on me for some reason. I 'answered him back', whereupon he gripped my wrist, twisted it round and bent my forearm back upon itself in a hideously painful way. I remember his handsome, jeering red face bearing down upon mine. He was, I think, older than I, besides being enormously stronger. As he let go of me a terrible, wicked resolve formed itself in my heart. I would get back on him by hitting him when he did not expect it. It was a strategic moment, for the master who had been 'taking' the walk would be coming back almost immediately, and then there could be no fight. I let perhaps a minute go by, walked up to Hale with the most harmless air I could assume, and then, getting the weight of my body behind it, smashed my fist into his face. He was flung backwards by the blow, and some blood ran out of his mouth. His always sanguine face turned almost black with rage. Then he turned away to rinse his mouth at the washbasins.

'*All right!*' he said to me between his teeth as the master led us way.

For days after this he followed me about, challenging me to fight. Although terrified out of my wits, I steadily refused to fight. I said that the blow in the face had served him right and there was an end of it. Curiously enough he did not simply fall upon me there and then, which public opinion would probably have supported him in doing. So gradually the matter tailed off, and there was no fight.

Now, I had behaved wrongly, by my own code no less than

his. To hit him unawares was wrong. But to refuse afterwards to fight knowing that if we fought he would beat me – that was far worse: it was cowardly. If I had refused because I disapproved of fighting, or because I genuinely felt the matter to be closed, it would have been all right; but I had refused merely because I was afraid. Even my revenge was made empty by that fact. I had struck the blow in a moment of mindless violence, deliberately not looking far ahead and merely determined to get my own back for once and damn the consequences. I had had time to realize that what I did was wrong, but it was the kind of crime from which you could get some satisfaction. Now all was nullified. There had been a sort of courage in the first act, but my subsequent cowardice had wiped it out.

The fact I hardly noticed was that though Hale formally challenged me to fight, he did not actually attack me. Indeed, after receiving that one blow he never oppressed me again. It was perhaps twenty years before I saw the significance of this. At the time I could not see beyond the moral dilemma that is presented to the weak in a world governed by the strong: Break the rules, or perish. I did not see that in that case the weak have the right to make a different set of rules for themselves; because, even if such an idea had occurred to me, there was no one in my environment who could have confirmed me in it. I lived in a world of boys, gregarious animals, questioning nothing, accepting the law of the stronger and avenging their own humiliations by passing them down to someone smaller. My situation was that of countless other boys, and if potentially I was more of a rebel than most, it was only because, by boyish standards, I was a poorer specimen. But I never did rebel intellectually, only emotionally. I had nothing to help me except my dumb selfishness, my inability – not, indeed, to despise myself, but to *dislike* myself – my instinct to survive.

It was about a year after I hit Johnny Hale in the face that I left St Cyprian's for ever. It was the end of a winter term. With a sense of coming out from darkness into sunlight I put on my Old Boy's tie as we dressed for the journey. I well remember the feeling of that brand-new silk tie round my neck, a feeling of emancipation, as though the tie had been at once a badge of manhood and an amulet against Flip's voice and Sambo's cane. I was escaping from bondage. It was not that I expected, or even intended, to be any more successful at a public school than I had been at St Cyprian's. But still, I was escaping. I knew that at a public-school there would be more privacy, more neglect, more chance to be idle and self-indulgent and degenerate. For years I had been resolved – unconsciously at first, but consciously later on – that when once my scholarship was won I would 'slack off' and cram no longer. This resolve, by the way, was so fully carried out that between the ages of thirteen and twenty-two or three I hardly ever did a stroke of avoidable work.

Flip shook hands to say good-bye. She even gave me my Christian name for the occasion. But there was a sort of patronage, almost a sneer, in her face and in her voice. The tone in which she said good-bye was nearly the one in which she had been used to say *little butterflies*. I had won two scholarships, but I was a failure, because success was measured not by what you did but by what you *were*. I was 'not a good type of boy' and could bring no credit on the school. I did not possess character or courage or health or strength or money, or even good manners, the power to look like a gentleman.

'Good-bye,' Flip's parting smile seemed to say; 'it's not

worth quarrelling now. You haven't made much of a success of your time at St Cyprian's, have you? And I don't suppose you'll get on awfully well at public school either. We made a mistake, really, in wasting our time and money on you. This kind of education hasn't much to offer to a boy with your background and your outlook. Oh, don't think we don't understand you! We know all about those ideas you have at the back of your head, we know you disbelieve in everything we've taught you, and we know you aren't in the least grateful for all we've done for you. But there's no use in bringing it all up now. We aren't responsible for you any longer, and we shan't be seeing you again. Let's just admit that you're one of our failures and part without ill-feeling. And so, good-bye.'

That at least was what I read into her face. And yet how happy I was, that winter morning, as the train bore me away with the gleaming new silk tie (dark green, pale blue and black, if I remember rightly) round my neck! The world was opening before me, just a little, like a grey sky which exhibits a narrow crack of blue. A public school would be better fun than St Cyprian's, but at bottom equally alien. In a world where the prime necessities were money, titled relatives, athleticism, tailor-made clothes, neatly-brushed hair, a charming smile, I was no good. All I had gained was a breathing-space. A little quietude, a little self-indulgence, a little respite from cramming – and then ruin. What kind of ruin I did not know: perhaps the colonies or an office-stool, perhaps prison or an early death. But first a year or two in which one could 'slack off' and get the benefit of one's sins, like Doctor Faustus. I believed firmly in my evil destiny, and yet I was acutely happy. It is the advantage of being thirteen that you can not only live in the moment, but do so with full consciousness, foreseeing the future and yet not caring about it. Next term I was going to Wellington. I had also won a scholarship at Eton, but it was uncertain whether there would be a vacancy, and I was going to Wellington first. At Eton you had a room to yourself – a room which might even have a fire in it. At Wellington you had your own cubicle, and could make yourself cocoa in the evenings. The privacy of it, the grown-upness! And there would be libraries to hang about in, and summer afternoons when you could shirk games and mooch about the countryside alone, with no master driving you along. Meanwhile there were the holidays. There was the .22 rifle that I had bought the previous holidays (the Crackshot, it was called, costing twenty-two and sixpence), and Christmas was coming next week. There were also the pleasures of overeating. I thought of some particularly voluptuous cream buns which could be bought for twopence each at a shop in our town. (This was 1916, and food-rationing had not yet started.) Even the detail that my journey-money had been slightly miscalculated, leaving about a shilling over – enough for an unforeseen cup of coffee and a cake or two somewhere on the way – was enough to fill me with bliss. There was time for a bit of happiness before the future closed in upon me. But I did know that the future was dark. Failure, failure, failure – failure behind me, failure ahead of me – that was by far the deepest conviction that I carried away.

VI

All this was thirty years ago and more. The question is: Does a child at school go through the same kind of experiences nowadays?

The only honest answer, I believe, is that we do not with certainty know. Of course it is obvious that the present-day *attitude* towards education is enormously more humane and sensible than that of the past. The snobbishness that was an integral part of my own education would be almost unthinkable today, because the society that nourished it is dead. I recall a conversation that must have taken place about a year before I left St Cyprian's. A Russian boy, large and fair-haired, a year older than myself, was questioning me.

'How much a year has your father got?'

I told him what I thought it was, adding a few hundreds to make it sound better. The Russian boy, neat in his habits, produced a pencil and a small note-book and made a calculation.

'My father has over two hundred times as much money as yours,' he announced with a sort of amused contempt.

That was in 1915. What happened to that money a couple of years later, I wonder? And still more I wonder, do conversations of that kind happen at preparatory schools now?

Clearly there has been a vast change of outlook, a general growth of 'enlightment', even among ordinary, unthinking middle-class people. Religious belief, for instance, has largely vanished, dragging other kinds of nonsense after it. I imagine that very few people nowadays would tell a child that if it masturbates it will end in the lunatic asylum. Beating, too, has become discredited, and has even been abandoned at many schools. Nor is the underfeeding of children looked on as a normal, almost meritorious act. No one now would openly set out to give his pupils as little food as they could do with, or tell them that it is healthy to get up from a meal as hungry as you sat down. The whole status of children has improved, partly because they have grown relatively less numerous. And the diffusion of even a little psychological knowledge has made it harder for parents and schoolteachers to indulge their aberrations in the name of discipline. Here is a case, not known to me personally, but known to someone I can vouch for, and happening within my own lifetime. A small girl, daughter of a clergyman, continued wetting her bed at an age when she should have grown out of it. In order to punish her for this dreadful deed, her father took her to a large garden party and there introduced her to the whole company as a little girl who wetted her bed: and to underline her wickedness he had previously painted her face black. I do not suggest that Flip and Sambo would actually have done a thing like this, but I doubt whether it would have much surprised them. After all, things do change. And yet –!

The question is not whether boys are still buckled into Eton collars on Sunday, or told that babies are dug up under gooseberry bushes. That kind of thing is at an end, admittedly. The real question is whether it is still normal for a schoolchild to live for years amid irrational terrors and lunatic misunderstandings. And here one is up against the very great difficulty of knowing what a child really feels and thinks. A child which appears reasonably happy may actually be suffering horrors which it cannot or will not reveal. It lives in a sort of alien under-water world which we can only penetrate by memory or divination. Our chief clue is the fact that we were once children ourselves, and many people appear to forget the atmosphere of their own childhood almost entirely. Think for instance of the unnecessary torments that people will inflict by sending a child back to school with clothes of the wrong pattern, and refusing to see that this matters! Over things of this kind a child will sometimes utter a protest, but a great deal of the time its attitude is one of simple concealment. Not to expose your true feelings to an adult seems to be instinctive from the age of seven or eight onwards. Even the affection that one feels for a child, the desire to protect and cherish it, is a cause of misunderstanding. One can love a child, perhaps, more deeply than one can love another adult, but it is rash to assume that the child feels any love in return. Looking back on my own childhood, after the infant years were over, I do not believe that I ever felt love for any mature person, except my mother, and even her I did not trust, in the sense that shyness made me conceal most of my real feelings from her. Love, the spontaneous, unqualified emotion of love, was something I could only feel for people who were young. Towards people who were old – and remember that 'old' to a child means over thirty, or even over twenty-five – I could feel reverence, respect, admiration or compunction, but I seemed cut off from them by a veil of fear and shyness mixed up with physical distaste. People are too ready to forget the child's *physical* shrinking from the adult. The enormous size of grown-ups, their ungainly, rigid bodies, their coarse, wrinkled skins, their great relaxed eyelids, their yellow teeth, and the whiffs of musty clothes and beer and sweat and tobacco that disengage from them at every movement! Part of the reason for the ugliness of adults, in a child's eyes, is that the child is usually looking upwards, and few faces are at their best when seen from below. Besides, being fresh and unmarked itself, the child has impossibly high standards in the matter of skin and teeth and complexion. But the greatest barrier of all is the child's misconception about age. A child can hardly envisage life beyond thirty, and in judging people's ages it will make fantastic mistakes. It will think that a person of twenty-five is forty, that a person of forty is sixty-five, and so on. Thus, when I fell in love with Elsie I took her to be grown-up. I met her again, when I was thirteen and she, I think, must have been twenty-three; she now seemed to me a middle-aged woman, somewhat past her best. And the child thinks of growing old as an almost obscene calamity, which for some mysterious reason will never happen to itself. All who have passed the age of thirty are joyless grotesques, endlessly fussing about things of no importance and staying alive without, so far as the child can see, having anything to live for. Only child life is real life. The schoolmaster who imagines that he is loved and trusted by his boys is in fact mimicked and laughed at behind his back. An adult who does not seem dangerous nearly always seems ridiculous.

I base these generalizations on what I can recall of my own childhood outlook. Treacherous though memory is, it seems to me the chief means we have of discovering how a child's mind works. Only by resurrecting our own memories can we realize how incredibly distorted is the child's vision of the world. Consider this, for example. How would St Cyprian's appear to me now, if I could go back, at my present age, and see it as it was in 1915? What should I think of Sambo and Flip, those terrible, all-powerful monsters? I should see them as a couple of silly, shallow, ineffectual people, eagerly clambering up a social ladder which any thinking person could see to be on the point of collapse. I would no more be frightened of them than I would be frightened of a dormouse. Moreover, in those days they seemed to me fantastically old, whereas – though of this I am not certain – I imagine they must have been somewhat younger than I am now. And how would

Johnny Hale appear, with his blacksmith's arms and his red, jeering face? Merely a scruffy little boy, barely distinguishable from hundreds of other scruffy little boys. The two sets of facts can lie side by side in my mind, because those happen to be my own memories. But it would be very difficult for me to see with the eyes of any other child, except by an effort of the imagination which might lead me completely astray. The child and the adult live in different worlds. If that is so, we cannot be certain that school, at any rate boarding school, is not still for many children as dreadful an experience as it used to be. Take away God, Latin, the cane, class distinctions and sexual taboos, and the fear, the hatred, the snobbery and the misunderstanding might still all be there. It will have been seen that my own main trouble was an utter lack of any sense of proportion or probability. This led me to accept outrages and believe absurdities, and to suffer torments over things which were in fact of no importance. It is not enough to say that I was 'silly' and 'ought to have known better'. Look back into your own childhood and think of the nonsense you used to believe and the trivialities which could make you suffer. Of course my own case had its individual variations, but essentially it was that of countless other boys. The weakness of the child is that it starts with a blank sheet. It neither understands nor questions the society in which it lives, and because of its credulity other people can work upon it, infecting it with the sense of inferiority and the dread of offending against mysterious, terrible laws. It may be that everything that happened to me at St Cyprian's could happen in the most 'enlightened' school, though perhaps in subtler forms. Of one thing, however, I do feel fairly sure, and that is that boarding schools are worse than day schools. A child has a better chance with the sanctuary of its home near at hand. And I think the characteristic faults of the English upper and middle classes may be partly due to the practice, general until recently, of sending children away from home as young as nine, eight or even seven.

I have never been back to St Cyprian's. Reunions, old boys' dinners and such-like leave me something more than cold, even when my memories are friendly. I have never even been down to Eton, where I was relatively happy, though I did once pass through it in 1933 and noted with interest that nothing seemed to have changed, except that the shops now sold radios. As for St Cyprian's, for years I loathed its very name so deeply that I could not view it with enough detachment to see the significance of the things that happened to me there. In a way, it is only within the last decade that I have really thought over my schooldays, vividly though their memory has always haunted me. Nowadays, I believe, it would make very little impression on me to see the place again, if it still exists. (I remember hearing a rumour some years ago that it had been burnt down.) If I had to pass through Eastbourne I would not make a detour to avoid the school: and if I happened to pass the school itself I might even stop for a moment by the low brick wall, with the steep bank running down from it, and look across the flat playing field at the ugly building with the square of asphalt in front of it. And if I went inside and smelt again the inky, dusty smell of the big schoolroom, the rosiny smell of the chapel, the stagnant smell of the swimming bath and the cold reek of the lavatories, I think I should only feel what one invariably feels in revisiting any scene of childhood: How small everything has grown, and how terrible is the deterioration in myself! But it is a fact that for many years I could hardly have borne to look at it again. Except upon dire necessity I would not have set foot in Eastbourne. I even conceived a prejudice against Sussex, as the county that contained St Cyprian's, and as an adult I have only once been in Sussex, on a short visit. Now, however, the place is out of my system for good. Its magic works no longer, and I have not even enough animosity left to make me hope that Flip and Sambo are dead or that the story of the school being burnt down was true.

1947

Reflections on Gandhi

Saints should always be judged guilty until they are proved innocent, but the tests that have to be applied to them are not, of course, the same in all cases. In Gandhi's case the questions one feels inclined to ask are: to what extent was Gandhi moved by vanity – by the consciousness of himself as a humble, naked old man, sitting on a praying-mat and shaking empires by sheer spiritual power – and to what extent did he compromise his own principles by entering into politics, which of their nature are inseparable from coercion and fraud? To give a definite answer one would have to study Gandhi's acts and writings in immense detail, for his whole life was a sort of pilgrimage in which every act was significant. But this partial autobiography, which ends in the nineteen-twenties, is strong evidence in his favour, all the more because it covers what he would have called the unregenerate part of his life and reminds one that inside the saint, or near-saint, there was a very shrewd, able person who could, if he had chosen, have been a brilliant success as a lawyer, an administrator or perhaps even a businessman.

At about the time when the autobiography[1] first appeared I

---

[1] *The Story of my Experiments with Truth* by M. K. Gandhi, translated from the Gujarati by Mahadev Desai.

remember reading its opening chapters in the ill-printed pages of some Indian newspaper. They made a good impression on me, which Gandhi himself, at that time, did not. The things that one associated with him – homespun cloth, 'soul forces' and vegetarianism – were unappealing, and his medievalist programme was obviously not viable in a backward, starving, overpopulated country. It was also apparent that the British were making use of him, or thought they were making use of him. Strictly speaking, as a Nationalist, he was an enemy, but since in every crisis he would exert himself to prevent violence – which, from the British point of view, meant preventing any effective action whatever – he could be regarded as 'our man'. In private this was sometimes cynically admitted. The attitude of the Indian millionaires was similar. Gandhi called upon them to repent, and naturally they preferred him to the Socialists and Communists who, given the chance, would actually have taken their money away. How reliable such calculations are in the long run is doubtful; as Gandhi himself says 'in the end deceivers deceive only themselves'; but at any rate the gentleness with which he was nearly always handled was due partly to the feeling that he was useful. The British Conservatives only became really angry with him when, as in 1942, he was in effect turning his non-violence against a different conqueror.

But I could see even then that the British officials who spoke of him with a mixture of amusement and disapproval also genuinely liked and admired him, after a fashion. Nobody ever suggested that he was corrupt, or ambitious in any vulgar way, or that anything he did was actuated by fear or malice. In judging a man like Gandhi one seems instinctively to apply high standards, so that some of his virtues have passed almost unnoticed. For instance, it is clear even from the autobiography that his natural physical courage was quite outstanding: the manner of his death was a later illustration of this, for a public man who attached any value to his own skin would have been more adequately guarded. Again, he seems to have been quite free from that maniacal suspiciousness which, as E.M. Forster rightly says in *A Passage to India*, is the besetting Indian vice, as hypocrisy is the British vice. Although no doubt he was shrewd enough in detecting dishonesty, he seems wherever possible to have believed that other people were acting in good faith and had a better nature through which they could be approached. And though he came of a poor middle-class family, started life rather unfavourably, and was probably of unimpressive physical appearance, he was not afflicted by envy or by the feeling of inferiority. Colour feeling, when he first met it in its worst form in South Africa, seems rather to have astonished him. Even when he was fighting what was in effect a colour war he did not think of people in terms of race or status. The governor of a province, a cotton millionaire, a half-starved Dravidian coolie, a British private soldier, were all equally human beings, to be approached in much the same way. It is noticeable that even in the worst possible circumstances, as in South Africa, when he was making himself unpopular as the champion of the Indian community, he did not lack European friends.

Written in short lengths for newspaper serialization, the autobiography is not a literary masterpiece, but is the more impressive because of the commonplaceness of much of its material. It is well to be reminded that Gandhi started out with the normal ambitions of a young Indian student and only adopted his extremist opinions by degrees and, in some cases, rather unwillingly. There was a time, it is interesting to learn, when he wore a top-hat, took dancing lessons, studied French and Latin, went up the Eiffel Tower, and even tried to learn the violin – all this with the idea of assimilating European civilization as thoroughly as possible. He was not one of those saints who are marked out by their phenomenal piety from childhood onwards, nor one of the other kind who forsake the world after sensational debaucheries. He makes full confession of the misdeeds of his youth, but in fact there is not much to confess. As a frontispiece to the book, there is a photograph of Gandhi's possessions at the time of his death. The whole outfit could be purchased for about £5, and Gandhi's sins, at least his fleshly sins, would make the same sort of appearance if placed all in one heap. A few cigarettes, a few mouthfuls of meat, a few annas pilfered in childhood from the maidservant, two visits to a brothel (on each occasion he got away without 'doing anything'), one narrowly escaped lapse with his landlady in Plymouth, one outburst of temper – that is about the whole collection. Almost from childhood onwards he had a deep earnestness, an attitude ethical rather than religious, but, until he was about thirty, no very definite sense of direction. His first entry into anything describable as public life was made by way of vegetarianism. Underneath his less ordinary qualities one feels all the time the solid middle-class businessmen who were his ancestors. One feels that even after he had abandoned personal ambition he must have been a resourceful, energetic lawyer and a hard-headed political organizer, careful in keeping down expenses, an adroit handler of committees and an indefatigable chaser of subscriptions. His character was an extraordinarily mixed one, but there was almost nothing in it that you can put your finger on and call bad, and I believe that even Gandhi's worst enemies would admit that he was an interesting and unusual man who enriched the world simply by being alive. Whether he was also a lovable man, and whether his teachings can have much value for those who do not accept the religious beliefs on which they are founded, I have never felt fully certain.

Of late years it has been the fashion to talk about Gandhi as though he were not only sympathetic to the western left-wing movement, but were even integrally part of it. Anarchists and pacifists, in particular, have claimed him for their own, noticing only that he was opposed to centralism and State violence and ignoring the other-worldly, anti-humanist tendency of his doctrines. But one should, I think, realize that Gandhi's teachings cannot be squared with the belief that Man is the measure of all things, and that our job is to make life worth living on this earth, which is the only earth we have. They make sense only on the assumption that God exists and that the world of solid objects is an illusion to be escaped from. It is worth considering the disciplines which Gandhi imposed on himself and which – though he might not insist on every one of his followers observing every detail – he considered indispensable if one wanted to serve either God or humanity. First of all, no meat eating, and if possible no animal food in any form. (Gandhi himself, for the sake of his health, had to compromise on milk, but seems to have felt this to be a backsliding.) No alcohol or tobacco, and no spices or condiments, even of a vegetable kind, since food should be taken not for its own sake, but solely in order to preserve one's strength. Secondly, if possible, no sexual intercourse. If sexual intercourse must happen, then it should be for the sole purpose of begetting children and presumably at long intervals. Gandhi himself, in his middle thirties, took the vow of *bramahcharya*, which means not only complete chastity but the elimination of sexual desire. This condition, it seems, is difficult to attain without a special diet and frequent fasting. One of the dangers of milk drinking is that it is apt to arouse sexual desire. And finally – this is the cardinal point – for the seeker after goodness there must be no close friendships and no exclusive loves whatever.

Close friendships, Gandhi says, are dangerous, because 'friends react on one another' and through loyalty to a friend one can be led into wrong-doing. This is unquestionably true. Moreover, if one is to love God, or to love humanity as a whole, one cannot give one's preference to any individual person. This again is true, and it marks the point at which the humanistic and the religious attitudes cease to be reconcilable. To an ordinary human being, love means nothing if it does not mean loving some people more than others. The autobiography leaves it uncertain whether Gandhi behaved in an inconsiderate way to his wife and children, but at any rate it makes clear that on three occasions he was willing to let his wife or a child die rather than administer the animal food prescribed by the doctor. It is true that the threatened death never actually occurred, and also that Gandhi – with, one gathers, a good deal of moral pressure in the opposite direction – always gave the patient the choice of staying alive at the price of committing a sin: still, if the decision had been solely his own, he would have forbidden the animal food, whatever the risks might be. There must, he says, be some limit to what we will do in order to remain alive, and the limit is well on this side of chicken broth. This attitude is perhaps a noble one, but in the sense which – I think – most people would give to the word, it is inhuman. The essence of being human is that one does not seek perfection, that one *is* sometimes willing to commit sins for the sake of loyalty, that one does not push asceticism to the point where it makes friendly intercourse impossible, and that one is prepared in the end to be defeated and broken up by life, which is the inevitable price of fastening one's love upon other human individuals. No doubt alcohol, tobacco and so forth are things that a saint must avoid, but sainthood is also a thing that human beings must avoid. There is an obvious retort to this, but one should be wary about making it. In this yogi-ridden age, it is too readily assumed that 'non-attachment' is not only better than a full acceptance of earthly life, but that the ordinary man only rejects it because it is too difficult: in other words, that the average human being is a failed saint. It is doubtful whether this is true. Many people genuinely do not wish to be saints, and it is probable that some who achieve or aspire to sainthood have never felt much temptation to be human beings. If one could follow it to its psychological roots, one would, I believe, find that the main motive for 'non-attachment' is a desire to escape from the pain of living, and above all from love, which, sexual or non-sexual, is hard work. But it is not necessary here to argue whether the other-worldly or the humanistic ideal is 'higher'. The point is that they are incompatible. One must choose between God and Man, and all 'radicals' and 'progressives', from the mildest Liberal to the most extreme Anarchist, have in effect chosen Man.

However, Gandhi's pacifism can be separated to some extent from his other teachings. Its motive was religious, but he claimed also for it that it was a definite technique, a method, capable of producing desired political results. Gandhi's attitude was not that of most western pacifists. *Satyagraha*, first evolved in South Africa, was a sort of non-violent warfare, a way of defeating the enemy without hurting him and without feeling or arousing hatred. It entailed such things as civil disobedience, strikes, lying down in front of railway trains, enduring police charges without running away and without hitting back, and the like. Gandhi objected to 'passive resistance' as a translation of *Satyagraha*: in Gujarati, it seems, the word means 'firmness in the truth'. In his early days Gandhi served as a stretcher-bearer on the British side in the Boer War, and he was prepared to do the same again in the war of 1914–18. Even after he had completely abjured violence he was honest enough to see that in war it is usually necessary to take sides. He did not – indeed, since his whole political life centred round a struggle for national independence, he could not – take the sterile and dishonest line of pretending that in every war both sides are exactly the same and it makes no difference who wins. Nor did he, like most western pacifists, specialize in avoiding awkward questions. In relation to the late war, one question that every pacifist had a clear obligation to answer was: 'What about the Jews? Are you prepared to see them exterminated? If not, how do you propose to save them without resorting to war?' I must say that I have never heard, from any western pacifist, an honest answer to this question, though I have heard plenty of evasions, usually of the 'you're another' type. But it so happens that Gandhi was asked a somewhat similar question in 1938 and that his answer is on record in Mr Louis Fischer's *Gandhi and Stalin*. According to Mr Fischer Gandhi's view was that the German Jews ought to commit collective suicide, which 'would have aroused the world and the people of Germany to Hitler's violence'. After the war he justified himself: the Jews had been killed anyway, and might as well have died significantly. One has the impression that this attitude staggered even so warm an admirer as Mr Fischer, but Gandhi was merely being honest. If you are not prepared to take life, you must often be prepared for lives to be lost in some other way. When, in 1942, he urged non-violent resistance against a Japanese invasion, he was ready to admit that it might cost several million deaths.

At the same time there is reason to think that Gandhi, who after all was born in 1869, did not understand the nature of totalitarianism and saw everything in terms of his own struggle against the British Government. The important point here is not so much that the British treated him forbearingly as that he was always able to command publicity. As can be seen from the phrase quoted above, he believed in 'arousing the world', which is only possible if the world gets a chance to hear what you are doing. It is difficult to see how Gandhi's methods could be applied in a country where opponents of the régime disappear in the middle of the night and are never heard of again. Without a free press and the right of assembly, it is impossible not merely to appeal to outside opinion, but to bring a mass movement into being, or even to make your intentions known to your adversary. Is there a Gandhi in Russia at this moment? And if there is, what is he accomplishing? The Russian masses could only practise civil disobedience if the same idea happened to occur to all of them simultaneously, and even then, to judge by the history of the Ukraine famine, it would make no difference. But let it be granted that non-violent resistance can be effective against one's own government, or against an occupying power: even so, how does one put it into practice internationally? Gandhi's various conflicting statements on the late war seem to show that he felt the difficulty of this. Applied to foreign politics, pacifism either stops being pacifist or becomes appeasement. Moreover the assumption, which served Gandhi so well in dealing with individuals, that all human beings are more or less approachable and will respond to a generous gesture, needs to be seriously questioned. It is not necessarily true, for example, when you are dealing with lunatics. Then the question becomes: Who is sane? Was Hitler sane? And is it not possible for one whole culture to be insane by the standards of another? And, so far as one can gauge the feelings of whole nations, is there any apparent connexion between a generous deed and a friendly response? Is gratitude a factor in international politics?

These and kindred questions need discussion, and need it urgently, in the few years left to us before somebody presses the button and the rockets begin to fly. It seems doubtful whether civilization can stand another major war, and it is at least thinkable that the way out lies through non-violence. It is Gandhi's virtue that he would have been ready to give honest consideration to the kind of question that I have raised above; and indeed, he probably did discuss most of these questions somewhere or other in his innumerable newspaper articles. One feels of him that there was much that he did not understand, but not that there was anything that he was frightened of saying or thinking. I have never been able to feel much liking for Gandhi, but I do not feel sure that as a political thinker he was wrong in the main, nor do I believe that his life was a failure. It is curious that when he was assassinated, many of his warmest admirers exclaimed sorrowfully that he had lived just long enough to see his life work in ruins, because India was engaged in a civil war which had always been foreseen as one of the by-products of the transfer of power. But it was not in trying to smooth down Hindu–Moslem rivalry that Gandhi had spent his life. His main political objective, the peaceful ending of British rule, had after all been attained. As usual, the relevant facts cut across one another. On the one hand, the British did get out of India without fighting, an event which very few observers indeed would have predicted until about a year before it happened. On the other hand, this was done by a Labour Government, and it is certain that a Conservative Government, especially a government headed by Churchill, would have acted differently. But if, by 1945, there had grown up in Britain a large body of opinion sympathetic to Indian independence, how far was this due to Gandhi's personal influence? And if, as may happen, India and Britain finally settle down into a decent and friendly relationship, will this be partly because Gandhi, by keeping up his struggle obstinately and without hatred, disinfected the political air? That one even thinks of asking such questions indicates his stature. One may feel, as I do, a sort of aesthetic distaste for Gandhi, one may reject the claims of sainthood made on his behalf (he never made any such claim himself, by the way), one may also reject sainthood as an ideal and therefore feel that Gandhi's basic aims were anti-human and reactionary: but regarded simply as a politician, and compared with the other leading political figures of our time, how clean a smell he has managed to leave behind!

1949

Politics and the English Language

Most people who bother with the matter at all would admit that the English language is in a bad way, but it is generally assumed that we cannot by conscious action do anything about it. Our civilization is decadent, and our language – so the arguments runs – must inevitably share in the general collapse. It follows that any struggle against the abuse of language is a sentimental archaism, like preferring candles to electric light of hansom cabs to aeroplanes. Underneath this lies the half-conscious belief that language is a natural growth and not an instrument which we shape for our own purposes.

Now, it is clear that the decline of a language must ultimately have political and economic causes: it is not due simply to the bad influences of this or that individual writer. But an effect can become a cause, reinforcing the original cause and producing the same effect in an intensified form, and so on indefinitely. A man may take to drink because he feels himself to be a failure, and then fail all the more completely because he drinks. It is rather the same thing that is happening to the English language. It becomes ugly and inaccurate because our thoughts are foolish, but the slovenliness of our language makes it easier for us to have foolish thoughts. The point is that the process is reversible. Modern English, especially written English, is full of bad habits which spread by imitation and which can be avoided if one is willing to take the necessary trouble. If one gets rid of these habits one can think more clearly, and to think clearly is a necessary first step towards political regeneration: so that the fight against bad English is not frivolous and is not the exclusive concern of professional writers. I will come back to this presently, and I hope that by that time the meaning of what I have said here will have become clearer. Meanwhile, here are five specimens of the English language as it is now habitually written.

These five passages have not been picked out because they are especially bad – I could have quoted far worse if I had chosen – but because they illustrate various of the mental vices from which we now suffer. They are a little below the average, but are fairly representative samples. I number them so I can refer back to them when necessary:

1. I am not, indeed, sure whether it is not true to say that the Milton who once seemed not unlike a seventeenth-century Shelley had not become, out of an experience ever more bitter in each year, more alien (*sic*) to the founder of that Jesuit sect which nothing could induce him to tolerate.

Professor Harold Laski (Essay in *Freedom of Expression*)

2. Above all, we cannot play ducks and drakes with a native battery of idioms which prescribes such egregious collocations of vocables as the Basic *put up with* for *tolerate* or *put at a loss* for *bewilder*.

Professor Lancelot Hogben (*Interglossa*).

3. On the one side we have the free personality: by definition it is not neurotic, for it has neither conflict nor dream. Its desires, such as they are, are transparent, for they are just what institutional approval keeps in the forefront of consciousness; another institutional pattern

would alter their number and intensity; there is little in them that is natural, irreducible, or culturally dangerous. But *on the other side*, the social bond itself is nothing but the mutual reflection of these self-secure integrities. Recall the definition of love. Is not this the very picture of a small academic? Where is there a place in this hall of mirrors for either personality or fraternity?

Essay on psychology in *Politics* (New York).

4. All the 'best people' from the gentlemen's clubs, and all the frantic Fascist captains, united in common hatred of Socialism and bestial horror of the rising tide of the mass revolutionary movement, have turned to acts of provocation, to foul incendiarism, to medieval legends of poisoned wells, to legalize their own destruction to proletarian organizations, and rouse the agitated petty-bourgeoisie to chauvinistic fervour on behalf of the fight against the revolutionary way out of the crisis.

Communist pamphlet.

5. If a new spirit *is* to be infused into this old country, there is one thorny and contentious reform which must be tackled, and that is the humanization and galvanization of the B.B.C. Timidity here will bespeak canker and atrophy of the soul. The heart of Britain may be sound and of strong beat, for instance, but the British lion's roar at present is like that of Bottom in Shakespeare's *Midsummer Night's Dream* – as gentle as any sucking dove. A virile new Britain cannot continue indefinitely to be traduced in the eyes, or rather ears, of the world by the effete languors of Langham Place, brazenly masquerading as 'standard English'. When the Voice of Britain is heard at nine o'clock, better far and infinitely less ludicrous to hear aitches honestly dropped than the present priggish, inflated, inhibited, schoolma'amish arch braying of blameless, bashful mewing maidens!

Letter in *Tribune*.

Each of these passages has faults of its own, but, quite apart from avoidable ugliness, two qualities are common to all of them. The first is staleness of imagery: the other is lack of precision. The writer either has a meaning and cannot express it, or he inadvertently says something else, or he is almost indifferent as to whether his words mean anything or not. This mixture of vagueness and sheer incompetence is the most marked characteristic of modern English prose, and especially of any kind of political writing. As soon as certain topics are raised, the concrete melts into the abstract and no one seems able to think of turns of speech that are not hackneyed: prose consists less and less of *words* chosen for the sake of their meaning, and more of *phrases* tacked together like the sections of a prefabricated hen-house. I list below, with notes and examples, various of the tricks by means of which the work of prose construction is habitually dodged:

Dying metaphors. A newly invented metaphor assists thought by evoking a visual image, while on the other hand a metaphor which is technically 'dead' (e.g. *iron resolution*) has in effect reverted to being an ordinary word and can generally be used without loss of vividness. But in between these two classes there is a huge dump of worn-out metaphors which have lost all evocative power and are merely used because they save people the trouble of inventing phrases for themselves. Examples are: *Ring the changes on, take up the cudgels for, toe the line, ride roughshod over, stand shoulder to shoulder with, play into the hands of, no axe to grind, grist to the mill, fishing in troubled waters, rift within the lute, on the order of the day, Achilles' heel, swan song, hotbed.* Many of these are used without knowledge of their meaning (what is a 'rift', for instance?), and incompatible metaphors are frequently mixed, a sure sign that the writer is not interested in what he is saying. Some metaphors now current have been twisted out of their original meaning without those who use them even being aware of the fact. For example, *toe the line* is sometimes written *tow the line*. Another example is *the hammer and the anvil*, now always used with the implication that the anvil gets the worst of it. In real life it is always the anvil that breaks the hammer, never the other way about: a writer who stopped to think what he was saying would be aware of this, and would avoid perverting the original phrase.

Operators, or *verbal false limbs*. These save the trouble of picking out appropriate verbs and nouns, and at the same time pad each sentence with extra syllables which give it an appearance of symmetry. Characteristic phrases are: *render inoperative, militate against, prove unacceptable, make contact with, be subject to, give rise to, give grounds for, have the effect of, play a leading part (role) in, make itself felt, take effect, exhibit a tendency to, serve the purpose of,* etc. etc. The keynote is the elimination of simple verbs. Instead of being a single word, such as *break, stop, spoil, mend, kill*, a verb becomes a *phrase*, made up of a noun or adjective tacked on to some general-purposes verb such as *prove, serve, form, play, render*. In addition, the passive voice is wherever possible used in preference to the active, and noun constructions are used instead of gerunds (*by examination of* instead of *by examining*). The range of verbs is further cut down by means of the *-ize* and *de-* formations, and banal statements are given an appearance of profundity by means of the *not un-* formation. Simple conjunctions and prepositions are replaced by such phrases as *with respect to, having regard to, the fact that, by dint of, in view of, in the interests of, on the hypothesis that*; and the ends of sentences are saved from anticlimax by such resounding commonplaces as *greatly to be desired, cannot be left out of account, a development to be expected in the near future, deserving of serious consideration, brought to a satisfactory conclusion*, and so on and so forth.

Pretentious diction. Words like *phenomenon, element, individual* (as noun), *objective, categorical, effective, virtual, basic, primary, promote, constitute, exhibit, exploit, utilize, eliminate, liquidate*, are used to dress up simple statements and give an air of scientific impartiality to biassed judgements. Adjectives like *epoch-making, epic, historic, unforgettable, triumphant, age-old, inevitable, inexorable, veritable*, are used to dignify the sordid processes of international politics, while writing that aims at glorifying war usually takes on an archaic colour, its characteristic words being: *realm, throne, chariot, mailed fist, trident, sword, shield, buckler, banner, jackboot, clarion.* Foreign words and expressions such as *cul de sac, ancien régime, deus exmachina, mutatis mutandis, status quo, Gleichschaltung, Weltanschauung*, are used to give an air of culture and elegance. Except for the useful abbreviations *i.e., e.g.,* and *etc.*, there is no real need for any of the hundreds of foreign phrases now current in English. Bad writers, and especially scientific, political and sociological writers, are nearly always haunted by the notion that Latin or Greek words are grander than Saxon ones, and unnecessary words like *expedite, ameliorate, predict, extraneous, deracinated, clandestine, sub-aqueous* and hundreds of other constantly gain ground from their Anglo-Saxon opposite numbers.[1] The jargon peculiar to Marxist writing

[1] An interesting illustration of this is the way in which the English flower names which were in use till very recently are being ousted by Greek ones, *snapdragon* becoming *antirrhinum*, *forget-me-not* becoming *myosotis*, etc. It is hard to see any practical reason for this change of fashion: it is probably

(*hyena, hangman, cannibal, petty bourgeois, these gentry, lackey, flunkey, mad dog, White Guard*, etc) consists largely of words and phrases translated from Russian, German or French, but the normal way of coining a new word is to use a Latin or Greek root with the appropriate affix and, where necessary, the *-ize* formation. It is often easier to make up words of this kind (*deregionalize, impermissible, extramarital, non-fragmentatory* and so forth) than to think up the English words that will cover one's meaning. The result, in general, is an increase in slovenliness and vagueness.

Meaningless words. In certain kinds of writing, particularly in art criticism and literary criticism, it is normal to come across long passages which are almost completely lacking in meaning.[1] Words like *romantic, plastic, values, human, dead, sentimental, natural, vitality*, as used in art criticism, are strictly meaningless, in the sense that they not only do not point to any discoverable object, but are hardly even expected to do so by the reader. When one critic writes, 'The outstanding features of Mr X's work is its living quality', while another writes, 'The immediately striking thing about Mr X's work is its peculiar deadness', the reader accepts this as a simple difference of opinion. If

---

due to an instinctive turning-away from the more homely word and a vague feeling that the Greek word is scientific. [Author's footnote.]

[1] Example: 'Comfort's catholicity of perception and image, strangely Whitmanesque in range, almost the exact opposite in aesthetic compulsion, continues to evoke that trembling atmospheric accumulative hinting at a cruel, an inexorably serene timelessness... Wrey Gardiner scores by aiming at simple bullseyes with precision. Only they are not so simple, and through this contented sadness runs more than the surface bitter-sweet of resignation. (*Poetry Quarterly.*) [Author's footnote.]

words like *black* and *white* were involved, instead of the jargon words *dead* and *living*, he would see at once that language was being used in an improper way. Many political words are similarly abused. The word *Fascism* has now no meaning except in so far as it signifies 'something not desirable'. The words *democracy, socialism, freedom, patriotic, realistic, justice*, have each of them several different meanings which cannot be reconciled with one another. In the case of a word like *democracy*, not only is there no agreed definition, but the attempt to make one is resisted from all sides. It is almost universally felt that when we call a country democratic we are praising it: consequently the defenders of every kind of régime claim that it is a democracy, and fear that they might have to stop using the word if it were tied down to any one meaning. Words of this kind are often used in a consciously dishonest way. That is, the person who uses them has his own private definition, but allows his hearer to think he means something quite different. Statements like *Marshal Pétain was a true patriot*, *The Soviet press is the freest in the world*, *The Catholic Church is opposed to persecution*, are almost always made with intent to deceive. Other words used in variable meanings, in most cases more or less dishonestly, are: *class, totalitarian, science, progressive, reactionary, bourgeois, equality*.

Now that I have made this catalogue of swindles and perversions, let me give another example of the kind of writing that they lead to. This time it must of its nature be an imaginary one. I am going to translate a passage of good English into modern English of the worst sort. Here is a well-known verse from *Ecclesiastes*:

I returned, and saw under the sun, that the race is not to the swift, nor the battle to the strong, neither yet bread to the wise, nor yet riches to men of understanding, nor yet favour to men of skill; but time and chance happeneth to them all.

Here it is in modern English:

Objective consideration of contemporary phenomena compels the conclusion that success or failure in competitive activities exhibits no tendency to be commensurate with innate capacity, but that a considerable element of the unpredictable must invariably be taken into account.

This is a parody, but not a very gross one. Exhibit 3, above, for instance, contains several patches of the same kind of English. It will be seen that I have not made a full translation. The beginning and ending of the sentence follow the original meaning fairly closely, but in the middle the concrete illustrations – race, battle, bread – dissolve into the vague phrase 'success or failure in competitive activities'. This had to be so, because no modern writer of the kind I am discussing – no one capable of using phrases like 'objective' consideration of contemporary phenomena' – would ever tabulate his thoughts in that precise and detailed way. The whole tendency of modern prose is away from concreteness. Now analyse these two sentences a little more closely. The first contains 49 words but only 60 syllables, and all its words are those of everyday life. The second contains 38 words of 90 syllables: 18 of its words are from Latin roots, and one from Greek. The first sentence contains six vivid images, and only one phrase ('time and chance') that could be called vague. The second contains not a single fresh, arresting phrase, and in spite of its 90 syllables it gives only a shortened version of the meaning contained in the first. Yet without a doubt it is the second kind of sentence that is gaining ground in modern English. I do not want to exaggerate. This kind of writing is not yet universal, and outcrops of simplicity will occur here and there in the worst-written page. Still if you or I were told to write a few lines on the uncertainty of human fortunes, we should probably come much nearer to my imaginary sentence than to the one from *Ecclesiastes*.

As I have tried to show, modern writing at its worst does not consist in picking out words for the sake of their meaning and inventing images in order to make the meaning clearer. It consists in gumming together long strips of words which have already been set in order by someone else, and making the results presentable by sheer humbug. The attraction of this way of writing is that it is easy. It is easier – even quicker, once you have the habit – to say *In my opinion it is a not unjustifiable assumption that* than to say *I think*. If you use ready-made phrases, you not only don't have to hunt about for words; you also don't have to bother with the rhythms of your sentences, since these phrases are generally so arranged as to be more or less euphonious. When you are composing in a hurry – when you are dictating to a stenographer, for instance, or making a public speech – it is natural to fall into a pretentious, latinized style. Tags like *a consideration which we should do well to bear in mind* or *a conclusion to which all of us would readily assent* will save many a sentence from coming down with a bump. By using stale metaphors, similes and idioms, you save much mental effort, at the cost of leaving your meaning vague, not only for your reader but for yourself. This is the significance of mixed metaphors. The sole aim of a metaphor is to call up a visual image. When these images clash – as in *The Fascist octopus has sung its swan song, the jackboot is thrown into the melting-pot* – it can be taken as certain that the writer is not seeing a mental image of the objects he is naming; in other words he is not really thinking. Look again at the examples I gave at the beginning of this essay. Professor Laski (1) uses five negatives in 53 words. One of these is superfluous, making nonsense of the whole passage, and in addition there is the slip *alien* for akin, making further nonsense, and several avoidable pieces of clumsiness which increase the general vagueness. Professor Hogben (2) plays ducks and drakes with a battery which is able to write prescriptions, and, while disapproving of the everyday phrase *put up with*, is unwilling to look *egregious* up in the dictionary and see what it means. (3), if one takes an uncharitable attitude towards it, is simply meaningless: probably one could work out its intended meaning by reading the whole of the article in which it occurs. In (4) the writer knows more or less what he wants to say, but an accumulation of stale phrases chokes him like tea-leaves blocking a sink. In (5) words and meaning have almost parted company. People who write in this manner usually have a general emotional meaning – they dislike one thing and want to express solidarity with another – but they are not interested in the detail of what they are saying. A scrupulous writer, in every sentence that he writes, will ask himself at least four questions, thus: What am I trying to say? What words will express it? What image or idiom will make it clearer? Is this image fresh enough to have an effect? And he will probably ask himself two more: Could I put it more shortly? Have I said anything that is avoidably ugly? But you are not obliged to go to all this trouble. You can shirk it by simply throwing your mind open and letting the ready-made phrases come crowding in. They will construct your sentences for you – even think your thoughts for you, to a certain extent – and at need they will perform the important service of partially concealing your meaning even from yourself. It is at this point that the special connexion between politics and the debasement of language becomes clear.

In our time it is broadly true that political writing is bad writing. Where it is not true, it will generally be found that the writer is some kind of rebel, expressing his private opinions, and not a 'party line'. Orthodoxy, of whatever colour, seems to demand a lifeless, imitative style. The political dialects to be found in pamphlets, leading articles, manifestos, White Papers and the speeches of Under-Secretaries do, of course, vary from party to party, but they are all alike in that one almost never finds in them a fresh, vivid, home-made turn of speech. When one watches some tired hack on the platform mechanically repeating the familiar phrases – *bestial atrocities, iron heel, blood-stained tyranny, free peoples of the world, stand shoulder to shoulder* – one often has a curious feeling that one is not watching a live human being but some kind of dummy: a feeling which suddenly becomes stronger at moments when the light catches the speaker's spectacles and turns them into blank discs which seem to have no eyes behind them. And this is not altogether fanciful. A speaker who uses that kind of phraseology has gone some distance towards turning himself into a machine. The appropriate noises are coming out of his larynx, but his brain is not involved as it would be if he were choosing his words for himself. If the speech he is making is one that he is accustomed to make over and over again, he may be almost unconscious of what he is saying, as one is when one utters the responses in church. And this reduced state of consciousness, if not indispensable, is at any rate favourable to political conformity.

In our time, political speech and writing are largely the defence of the indefensible. Things like the continuance of British rule in India, the Russian purges and deportations, the dropping of the atom bombs on Japan, can indeed be defended, but only by arguments which are too brutal for most people to face, and which do not square with the professed aims of political parties. Thus political language has to consist largely of euphemism, question-begging and sheer cloudy vagueness. Defenceless villages are bombarded from the air, the inhabitants driven out into the countryside, the cattle machine-gunned, the huts set on fire with incendiary bullets: this is called *pacification*. Millions of peasants are robbed of their farms and sent trudging along the roads with no more than they can carry: this is called *transfer of population* or *rectification of frontiers*. People are imprisoned for years without trial, or shot in the back of the neck or sent to die of scurvy in Arctic lumber camps: this is called *elimination of unreliable elements*. Such phraseology is needed if one wants to name things without calling up mental pictures of them. Consider for instance some comfortable English professor defending Russian totalitarianism. He cannot say outright, 'I believe in killing off your opponents when you can get good results by doing so'. Probably, therefore, he will say something like this:

> While freely conceding that the Soviet régime exhibits certain features which the humanitarian may be inclined to deplore, we must, I think, agree that a certain curtailment of the right to political opposition is an unavoidable concomitant of transitional periods, and that the rigours which the Russian people have been called upon

to undergo have been amply justified in the sphere of concrete achievement.

The inflated style is itself a kind of euphemism. A mass of Latin words falls upon the facts like soft snow, blurring the outlines and covering up all the details. The great enemy of clear language is insincerity. When there is a gap between one's real and one's declared aims, one turns as it were instinctively to long words and exhausted idioms, like a cuttlefish squirting out ink. In our age there is no such thing as 'keeping out of politics'. All issues are political issues, and politics itself is a mass of lies, evasions, folly, hatred and schizophrenia. When the general atmosphere is bad, language must suffer. I should expect to find – this is a guess which I have not sufficient knowledge to verify – that the German, Russian and Italian languages have all deteriorated in the last ten or fifteen years, as a result of dictatorship.

But if thought corrupts language, language can also corrupt thought. A bad usage can spread by tradition and imitation, even among people who should and do know better. The debased language that I have been discussing is in some ways very convenient. Phrases like *a not unjustifiable assumption, leaves much to be desired, would serve no good purpose, a consideration which we should do well to bear in mind*, are a continuous temptation, a packet of aspirins always at one's elbow. Look back through this essay, and for certain you will find that I have again and again committed the very faults I am protesting against. By this morning's post I have received a pamphlet dealing with conditions in Germany. The author tells me that he 'felt impelled' to write it. I open it at random, and here is almost the first sentence that I see: '(The Allies) have an opportunity not only of achieving a radical transformation of Germany's social and political structure in such a way as to avoid a nationalistic reaction in Germany itself, but at the same time of laying the foundations of a co-operative and unified Europe.' You see, he 'feels impelled' to write – feels, presumably, that he has something new to say – and yet his words, like cavalry horses answering the bugle, group themselves automatically into the familiar dreary pattern. This invasion of one's mind by ready-made phrases (*lay the foundations, achieve a radical transformation*) can only be prevented if one is constantly on guard against them, and every such phrase anaesthetizes a portion of one's brain.

I said earlier that the decadence of our language is probably curable. Those who deny this would argue, if they produced an argument at all, that language merely reflects existing social conditions, and that we cannot influence its development by any direct tinkering with words and constructions. So far as the general tone or spirit of a language goes, this may be true, but it is not true in detail. Silly words and expressions have often disappeared, not through any evolutionary process but owing to the conscious action of a minority. Two recent examples were *explore every avenue* and *leave no stone unturned*, which were killed by the jeers of a few journalists. There is a long list of fly-blown metaphors which could similarly be got rid of if enough people would interest themselves in the job; and it should also be possible to laugh the *not un-* formation out of existence,[1] to reduce the amount of Latin and Greek in

---

[1] One can cure onself of the *not un-* formation by memorizing this sentence. *A not unblack dog was chasing a not unsmall rabbit across a not ungreen field.* [Author's footnote.]

the average sentence, to drive out foreign phrases and strayed scientific words, and, in general, to make pretentiousness unfashionable. But all these are minor points. The defence of the English language implies more than this, and perhaps it is best to start by saying what it does *not* imply.

To begin with, it has nothing to do with archaism, with the salvaging of obsolete words and turns of speech or with the setting-up of a 'standard English' which must never be departed from. On the contrary, it is especially concerned with the scrapping of every word or idiom which has outworn its usefulness. It has nothing to do with correct grammar and syntax, which are of no importance so long as one makes one's meaning clear or with the avoidance of Americanisms, or with having what is called 'a good prose style'. On the other hand it is not concerned with fake simplicity and the attempt to make written English colloquial. Nor does it even imply in every case preferring the Saxon word to the Latin one, though it does imply using the fewest and shortest words that will cover one's meaning. What is above all needed is to let the meaning choose the word, and not the other way about. In prose, the worst thing you can do with words is to surrender them. When you think of a concrete object, you think wordlessly, and then, if you want to describe the thing you have been visualizing, you probably hunt about till you find the exact words that seem to fit it. When you think of something abstract you are more inclined to use words from the start, and unless you make a conscious effort to prevent it, the existing dialect will come rushing in and do the job for you, at the expense of blurring or even changing your meaning. Probably it is better to put off using words as long as possible and get one's meanings as clear as one can through pictures or sensations. Afterwards one can choose – not simply *accept* – the phrases that will best cover the meaning, and then switch round and decide what impression one's words are likely to make on another person. This last effort of the mind cuts out all stale or mixed images, all prefabricated phrases, needless repetitions, and humbug and vagueness generally. But one can often be in doubt about the effect of a word or a phrase, and one needs rules that one can rely on when instinct fails. I think the following rules will cover most cases:

i. Never use a metaphor, simile or other figure of speech which you are used to seeing in print.
ii. Never use a long word where a short one will do.
iii. If it is possible to cut a word out, always cut it out.
iv. Never use the passive where you can use the active.
v. Never use a foreign phrase, a scientific word or a jargon word if you can think of an everyday English equivalent.
vi. Break any of these rules sooner than say anything outright barbarous.

These rules sound elementary, and so they are, but they demand a deep change of attitude in anyone who has grown used to writing in the style now fashionable. One could keep all of them and still write bad English, but one could not write the kind of stuff that I quoted in those five specimens at the beginning of this article.

I have not here been considering the literary use of language, but merely language as an instrument for expressing and not for concealing or preventing thought. Stuart Chase and others have come near to claiming that all abstract words are meaningless, and have used this as a pretext for advocating a kind of political quietism. Since you don't know what Fascism is, how can you struggle against Fascism? One need not swallow such absurdities as this, but one ought to recognize that the present political chaos is connected with the decay of language, and that one can probably bring about some improvement by starting at the verbal end. If you simplify your English, you are freed from the worst follies of orthodoxy. You cannot speak any of the necessary dialects, and when you make a stupid remark its stupidity will be obvious, even to yourself. Political language – and with variations this is true of all political parties, from Conservatives to Anarchists – is designed to make lies sound truthful and murder respectable, and to give an appearance of solidity to pure wind. One cannot change this all in a moment, but one can at least change one's own habits, and from time to time one can even, if one jeers loudly enough, send some worn-out and useless phrase – some *jackboot, Achilles' heel, hotbed, melting pot, acid test, veritable inferno* or other lump of verbal refuse – into the dustbin where it belongs.

1946

ORWELL'S EARLY NOVELS

BURMESE DAYS

Based on his experiences as a policeman in Burma, George Orwell's first novel presents a devastating picture of British imperialism in a society where, 'after all, natives were natives'. When Flory, a white timber merchant, befriends Indian Dr Veraswami, he defies this orthodoxy. The doctor is in danger: U Po Kyin, a corrupt magistrate, is plotting his downfall. The only thing that can save him is membership of the all-white Club, and Flory can help. Flory's life is changed further by the arrival of beautiful Elizabeth Lackersteen from Paris, who offers an escape from the loneliness and the 'lie' of colonial life.

A CLERGYMAN'S DAUGHTER

Intimidated by her father, the Rector of Knype Hill, Dorothy performs her submissive roles of dutiful daughter and bullied housekeeper. Her thoughts are taken up with the costumes she is making for the church school play, by the hopelessness of preaching to the poor and by debts she cannot pay. Suddenly her routine shatters and Dorothy finds herself down and out in London. She is wearing silk stockings, has money in her pocket but cannot remember her name. Orwell leads us through a landscape of unemployment, poverty and hunger, where Dorothy's faith is challenged and her life changed.

www.penguinclassics.com

ORWELL'S PRE-WAR ENGLAND

KEEP THE ASPIDISTRA FLYING

Gordon Comstock loathes dull, middle-class respectability and worship of money. He gives up a good job in advertising to work part-time in a bookshop, giving him more time to write. But he slides instead into a self-induced poverty that destroys his creativity and his spirit. Only the ever-faithful Rosemary has the strength to challenge his commitment to his chosen way of life – but will he sell out? Through the character of Gordon Comstock, Orwell reveals his own disaffection with the society he himself once renounced.

COMING UP FOR AIR

George Bowling, forty-five, mortgaged, married with children, is an insurance salesman with an expanding waistline, a new set of false teeth – and a desperate desire to escape his dreary life. He fears modern times – since, in 1939, war is imminent – foreseeing food queues, soldiers, secret police and tyranny. So he decides to escape to the world of his childhood, to the village he remembers as a rural haven of peace and tranquility. But what will he find when he gets there?

www.penguinclassics.com

ORWELL'S GREAT POLITICAL NOVELS

ANIMAL FARM

When the downtrodden animals of Manor Farm overthrow their master Mr Jones and take over the farm themselves, they imagine it is the beginning of a life of freedom and equality. But as a cunning, ruthless élite among them starts to take control, the other animals find themselves hopelessly ensnared as one form of tyranny is gradually replaced with another. Written at the end of 1943 but almost not published for its attack on Britain's wartime ally Stalin, Orwell's chilling 'fairy story' is a timeless and devastating satire of idealism betrayed by power and corruption.

NINETEEN EIGHTY-FOUR

Hidden away in the Record Department of the sprawling Ministry of Truth, Winston Smith skilfully rewrites the past to suit the needs of the Party. Yet he inwardly rebels against the totalitarian world he lives in, which demands absolute obedience and controls him through the all-seeing telescreens and the watchful eye of Big Brother. In his longing for truth and liberty, Smith begins a secret love affair with a fellow-worker, Julia, but soon discovers a nightmare world where love is hate, war is peace and the true price of freedom is betrayal.

www.penguinclassics.com

ORWELL AMONG THE UNDERCLASS

DOWN AND OUT IN PARIS AND LONDON

'You have talked so often of going to the dogs – and well, here are the dogs, and you have reached them.'

George Orwell's vivid memoir of his time among the desperately poor and destitute in London and Paris is a moving tour of the underworld of society. Here he painstakingly documents a world of unrelenting drudgery and squalor – sleeping in bug-infested hostels and doss houses, working as a dishwasher in the vile 'Hôtel X', living alongside tramps, surviving on scraps and cigarette butts – in an unforgettable account of what being on the streets is really like.

THE ROAD TO WIGAN PIER

A searing account of George Orwell's experiences of working-class life in the bleak industrial heartlands of Yorkshire and Lancashire, *The Road to Wigan Pier* is a brilliant and bitter polemic that has lost none of its political impact over time. His graphically unforgettable descriptions of social injustice, slum housing, mining conditions, squalor, hunger and growing unemployment are written with unblinking honesty, fury and great humanity.

www.penguinclassics.com

ORWELL FROM ABROAD

HOMAGE TO CATALONIA

When George Orwell joined up to fight in the Spanish Civil War, it seemed like the beginning of 'an era of equality and freedom'. In *Homage to Catalonia* he vividly chronicles his experiences: the revolutionary euphoria of Barcelona, the courage of the ordinary Spanish men and women he fought alongside, the terror and confusion of the front, his near-fatal bullet wound and the cynical betrayal of his allies. Here he brings to bear all the force of his humanity, passion and integrity to describe the bright hopes and desperate disillusionment of a chaotic, brutal war.

SHOOTING AN ELEPHANT AND OTHER ESSAYS

Shooting an Elephant is Orwell's searing and painfully honest account of his experience as a police officer in imperial Burma; killing an escaped elephant in front of a crowd 'solely to avoid looking a fool'. The other masterly essays in this collection include classics such as 'My Country Right or Left', 'How the Poor Die' and 'Such, Such were the Joys', his memoir of the horrors of public school, as well as discussions of Shakespeare, sleeping rough, boys' weeklies and a spirited defence of English cooking. Opinionated, uncompromising, provocative and hugely entertaining, all show Orwell's unique ability to get to the heart of any subject.

www.penguinclassics.com

ORWELL IN ESSENCE

WHY I WRITE (PENGUIN GREAT IDEAS)

Whether talking about his own political writing, puncturing the lies of politicians, wittily dissecting the English character or telling unpalatable truths about war, these timeless, uncompromising essays from George Orwell are more relevant, entertaining and essential than ever.

BOOKS V. CIGARETTES (PENGUIN GREAT IDEAS)

Beginning with a dilemma about whether he spends more money on reading or smoking, these witty and provocative essays go on to explore everything from the perils of second-hand bookshops to the dubious profession of being a critic, from freedom of the press to what patriotism really means.

www.penguinclassics.com

THE 'PERPETUAL DISSIDENT'

THE PENGUIN ORWELL LIBRARY
The stories behind the ideas. The ideas behind the stories.

FICTION
Burmese Days
A Clergyman's Daughter
Keep the Aspidistra Flying
Coming Up for Air
Animal Farm
Nineteen Eighty-four

NON-FICTION
Down and Out in Paris and London
The Road to Wigan Pier
Homage to Catalonia
Shooting an Elephant and Other Essays
Why I Write (Penguin Great Ideas)
Books v Cigarettes (Penguin Great Ideas)

'I am not able, and I do not want, completely to abandon the world-view that I acquired in childhood. So long as I remain alive and well I shall continue to feel strongly about prose style, to love the surface of the earth, and to take pleasure in solid objects and scraps of useless information. It is no use trying to suppress that side of myself. The job is to reconcile my ingrained likes and dislikes with the essentially public, non-individual activities that this age forces on all of us'
Why I Write

www.penguinclassics.com